Speculations about GOD and the COSMOS

STAN GUDDER

SPECULATIONS ABOUT GOD AND THE COSMOS

iUniverse books may be ordered through booksellers or by contacting:

iUniverse
1663 Liberty Drive
Bloomington, IN 47403
www.iuniverse.com
1-800-Authors (1-800-288-4677)

Because of the dynamic nature of the Internet, any web addresses or links contained in this book may have changed since publication and may no longer be valid. The views expressed in this work are solely those of the author and do not necessarily reflect the views of the publisher, and the publisher hereby disclaims any responsibility for them.

Any people depicted in stock imagery provided by Thinkstock are models, and such images are being used for illustrative purposes only. Certain stock imagery © Thinkstock.

ISBN: 978-1-4917-7315-4 (sc)
ISBN: 978-1-4917-7314-7 (e)

Library of Congress Control Number: 2015913218

Print information available on the last page.

iUniverse rev. date: 08/24/2015

Preface

In Chapter 12 of this book, the character, Robert Freeman, says: "The road to knowledge begins with asking the right questions." But what are the right questions and to whom do we ask these questions? The right questions are the deep and penetrating ones. They lie far below the surface and require great insight and ingenuity to answer. We can ask ourselves, our friends, experts in the field or ultimately God. But we must be prepared for the fact that some questions cannot be answered, not even by God. When experts consider a question to which they don't know the answer, they frequently go to the laboratory or into the field and perform experiments. If the experiments are successful, the results give partial answers to the questions. Theoretical scientists usually try to answer questions using theories and computations. If the question is of a scientific nature it is probably best to go to an expert. If the question is spiritual it is best to go to a spiritual leader or to the ultimate source, God.☺ If you don't believe in God, this book might change your mind. Or it might not.☹ If you do believe in God, he might be similar to the one described here and he will answer some of your questions.

Some of the scientific questions asked in this book are: why is there more matter than antimatter, what are dark matter and dark energy, is time-travel possible, is faster-than-the-speed-of-light-travel possible, how did the universe begin and how is it evolving, what principles govern the workings of the universe, is there one universe or many parallel universes, what is reality? You must remember that this book is a work of fiction! Some of the answers to these questions as offered here are close to the truth, but they are not always precise and perfectly accurate. Some others are pure speculation. I think you will be able to tell the difference and if you can't, just remember that you are reading a novel and no harm will be done.

Some of the spiritual questions asked are: is there a heaven, is there a hell, is there a God, are there angels, do we have souls, if so where do they go when we die, does God hear our prayers, does God care, does God intervene, are there angels here on Earth? Answers to these questions will be given by God himself. A question that people have asked for centuries is: if there is a benevolent God, why is there so much evil? Why is there so much pain, suffering and despair? Some possible answers will be given in the story presented here. Whether you believe these answers is up to you. If it just gives you food for thought, then I will have achieved my goal.

Some of the characters in this book were inspired by actual persons. Two of the obvious ones are Walter Cronkite and Richard Feynman. But these characters were only inspired by these individuals, they are not intended to be accurate depictions of them. I have used names similar to the names of real people because it enabled me to visualize them in their actions. I did not intend to offend anyone, so if you see a name that's similar to yours, please consider it the compliment I intended and do not sue me.

Although I usually began each chapter with a premise, it did not feel as though I wrote this book consciously. Instead, the words seemed to simply flow naturally and logically onto the page, without obvious effort on my part. Of course, the underlying themes are the title of the book. This is my first novel and my main credential for writing it, is that when it was completed, I was 78 years old. Not many first time novelists can make this claim and I believe that this ripe age has given me some experience and wisdom. Most of my career has been devoted to applying mathematics to solve problems in physics. This field has enjoyed a long tradition beginning with Archimedes, continuing to Isaac Newton and in modern times, John von Neumann. As a professional mathematical physicist, I can certainly say that I know more mathematics and physics than the average person. I cannot make this claim about spiritual matters. But what does it mean to be an expert in spiritual knowledge? Does it mean someone who knows about the various religions and how they compare? Does it mean someone who knows a lot about God? I don't think so. Spiritual knowledge is a very personal matter, that only comes from experience and deep thought.

A recurring theme is the important role that mathematics plays in the cosmos. In order for you to understand this, I have included a dose of mathematics. But this dose is given with a spoonful of sugar, and I think you can easily digest it. The only thing required is a little high school algebra. Just take a deep breath and you might even enjoy it. If you find the mathematics too intimidating you can skip it, if you must, and there will still be a worthwhile story to read.

I would like to thank my best friend and partner, Paula, who typed the manuscript and served as a thoughtful critic. Also, I would like to thank my family and friends who read the manuscript, made corrections and suggested improvements. In particular, I am deeply indebted to my dear daughters, Dolly and Gail, who spent many hours editing the manuscript. Although it wasn't planned, this book has become a gratifying family project.

Stan Gudder

Contents

Chapter 1

Compassion

My name is Emma Hartman and I live in Denver, Colorado. I am fourteen years old. I live in a nice, four bedroom house in a neighborhood called Park Hill with my father, Gary, and our shelty, Daisy. Gary works as a lawyer for an environmental law firm. He says he wants to go to the University of Colorado Engineering School to learn more about environmental science. My Dad and I love going hiking and camping in the mountains, except in the winter when we go skiing practically every Saturday. You may wonder why we live in such a big house with only two of us. This is the story of how it happened. This story is very sad and until now I couldn't tell you about it without crying, but now I think I'm ready to share. It would make me feel better if I could get it out of my system. The only person I have talked to about this is my Dad and he has filled me in on details that I did not directly witness.

Two years ago, we were a fairly happy family of five. Besides Dad and I, there were my Mom, Ellen, my sister, Diane who was then nine and my brother, Jimmy, who was seven. I loved, loved, loved my room and I spent a lot of time there. I had a large bed with a beautiful floral bedspread. Next to my bed was an ornate cabinet with glass doors that contained my doll collection. The ceiling was quite high and hanging on the walls right below there was a row of hats collected by my Mom and me. On the wall across from my bed there was a calendar with a picture of a wild animal for each month. Below the Siberian tiger the date July 1976 was displayed. Everyone used to say that I was very pretty. But I was more interested in soccer, tennis, skiing and nature than I was in wearing lipstick, dressing up and that kind of stuff. My parents' friends and our relatives used to say that Diane and Jimmy were really cute and I guess they were. Diane had blond hair and freckles under her eyes. She had a cute, impish little smile and she laughed a lot. Jimmy had long hair and loved to goof around. His favorite pursuit was to jump up on a statue and pretend he was part of it. He did look like a boy in one of those Greek statues.

Diane and Jimmy were inseparable and loved to play together. They would fold up an old blanket like a sled and slide down our back steps to the rec room in the basement.

1

They would bounce a ball down the steps and see if it would land inside a plastic pitcher. This would happen only once out of every twenty or thirty tries accompanied by a lot of excitement and cheering. They would play a lousy game of ping pong in the rec room with Daisy barking and running back and forth under the table. A lot of times the ball wouldn't hit the table but would fly off against a wall or ceiling. Then Daisy would grab the ball and start chewing it. Getting the ball out of her mouth was great fun. We didn't have a ping pong ball without holes and chew dents. Diane and Jimmy would run around the house laughing, giggling and throwing paper airplanes with Daisy yapping behind trying to catch the planes. I feel guilty now that I was such a bitch, but they were really annoying. I think they aggravated me more than Mom and Dad.

Diane and Jimmy lived in a world of play and fantasy. They would make up stories of imaginary places and people. They would participate in elaborate adventures. They dressed up in Mom's, Dad's and my old clothes. We called them dress-up clothes and Mom kept them in a chest in our rec room. Their favorite game was to attach old cardboard boxes together to form a make believe mansion. They drew windows and cut out doors. The occupants of this mansion were small dolls and trolls. Diane and Jimmy furnished their house with doll house furniture, old thread spools and anything they could get ahold of, including things they found in my room. They even had roads, cars and trucks going around their mansion.

To me they were a nuisance and a pair of little pests. "Mom, will you tell them to shut up? They're making a big racket and getting Daisy all excited and barking. I'm trying to do my homework and need some quiet."

"You know, Emma, they have a right to play and make a little noise if they want. But I'll tell them to tone it down a bit."

"I hate them, Mom, and I don't like you either. Just cause there's two of them and one of me, you always stick up for them. They're always making loud noises, they go into my room when I'm not there. They get into my dolls and stuff and mess up everything. I never know where anything is."

"All right, young lady that's enough of the ugly talk. Daddy's at work right now, but I think the three of you should get together with me for a little family conference."

So we all sat around the dining room table for a conference. This was not unusual, by the way.

Without hesitation, Diane began the conversation, "she's always picking on us, Mom. She yells at us and she sometimes pushes us."

"Yesterday she said I was bothering her," Jimmy added defiantly, "and she hit me in the arm. It really hurt."

I couldn't let those brats have the last word, "the reason I hit him is because the little pervert snuck into my room and was watching me when I was getting dressed. I told the little creep if I caught him doing that again, I'd scratch his eyes out. My bedroom is between theirs and they play upstairs a lot. They make all kinds of noise, jump up and down and sometimes they even knock against the walls. Why can't they just play downstairs in the rec room?"

"We always played in the rec room," Diane whined, "and remember what happened? One day after we all left, Daisy ate some of our trolls, got sick and puked all over our troll house."

"Yeah," Jimmy joined in, "another time, she was really mad when we left her in the house alone. She ate one of our doll couches and pooped all over our beautiful mansion."

After this went on for a while, Mom interjected, "all right, all right, there doesn't seem to be much I can do here. I think the three of you need to talk together like civilized people and work things out. I'm leaving you here and when I come back I expect a little mutual accommodation. I will say one thing, though, Jimmy, stay out of Emma's room, especially when she's dressing."

We puzzled awhile about what mutual accommodation meant. But that was good because at least we were talking and we worked things out as best we could. But this episode was typical and we tolerated each other and hoped things would get better when we got older. When I think back now, I know that I really loved them and I miss them very much. It's so quiet now and I feel lonesome. Of course, a twelve year old doesn't tell her siblings that she loves them, but I'm sorry I didn't. Why did I think of them as little brats? After all, they were kind of cute. I could have read to them. I could even have played with them. Now that I'm all of fourteen, I think about making it up with children of my own. I know that Diane and Jimmy worshipped me. They looked up to me as the coolest person on earth. Perhaps the reason they were so close was because they didn't have me. I was a typical teenager and I couldn't be bothered with the likes of them. I had not learned about compassion and humanity.

In my defense, sometimes I acted decently. One evening, Diane complained about some bullies at our school. "This girl in my class, Katie, is really mean. She and her two friends Mindy and Sarah are always picking on me."

"What are they picking on you about, honey?" asked Mom.

"They make fun of my clothes. They say I'm ugly and my teeth stick out. They say I have big ears and look like Dumbo. Katie and the other two bump into me and push me around. They strut around like they own the school. Katie is the worst and her two friends do whatever she says."

"Well dear, I think your clothes are fine and you have very nice ears. You do have a little overbite and the orthodontist will fit you with braces next year when your mouth is more developed. Do they pick on other kids in the class?"

"They try to boss everyone around but they're especially hard on me and this shy little kid, Bobby. The other boys just seem to think they're amusing. Anyway, they're too busy with their trucks, planes and war games to pay much attention to them."

"Why don't you try to ignore them like those boys do? You could just play with the other girls in your class."

Not to be left out of such an interesting conversation, I jumped in, "I can't believe that Katie is such a brash bully. Her older sister Lydia is in my class and she's very quiet and meek. She's afraid of her own shadow. Lydia isn't a member of the 'in group' like me. She told me she'd like to be part of our group but nobody ever listens to her. How could Lydia's baby sister be so different from her? Are you sure you're not exaggerating?"

The three of us went to the same grade-school and it was my job to collect Diane and Jimmy after school and walk them home. I complained to Mom and Dad that I would rather be with my friends after school but they told me it was my responsibility as an older sister. A week after our bully conversation, I was a little late picking them up after school because I was hanging out with my friends by the lockers. I didn't see what happened, but Diane filled me in later and this is what she told me. Jimmy was playing on the jungle gym and Diane was in the playground leaning against the school building reading a book. Katie and her cohorts approached Diane. "Well look who it is, none other than Bugs Bunny," said Katie.

"Leave me alone, I'm waiting for my sister."

"I don't see your big sister anywhere." Mindy responded with a wicked glint in her eye. "Too bad she's not here to protect you."

The three girls surrounded Diane and pushed her from one to the other around in a circle. One of the pushes was too hard and Diane fell to the ground. Katie was wearing a dress that she lifted up and sat down on Diane's face. The three bullies laughed while Katie swung her butt back and forth.

"I'm going to blow out some gas," Katie laughed, "do you smell that, Bugs?"

That was all Diane could take. She thrashed about and scratched Katie on the arm. This resulted in a lot of punching. A punch landed on Diane's nose and it started bleeding. The bleeding nose scared the three bullies and they ran away, leaving Diane lying on the ground, crying. Just then I arrived at the pathetic scene. I soothed Diane, grabbed a bandana from my backpack and pressed it on Diane's bleeding nose. I helped her up, put my arm around her and walked Diane and Jimmy home. Diane held the bandana on her bleeding nose and laid her head on my shoulder. I had a soft and tender feeling toward her. These were emotions that I had seldom experienced.

When we got home, Mom put an icepack on Diane's nose and stopped the bleeding. After Diane told us what happened, Mom said, "I'm going to talk to the Principal and Katie's mother about this." Diane protested that that would make things worse and Katie would be mad and pick on her more. Then I said, "how about this? I'll talk to Katie's sister Lydia. She's been asking me to be her friend. I'll tell Lydia I'll be her friend if she asks Katie to let up on you, Diane." This made Diane feel better and the bullying actually stopped. As a bonus, Lydia turned out to be a good friend. This experience seems minor compared to the terrible thing that happened next.

Two years ago on a Friday evening in July, 1976 while we were eating dinner, Dad said, "remember, tomorrow we're getting up real early and going camping. I've reserved a campsite at the Big Thompson campground. It will take about two hours to drive up there and we'll pack up the station wagon tonight so we'll be ready to go tomorrow morning. We can't take Daisy because she keeps running after squirrels and we have a devil of a time getting her back. We'll take Daisy over to Namma and Poppa's house on the way out of town. After we wash dishes, I want you to get your stuff together in your duffle bags, so I can put them in the wagon."

While we kids got our clothes, hiking boots, some toys and favorite blankies packed, Dad retrieved our five person tent, sleeping bags, air mattresses, cooking equipment, Coleman lantern and other camping gear from the basement storeroom. Mom put together boxes and coolers of food, helped us pack and got her and Dad's clothes out. "How long are we going for, Dad?", I asked. "We'll be gone Saturday, Sunday and come home Monday afternoon" he replied. So we all scrambled around, got everything ready, packed our station wagon to the brim, including a carrier on the top, and were ready to go Saturday morning. We got up about 6:00 a.m. and left at 7:30. Mom and Dad sat in the front seat and we kids were in the back.

The first hour of driving was lots of fun. Dad lead us in songs like: *I've Been Working on the Railroad, Who's Going to Shoe Your Pretty Little Feet* and *This Land is Your Land*. We told jokes and played games like counting Volkswagens, finding objects that began with A,B,C,... and Guess What I See. After about an hour, we started getting fidgety and things began to disintegrate. Each of us had something to say.

I spoke up first, "when are we getting there? I'm getting bored."

"Stop the car, Daddy. I've got to pee," Jimmy shouted.

Not to be left out, Diane added, "I'm hungry and I want some water."

Sitting next to Jimmy was a disaster for me because he would continually nudge, pinch and tickle me so Diane would always sit in the middle.

"It's crowded back here and Diane's hogging all the room and pushing me against the door," I protested.

Moments later Diane squirmed in her seat and said, "P U, Jimmy just farted, open the window, it stinks in here."

Dad grumbled, "Emma, you're kicking the back of my seat. I'm trying to drive and I can't concentrate with all your arguing and bickering. If you guys don't quiet down, I'm going to stop the car, come back there and give each of you a big juicy kiss."

This shut us up for awhile, but then it started again.

After about two and a half hours we arrived at the Big Thompson campground. It was a beautiful campsite. We had a large clearing in the forest to set up our tent. There was a magnificent view of the mountains and the day was bright and sunny. The Big Thompson River which was really a fairly small creek, gurgled about a hundred yards away. There were a few other families camping there, but they were pretty far away. We couldn't hear them and could barely see them. The first thing we did was unpack our low lawn chairs and relax on them to enjoy the scenery. There were lots of birds chirping in the trees, butterflies twittering about and colorful wildflowers peaking from the ground. There were a few bees buzzing about the flowers but they didn't bother me and I didn't notice any pesky flies or mosquitos. I was amazed when I heard a surprisingly loud buzzing sound and looked around to see a wonderfully colored red and green humming bird. I watched it for a long time as it darted in and out of the trees and among the wild flowers. Finally it flew away and I didn't see it again. I felt like this was an enchanted, magical place that I never wanted to leave.

Our first big job was to set up the tent. This was a heavy, floored, canvas tent that Mom and Dad struggled to lift into the back of the station wagon. Now all five of us pulled and groaned to get it out and carry it from the wagon to the campsite. First Jimmy fell down and he pulled Diane and me with him. Then Mom and Dad decided to join the fun so they fell down and we found ourselves in a big jumble on the folded tent, laughing. It seemed like we laughed for ten minutes. When a couple of us stopped, someone would start laughing and it would go on over again. After we finally stopped laughing, we actually cooperated very well and got the tent set up.

We packed up some sandwiches for lunch and started out on a three hour hike. Mom, Dad and I liked hiking but I can't say the same for my siblings. They complained they were tired, it was too hot and the trail was too steep. The trail first went through a fairly dense forest, then up some rock fields and finally above timberline at 11,000 feet. We sat on some large boulders and got out our sandwiches and apples for lunch. The view was breathtaking. We were surrounded by high mountains, some over 14,000 feet high. There were fields of wildflowers, white, blue, yellow and red. Besides that we could see a large deep blue lake about a half mile away. After lunch, we kids ran to the lake (with no complaints from the younger ones). We saw fish and had a great time skipping rocks on the lake's surface. Even though it took us over two hours to climb up, we got back down to the campsite in less than an hour. Most of the time, we three kids were laughing and running down the mountain with our parents in serious conversation walking way behind.

That evening we cooked a delicious dinner on a campfire. We unpacked our sleeping bags and our air mattresses and got our tent ready for the night. We didn't have air pumps and blowing up the air mattresses was not easy. The best way to do it without getting dizzy was to lay on the ground with the nozzle of the mattress in your mouth and breath in through your nose and out heavily with your mouth. Diane and Jimmy needed some help with this and we all gladly pitched in. It got dark about 9:00 p.m. and we roasted marshmallows and sat around our campfire telling stupid ghost stories. After we tired of that we did what I liked best which was a game we invented called "I remember."

"Me first," Jimmy said excitedly, "I remember when we were skiing and it was the first time I went on a chair lift. At the end of the lift was a steep little hill where we were supposed to get off. On the support pole before the hill there was a sign that said 'Keep Ski Tips Up.' I couldn't read then and I didn't pay any attention to the picture of a person with their ski tips up. Well, when we got to the end, my skis went right into the hill. They stuck in the hill and flew off my boots as the chair swung around and continued on. I jumped off the lift and tumbled down the other side of the hill. Mom was sitting next to me and she fell down when I got in her way. The rest of you guys were in the next chair and you all fell down trying to avoid us. The attendant stopped the lift and retrieved my skis and we all laid at the bottom of the hill in a giggling pile." We all laughed at the memory.

"That reminds me of another mishap on a chair lift," Diane began, "I was sitting next to Jimmy and you guys were in the chair behind us. There was a sign that said check for loose equipment. We didn't know exactly what that meant but we looked down at the snow and all around but didn't see any equipment that was loose. Well, it turned out that Jimmy's coat was unzipped and stuck in the chair. At the end of the ride, I got off and the chair swung around with Jimmy hanging with his jacket stuck. When the attendant stopped the lift, Jimmy's feet were dangling about four feet off the ground. I jumped up, grabbed his ankles and pulled him down."

"Ha," I laughed, "speaking of Jimmy, I remember that time in Wisconsin when we were on that beach on Lake Michigan. Jimmy and I decided to go to the end of a wharf in the lake while the rest of you remained on the beach. At the end of the wharf there was a heavy rope attached to the pier. Well, Jimmy decided to untie the rope and throw one end into the water. The only trouble was he forgot to let go of the rope and into the water he went. He was not a very good swimmer then and all I could see was his head bobbing up and down under the pier. You guys were too far away to do anything and I heard you yelling and screaming to reach in for him. I couldn't reach him so I jumped in, grabbed him and pushed him up so he could hang onto the pier. You guys came running over and pulled us out. I was treated like a real hero and it felt good."

"I remember a time when I was really scared." Mom said, changing the tone. "When Diane was a baby, we sometimes strapped her into her infant seat, put the seat on the table and fed her. For some reason, this was more convenient than a high chair. Well, one time, I was feeding her this way and left her for a second when the phone rang. The next instant, she was on the floor crying and bleeding like mad. Luckily, the top of the seat absorbed most of the blow but she had bitten the tip of her tongue. Dad and I were frightened to death and we rushed her to the emergency room. They stitched up her tongue but she still has a little bump there. I'm sorry, dear."

Then Dad said, "I think we need a story about Emma. Last year we had a big party in our back yard and invited all our friends. As part of the refreshments we had a big bowl of rum punch. Well, Emma took a sip and decided she liked it. After about an hour, we had a very drunk daughter on our hands."

"Remember early April, when we went on a hike at Hanging Lake Trail?" We all nodded, as Mom began her story. "The trail head was right off Interstate 70 near Glenwood Springs. It was still kind of cold and there was a little snow and ice on the ground when we started up the trail. The trail was very steep and went up to a high mountain lake. A little way up, we ran into a lot of ice and snow. Jimmy was climbing the trail a little in front of us. Just as I was beginning to think we should turn back, I saw Jimmy fall and he started sliding down the trail, head first, right past us. He was going really fast. Dad and I tried to grab him as he went by, but we couldn't reach him. After sliding about 30 feet, he came to a stop with a loud thump, when his head hit a boulder. I thought, 'Oh my gosh, he probably got a concussion.' At the very least, he's going to have a big bump and bloody head. Well, he got up, shook his head and started climbing back up the trail as if nothing happened. I said, 'that's it, it's time to go back.'"

About 10:30 p.m. we were all tired, so we went to bed. I convinced my parents that I could sleep outside by myself near the tent. My reasoning was, that I wouldn't have to smell all the farting and hear my siblings joking and giggling. Besides that, Mom and Dad were usually laughing and whispering in Mom's shared sleeping bag. One time when we were camping, I heard Mom say, "don't you dare, not with the children here." I had no idea what she was talking about. That reminds me of the time that one of my girl friends at school told me, "watch out for boys, they're only interested in one thing." When I asked her what that was, she said, "I don't know, nobody will tell me."

It was pitch dark outside except for a wisp of a moon. Even though it was the middle of summer, it was cold in the mountains at night, about 50 degrees. I laid there on my back looking up at the stars. They were very bright and there must have been millions of them. I could see the milky way, the big dipper and Orion. The stars were much clearer here than in the city. I felt a sense of awe in this vast universe. Could there be a higher power keeping all of this running? It was so peaceful and quiet. I felt safe and content. I was very happy. I wanted it to last forever.

We woke up kind of late Sunday morning. The sky was gray and big black clouds were moving toward us. After a great pancake and syrup breakfast, we sat on our lawn chairs and watched the clouds build up. We took turns describing the shapes. Then I saw an amazing sight in the forest. A huge buck deer walked slowly by about 50 yards from us. I silently motioned to the others and then we saw a doe and three fawns nearby. We watched them in amazement as they nibbled on a patch of grass. Then they stared at us for a long time and ambled deeper into the woods until we could no longer see them.

Then it started to rain. At first it was only a misty drizzle and felt good on our skin. But soon, it started raining harder and we had to retreat into our tent. It rained the rest of the day. Luckily we brought some books and board games so we spent the afternoon playing games and reading. Sometimes we read together and sometimes by ourselves. Jimmy and Diane were unusually quiet and we didn't squabble or argue. This might have been because they were a little frightened from the heavy rain hitting the tent and all the lightning and thunder. Our parents warned us not to touch the sides of the tent because we might cause it to leak. The wind was blowing hard and the tent was shaking.

I didn't sleep very well that night with the tent poles shaking and the loud noise of the rain. We soon felt water sloshing around below the canvas floor of the tent. At first it was funny but then I got a little seasick from the tent swaying and the water making waves under the floor. Everyone else ignored it and fell asleep. Then I noticed that the tent was leaking and our stuff was getting wet. I didn't say anything because I didn't want to disturb anyone.

We woke up early Monday morning. It was still raining hard and our sleeping bags and clothes that were not in waterproof duffles were wet. I felt like there was a foot of water sloshing around below the tent. We looked out of the front flap and there seemed to be water everywhere. After we quickly got dressed and were assessing the situation outside, a forest ranger drove up in a Jeep. The water was high up on his boots when he approached our tent. He told my parents that the Big Thompson was rising and there were flash flood warnings. He said that we should leave immediately and head for high ground. He warned us that things were very dangerous and we shouldn't try to wait it out. As the ranger was leaving, Dad said we should grab what we could and throw it in the wagon. This was an emergency and we didn't have time to take the tent. We would come back for it later if we could.

So we grabbed our essentials, piled into the wagon and drove off. We were wet, muddy and miserable as we drove out of the campground. I usually say goodbye when we leave a nice place that I've enjoyed but I didn't even think of it this time. It was raining very hard, the water was over a foot high and Dad could hardly see where he was going. He planned to drive on the gravel camp road to the main highway which was on high ground about ten miles away. The wipers couldn't keep up with the deluge of rain and we could barely see anything out the windows. We didn't know what was going to happen and we were all really scared. After we drove for about ten minutes, a huge wall of water came crashing down the canyon and swept our wagon off the road. We went careening down a steep embankment. We kids were screaming and crying and our parents had panicked expressions on their faces.

After that, all I can remember is a terrifying rush down a steep hill, the wagon bouncing off of trees and turning over a few times. I hit my head and was unconscious for a minute. When I woke up, I felt dizzy and sick and my head hurt really bad. After my eyes opened I couldn't believe what I was seeing. Our car had landed upside down at the bottom of the swollen Big Thompson River! We were under ten feet of foaming fast-moving water and there were waves and a huge amount of bubbles flowing past our windows. I could feel the car scraping along the bottom of the river as the current moved us along. The water was leaking in and there were already a couple of inches on the ceiling which was now our floor. Diane, Jimmy and I were hanging upside down with our seat belts holding us. They were quiet, still and pale and it looked like they were dead. Mom, in front was also hanging by her seat belt. It looked like she had hit her head against the windshield. She had a big gash on her forehead and was bleeding profusely. My whole world had come to an end and I wanted to die. I couldn't stand it and started crying hysterically.

Then I saw my Dad. He had released his seatbelt and was crouching on the ceiling next to the window. He turned around to me and said in a steady, reassuring voice, "I know this is really, really terrible sweetheart, but I need you to stop crying and be very brave, so we can survive this. Water is leaking in fast and we'll all drown if we don't get out of the car." I mustered all the strength I could manage and stopped crying. I suddenly felt a great will to live. I even had hope that we might all get through this. Dad helped me get out of my seatbelt and told me to take off my boots and sit right next to him. The blood from Mom's forehead was dripping down on me but I tried to ignore it and be brave.

Trying to maintain his calm, Dad instructed, "now I want you to take a deep breath.

I'm going to lower the window and the water will rush into the car. We'll have to let the water fill the car. I know you're a good swimmer, so you can follow me when I leave through the window and swim up to the surface."

I took a breath and barely blurted out, "but what about the rest of the family?"

"I'll have to get you out first. Then I'll come back for them."

Dad tried to roll down the window but it was stuck. The big dent in the car ceiling must have been pressing against it.

"O.K., my only choice is to kick the window out. Remember, be brave, cover your eyes and take a deep breath."

He kicked the window with both feet as hard as he could. There was a shattering of tiny bits of glass and a huge incoming wave of water immediately filled the inside of the car. I could see dad push himself out the open window. He turned back and reached his hand out to me. I grabbed it and he pulled me out. I remember thinking that there was no way I could do this. The water was freezing cold, the pressure on my ears was tremendous and the strong current was pushing us downstream. We kicked our legs and flapped our arms in a gigantic effort to reach the surface from ten feet below. After what seemed forever, we got to the surface and took in explosive breaths of air. Dad and I struggled to swim to the shore. I went under a few times but Dad pulled me up. We finally got to shore but I never would have made it without him. We crawled out of the water and climbed up a few feet from the river's edge.

Dad gave me a big hug and said, "I want you to stay here. I've got to go back." He dove back into the water. My teeth were chattering. I was very cold and exhausted. I was scared that he wouldn't make it in that fearsome current. I didn't think I would ever see any of my family again. I started crying. I felt a big bump on my head and fell into a state of deep depression.

Just as my despair reached its highest level, I saw an amazing sight I will remember for the rest of my life. Looking at the swollen river, I saw three small bright sparks rise from the surface. They flittered above the water like butterflies, first in circles, then criss-crossing each others' paths playfully. Then as if they could see me, they flew over in my direction. They then lighted gently onto my outstretched palm. I closed my hand around them and I could feel a warm tingly sensation. I opened my hand and they lingered there for a few seconds. Then they seemed to answer a call and sped straight up into the air. I watched as they rose higher and higher and disappeared into the dark clouds.

Meanwhile, Dad was struggling in the river against the current. I couldn't see him, but he later told me what happened. He had a hard time finding the car. We had been swept downstream but the car was moving downstream at a slower rate. He finally found it and dove down. He looked into the broken window and saw three lifeless bodies still hanging upside down. He squeezed through the window and tried to release Mom's seatbelt, but it was jammed. His lungs were stinging and felt like they would burst so he reluctantly surfaced, took a big breath of air and dove down again. He took one last look into the car and knew the situation was hopeless. By the time he pulled himself out of the river he was a good hundred yards downstream from where I was sitting. We both summoned up our last bit of energy and dragged ourselves toward each other. He held me tightly and we swayed back and forth. "I tried, I really tried. Should I have done something differently?" he sobbed. We clung to each other for a long time and cried. After a long embrace, my head stopped hurting and I had a warm feeling.

I told Dad about the sparks and he stroked the bump on my head and said it may have been delusions caused by my injury. Or it could have been sparks coming from the car battery.

"How did this happen, Daddy?"

"I don't know for sure, sweetheart. It might have been a natural disaster that couldn't be prevented or it might have been caused by mankind's neglect of the environment. Such things as climate change, pollution and erosion could be partly responsible. I may specialize in environmental law but I'm not a scientist so I don't know the detailed mechanisms behind these phenomena. Right now I'm exhausted and confused." (A few weeks later, Dad told me that he couldn't say exactly what he would do. But he wanted to learn more and thought he'd go back to college to get better educated in environmental science. He didn't want anything like that to happen again and was willing to devote the rest of his life to prevent such situations.)

"But Dad, why did it have to happen to us?"

"I guess we were just very unlucky. We were in the wrong place at the wrong time. We did nothing wrong and we did nothing to deserve this. There is no higher power that's punishing us. I think it just happened for no reason. Although this is the worst experience we will have for the rest of our lives, I think we have learned something from it. We have learned compassion. Compassion for each other, compassion for our lost family, compassion for the world. We do have each other and I will do everything in my power, to allow you to have a great life. I want us both to do things that will make them proud."

"Daddy, do you believe in God?"

"I would like to believe but I just don't know. Your Mom and siblings lived in an enchanted fantasy world and I know that they believed. They even believed in fairies, trolls and Santa Claus. But I'm more of a realist and I think I need more proof. What about you?"

"I guess I don't know yet. Will we ever be with them again, Daddy?"

"Yes, sweetheart, we will. I'm sure we will."

I could only hope that he was right.

Then it stopped raining. The clouds parted slightly and the sun shown through. We began feeling a little dry. As we started thinking about how we were going to get home, we looked at the river again. To our great surprise we saw our tent sailing majestically downstream. We both laughed with a kind of bittersweet sense of release and scrambled up the hill to the road.

Chapter 2

A Taste of Heaven

The three sparks are not a delusion. They are real and they rise through the clouds and into the blue sky. They pick up velocity and fly at the speed of light through the atmosphere. It's not clear how long they travel but it could be a long time because they land on a golden alter in a pure white marble temple at a place where space and time are different than our own. The temple is one of thousands of temples all situated on a marble floor that stretches in every direction as far as the eye can see. But in fact, the eye can really not see and this whole incredible edifice is invisible to humans because it lies in a four-dimensional space instead of stretching into three dimensions.

The three sparks suddenly transform into three white robed figures, one adult and two children. These figures closely resemble Ellen, Diane and Jimmy. Closely resemble because they're a little too perfect. Diane had some mosquito bites on her leg which are now gone. Ellen had a mole on her face near her right eye and it's gone. The scab on Jimmy's knee is no longer there. The three figures embrace in a big family hug but it's a little strange because they can't feel each other.

A tall stately woman, again in a white robe, appears at the front of the marble room and ushers the three to be seated in comfortable white leather chairs. "Let me introduce myself," she says. "My name is Joan Starr and I am an angel. Welcome to the Academy or as you previously called it, heaven. You probably feel a little unusual now but you will soon get used to it. You no longer can feel, see and hear in the way you could before. You are not composed of matter, but of pure energy and we are communicating by means of thought waves. The sparks from which you transformed are called your souls and souls cannot be destroyed. The reason you and I appear the way we do is because we are comfortable having these forms. For example, I died about 2,000 years ago at the age of 60 but I feel better when I look like I'm 30. You can take any form you please but I suspect you like the way you are for now. It may appear that I am talking to you but you are actually sensing high frequency thought waves. Most angels communicate directly with these waves without the pretext of moving their mouths which aren't real anyway.

13

I can tell by your quizzical expressions that you are quite confused and that's only natural. I will only continue this introduction for a little while longer and let you have time to absorb and rest. Even angels have to rest to recharge their energies. The Academy is a place of learning, study and investigating. While your previous world was $3 + 1$-dimensional, meaning three dimensions of space and one dimension of time, the Academy of your present world is $4 + 2$-dimensional, meaning four dimensions of space and two dimensions of time. Because of these additional dimensions, you can do some really wild things and you will have ample opportunity to experiment and have fun. Your present status at the Academy is that of apprentice. This status will last about 1,000 years but time is quite different here because it's two-dimensional and can't be compared to linear time. If you succeed well with your studies you will be promoted to the status of angel like me. Angels exist in a $4 + 3$-dimensional world so we have an additional dimension of time freedom, which can be quite enjoyable. Angels who truly excel in research can be promoted to $4 + 4$-dimensional archangels.

You will learn more about these things as you progress in your studies and there really is a lot to learn. One thing you will learn about is that, although we are composed of pure energy, we have the ability to convert some of that energy into mass. This is because mass and energy are equivalent and each can be converted into the other. Before we recess, there is one more being I should mention. Last but not least, is a $5 + 5$-dimensional being called God. None of us have a gender here and it's only by tradition that we refer to God as 'he.' By the way, some angels and archangels refer to him as 'Mr. G.,' but for reverence I prefer to call him God. We will meet again before you begin your apprentice classes, but for now do you have any questions?"

"Will we ever see Gary and Emma again?" Ellen asked.

"It may take awhile," Joan assured her, "but when they are elevated to the Academy, you will be reunited. You will then be together forever."

With some hope in her voice Diane asked, "what about Daisy? Can she come here too?"

"I'm sorry dear, but there are no real dogs at the Academy. But we do have Earth simulations, where you can find dogs that are almost real. They run, jump, play and lick but they don't eat, pee and poop like real dogs."

Not to be left out, Jimmy poses his question, "do you have toys here?"

"Yes dear, we have lots of toys. We have old toys and toys like you've never seen before. Now, I'll take you all on a little tour of the Academy."

Joan leads them along a marble path lined with magnificent parks, temples and buildings. "You'll be interested in this playground, Jimmy. It has every kind of jungle gym, hanging bars, slides and swings you can imagine. The next building contains classrooms where you and Diane will learn about fascinating subjects. Next are seminar buildings where you will discuss the structure of the cosmos, Ellen. Then we have laboratories and observatories where experiments and investigations are conducted. That temple is called God's Hall. I'll take you in to meet God."

Ellen, Diane and Jimmy enter the temple. In the center of the marble floor is a large Persian rug on which is seated a smiling figure with a flowing white beard. He directs them to sit before him and begins speaking. "I am the leader of the Academy and you can call me God. First, I must tell you that I am sorry that your lives on Earth were cut so short. This has deprived you of the many experiences that you might have had on Earth. I am confident that we can make this up to you here. I hope you did not suffer when you died. It is clear that you did nothing wrong to deserve this. You are completely innocent and there was no question that you would come here to the Academy, or as you call it, heaven. I suspect that your first question is why this happened to you and why, being God, didn't I prevent this from happening. It happened because it was the natural flow of events. I could not prevent it because my intervention would have interfered with this natural flow. Such interference would cause inconsistencies that could destroy your universe. You will learn more about this in your classes and seminars. I know that you have many questions but I think it is best to leave them for later meetings. It is now time for you to rest and recharge your energies."

After sufficient rest, the three new apprentices begin their heavenly activities. Jimmy runs directly to the playground where he is eager to try his recently acquired physical skills. Since he is composed of pure energy and elementary particles, he feels light as a feather. He can jump incredibly high, do huge flips and even fly. He can negotiate a monkey-bar set a hundred yards long. Then he sees others in the playground who are having as much fun as he.

Jimmy was used to playing with children on Earth whose races were different than his own. But here the situation is more extreme. The other children are about his size but that's where the similarities frequently end. Three are Earthlings of other races, but there are also children with three legs and one arm, there are children with no ears and one eye. In fact, there are as many variations as one can imagine. The other children greet Jimmy eagerly and he quickly makes friends. They become involved in playing various games. Some are new to Jimmy and others are like games he played on Earth. He learns that there is one important rule that is the guiding principle for everything. This rule is that one must have compassion for all other beings. In particular, Jimmy learns not to make fun of others because they look or act differently.

Jimmy and some of the other children play tag. He finds that he can do some amazing things to tag someone. He can suddenly disappear and then reappear somewhere else. He can be at two different places at the same time. He can protrude part of himself quickly forward and then the rest of him snaps in to meet the first part. He finds himself wondering how it is possible for him to perform these wild stunts. He doesn't know that he will later learn these things in spacetime seminars. For now he is having the time of his life (or should we say afterlife?).

Jimmy soon learns that life in the Academy is not all fun and physical games. A large portion of time is devoted to intellectual and mental pursuits. One of Jimmy's friends tells him about this great children's math class taught by Angel Galois. In this course, the students learn math by doing puzzles. This sounds fascinating, so Jimmy joins his friend at the class.

After introducing himself to the new students, Angel Galois begins, "I will give you five puzzles. You will then have time to work on the puzzles by yourself or with others. After that you are invited to present your answers to the class.

Puzzle 1. You have three pitchers. The first holds three cups of water, the second holds five cups of water and the third is larger than the second but its size is unknown. How can you obtain four cups of water using these three pitchers?

Puzzle 2. Replace each letter with one of the digits $1, 2, 3, 4$.

$$\frac{A}{B} + \frac{C}{D} = 5$$

Puzzle 3. Each of the digits 1 through 9 belongs in the squares. Some row sums and column sums are given. Place the correct digits in the squares.

	3		12
		5	
6			17
12	21		

Puzzle 4. Cross out two of the numbers in the following array so that the sum of the numbers in each row and column is a multiple of three.

1	3	5	6
4	9	2	1
2	3	9	4
8	7	5	8

Puzzle 5. If N is a factor of 72, a multiple of 6 and is divisible by 8, find N.

Those are the puzzles. If you solve all five as a class, I'll let you fly on the back of my giant winged dragon and play on our amazing new fifty meter 4-dimensional sliding board. Good luck, enjoy."

The children work enthusiastically on the puzzles. Most of them work in groups and have many animated discussions. After a considerable amount of time, Angel Galois asks for volunteers to present solutions. A three-eyed child with a beak-like orange nose raises his six-fingered hand, "Here's how my group solved Puzzle 1. Fill the second pitcher with five cups of water and pour out three cups to fill the first pitcher. This leaves two cups of water in the second pitcher. Pour these two cups into the third pitcher. So as not to waste water, empty the first pitcher into the second pitcher. Now fill the second pitcher with new water and proceed as before to obtain four cups of water in the third pitcher."

"Well done," says Galois. "How about Puzzle 2?"

Our very own, Jimmy raises his hand. "We thought this one was the easiest. Just let $A = 3$, $B = 1$, $C = 4$ and $D = 2$."

The volunteer for Puzzle 3 begins, "after some trial and error, we decided that we should first do the third column. To add up to 21 we needed the larger numbers 7, 8 or 9. After some more trial and error we put a 7 at the top and a 9 at the bottom. This then determined the other numbers and we got this solution."

2	3	7
4	8	5
6	1	9

The children cheer and the next volunteer steps up. "For Puzzle 4 we first noticed that all the rows and columns summed to a multiple of three except rows two and four and columns two and four. Cross out the one in row two and the seven to get the solution."

"Great job," cheers Galois. "Finally, we have Puzzle 5."

The volunteer for this puzzle says, "The multiples of 6 are: $6, 12, 18, 24, 30, 36, \ldots$. Only 24 is divisible by 8. Since 24 is a factor of 72, the answer is 24."

Everyone jumps up and applauds. Galois says, "that's enough for now. Enjoy the dragon and sliding board." Jimmy decides that this was much better than any math class he had on Earth.

Diane attends a class entitled Planetary Sets. The instructor, Angel Alexis is saying, "in this class you will learn how sets are described in various planets. A set is just a collection of objects with certain properties. The objects are usually called elements or members of the set. For example, $\{a, b, c\}$ is a set with the three members a, b and c. Notice that we usually enclose the members of a set in curly brackets. We also have a special set called the empty set $\emptyset$ that has no members.

On the planet Earth, the elements of a set can be arbitrary. We could have a set of oranges or a set of numbers or a set of anything. On Earth, they usually start with a universal set $S = \{a_1, a_2, \ldots, a_n\}$ and consider subsets of S. A *subset* of S is $\emptyset$ or a set whose elements come from the elements of S. For example $\{a_1\}$, $\{a_2\}$, $\{a_2, a_3\}$, $\{a_2, a_3, a_4\}$ and S are subsets of S if $n \geq 4$. For subsets A and B of S we say that A is *included in B* and write $A \subset B$ if A and B are different and the members of A are also members of B. For example, $\emptyset \subset \{a_1\}$, $\{a_2\} \subset \{a_1, a_2, a_3\}$ and $\{a_1, a_2\} \subset \{a_1, a_2, a_4\}$. If A is not included in B we write $A \not\subset B$. For instance, $\{a_1\} \not\subset \{a_2\}$ and $\{a_2\} \not\subset \{a_1, a_3\}$. The inclusion relation $\subset$ has two important properties. These are $A \not\subset A$ (irreflexivity) and $A \subset B$, $B \subset C$ imply $A \subset C$ (transitivity). Irreflexivity holds because A and A are the same and transitivity holds because any member of A is also a member of B and thus is a member of C.

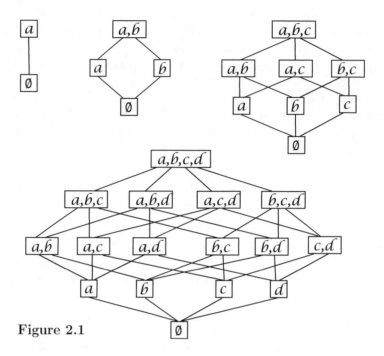

Figure 2.1

To understand the relationships between subsets of a set S we can draw diagrams of these subsets. These are called *Hasse diagrams* and are obtained as follows. If $A \subset B$ and there is no subset C with $A \subset C \subset B$ then we draw a rising line from A to B. Figure 2.1 illustrates the Hasse diagrams for universal sets with one, two, three and four elements. For ease of reading we incase the members of subsets in rectangles. The Hasse diagrams in Figure 2.1 are examples of *Boolean algebras*.

Let's now see how sets are described on the planet Xen. It seems that the inhabitants of this planet, the Xenons, developed their set theory at a later stage than the Earthlings. When the Xenons developed their set theory, their physics was quite advanced. In fact, they were aware of matter and antimatter. For this reason, their sets were composed of two types of members that they called elements and anti-elements. The Xenons had seen experiments in which matter and antimatter of the same type annihilated each other when brought close together. For example, if an electron and positron (anti-electron) meet, their matter disappears and nothing remains but pure energy. Because of this behavior, the Xenons refused to allow an element a and its corresponding anti-element $\bar{a}$ to exist together in a set.

Suppose we have a pegboard with three holes of different shapes numbered 1, 2 and 3 and three pegs each having the shape of one of the holes also numbred 1, 2 and 3. We can represent the pegs by the set $\{1,2,3\}$ and the holes by the set $\{\bar{1},\bar{2},\bar{3}\}$. If a peg comes in contact with its corresponding hole, we assume that it is placed in the hole. In this way, a peg together with a hole of the same shape results in neither a peg nor a hole. For example, there would be no set of the form $\{1,2,\bar{2},3,\bar{3}\}$, only sets in which a number and its anti-number do not appear together. Instead of $\{1,2,\bar{2},3,\bar{3}\}$ we would have the set $\{1\}$.

As another example, suppose there are certain pairs of Xenons that hate each other and the sets represent committees. We would not want such pairs to appear together in a committee. At the opposite extreme, suppose there are certain pairs of Xenons that are in love and again the sets represent committees. If such a pair are in the same committee, they would either wander off together or be so interested in each other that they would be ineffective members.

The Xenons use a different inclusion relation than the Earthlings. They reason that the more elements a set contains the larger it is, and the more anti-elements the smaller. They use the symbol $\sqsubset$ for inclusion and they assume that $A \sqsubset B$ if A and B are different, if every element in A is also in B and every anti-element in B is also in A. As with the inclusion relation *subset* on Earth, the inclusion relation $\sqsubset$ satisfies irreflexivity and transitivity. As an example, suppose we begin with the collection $S = \{a,b,\bar{b}\}$. The Xenian subsets of S are $\emptyset$, $\{a\}$, $\{b\}$, $\{\bar{b}\}$, $\{a,b\}$, $\{a,\bar{b}\}$. We have that $\{\bar{b}\} \sqsubset \emptyset$, $\{a,\bar{b}\} \sqsubset \{a\}$ and $\{a\} \sqsubset \{a,b\}$.

Figure 2.2 presents the Hasse diagrams of subsets for the Xen collections $\{a\}$, $\{a,\bar{a}\}$, $\{a,\bar{a},b\}$ and $\{a,\bar{a},b,\bar{b}\}$. Notice that, except for the first one, these Hasse diagrams do not have the same structure as those in Figure 2.1. This shows that the Xen Hasse diagrams do not give a Boolean algebra.

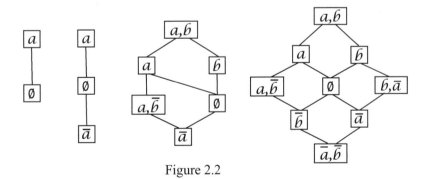

Figure 2.2

Finally, we consider set theory on the planet Ne. The Neons knew nothing about matter and anti-matter when they developed their set theory so it is entirely different from that of the planet Xen. It is also different from set theory on Earth. It seems that in their early history, the Neons developed superstitions about odd numbers. They were similar but stronger than the Earthlings' superstitions about the number 13. The very fact that Earthlings call such numbers "odd" indicates they have certain reservations about them also. In any case, the Neons refused to consider sets with an odd number of members.

On the planet Ne, the set $S = \{a, b, c, d\}$ only has the subsets $\emptyset$, $\{a, b\}$, $\{a, c\}$, $\{a, d\}$, $\{b, c\}$, $\{b, d\}$, $\{c, d\}$ and S. The inclusion relation on Ne is the same as used on Earth. The Hasse diagram for the subsets of this set S is given in Figure 2.3. This shows that the set theory structure on Ne is different than that on Xen and Earth. Well, that ends our lesson for now. See you next time." Diane found the Planetary Sets class to be fascinating. It was much better than any math class she had taken on Earth.

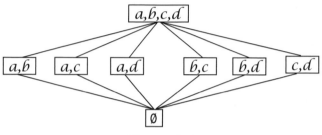

Figure 2.3

Because of her maturity, Ellen did not attend classes. She took graduate-level seminars. After she had attended several seminars, we find her in discussion with one of her new friends, Sandy. "How long have you been here at the Academy, Sandy?"

"I've been here about 200 Earth years, Ellen. Why do you ask?"

"Well, there are some things I'm confused about. You've had a lot of experience at the Academy and I was wondering if you would answer a few questions."

"I'd be glad to answer anything you ask. I must remind you that I'm not an angel or archangel so I don't know as much as they do, but I'll do my best."

"I've found the seminars I've attended to be fascinating. I've learned many new things about science, math and the universe. I have broadened my knowledge about literature, cultures and music. But I no longer have my human brain. How am I able to remember things? How am I able to learn and reason? Why is it that these things even come easier to me than they did on Earth? I feel like the straw man in the *Wizard of Oz*. I don't have a brain but my mind has great power."

"You may not have an ordinary body and brain, but you do have energy and interacting elementary particles. Some of these particles have come together to form what we call a data bank. Your data bank is much better than a human brain. While a brain works like an ordinary computer, your data bank operates like a quantum computer. Quantum computers have much more memory and process information faster than a typical computer.

I don't know all the details, but you will learn more about these things in seminars. It's all very amazing."

"Thank you, Sandy, that helps a lot. Now I have another question and it may be harder to answer. You have been at the Academy a few hundred years. Others have been here for thousands and millions of years. I know that academicians learn fascinating things, have stimulating discussions and conduct awesome research. You have an idyllic existence, but there must be more. To put it bluntly, don't you sometimes get bored?"

"You're right, Ellen, there is more. You just haven't been here long enough to find it. One can get bored with a perfectly smooth and idyllic existence in which nothing bad ever happens. On Earth we had experiences like pain, suffering and misery. Some say we need such experiences for contrast if we want the pleasures of joy, happiness and contentment. All of us still carry our own versions of pain, suffering and misery on our shoulders. Our souls can release these emotions as if we were living through our worst nightmares. We have a place in the Academy where we can obtain such release. It's called the cave of souls, but you might not want to go there."

Ellen decides that sooner or later she would have to visit the cave of souls. "I might as well try it now. After all, what could happen? I am in heaven, aren't I?"

Ellen concentrates on the words "cave of souls" and sure enough she finds herself approaching the entrance of a large cave. Immediately after entering she feels a transformation. Her earthly body has returned. She's wearing a shirt and jeans. She pinches her arm and feels the pain. An insect bite on her leg itches and her stomach growls with hunger pangs. The cave is cold and damp. She feels miserable. Upon noticing lot of spiders crawling on the wall, Ellen decides to turn back and get out of there. But the cave entrance closes with a stone wall. She claws at the stones to no avail. Her only choice is to turn around and continue into the cave. The cave is dark except for a burning torch attached to the wall. Blocks away, down a narrow corridor she can barely make out another torch. Her heart races when she spies a bunch of rats scurrying near her feet. Ellen walks quickly to get away from them.

A huge, menacing creature jumps out behind her from a side corridor. It's a gorilla-like monster with one large eye in the center of its forehead. The monster has immense fanged teeth and huge sharp claws. White saliva is drooling from its mouth. The creature is so grotesque that Ellen turns away paralyzed with fear. The monster approaches her and swipes a claw along her back. Her shirt is ripped open leaving a long bleeding gash. The gash stings intensely and Ellen starts running away as fast as she can. This is like a combination of all her nightmares. But it's worse because it is so real.

As she is running, Ellen can hear the creature lumbering behind her and feel his hot breath. The cave narrows into a tunnel that is barely large enough for her to crawl into. Luckily the creature is too large to get in and she hears him growl in frustration as she crawls away. The tunnel gets narrower and Ellen has to hold her breath in order to proceed. Then she is stuck. She can't go forward and, with the monster nearby, she can't go back. She's in complete misery with visions of dying alone in this awful place.

21

Ellen realizes that the tunnel walls are made of mud. She can claw at the walls and make the opening a little bit larger. Also, she sees a light ahead. She squeezes through and pulls herself out into an open cavern. Before she can heave a sigh of relief, the gorilla creature pounces on her. Its fangs pierce deeply into her neck and she bleeds profusely. She screams from the unbearable pain. She can feel the creature sucking her neck as she bleeds out and dies.

After what seems a short time, Ellen awakes in her white robed heavenly state. She's seated at a table under a blue sky in the outdoor patio of a French café. In front of her is an elegant cup containing cosmic tea. She drinks the tea and feels exhilarated. The pain is gone and she feels light again. She jumps high into the air, makes a huge somersault and comes down gently to the ground. The contrast between what she felt before and how she feels now is spectacular. "There's a little bit of hell in heaven," she thinks. "Also, there's a little bit of Earth in heaven, but heaven is much better."

Chapter 3

Consistency

Two white robed angels stroll along one of the many marble paths of the Academy. One is tall, young, handsome and has a well-trimmed beard. The other is shorter, stocky and has a scruffy beard. Although most members of the Academy do not wear jewelry, the taller angel sports a medallion around his neck in the shape of a cross and the shorter angel has a medallion in the shape of a peace symbol. The scruffy angel turns to the other angel and says, "don't you think it would be more pleasant if we got off this marble road and walked through the forest simulator, Jesus?" The other angel replies, "yes, Moses, I like the forest simulator, it reminds me of my time on earth."

The scene gradually turns into a lush forest and the path becomes well-trimmed grass. The white sky turns dark blue with a few well-placed clouds. Again, the forest is a little too perfect. Although there are butterflies and birds, there do not seem to be bugs. Wild flowers appear in abundance but there is no dead vegetation or fallen trees.

"Do you miss Earth, Jesus?"

"Yes I do and what about you, Moses?"

"Well, some things I don't miss. Like the pain in my leg, the sunburn and the constant itching. But that was all part of being human and it reminded me I was alive. There were a lot of good things too. Like the tastes and the smells. The sex was really great; one of the perks of being a great leader. I know we can get all these things in the Earth simulator, but they're just not as intense. What about you? I bet with all those groupies hanging around, you did a lot of fucking."

"I did my share of loving, but please Moses don't use that kind of language. You know that God doesn't like cursing."

"I don't pretend he doesn't hear me. Mr. G. is everywhere. But I don't think he really minds. He's got a lot of compassion and a great sense of humor. Anyway, even if our language is perfectly polite, I don't think our chances of ever returning to Earth are very good. Especially after all the crazy stunts you pulled, you asshole. You were lucky the archangel committee agreed to have the seed of your soul inserted in Mary. But then you started pulling those do-gooder 'miracles' like curing blindness and epilepsy. You know those people were getting better on their own. Then there was that cheap walking on water trick. How did you ever think of that? But the crowning glory was that resurrection from the dead stunt. That was a real beaut. You really ruined things for the rest of us, you fuckin' prick. You know how concerned Mr. G. is about contradictions and inconsistencies. You were fuckin' close to them right and left."

"God dammit, Moses, I told you to watch the cussing. You should talk about ridiculous stunts. What about that stupid burning bush trick? And who thought of those idiotic ten plagues? The parting of the Red Sea stunt must have taken a lot of conniving and your admonitions about worshipping the golden calf took the cake. Then there was your sojourn to the top of Mount Sinai. Everyone knew you chiseled those commandments into the tablets yourself. Why else would it have taken so long? God could have done it in a couple of seconds. Besides, he certainly wouldn't have written those things in such a ridiculous way. But what really showed your true shit-head colors was that wandering in the desert for forty years. What was that all about? Don't give me that generation of slaves having to die crap. You were only a few hundred miles from the Land of Israel. I could have led the Hebrews there in a couple of months."

"Look, Jesus, that's all water under the bridge. Let's not get all worked up about these things. There's nothing we can do about them now. We were both inexperienced and wanted to do what was best for our people. We now know that Mr. G. is very concerned about consistency but we didn't know that then and we got close to crossing the line. We're just two good Jewish boys trying to do our best. You know I love you. Let's talk about something else."

The two angels give each other a big bear hug and Jesus asks, "do you want to connect?"

"Sure, why not?", says Moses.

They embrace and meld into a blob resembling a giant amoeba. The blob rises above the ground sways back and forth and twirls about. It then flies around in great circles and dances in the air. This goes on for quite a while but finally the blob alights gently on the ground and separates back into the two angels.

"Wow, that was nice," Moses says. "We ought to do that more often."

"You're right Moses, we should."

The two angels are pretty much alone except every once in a while another angel or two walks or glides down the path. One of these angels approaches them and says, "is that you Moses?"

"Yes, it's me. I'm sorry but I'm having a hard time processing your name."

The angel replies, "I'm Shalamat, we were both in Egypt 3,500 years ago."

"You do look familiar and whatever I did to you, please forgive me."

"I don't know if I can do that. You were a complete jerk in those days. You were a hot shot prince, son of the royal pharaoh and I was your lowly camel bearer."

"Look, Shalamat, things were a lot different in those days. The pharaoh was supposed to be a god and he told me that I was part of the divine reign. I was informed that the usual laws of man did not apply to me and I could do whatever I wanted."

"Well, you certainly learned that lesson well. You sat up tall and straight on your camel while I led it along narrow crowded streets. One time the camel crapped on the steps of your magnificent temple and you shoved my face into the camel shit. How do you think that felt? I'll tell you, it was really disgusting. Another time you slipped off the camel and said it was my fault. You pulled off my shirt and whipped me with your camel whip. My back was covered in scratches and blood and it stung for days. The scars were there for the rest of my life. I still can't believe what a schmuck you were."

"All I can say is, that I was very young then and didn't know the ways of the world."

"I'm not finished yet. You remember my wife, Shasha? She was a very good looker. You grabbed her and rode off with her into the desert on your camel. You spent some time with her and then brought her back. When she told me about it I was livid and said I would kill you. She reminded me what would happen to us if I killed a prince. Besides, she confessed that she flirted with you, the hot shot royalty and it felt kind of good. I forgave her and decided to let the whole thing go. In any case, it wasn't her fault and nothing can excuse your terrible behavior."

"I'm very sorry, Shalamat. You're right, nothing can excuse my behavior. I didn't learn humility and compassion until I was about 50. The last 100 years of my life were much better though. You remember, I killed the Egyptian when I saw him beat a Hebrew?"

"Yes, but you **killed** the Egyptian. You're not supposed to go around killing people. How in the world did you get admitted to the Academy when you acted like that?"

"I guess I redeemed myself later. You have every right to hate me. I'll tell you what. If it will make you feel better, you can hit me."

"Okay, let's try it."

Shalamat winds up his fist and hits Moses in the jaw with all his might. The only problem is that his fist goes right through Moses' face and comes out the other side.

"Whoops, I forgot, I'm mostly energy now. I'll put more mass into my face and you can try again."

Shalamat tries again and this time he hits solid mass and there is a loud crack.

"Ouch, that really hurt. Do you feel better now?"

"That hurt my fist too. I feel a little better, but not much."

"Okay, let's try this. How would you like to kick my ass?"

"That sounds good. Let's do it."

Moses bends over, throws up his robe and exposes his big fat ass.

"Wait a minute, something's wrong. That doesn't look right to me," says Salamat.

Moses thinks for a second, gives a few grunts and grows a lot of hair on his bottom half. He then exposes his big, fat, hairy ass. Shalamat gives him a swift hard kick that knocks him over and he lands with his face in the dirt. While Moses gets up and wipes himself off, Shalamat walks away with a satisfied smile. The two angels continue their walk with Jesus sporting a large grin and chuckling to himself. They are soon confronted by another angel who looks at them and says, "Jesus, is that you, you big schmuck?"

"It looks like it's your turn, Jesus. This is going to be fun," Moses says with a satisfied chuckle.

"Yes, it's me," Jesus replies to the angel, ignoring Moses, "what is your problem, my son?"

"You probably don't remember me, the last time we saw each other was 2,000 years ago. My name is Wobegon and you're my problem."

"I'm sorry if I offended you, Wobegon. Please tell me what happened." Jesus humbly bows his head.

"I was lying on my death bed with a terrible disease and along comes this arrogant, contemptible person, Jesus. You performed one of your ridiculous miracles and cured me."

"I don't see anything wrong with that. It's what I did in those days."

"Well, your stupid meddling caused me all sorts of grief. Instead of dying a peaceful death, the disease left me in a weakened state. I couldn't work and became a beggar for twenty years."

"At least I gave you twenty extra years."

"Let me tell you, I was miserable. How would you like being a beggar for twenty years? People spit on me, kicked me and cursed me. Children taunted me and threw rocks at me. I was homeless, hungry and without a decent bath for weeks on end. I stunk and was covered with flies, flees and other bugs. I was boiling hot in the summer and freezing cold all winter. I was in pain and suffering for twenty years. But that wasn't the worst of it. Because I was the recipient of your idiotic miracle, the Romans called me a Christian and threw me and some other unfortunate people into a coliseum with a bunch of hungry lions. A lion bit off one of my legs. Blood was gushing out and I was in excruciating pain. I yelled and cried and the louder I screamed the more a crowd of 100,000 people laughed and cheered. The lion was having a great time. He chewed the meat off my bone and licked the blood off his lips. Then he licked the blood off the stub of my leg, gave a loud purring sound and bit off my other leg. It took him a few minutes to eat the meat off my thighs while I was suffering enormously. I don't blame the lion. That's what lions do. But how can that cheering crowd enjoy the agony of others like that? I was still conscious when he bit off both my arms. I passed out mercifully while he was sucking out my eyeballs. Can you imagine my pain and suffering? It's the worst way I can think of to die. And people lamented about your little crucification."

"What can I say? I have no reply except my deepest sorrow. I will do anything you ask. What is your bidding?"

"You say you have compassion. Doesn't that mean you can feel other people's suffering?

"Yes it does. But what can I do to make this up to you?"

"I'd like to chew off your hand. But I don't want a fake hand. I want a real hand with flesh, bones, blood and nerves."

"All right, here it is."

Jesus pulls up the sleeve of his robe and extends his right arm. Wobegon grabs it with both hands and flashes a set of bright teeth. They are large, long and pointed like the teeth of a lion. Wobegon bites down hard and pulls off five fingers with his teeth. He spits out blood, bones and pieces of flesh while Jesus screams. Then he bites down again around the wrist. With Jesus screaming uncontrollably, he bites down a third time in the middle of Jesus' forearm. Then Jesus falls to his knees, crying and holding the stub of his right arm with his left hand.

"Now you know a fraction of my pain. Goodbye," Wobegon says angrily.

As Wobegon walks away, Jesus pops out a new right arm. "Wow, that was terrible. It made my crucification seem like nothing. I guess I still have a lot to learn."

"I'm glad that's over." Moses sighs, "it was beginning to be more than I could take. I hope we don't meet any others that we knew in the old days."

The two angels continue walking, but now in silence. The stillness is broken when Jesus says, "do you know what a natural number is?"

"Do you think I'm an idiot?" Moses growls, "I may be dumb but I'm not stupid. Of course I know what a natural number is. I've been going to the number theory seminars given by Mr. G. and some archangels. In fact, I suspect that among other things, Mr. G. is a mathematician. In any case, I know that mathematics is his favorite subject. Anyway, a natural number is a whole number or counting number like $1, 2, 3, \ldots$ The set of natural numbers is denoted by $\mathbb{N} = \{1, 2, 3, \ldots\}$ where the three dots indicate that the list goes on indefinitely. The curly brackets denote a set whose elements are listed inside. For example, the first three natural numbers form the set $\{1, 2, 3\}$. The natural numbers between five and ten inclusively form the set $\{5, 6, 7, 8, 9, 10\}$."

Jesus replies, "that's right. Now maybe you can tell me what an even number is."

"That's easy. An even number is a natural number that's divisible by 2. Thus, if you divide an even number by 2, you get another natural number. The even numbers form the set $\{2, 4, 6, 8, \ldots\}$. Notice all these numbers are divisible by 2. Another way of saying this is that even numbers are natural numbers that have 2 as a factor. Thus, they can be written as 2 times some natural number. For example, we have $2 = 2 \times 1, 4 = 2 \times 2, 6 = 2 \times 3, 8 = 2 \times 4, \ldots$ These have the factor 2."

"Sometimes it's useful to do this symbolically. Let a represent a natural number. If a is even then $\frac{a}{2} = b$ where b is a natural number. Multiplying both sides by 2, we can write this as $b = 2 \times a$ so we see that 2 is a factor. We usually write $2 \times a$ as $2 \cdot a$ or $2a$ because it's shorter."

"I'm glad that we're now talking to each other civilly." Moses says, the edge gone from his tone, "it's my turn to ask you the next question. What's an odd number?"

Jesus smiles, glad to have moved the conversation, "I could say that an odd number is a natural number that's not an even number but that wouldn't be very informative. It would be better to say that an odd number is a natural number that is not divisible by 2. That is, an odd number is a natural number that does not have 2 as a factor. The odd numbers form the set $\{1, 3, 5, 7, \ldots\}$. Symbolically, odd numbers can be written as $2a - 1$ where a is a natural number. Notice that such numbers are not divisible by 2 because if we divide $2a - 1$ by 2 we get $a - \frac{1}{2}$ which is not a natural number."

"Do you know where the names for the different types of numbers come from?"

"The natural numbers come up directly from nature. God told me that mathematics ticks off time starting from the big bang using natural numbers, $1, 2, 3, \ldots$ Even numbers come from the fact that they divide evenly into two parts. If you have a pile of ten sticks, it divides evenly into two five stick piles. Odd numbers divide evenly with one odd-ball left over. If you have a pile of thirteen sticks, it divides evenly into two six stick piles plus an odd stick left over."

"It looks like the sum of two even numbers is even. For example, $2 + 2 = 4$ which is even, $4 + 8 = 12$ which is even, $6 + 10 = 16$ which is even. Each of the two even numbers has a factor of 2 so the sum should have a factor of 2. Is that always true?"

"Yes, it is. The best way to show this is to take two even numbers a and b. We can write them as $a = 2c$ and $b = 2d$ so the sum is

$$a + b = 2c + 2d = 2(c + d)$$

Since $a + b$ has 2 as a factor, it's even. What about the sum of two odd numbers?"

"Okay," Moses says, "let's test this with some numbers, $1+3 = 4$ which is even, $3+5 = 8$ which is even, $7+11 = 18$ which is even. It looks like the sum of two odd numbers is always even. We can prove this by letting a and b be odd and writing $a = 2c - 1$ and $b = 2d - 1$ where c and d are natural numbers. Then

$$a + b = 2c - 1 + 2d - 1 = 2(c + d) - 2 = 2(c + d - 1)$$

Thus, $a + b$ has 2 as a factor so it's even."

"Hmm," Jesus picks up the line of thinking, "let's test the sum of an even number and an odd number. We have $2 + 1 = 3$ which is odd, $2 + 3 = 5$ which is odd, $6 + 9 = 15$ which is odd, $4 + 13 = 17$ which is odd. It appears that the sum of an even number a and an odd number b is always odd. To prove this we can write $a = 2c$ and $b = 2d - 1$ so the sum becomes

$$a + b = 2c + 2d - 1 = 2(c + d) - 1$$

and it follows that $a + b$ is odd."

"If $a = 2c, b = 2d$ are even, then their product

$$a \cdot b = (2c) \cdot (2d) = 4(c \cdot d) = 2 \cdot 2(c \cdot d)$$

has a factor of 2, so it's even. If $a = 2c$ is even and $b = 2d - 1$ is odd, then their product

$$a \cdot b = 2c \cdot (2d - 1) = 2 \cdot [c(2d - 1)]$$

has a factor of 2, so it's even. Some examples are: $2 \cdot 4 = 8$, $4 \cdot 10 = 40$, $2 \cdot 3 = 6$, $4 \cdot 7 = 28$."

"If $a = 2c - 1, b = 2d - 1$ are odd neither has a factor of 2 so their product shouldn't have a factor of 2. This would show that $a \cdot b$ is odd. Let us check this,

$$a \cdot b = (2c - 1)(2d - 1) = (2c - 1) \cdot (2d) - (2c - 1) \cdot 1$$
$$= 4cd - 2d - 2c + 1 = 2(2cd - d - c + 1) - 1$$

and this does it. Some examples are: $3 \cdot 5 = 15$, $7 \cdot 3 = 21$, $5 \cdot 9 = 45$. Figure 3.1 summarizes what we have done. It's curious that even numbers come up more often than odd numbers on the right side of the equations in Figure 3.1. This shows that if you do a lot of arithmetic operations on natural numbers, then you are more likely to end up with an even rather than an odd number."

even + even = even
odd + odd = even
even + odd = odd

sums

even × even = even
odd × odd = odd
even × odd = even

products

Figure 3.1

"There are other interesting numbers besides the even and odd numbers." Moses offers, "for example, there are the square numbers, $1, 4, 9, 16, 25, 36, 49, \ldots$ These are numbers of the form $n = m^2$ where m is a natural number. The first few square numbers are illustrated in Figure 3.2."

Figure 3.2

"I, myself, like the triangular numbers $1, 3, 6, 10, 15, \ldots$," Jesus adds excitedly, "these are numbers of the form

$$a = \frac{b(b+1)}{2}$$

where b is a natural number. The first few triangular numbers are illustrated in Figure 3.3. Notice that 10 has the shape of pins in bowling."

"Hey, I just noticed something amazing." exclaims Moses.

"What's that?"

"If you add two successive triangular numbers, you get a square number."

"Wow, if that's true, it would be really exciting. How would you prove that?"

"Well, take the triangular number 3 in Figure 3.3. Turn the three dots upside down and look at it with the next triangular number which has six dots. Taken together we have three dots in each of three rows and this gives nine dots which is a square number. I think this works with any two successive triangular numbers."

"That's a fascinating discovery," replies Jesus. "Let's see if we can prove that algebraically. Take a triangular number $b(b+1)/2$. The next triangular number is $(b+1)(b+2)/2$."

"Let me have the fun of finishing this," admonishes Moses. "If we add them together, we get

$$\frac{b(b+1)}{2} + \frac{(b+1)(b+2)}{2} = \frac{(b+1)(2b+2)}{2} = \frac{2(b+1)(b+1)}{2} = (b+1)^2$$

But $(b+1)^2$ is a square number so we proved it. I think this makes us mathematical geniuses!"

"I don't know about that, but we certainly are having a good time," exclaims Jesus. "Let's keep going with this. Another important kind of numbers is the set of prime numbers. Do you know what they are?"

Figure 3.3

"Of course, I know what a prime number is." Moses says, rolling his eyes, "it's a natural number, greater than 1 that's divisible only by 1 and itself. For example, the first few prime numbers are $2, 3, 5, 7, 11, 13, 17, 19, 23, \ldots$.The important thing is that any natural number greater than 1 is a prime or a product of primes. Some examples are: $6 = 2 \cdot 3$, $8 = 2 \cdot 2 \cdot 2$, $10 = 2 \cdot 5$, $24 = 2 \cdot 2 \cdot 3 \cdot 3$, $100 = 2 \cdot 2 \cdot 5 \cdot 5$. Do you know anything else about prime numbers?"

"I remember Mr. G. once telling me that there are infinitely many primes and he told me the proof. Do you remember it?"

"It's clear that the set of natural numbers $\mathbb{N}$ is infinite. We just keep counting forever. It follows that the set of even numbers is infinite. We just multiply all the natural numbers by 2. In a similar way, the set of odd numbers is infinite we just subtract 1 from the even numbers. However it's not so clear that the set of prime numbers is infinite. As I recall, there is a simple proof going back at least 2,000 years due to the Greek mathematician Euclid. He is an archangel and we could ask him. But what the hell, let's try to do it ourselves. Let's begin by assuming there are only a finite number of primes. We can list them $p_1, p_2, \ldots p_n$ where p_1 is the smallest prime, 2, p_2 is the next prime, 3 and so on, while p_n is the largest prime."

"I remember now. We next form the number N as the product of all the primes plus 1,

$$N = p_1 p_2 \cdots p_n + 1$$

Now N is not prime because N is larger than the largest prime p_n. Since N is not prime, N must be divisible by at least one of the primes, say p_j. If we divide both sides of our equation by p_j, we get

$$\frac{N}{p_i} = p_1 p_2 \cdots p_{j-1} p_{j+1} \cdots p_n + \frac{1}{p_j}$$

Now N/p_j is a natural number, $p_1 p_2 \cdots p_{j-1} p_{j+1} \cdots p_n$ is a natural number and $1/p_j$ is a fraction."

Moses interrupts, "this is fun, let me finish. We have a whole number equal to a whole number plus a fraction. If this were true we would reach a contradiction and mathematics would be inconsistent. But as Mr. G. (and everyone else) keeps emphasizing, mathematics is consistent. So where are we? Our original assumption that there are finitely many primes must be false! Thus, there are an infinite number of primes."

"I think the name prime comes from the fact that these numbers are the primary building blocks of all the natural numbers." Jesus pauses contemplatively, "remember every natural number greater than 1 is prime or a product of primes. There is another interesting result about numbers going back some 2,000 years due to the ancient Greek school of Pythagoras. Recall that a number is rational if it's a ratio of two natural numbers. For example, $1/2, 1/3, 2/3, 3/4$ are rational numbers. Rational numbers are also called fractions. We can always reduce a rational number to lowest terms. Thus, $\frac{6}{8} = \frac{3}{4}$ to lowest terms and $\frac{5}{10} = \frac{1}{2}$ to lowest terms. Of course, natural numbers are also rational because we can always divide by 1; for example $2 = \frac{2}{1}$, $3 = \frac{3}{1}$ and so forth. The ancient Greek school of Pythagoreans believed that the physical world could be completely described by rational numbers. There may be other numbers but they would be suspicious and have nothing to do with the real world. The Greek's beautiful edifice came tumbling down when they discovered numbers in simple geometry that were not rational. Appropriately, they called these numbers irrational."

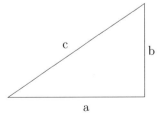

Figure 3.4

"Yes," Moses adds, "they found irrationals in their geometric study of triangles. According to the famous theorem of Pythagoras, if you take a right triangle whose legs have length a and b and whose hypotenuse has length c, then $a^2 + b^2 = c^2$ (Figure 3.4).

A simple example is a right triangle with $a = 3$, $b = 4$ and $c = 5$. In this case we have $3^2 + 4^2 = 5^2$ which is certainly true. Another simple example is a right triangle with $a = b = 1$. We would then have that $c^2 = 1^2 + 1^2 = 2$ or $c = \sqrt{2}$."

Moving ahead, Jesus explains, "the ancient Pythagoreans were dumbfounded when they discovered that $\sqrt{2}$ is irrational. Their proof went like this. Assume that $\sqrt{2}$ is rational. Then we can write $\sqrt{2}$ as a ratio of natural numbers $\sqrt{2} = \frac{m}{n}$ where this fraction is reduced to lowest terms. Squaring this expression we obtain $2 = \frac{m^2}{n^2}$ or $2n^2 = m^2$. Since m^2 is a multiple of 2, m^2 is an even number. But m^2 is the product of m with m and we have seen that a product of two odd numbers is odd. We conclude that m must be even. We can then write $m = 2p$ for some natural number p. Hence,

$$2n^2 = m^2 = 4p^2$$

so $n^2 = 2p^2$. By the same reasoning as before, we conclude that n is even. But then m and n have a common factor, 2. However, we assumed that m/n was reduced to lowest terms so m and n cannot have a common factor (a common factor would have been cancelled out). This gives a contradiction. But mathematics is consistent so no contradictions are allowed. Thus, our original assumption that $\sqrt{2}$ is rational must be false. We conclude that $\sqrt{2}$ is irrational."

Moses, becoming more animated, says, "wow, this is exciting. I'll bet we can prove that $\sqrt{3}$ is irrational in a similar way. Let's see, assume $\sqrt{3}$ is rational so we write $\sqrt{3} = \frac{m}{n}$ where m and n are natural numbers and the fraction is reduced to lowest terms. Then $3 = \frac{m^2}{n^2}$ or $3n^2 = m^2$. Now m^2 has 3 as a factor. But then m has 3 as a factor because if m doesn't have 3 as a factor how could you multiply two copies of m together to get a 3 in m^2? Hence, $m = 3p$ for some natural number p. We then have

$$3n^2 = m^2 = 9p^2$$

But then $n^2 = 3p^2$ so as before n has a factor 3. Again, this contradicts the fact that $\frac{m}{n}$ was reduced to lowest terms."

"In the same way we can show that $\sqrt{5}, \sqrt{7}, \sqrt{11}, \ldots$ are irrational." Jesus says, with a nod, "so the square root of any prime is irrational. Since there are infinitely many primes, we conclude that there are infinitely many irrationals. The ancient Pythagoreans would be horrified if they knew this."

"Math is really fun. We'll have to do more of it sometime. If we keep this up we may discover some new math results ourselves."

"Moses, do you think we'll ever get to go back to earth?"

"I really don't know. Mr. G. was not very pleased with some of our antics the last time we were there. For instance, why didn't you defend yourself in court so they wouldn't crucify you? You might have avoided that whole spectacle."

"I thought it was God's will for me to return to the Academy, so I was just doing his bidding. I thought I saw a vision in which he was telling me that my work was done and it was time to return."

"You should ask Mr. G. about that. I doubt if it was his will for you to draw all that attention to yourself."

"So do you think we'll ever be promoted to the status of archangel? After all, we are very well known."

"Well, as I said, Mr. G. is not that pleased with us now. Besides that, we haven't excelled very much in research. Maybe in a few hundred years he'll think better of us. In any case, I'll bet that I make archangel before you do."

"Are you kidding? I have much better credentials than you. Your glory days are over. Around here you are thought of as a lazy buffoon. Anyway, what would we bet? We have no use for material things and I can't think of anything I would want."

"I"ll ignore that buffoon comment and confide that I would like some kind of remembrance of Earth. I'll tell you what, the loser of the bet will sneak back to earth, retrieve a small sea shell and give it to the winner."

"Just as I thought, you really are crazy. How can we do that? You know we can't return to Earth without permission. Also, we don't want to upset the balance of nature. You've heard of the butterfly effect. That might lead to a disastrous inconsistency."

"You're referring to the wind from the wings of a butterfly in Brazil causing a hurricane in Florida a year later. Let me tell you, that's nonsense. That comes from the theory of chaos while butterflies and hurricanes are not chaotic systems. They follow well established rules of science. First of all, missing one little sea shell will surely be inconsequential. Secondly, nobody will notice. Mr. G. and the archangels are so busy with their research and their exponentially growing multi-universe that they wouldn't know."

"Now that I think about it, it would be nice having a sea shell in a hidden pocket inside my robe. All right, it's a bet. I guess the worst possible case is we could get demoted to apprentices and have to start all over. I would be a little embarrassed going from Jesus Christ to an apprentice. Also, all my disciples would be mortified."

A few hundred years later a couple are making love on a desolate moonlit Mediterranean beach. The trees sway gently in the breeze and the sea water breaks in undulating waves on the beach. As they pause to glance at the sea, they notice a white robed figure walking along the water's edge in the distance. As they watch in astonishment, the figure stoops down, picks something up and vanishes into a puff of sparks. The couple look into each others eyes in wonder and go back to what they were doing.

Chapter 4

God's Story

Let me introduce myself. My name is God and I am about to tell you the story of the universe. To be precise, there are many universes, so this is really the story of the multi-universes. Scientists on Earth are actually studying this subject, they call it the theory of the multiverse. This story will be nontechnical and for a more detailed and technical version I advise you to attend my cosmic seminars. For want of a better word, let us call all that we can experience or imagine, the world.

The world consists of two parts, the world of thought and reasoning called the world of intelligence and the world we experience with our senses called the cosmos. These two worlds overlap. We can think and reason about the cosmos and the cosmos supplies us with "thought waves." For example, we can "read each other's thoughts." There are two principles that govern the smooth operation of the world and these are compassion and reality. These two principles are necessary and sufficient for the world to exist in a unified harmonious manner.

Let us first discuss compassion. There are various ways to define compassion. To have compassion is to care for other people and their feelings. More broadly, one can care about animals, plants and other living beings. One can care about the environment and all the products of nature. Compassion includes sympathy and empathy. It is an essential ingredient for being human. Unfortunately, not everyone has great compassion. But it is something that can be learned and developed. It is a quality that everyone should strive for. When Moses brought his ten commandments down from Mount Sinai, he said they came from me in order to give them authority. For him, these were the appropriate rules for the orderly conduct of a civilized society. I don't care whether people worship me or idols, I do care about compassion and the qualities that derive from it. For me, there is but one commandment. Thou shalt have compassion. From compassion comes love, friendship, caring and the other qualities that make life worth living.

Even though I am God, I don't know everything. I am constantly learning, exploring and investigating. My apprentices, angels and archangels are always asking questions and challenging themselves and others to answer them. We formed a society devoted to pure thought called the Academy. The cosmos began approximately 13.75 billion years ago. When the cosmos was created, I was created too. The reason that I will exist as long as the cosmos exists is because I have no material body. I do not have cells that decay and die as you do. I consist of tiny elementary particles and energy. The particles and energy are interchangeable because of Einstein's equation $E = mc^2$ where E is the amount of energy, m is the mass of the particle and c is the speed of light. Not only did I not create the cosmos, I do not control the evolution of the cosmos. Because of this, you might think that there is a higher power than me that created and controls the cosmos. In a sense, there is; but it would be better to call it another power rather than a higher power because it doesn't have compassion as I do. This other power is reality and we shall discuss this later.

I was not created with compassion, I learned it and I will now explain how. Soon after the big bang the cosmos was composed of matter, antimatter and energy. (There was also dark energy and dark matter, but these are not important for our present discussion.) There was considerably more energy available and matter and antimatter appeared in equal amounts. The matter consisted of various kinds of particles and the antimatter consisted of various kinds of antiparticles. The particles and the antiparticles of the same kind were identical except for their electric charge. According to Einstein's equation, a certain amount of energy can transform into a particle-antiparticle pair which zoom off in opposite directions. Conversely, if a particle-antiparticle pair come in close proximity, they annihilate each other into a puff of energy.

During the first billion years trillions of stars were formed and clustered into billions of galaxies. In that time period there were no planets with intelligent life, so I was almost alone in the cosmos. But I was not really alone, far from it. While I was composed of tiny particles and pure energy, I had a magnificent counterpart composed of antiparticles and pure energy. Let us call my counterpart the Goddess. For a billion years the Goddess and I had a glorious time. We would twirl about the cosmos. We would hug in huge cosmic embraces. We were like two giant eagles mating in midair. I adored her and she adored me. We cared for each other and we were in love. We did not have sex in the usual sense because we didn't have material bodies. But we would connect and become one. Our energies would annihilate and vanish into delightful, tingly puffs of energy. Some of our intertwined energy would create particle-antiparticle pairs which became part of us.

One of our favorite pastimes was to race with photons which are particles of light or light beams. At first they were always faster than us. But we felt sorry for them because they could only go one speed, called c, and had to follow the curvature of the universe, while we could turn any way we wanted and slow down and speed up. But then a delightful thing happened. We found that we could travel faster than the speed of light! The light beams were quite miffed when we flew past them. Not only could we fly faster but the faster we went the easier it was. It was easier to fly at speed $2c$ that it was at speed c; it was easier to fly at speed $10c$ than at speed $2c$. We found ourselves darting about at speeds thousands of times c. We could traverse millions of light-years in less than a year.

36

We sped across an entire universe in what seemed like no time at all. You have probably heard that nothing can travel faster than c, so how did we do it? Also, why is it easier to go faster and faster? It has to do with the dimension of time. You will find out more about the subject later in this book.

Our relationship was not just physical. We had intelligence and we could interact and communicate via thought waves, a form of electromagnetic radiation at frequencies not yet well utilized by humans. What did we communicate about? The cosmos itself. The cosmos was an immense and complicated puzzle and we were a part of it. It contained a myriad of universes growing exponentially in complexity. We observed it, studied it and discussed it. We were overjoyed with our power and what we could do. The cosmos was our enormous playground and existence was wonderful. We both wanted it to last forever. We were intimately aware of each other and had compassion for each other. But I really learned compassion when I lost her.

I don't know how it happened, but a contradiction occurred in the antimatter realm. I have studied and pondered for billions of years, but I still don't know what caused it. This is one of the great mysteries of the cosmos and I call it the cosmic inconsistency. A contradiction caused another contradiction which caused still another contradiction. We became aware of a cascading avalanche of destruction. It was like the collapse of a monumental house of cards. She communicated to me that she had to try to save the collapsing antimatter realm. I begged her not to go and to stay with me in our beautiful paradise. I could not help her because my matter particles would only make things worse. I knew she had to do what she had to do. I watched her disappear in a colossal explosion of pure energy that destroyed most of the antimatter in the cosmos. There remained a small amount of antimatter, but she was only a minute remnant of her previous self, we lost all means of communication and things were never the same again.

I grieved for eight billion years! I missed her and I was all alone. I lost interest in the cosmos evolving and changing around me. It seemed cold and sterile. I was lonesome and I longed for her. The memory of what we once had did not console me. Just at the height of my depression, despair and loneliness a miracle happened. I cannot claim credit for this miracle. I wish I could and you wouldn't know differently, but being God, I must set an example and not lie. About five billion years ago, life started appearing on a few planets and this was the miracle. It began slowly with some single celled amoeba in bodies of water. The cells multiplied and formed more complex organisms. Some of the organisms crawled out of the water and developed intelligence. I was no longer alone! I felt alive again. There was other intelligence in the cosmos. There were beings who could reason, who had consciousness and souls.

But I established an important rule. Do not intervene. Intervention might lead to a contradiction and this might result in disaster. I had seen cosmic destruction before and could not let it happen again. I could not interact directly with the intelligent life. This is difficult for me because I have compassion and cannot stand human pain and suffering. Part of me shakes and quivers when I see such things. When I see innocent children shivering in fear being led to gas chambers, I cry and I scream and cry again. But I am the guardian of consistency and know that the cosmos itself could die without it.

So I established the Academy. This enabled me to have contact with other intelligent beings without interfering with the evolving cosmos. One of my powers is that I have control over dimension. The cosmos is in reality part of a $5 + 5$-dimensional manifold, 5 dimensions of space and 5 dimensions of time. I am a $5 + 5$-dimensional being. Although you have the ability to visualize such a manifold in your imagination and to describe it mathematically, you only have physical access to a $3 + 1$-dimensional manifold, three dimensions of space and one dimension of time. From your earthly platform, you cannot make contact with these higher dimensions. What you can sense, even with the aid of your most accurate instruments, is a four-dimensional projection of this ten-dimensional manifold. To take an example, suppose you are observing your shadow on the ground on a sunny day. The shadow can be regarded as a two-dimensional projection of your three-dimensional body. You can obtain a considerable amount of information about your body by looking at your shadow but it would be very difficult, if not impossible, to reconstruct the entire three-dimensional object in this way.

I not only have the power to control dimension, I can bestow this control to other intelligent beings and this is how I was able to build the Academy. I noticed that intelligent beings possess a soul or, you might call it a spirit, and that the soul exists forever and cannot be destroyed. When an intelligent being dies, the soul lives on. I can take this soul and elevate it to a higher dimension. This is not an intervention because the being has died and so the course of events in the usual physical world is not changed. These elevated souls become members of the Academy or, as we call them, academicians. I soon realized that I couldn't do everything myself. I'm only God, for God's sake, and the cosmos is growing exponentially. Polynomial growth, I can handle, but exponential growth is beyond even me. I called the first few elevated souls archangels and I bestowed upon them the power to elevate other worthy souls. We soon had a hierarchy of academicians called apprentices, angels and archangels. The Academy became a citadel of study, learning and investigation.

Until now I have discussed compassion. I'll next consider the other basic principle of the world, reality. How do we define reality? People seem to have a hard time defining this word. If you look in a dictionary, you will find something like, reality: that which is actual. So you look to the definition of actual: that which is real. This doesn't help very much. You might also find the definition, reality: that which exists independently of our perceptions. That's getting closer but it's still not very enlightening. Let's see what some famous people say about reality.

Albert Einstein famously said, "reality is merely an illusion, albeit a very persistent one."

Lilly Tomlin said that reality "is for people who can't cope with drugs."
These are all amusing, but they still don't help. Let's use the working definition: reality is that which is consistent and permanent. If you think about it for a while, you will come to the conclusion that not much is real. In fact, I challenge you to tell me something that's

real. The chair you're sitting in is not real. Your house and your car are not real. This Earth itself will only last about five billion more years, so it's not real. The cosmos will probably not last forever. It is likely that it will stop expanding and then contract into a "big crunch." That may be the end or it might be the beginning of another big bang. Even I don't know.

You might suggest that God is real. But there are many who do not believe I exist, so for them I certainly am not real. More to the point, I am not consistent. I claim to be compassionate, yet I must admit I have no compassion for Adolf Hitler and his Nazi hoodlums. Also, I am not permanent. I am part of the cosmos and we decided this will probably not last forever.

Before continuing, we need a precise definition of consistent. An entity is consistent if it is without contradiction. A contradiction occurs if there is a proposition that is both true and false. Another way of saying this is that there is a proposition that is true and whose negation is also true. This is equivalent to a proposition that is false and whose negation is also false. Let's look at an example. Consider the proposition:

A = "The word THE contains the letter H."

The negation of A is the proposition:

$NOT(A)$ = "The word THE does not contain the letter H."

In this case the proposition A is true while the proposition $NOT(A)$ is false.

So what is real? We couldn't find a concrete object that is real so what about something abstract like language. The English language is not real because it is not permanent. Also, the English language is inconsistent. Here's an example. In the small town of Trent, Iowa, there is a barber who only shaves those Trent men who do not shave themselves. Consider the proposition: "The barber shaves himself." This proposition is false because the barber only shaves those men who do not shave themselves. By the same reasoning the negation: "The barber does not shave himself" is also false. This gives a contradiction so the English language is inconsistent.

What about a science like biology? Part of biology is artificial and human-made like the classification of species. The other part is chemistry. So what about chemistry? Again, part of chemistry is artificial and human-made. The laws of chemistry are not permanent. For example, 150 years ago atoms and molecules were unknown. The other part of chemistry is physics. Part of physics is human-made and the rest is mathematics. For example, Newton's laws of physics have been superseded by quantum mechanics and general relativity. We have come to the end of the line. Mathematics is real! And mathematics is the only thing that is real. Mathematics is permanent, it would exist even if there were no cosmos or universe. Mathematics is consistent because it is built upon consistent axioms and postulates. Who built it? No one, it built itself and was always there.

We conclude that the governing principles of the cosmos are compassion and mathematics. Compassion is necessary for intelligent beings and doesn't apply to physical objects. Reality (mathematics) is needed for everything in the cosmos. Math is not just numbers. Geometry, logic and methods of reasoning are part of math. There are other parts of math such as topology, algebra, analysis, probability and combinatorics. I would like to give you an example of a mathematical structure called a graph. The theory of graphs is not only interesting in its own right, it has important applications to the everyday world. In particular, graphs can be used to describe the structure of the cosmos.

A graph is a finite set V together with a collection E of two element subsets of V. The elements of V are called *vertices* and the elements of E are called *edges*. A graph is diagramed as follows. Draw the vertices as small circles and if two vertices belong to an edge, join the corresponding circles with a line. In Figure 4.1 all the graphs with one, two or three vertices are diagrammed. Table 4.1 gives the vertex set and the edge set of each of the graphs diagrammed in Figure 4.1. The symbol $\emptyset$ represents the empty set, the set with no elements.

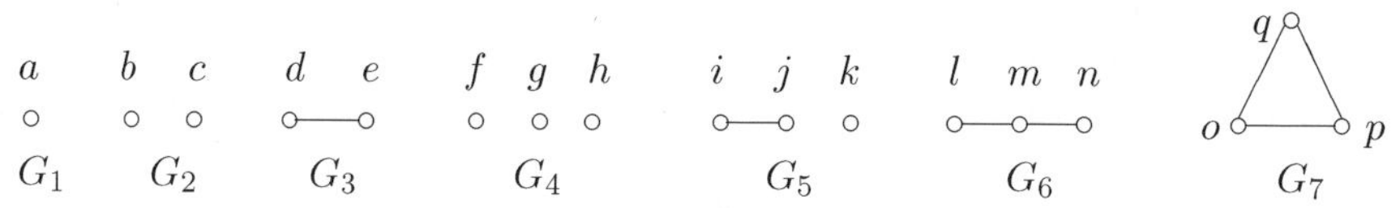

Figure 4.1

Graph	Vertex Set	Edge Set
G_1	$\{a\}$	$\emptyset$
G_2	$\{b,c\}$	$\emptyset$
G_3	$\{d,e\}$	$\{\{d,e\}\}$
G_4	$\{f,g,h\}$	$\emptyset$
G_5	$\{i,j,k\}$	$\{\{i,j\}\}$
G_6	$\{l,m,n\}$	$\{\{l,m\},\{m,n\}\}$
G_7	$\{o,p,q\}$	$\{\{o,p\},\{p,q\},\{o,q\}\}$

Table 4.1

In the diagram of a graph, the position of the vertices is immaterial as long as the edges are correctly represented by lines. Also, the lines representing edges need not be straight lines. Figure 4.2 gives three diagrams that represent the same graph $G = (V, E)$ where $V = \{a, b, c, d\}$ and

$$E = \{\{a, b\}, \{a, d\}, \{b, c\}, \{b, d\}\}$$

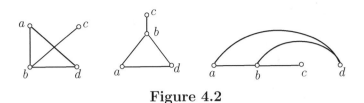

Figure 4.2

If $e = \{u, v\}$ is an edge, then u and v are called *adjacent* vertices. Thus, in graph G_7 any two vertices are adjacent. In graph G_6, l and m are adjacent and m and n are adjacent, but l and n are not adjacent. If two distinct edges have a vertex in common, then the edges are *adjacent*. For example, any two edges of G_6 or G_7 are adjacent. For the graph in Figure 4.2, edge $\{b, c\}$ is adjacent to edges $\{a, b\}$ and $\{b, d\}$ but is not adjacent to edge $\{a, d\}$. To make the notation simpler an edge $\{u, v\}$ is usually denoted by uv or vu. A *path* in a graph is a sequence of edges

$$v_1 v_2, v_2 v_3, v_3 v_4, \ldots, v_{n-1} v_n$$

where each edge is adjacent to the next edge. We also call this a path from v_1 to v_n. For example, in Figure 4.2, two paths from a to c are ab, bc and ad, db, bc. A graph is *connected* if for any two of its vertices a and b, there is a path from a to b. For example, G_3, G_6, G_7 and the graph in Figure 4.2 are connected while G_1, G_2, G_4 and G_5 are not connected.

Suppose you have the job of designing a safe and economical highway system. Certain areas must be linked by highways and you are to decide where the highways are to be placed. Since intersections are inconvenient and unsafe for high-speed driving and underpasses and overpasses are costly to construct, the best highway system will keep the number of crossing roads to a minimum. If you represent the different areas by vertices and the highways by edges, you will have a graph. What you need is a graph with edges that don't cross.

There are other important uses of graphs with edges that do not cross. Such graphs are needed in the design of miniature electronic circuits. The conductors in these circuits are printed on a thin wafer as a fine silver or copper line. These lines cannot cross so must be represented by graphs with noncrossing edges.

A graph is *planar* if it can be diagramed on a plane so that distinct edges do not cross. All the graphs we have considered, so far, are planar. Although two edges cross in the first diagram of Figure 4.2, the graph is redrawn in the second two diagrams with noncrossing edges. Another example of a planar graph is diagramed in Figure 4.3. Although the left diagram has crossing edges, it is redrawn in the right diagram with noncrossing edges.

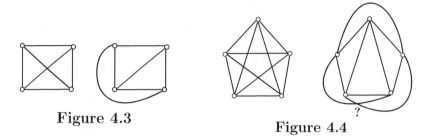

Figure 4.3   Figure 4.4

An example of a nonplanar graph is the pentagram diagramed on the left in Figure 4.4. The pentagram has appeared in many places in history, for example King Solomon's seal. It was used in the magic symbol of the ancient Pythagoreans. The pentagon appeared in the inner face of Sir Gawain's shield to remind him of the power of his five virtues and the strong interconnections between them. The right diagram in Figure 4.4 is an attempt to make noncrossing edges but any such attempt is doomed to failure.

Another nonplanar graph is given by the story of the three cabins and the three wells. There were paths from each cabin to each of the wells, but since the inhabitants of the different cabins did not like each other, they decided to construct paths from their cabins to each of the wells so that the paths did not cross. In this way they would not have to come in contact with a neighbor. But no matter how hard they tried, they could not construct the paths. This graph is diagramed in Figure 4.5.

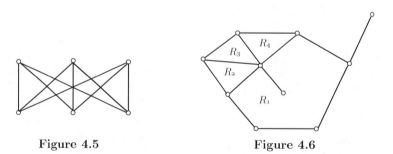

Figure 4.5   Figure 4.6

When planar graphs are considered, it will always be assumed that they are diagramed on the plane so that distinct edges do not cross. Given a planar graph G, a region is a minimal portion of the plane inside G whose boundary are edges of G. For example $G_1 - G_6$ have no regions, G_7 has one region, the graph in Figure 4.2 has one region, and the graph in Figure 4.3 has three regions. The planar graph diagramed in Figure 4.6 has four regions labeled R_1, R_2, R_3, R_4.

Let G be a connected planar graph with v vertices, e edges and r regions. An amazing formula relating these three numbers was discovered by the great Swiss mathematician Leonhard Euler over 250 years ago. See if you can guess this formula. In Figure 4.7, v, e and r have been found for four graphs. Can you make a conjecture from these examples?

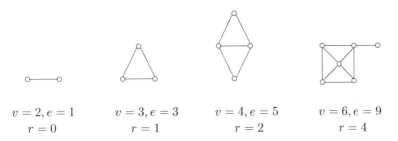

$$v = 2, e = 1 \qquad v = 3, e = 3 \qquad v = 4, e = 5 \qquad v = 6, e = 9$$
$$r = 0 \qquad\qquad r = 1 \qquad\qquad r = 2 \qquad\qquad r = 4$$

Figure 4.7

In case you haven't figured it out, here it is. Euler's formula: If G is a connected planar graph with v vertices, e edges and r regions, then $e = v + r - 1$.

You should check the graphs in Figure 4.7 to see if Euler's formula works. Let's look at Figure 4.6. We have $v = 10$, $e = 13$, $r = 4$ and

$$v + r - 1 = 10 + 4 - 1 = 13 = e$$

What happens if we have a planar graph that's not connected? We just look at its connected parts which are called *components*. For example, the graph in Figure 4.8 has three components.

Figure 4.8

Now we have an Euler's formula for each component. If we add these formulas we get the total number of edges equals the total number of vertices plus the total number of regions minus the number of components. We thus obtain the following formula.

The general Euler's formula: if G is a planar graph with v vertices, e edges, r regions and c components, then

$$e = v + r - c$$

Of course, if G is connected then $c = 1$ and the general formula reduces to Euler's formula. Let's check the general formula with the graph in Figure 4.8. We have that $v = 8$, $e = 8$, $r = 3$, $c = 3$. Then

$$v + r - c = 8 + 3 - 3 = 8 = e$$

so it works. Notice we can write this formula in a prettier way as $v + r = e + c$.

If you come to my cosmic seminar you will see that the structure of the cosmos is described by a certain kind of graph. In fact, mathematics is indispensable for describing your universe and how it operates. But mathematics does much more. Remember I said there was another power that created and controlled the cosmos. I called it reality, but now we know it is mathematics. Before the cosmos existed there was mathematics. But mathematics needed to express itself. It **had** to express itself so it created the cosmos out of the void! If you had infinite potential and unlimited reasoning power, wouldn't you will yourself into existence? That's what mathematics did.

How can an entity as grand as a universe be created out of nothing? Doesn't it take energy or something? According to a principle of quantum mechanics, energy can be borrowed from nothing as long as it is not borrowed for very long and is then returned. This principle is called the Heisenberg uncertainty principle and one form of it is described mathematically by $\Delta E \Delta t \geq \hbar$ where ΔE is the uncertainty of energy, Δt is the uncertainty of time and $\hbar$ is a very small number called Planck's constant. As long as a time interval Δt is very small, an amount of energy ΔE satisfying $\Delta E \Delta t \geq \hbar$ can be borrowed and returned during that time interval. But if energy is borrowed and almost immediately returned, doesn't that make the total energy zero most of the time? How can something as vast and complicated as a universe exist with no energy? It can exist because of gravity and gravity is caused by the curvature of a universe. The curvature of the universe is negative which means that gravitational energy is negative. A universe is composed of particles and positive energy where the particles have an equivalent amount of energy given by $E = mc^2$. Particles can also have positive kinetic energy due to their motion. If you add up all this positive energy and the negative energy due to gravity, you obtain zero.

In this way, mathematics created the cosmos from nothing. But it also controls the way a universe evolves in time. A universe expands in discrete time steps $1, 2, 3, 4, \ldots$, and this is one way that mathematics expresses itself. At each time step, a scaffolding in the form of a graph composed of vertices and edges expands one vertex at a time. At time 1 a universe looks like graph G_1 and at time 2 it looks like graph G_2 or G_3 of Figure 4.1. After this the structure of the scaffolding becomes more complicated and is described by a mathematical system called a causal set. If you attend my cosmic seminar you can get more details about this.

There is one last subject I'd like to discuss. I said earlier that I am a $5 + 5$-dimensional being. In fact, the cosmos itself is $5 + 5$-dimensional. Your physicists are getting close to the reason for this. The two great theories of physics are general relativity and quantum mechanics. General relativity is the study of gravity and quantum mechanics is the study

44

of subatomic particles and their interactions. Quantum mechanics describes particles like neutrinos, quarks, electron, photons and protons very well and general relativity describes large objects like planets, stars and galaxies very well. However, these two theories as they now stand are incompatible. Your physicists are hard at work trying to find a unifying theory that encompasses them both. The main candidate that they are studying for this purpose is string theory. In string theory, elementary constituents like neutrinos, electrons and quarks are not represented by particles but by small one-dimensional vibrating strings. To make a long story short, they have derived a lot of complicated equations and formulas. But the only way these equations are consistent is if the underlying manifold is ten-dimensional.

So if they are right, mathematics determines the dimension of the cosmos. I won't say if they're right or not because I don't want to influence their work, but I will give you a little hint. The string theorists assume that the cosmos is $9 + 1$-dimensional, nine dimensions of space and one dimension of time. Now Albert Einstein, in his investigations in relativity theory, taught that space and time should have an equal footing. But this is a little strange because he was working on a $3 + 1$-dimensional manifold, so space and time were allotted different dimensions. In the same way, the cosmos should be $5 + 5$-dimensional and not $9 + 1$-dimensional.

String theorists are frequently asked the following question, "If the universe is $9 + 1$-dimensional, why can we only detect $3 + 1$ dimensions? What happened to the other six dimensions?" They answer that the other six dimensions are folded up and tucked away in a very small region of the universe. For this reason, they are inaccessible to humans and they will never be able to find them. The right reason is that humans are $3 + 1$-dimensional beings and it is impossible for you to experience higher dimensions. It's like asking a worm who is constrained to the two-dimensional surface of the Earth what it feels like to fly.

Let me end by telling you that this book you're reading is very good. I have read the whole thing and I highly recommend it. Needless to say, it's hard to find a book that is recommended by God. By the way, the cosmic seminar that I've mentioned a few times can be found in Chapter 8. In the next chapter you will learn more about physics and elementary particles.

I'll leave you with a parting thought. If you ever need me, remember I'm a ten-dimensional being. Just look at the ten fingers on your hands and I'll be there.

Chapter 5

Philosophy of Physics and Religion

Fine Hall is a stately red brick building at Princeton University. Its ceilings are high and its windows are tall. Its corridors are long and lined with polished dark wood. Lecture Room 8 is steeply inclined so that all students can see the speaker at the podium below. The room holds about 100 students and it is almost full. This is the first class of a popular course called "The Philosophy of Physics and Religion." The course is taught by an equally popular Israeli professor who has only been at Princeton for three years. The professor is a young man but has Ph.Ds in both physics and philosophy. He has already done important research in nuclear fission. Listen carefully, he is beginning to speak.

Welcome students to the philosophy department of Princeton University. I am Itamar Pitowski, visiting professor of philosophy and physics. This will be an introductory lecture on some of the things we know about our universe and some unanswered questions concerning physics and religion. It's embarrassing to say that there is a lot more that we don't know than we do know. But that's what makes life interesting isn't it? Nature has presented us with a wonderful gift. This gift is the puzzle of our vast and complicated universe. By experiment and observation we can ask nature questions. If we are clever enough to ask the right questions she will divulge her secrets and her response may be difficult to interpret but answer she must. We can piece these answers together and apply our powers of reasoning to construct theories about the workings of the universe. By further experiments, we can test our theories to see if they give correct predictions. If these predictions are not correct, we must abandon or alter our theories. If the predictions are correct we can expand the boundaries of our theories to new phenomena by asking more questions. This process is called the scientific method.

Will this cycle ever end? Will we ever discover a final ultimate theory of everything? Put another way, does such a theory actually exist? No one knows and this is a basic unsolved mystery of nature. Another mystery is that, until now all theories of physics have been formulated mathematically. Why is mathematics the language of physics? Besides that, other than experiment, solving mathematical problems is the way physics advances.

The Nobel laureate, Eugene Wigner, once wrote an article titled "The unreasonable effectiveness of mathematics in the physical sciences." He and many others have pondered this mystery, but have not arrived at definitive answers. You, as future researchers, will have a lifetime opportunity to pursue these and other exciting intellectual adventures.

We now possess two basic theories for the natural world, quantum mechanics and general relativity. Quantum mechanics describes the world of the very small. These are the elementary particles and their interactions. Quantum mechanics developed during the period 1900 to 1925 and was the culmination of the work of many famous contributors. Among these were Planck, Einstein, Bohr, Born, Heisenberg, Schrödinger, Dirac and Pauli. General relativity describes the world of the very large, such as planets, stars, galaxies and black holes. This includes cosmology which studies the origin of the universe. General relativity which investigates the force of gravity developed during this same period and was mainly the work of one man, Albert Einstein. Everyday objects such as baseballs, cars and airplanes are composed of huge numbers of elementary particles and quantum mechanics applies to them as well. However, quantum mechanics does not include gravity in its realm and these two great theories appear to be incompatible. Our description of the very small and the very large are quite different and another important unsolved mystery of physics is to find a theory that encompasses both quantum mechanics and general relativity. Such a theory, if it exists has been called a unified field theory. Physicists have proposed various candidates for a unified field theory. Two of these are called quantum gravity and string theory.

There are four known forces of nature. In decreasing order of relative strength, these are the strong nuclear force, weak nuclear force, electromagnetic force and gravity. The strong nuclear force holds elementary particles together. For example, the nucleus of an atom consists of protons and neutrons, except for a hydrogen atom that consists of a single proton. Experiments have shown that protons and neutrons themselves are composed of elementary constituents called quarks. (There is a delicious German cheese called quark, but this is different.) The Nobel laureate Murray Gell-Mann, coined the name quark which he got from a line in a James Joyce poem, "Three quarks for muster mark..." These quarks are held together by the strong nuclear force which also holds the protons and neutrons in the nucleus together.

The weak nuclear force is responsible for radioactive decay. For instance, radon, radium and uranium decay into lighter elements and other particles due to the weak nuclear force. Another example is that an isolated neutron decays into a proton, an electron and a neutrino. As indicated by its name, electromagnetism is the force responsible for electricity and magnetism. Some particles have electric charge such as electrons with their negative charge and positrons with their positive charge. Particles with the same charge sign repel each other and particles with opposite charge sign attract. Thus, two electrons repel and an electron, positron pair attract. Protons inside an atomic nucleus would repel each other except the strong nuclear force overpowers the electromagnetic force and holds the protons together. It turns out that a changing electric force causes magnetism. For example, electrons streaming through a coil of wire give an electric current. Since this current changes direction as it moves around the coil, a magnetic force is created through the middle of the coil. Conversely, a moving magnet causes electricity. This is how electricity is generated in steam, water power and nuclear power plants.

Finally, the gravitational force is only attractive. This attraction keeps us from falling off the surface of the Earth and keeps the Earth in its orbit around the sun. According to Einstein's general relativity theory, gravity is due to the curvature of the universe. Scientists believe that near the time of the big bang, there was only one force and that as the universe cooled down, this force separated into the four we now have. How this happened is another great mystery.

What causes these forces? If we hang two positively charged spheres from strings attached to the ceiling, we can see that they repel each other. Suppose we perform this experiment in a vacuum. There is nothing between the spheres and they still repel, so what's pushing them apart? This puzzling phenomenon is called "action at a distance." For many years, it was believed that there were electromagnetic waves between the spheres causing the repulsion. But if there is a wave, something should be waving. However, there is nothing between the spheres and experiments could not detect anything waving. Physicists believe they have now solved this puzzle. The forces are caused by other elementary particles.

An electrically charged object like an electron is continuously emitting and absorbing particles called photons. Photons are also known as light quanta and there are many types of photons characterized by numbers called their frequency. The light that we see is the result of photons hitting the retinas of our eyes. Different frequencies give different light colors. Heat is caused by low frequency photons. Radio, television, telephones, internet and other communication channels are photons. High frequency photons are responsible for x-rays, gamma-rays and cosmic-rays. If two electrons are in proximity one electron can emit a photon and the second electron can absorb that photon. Photons travel at the speed of light and have energy E proportional to their frequency ν. The energy is given by the formula $E = h\nu$ where h is Planck's constant. This energy pushes the second electron back. The first electron is also pushed back and it appears as though the electrons are repelling each other.

There is a picturesque way of illustrating this phenomenon. Suppose Alice and Bob are ice skating together and Alice throws a heavy lead ball to Bob. (Scientists like to use Alice and Bob because it is more personal than A and B. If someone watches Alice and Bob, she is appropriately named Eve.) By throwing the ball, Alice is pushed back and by catching the ball, Bob is also pushed back so the couple move away from each other. How would the couple attract? Well, suppose the couple face away from each other and Alice throws a heavy boomerang. This will push Alice toward Bob. If the boomerang flies through the air and Bob catches it, then Bob will be pushed toward Alice. Granted, electrons don't act like this, but the precise mechanism describing the phenomenon is given by the mathematics.

Physicists call the particles that cause the four basic forces, force-mediating bosons.

We have already mentioned that the electromagnetic mediating bosons are photons. The bosons mediating the strong nuclear force are called gluons. Those mediating the weak nuclear force are electroweak-bosons or W^+, W^- and Z particles and those mediating the gravitational force are gravitons. It is a puzzling fact that gravitons have not yet been detected. This is strange for two reasons. The first is that the other force-mediating bosons have been observed either directly or indirectly in many experiments. The second is that, of the four forces, gravity is the one that we are most aware of and the one that has been know the longest. It is believed that the reason for the failure to detect gravitons, is because they are quite massive and very high energies that we have not yet obtained, will be needed to observe them.

Besides the photons and gluons, all the elementary particles have mass. The neutrinos' mass is almost imperceptible and is by far the smallest. It is believed that the mass of an elementary particle is caused by its interaction with still another particle called a Higgs boson. The idea of such a particle originated with the Scottish physicist, Peter Higgs. Because of its mass bestowing power, people sometimes call the Higgs boson "God's particle." Whether God would approve of this name is unknown. Although the Higgs boson was postulated to exist about 50 years ago, it has only recently been observed at the large hadron collider (LHC). The LHC is an immense particle accelerator in the shape of a 35 mile circle below ground on the border between France and Switzerland. The accelerator collides beams of protons at energies previously unobtainable by mankind. They have now reached energies that are sufficient to detect the elusive Higgs boson as well as other particles of interest.

Besides mass, elementary particles have two other important properties called charge and spin. Charge is an electric charge and is either 0 or an integer multiple of one third an electron charge e_0. Spin is analogous to the spin of a top but it is much stranger because elementary particles can spin in every direction simultaneously! If a spin measurement is performed in a certain direction, it forces the particle to settle down to a spin in that direction and have a value of 0 or an integer multiple of $\frac{1}{2}\hbar$. Particles with spin an even multiple of $\frac{1}{2}\hbar$ are called bosons and those with an odd multiple of $\frac{1}{2}\hbar$ are called fermions. When we designate a charge or spin we usually omit the e_0 and $\hbar$.

Let's now summarize the known elementary particles. First consider the force-mediating bosons. Photons are massless, chargeless, spin-1 bosons, that move only at the speed of light. Electroweak-bosons are massive (that is, have mass) spin-1 particles with charge 0 or ±1. There are actually three of these called W^+, W^- and Z. Gluons are massless, chargeless spin-1 bosons. There are also three of these designated red, green and blue gluons. These have nothing to do with ordinary colors and are just used to distinguish the three types. In fact the strong nuclear force is sometimes called the color force and its study is called quantum chromodynamics. Finally, gravitons are massive, chargeless spin-2 particles.

We next have the leptons. Each lepton has three generations. The electron is a massive, spin-$\frac{1}{2}$ fermion with charge -1. The next two generations are called the muon and the tauon. These have the same properties as an electron except the muon has more mass and the tauon still more mass. We also have the three types of neutrino: electron-neutrino, muon-neutrino and tauon-neutrino. These have zero charge and spin-$\frac{1}{2}$. Their masses are minute but increase with generation. Because the electron-neutrino has no charge and infinitesimal mass and size, it practically does not interact with any other particle and flies along unhindered at close to the speed of light. Nuclear reactions produce neutrinos in large quantities. For example, billions of neutrinos from the sun pass through a person's body per second. Trillions of trillions of neutrinos pass through the Earth per second, practically unimpeded. In fact, there are more neutrinos than any other particle in the universe. Even more amazing is the fact that the mass of the neutrinos in the universe is much larger than the mass of all visible matter.

The next class of elementary particles are the quarks. In the first generation we have the down quark which is a massive spin-$\frac{1}{2}$ fermion with charge $-\frac{1}{3}$ and the up quark which is a massive spin-$\frac{1}{2}$ fermion with charge $\frac{2}{3}$. The higher generations have the same properties except are more massive. The second generation consists of the strange and charmed quark. The third generation consists of the bottom and top quark. Physicists do not like to make up new names so they use whimsical names that are already in the language like the colors and strange and charm. Initially it was thought that only two quarks, the down and up quarks were needed to describe the known particles like protons and neutrons. But then more exotic particles turned up in scattering experiments and new quarks were needed for their description. The next quark was called strange because it was a constituent of very short lived particles with unusual behaviors.

The elementary particles have their antimatter counterparts. These have the same properties as the matter particles except their charges are reversed. For example, the antimatter partner of the electron is the positron with charge $+1$ and the antimatter partner of the down quark is the antidown quark with charge $+\frac{1}{3}$. If a particle and its antiparticle partner come into proximity, they annihilate each other and form pure energy. Another great mystery of physics is the matter-antimatter asymmetry. By symmetry, one would expect about the same amount of antimatter as matter in the universe. But this isn't the case, there is a lot more matter than antimatter. In the early universe, for some unknown reason, there must have been an unbalance of more matter than antimatter. The matter annihilated most of the antimatter and now there is practically none left.

So far I have discussed the elementary particles. These are the basic constituents of matter (and antimatter). Most of our knowledge about these and other small particles comes from scattering experiments involving particle accelerators like the LHC or cosmic-ray experiments. In a particle accelerator, beams consisting of billions of protons or electrons can be accelerated to very high velocities using large magnetic and electric fields. The beams are then focused and forced to collide. The resulting collisions break up the beam or target particles and produce a large number of scattered particles that are then focused into sensitive detection chambers. Inside these chambers various measurements are performed. The results of the measurements are fed into large computer data banks that are later analyzed. The cosmic-ray experiments take high energy photons from outer space that interact with particles in detection chambers where the scattered remnants are analyzed. The cosmic-rays actually produce more energetic particles than accelerators but they don't involve as many particles and cannot be as easily controlled so the results are not as useful.

In any case, these experiments have produced a veritable zoo of particles. Hundreds of new exotic particles have been discovered in this way. Most of these particles do not naturally occur and only exist for a small fraction of a second and then decay into pure energy or naturally occurring particles. All of these new particles are composed of elementary particle constituents. The particles that have been discovered are called hadrons and the hadrons have been classified into two types, mesons and baryons.

The mesons have a very short lifetime and are composed of a quark and an antiquark. For example, a pi-meson consists of an up quark and a strange antiquark. Over fifty types of mesons have been discovered. The baryons consist of three quarks and over a hundred types of baryons have been found. We have the proton with its down quark and two up quarks, the neutron with its up quark and two down quarks, the Σ^- with two downs and a strange quark, the Σ^0 with a down, a strange and an up quark, the Σ^+ with a strange and two up quarks, the Ξ^- with a down and two strange quarks, the Ξ^0 with an up and two strange quarks and the Ω^- with three strange quarks. Of all the hadrons, only the proton and neutron occur in the stable matter observed in the universe. These two baryons together with electrons are the constituents of the periodic table of about 100 elements that form the observed matter around us. What is the purpose of all these other exotic short-lived particles? That is another great mystery.

The particles that we have discussed can be organized and classified using multigraphs. A multigraph is like a graph except multiple edges and loops are all allowed. For multiple edges we can have more than one edge joining two vertices and a loop is an edge that begins and ends at the same vertex. Figure 5.1 gives an example of a multigraph. A loop encloses a region and two nearby edges joining the same two vertices enclose a region. Thus, the multigraph in Figure 5.1 has $e = 11$ edges, $v = 4$ vertices and $r = 8$ regions. Euler's formula holds for planar multigraphs and we have $v + r - 1 = 4 + 8 - 1 = 11 = e$.

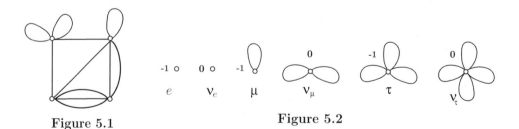

Figure 5.1   Figure 5.2

Figure 5.2 presents the diagrams for the leptons. We have the electron e, the muon μ, the tauon τ, the electron neutrino ν_e, the muon neutrino ν_μ and the tauon neutrino ν_τ. The numbers by the vertices are the electric charge. Notice that the first generation has no loops, the second generation has one or two loops and the third generation has three or four loops. The loops represent paths for electro-weak bosons.

Figure 5.3 presents the diagrams for the six quarks. These are the down d, up u, strange s, charmed c, bottom b and top t quarks.

Figure 5.3

Figure 5.4 presents the diagram for some of the mesons. The vertices are quark-antiquark pairs which we haven't labeled. For example, the π meson could be a down-antiup pair giving a charge -1 meson π^- or it could be an up-antidown pair giving a charge $+1$ meson π^+. We know that a quark with one loop as in the κ-meson is either strange or antistrange with similar observations for multiple loops. The edges that are not loops represent paths for gluons.

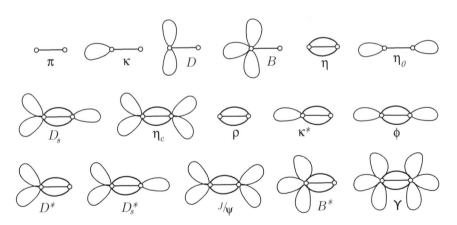

Figure 5.4 (Mesons)

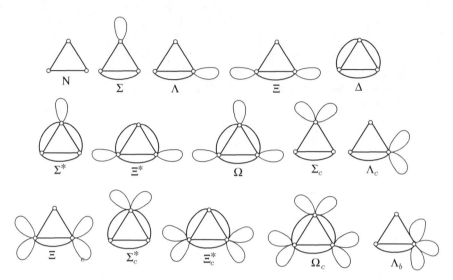

Figure 5.5 (Baryons)

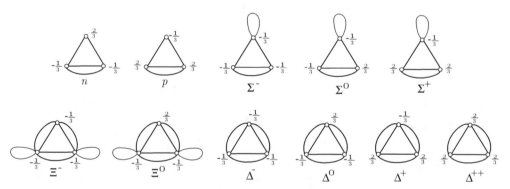

Figure 5.6 (Isospin-Multiplets)

Figure 5.5 presents the diagrams for some of the baryons. The vertices are all quarks. The first eight baryons is called the "eightfold way." The Ω baryon with its three strange quarks was theoretically predicted by Murray Gell-Mann before it was found experimentally. For awhile it was thought that all the baryons had been accounted for but then Σ_c was discovered with its charmed quark. The first baryon found with a bottom quark was Λ_b.

The diagrams in Figures 5.4 and 5.5 actually represent more than one particle because we did not distinguish between the down and up quarks for simplicity. If we do distinguish between down and up quarks we obtain isospin-multiplets. The isospin-multiplets form groups of very similar particles except for their electric charge. For example, the neutron n and proton p form an isospin-multiplet where the neutron has charge 0 and the proton charge +1. Figure 5.6 illustrates some isospin-multiplets.

Although there is much that we don't know about the elementary particles, their interactions and their formations as constituents of more complex particles, physicists have made important strides in their investigations. Due to researchers including Fermi, Bethe, Feynman, Schwinger, Gell-Mann and others, a very successful theory of elementary particles has been developed. This theory is called the standard model. The standard model has accurately described the properties of the elementary particles and the compound particles they compose. It has made predictions that have been verified in the laboratory and has not been contradicted by any experiments. The standard model is based upon the tenets of quantum mechanics and a discipline of mathematics called group theory. Unfortunately, the standard model appears to be incompatible with general relativity and a unification of these two great theories is actively sought.

General relativity describes the force of gravity and gravity is necessary for studying the large scale properties of the universe. For the description of most large scale properties, quantum mechanics and the standard model are not necessary. One exception is the life of a star. A "living" star is a sphere composed of hot gases, mainly hydrogen, helium, neutrinos and high frequency radiation. This immense heat is powered by nuclear fusion reactions below the surface of the star. After billions of years, a star depletes its nuclear fuel and gravity causes it to collapse into a dead dwarf star, a neutron star or a black hole depending on its original size. To describe such processes, quantum mechanics and the standard model are needed. These are especially important in the description of black holes. Black holes are so dense that gravity prevents even light from escaping, so they are invisible. The only way we detect them is through their influence upon nearby stars. In fact, their gravitational field is so large that they gobble up nearby stars and anything else they can get a hold of. Sometimes they get so fat that they explode and form a new galaxy. Because they are so difficult to observe, it was first thought that black holes were rare. However, it is now believed that there are billions of them. They appear at the centers and are dispersed throughout most galaxies. Because of the great density of black holes, their constituent particles are very close together and quantum effects become important.

Another exception is cosmology which is the study of the early universe. Immediately after the big bang, the universe consisted of a hot soup composed of the elementary particles, neutrinos, electrons, quarks and high frequency radiation. It took awhile (less than a second) for this soup to start coalescing into protons, neutrons and light elements like hydrogen and helium. Of course, the description of this hot soup requires quantum mechanics and the standard model.

Other mysteries are presented by our evolving universe. Our instruments indicate that the expansion of the universe is speeding up. This can only be caused by the pull of gravity of the matter and energy present. But the matter and energy that we have observed and detected, even including black holes and neutrinos, is completely inadequate to account for this required gravity. This means that there must be a huge amount of dark matter and dark energy out there, much more than we have observed. Where is it? What are its properties and composition? Now these are good questions.

I have outlined some of the big questions in the philosophy of physics. In this outline I did not give many detailed specifics like the charge of an electron, the masses of particles or the value of Planck's constant. These details are not necessary for a preliminary understanding and we will discuss them in later lectures. In the brief time we have left today, I would like to talk about the philosophy of religion.

Science and physics, in particular, are based upon the "scientific method." The scientific method dictates that we can describe and understand our world by observation. Observation and experiment together with reasoning and logic enable us to formulate "physical laws." As we discussed earlier, these physical laws explain our world within certain limits. On the other hand organized religion is based upon faith. We must trust and have faith in the tenets and teachings of the religion. In religion, there is no need for detailed observations, our senses give us enough information to get by. The answers to deep questions are already within us or they are provided by a higher calling. There is a higher power or force than us. This higher power created the universe, is ubiquitous and eternal. This power takes care of us and sets our moral standards.

Religion gives us a certain amount of comfort. We don't have to think as hard because it answers some of our questions and helps us make decisions. It forgives our transgressions and promises us salvation. It assures us that if we lead a good life we will go to a better place when we die. It teaches that good will prevail and evil will be overcome.

There are many unanswered questions in the philosophy of religion. Of course, the greatest question is: Does God exist? Other related questions are: Is there a heaven? Is there a hell? Does God care about us? Does God hear and answer our prayers? Is there reincarnation? Do we have a soul? Are the bible, Koran and other religious scriptures written by God, are they sent by God to mankind and then written or are they strictly a product of mankind? Do angels exist? If so, how are they born, where do they come from? What is heaven like? What do the beings in heaven do? If they exist forever, don't they get bored? How are people chosen to go to heaven or hell? Does God communicate and interact with us? If there is a God, why is there evil? Can science and religion coexist? Did God create the universe? If so, how? Did God create life? Since religion teaches us to be kind and love peace, why have more people been killed in the name of religion, than for any other cause? Are my questions loaded?

I am sure there are many other questions that we can ask. We shall discuss all these in later lectures. It is also interesting to speculate whether questions in physics or in religion are easier to answer. For now we have time for you to ask me a few questions about what I discussed today.

A student in the first row raises his hand and asks, "how do we know that neutrinos exist?"

"It's true that we cannot detect neutrinos directly," Pitowski explains, "but there are indirect methods. When a neutron decays, we can directly detect the decay products consisting of a proton, an electron and a γ-ray. The energy and momentum of these products and the original neutron can be measured. Now, energy and momentum are conserved in the decay. If we add up the energy and momentum of the decay products and compare this to that of the neutron, we find there is energy and momentum missing. We conclude that there must be another particle carrying this missing energy and momentum and this is the elusive neutrino."

From the back of the room, another student calls out, "I have read that scientists have transmitted neutrino beams from the LHC to a laboratory in Italy a few hundred miles away to determine their velocity. If neutrinos are so elusive, how do they detect them?"

Pitowski responds, "the LHC produces beams consisting of billions of protons. Such a beam can be narrowly focused to impinge upon a target screen. The protons in the beam collide with protons in the target screen and produce fragments composed of neutrinos and other particles. Most of the other particles have electric charge and can be guided away with powerful magnets and photons can be absorbed by thin membranes leaving a beam of pure neutrinos. Although the neutrino beam cannot be controlled or focused, a detection chamber in Italy can be set up in their path. Typically, such a chamber contains millions of gallons of water or other liquid. Of the billions of neutrinos, a few (maybe 10 or 11) will collide with a proton in the liquid. Sensitive detectors imbedded in the liquid will respond to the 'kicked' protons and record a reading in a computer. Using these readings the velocities of the neutrinos can be calculated."

There are excited murmurs through the class as another students says, "in science fiction episodes such as *Star Trek*, people are teleported from one place to another. Is this really possible?"

Pitowski, smiles to himself knowing he has the students thinking and says, "yes, it is theoretically possible. In fact, electrons have been teleported in laboratories. Of course, the jump from an electron to a person is immense, so it would be prohibitively complicated and expensive to do this with people. So my answer would be: people, no; small objects like atoms or molecules, yes. The way it works with electrons is roughly like this. All electrons have the same mass and charge and the only difference is their spin direction. Suppose Alice has an electron that she would like to teleport to Bob who could be many miles away. Alice and Bob first isolate a pair of electrons e_1 and e_2 in Alice's lab. This pair of electrons is prepared in what is called an entangled state and this is frequently performed in physics labs all over the world. Alice keeps her electron e_1 in her lab and Bob takes his electron e_2 back to his lab for later use. Now Alice wants to teleport an electron e to Bob in his lab many miles away. Neither Alice nor Bob know the spin of e. First Alice interacts the two electrons e and e_1. She then makes a spin measurement on her electron e_1. This measurement changes the original spin of e in an uncontrollable way and instantaneously alters the state of Bob's electron e_2 because e_1 and e_2 were entangled. Alice emails Bob and tells him the result of her measurement on e_1. Using this information, Bob makes a certain spin measurement on e_2 and transforms it into an electron with the original spin of e. Thus, Alice's original electron e has been essentially destroyed but it is reproduced from Bob's electron e_2."

A question from another student comes, "in *Star Trek* and other science fiction stories, rocket ships have to go at warp speed, that is faster than the speed of light because otherwise it would take thousands of years to get to other planets or worlds. Is this really possible?"

"My best guess is no," Pitowski says thoughtfully. "The basic tenant of special relativity is that no object or signal can travel faster than the speed of light. This has been tested thousands of times with a variety of experiments. It is so basic that if it is contradicted, a huge amount of physics would have to be thrown out. One of the catastrophic difficulties would be that as an object approaches the speed of light, its mass increases. Unlike the sound barrier, which is easily exceeded, to go past the speed of light barrier would require an infinite mass and hence an infinite amount of energy which is obviously impossible. One way to speed things up that might be possible is to take a shortcut through a wormhole."

"Professor Pitowski, do you believe in God?"

"Let me first say that some scientists believe in God," Pitowski says in response to the question. "They employ the scientific method in their work. However, they find that there are unanswered questions such as the origin of the universe that requires a higher power for an answer. I, myself, and most scientists, do not believe in God. The reason is not so much that God has not been observed, it's that even in our imagination there is no possible way to observe God in the future. There is no conceivable test for God's existence. For example, a few years ago, we had not observed the Higgs boson, but we could imagine and design experiments that would test for its existence. You might say, all we have to do is look around and see the wonderful beauty, variety and complexity of the universe to prove that God exists. But science has come a long way toward explaining the workings of the universe and we are confident that it is capable of explaining future phenomena that we encounter. In other words, God is not needed, so why should we invent something that is unnecessary?"

A young student in the front row asks thoughtfully, "if you don't believe in God, why do you study religion?"

Pitowski responds gently "I study religion because I am interested in the human condition. I try to understand what motivates people and what makes them tick. I want to understand the basic principles underlying our civilization. A political scientist may not believe in communism. Yet she studies it because she wants to investigate political systems."

Many hands go up with more questions. "If you don't believe in God, aren't you afraid that you won't go to heaven?" asks another student.

"Well, that's a loaded question. Since I don't believe in God, I don't believe in heaven either. I suppose I could believe in heaven without a God. But then who would elevate me to heaven. Besides, even if there is a God, how does he decide who goes to heaven? Can only people who believe in him be candidates for heaven? And if you believe in him, must you have a certain religion to be a candidate? Can only Christians go to heaven? Only Catholics? Only Muslims? What about intelligent beings on other planets? What about dogs, can they go to heaven? What about ants? What about blades of grass? If God asks questions like these, he isn't worth much salt as a God. Besides, life on earth is finite with millions of people dying every year, while existence in heaven should be eternal. The universe has evolved for billions of years and will continue for billions more. How could there be room for all these souls in heaven?

Well students, we have now run out of time. Please think about what we have said. I am only human and have answered your questions as best as I could. Perhaps you have better answers. I'll close with a joke. What's the difference between a philosopher and a physicist? *Pause.* A physicist has a waste basket. *Pause.* By the way, I'm reading a book on anti-gravity. I can't put it down. See you next week."

As the students shuffle out of the classroom, one student remains and approaches the professor. "Professor Pitowski, my name is Jerry Lamb and I'm a senior physics major in your class. Last year I spent a semester abroad at Queen's College of the University of London and I would like to relate an experience I had. I didn't want to ask you about this during class time because the other students might think it was silly. Besides that, they probably wouldn't believe me. I found this experience very puzzling and it might be related to your studies in the philosophy of physics and religion. Do you have time for me to tell you about it now?"

Pitowski, clears his lectern in preparation for his next class, "I always have time to listen to an interesting story. No matter how wild it is, I assure you I'll keep an open mind. Go ahead, Jerry."

"At the beginning of the semester at Queen's College," Jerry begins, "I met a lovely student named Susie Sands. She was from Nottingham and was also a physics major. We had many common interests and became very good friends. One thing led to another and we moved in together for about three months. Since then I have been hoping she would come to America and we could get married. Anyway, one of our mutual interests is William Shakespeare. About a month after we met, we went to a Shakespeare play at the National Theater, South Bank. The play was very moving and after it was over we strolled out to the large balcony of the theater. The other playgoers had all left and we were alone on the balcony, except for another couple who were necking at the far end. It was a beautiful, warm, moonless night and the sky was dark, except for a few high gray clouds. The balcony overlooks the Thames River which was about 50 yards away. Across the river, in the distance, was a magnificent view of the city lights. As we looked up at the sky, Susie pointed out a light in the clouds. We both thought it was one of those search lights that they shine up for advertising. But then the light started coming down out of the clouds. It wasn't a light at all. It was a shiny metal disk. The disk came closer and closer to us and after about 30 seconds, it hovered over the river about the same height above the water as we were. I estimate the disk was three or four feet in diameter and about 70 yards away from us. The disk was very bright, as if a light was shining on it, but there was no light source in sight.

The disk started rotating at a moderate angular velocity about an axis along a diameter. This went on for about a minute. It then stopped and started rotating about an axis along a diameter perpendicular to the first. After another minute it stopped and hovered motionlessly. A few seconds later it started rotating about an axis through its center perpendicular to its plane and almost immediately sped off into the sky. It rose very quickly and was gone in less than ten seconds. The whole experience lasted less than four minutes. I swear that I am not making this up. I really saw it. Susie saw it and I could tell that the other couple saw it. They did not seem very impressed and Susie was mildly impressed. I was very excited. I kept saying, wow, do you see that, awesome, do you see that? What is it? I heard the other woman say, "it must be some kind of a computer." That didn't make any sense to me, so I just ignored them and they went back to their necking.

The disk had no visible means of propulsion. It was completely smooth. There were no jets and no jet stream. It was utterly quiet, except for a slight flapping noise of the wind hitting it when it rotated. Being a physics major, I can tell you that there is no human technology that could be responsible for this. I can't believe it was some secret government project. I checked in the *London Times* and watched newscasts for the next couple of days and there was no mention of this sighting. It seemed as if we were the only people to see this and the whole incident was covered in a shroud of silence. Can you explain this? Do you think it came from another planet? Or maybe someplace else?"

Pitowski considers his words carefully, "this is something that I know very little about, Jerry. Unidentified flying objects (UFOs) have been sighted for hundreds of years. Most of these sightings have been explained as known natural or man-made phenomena or hoaxes. A few remain unexplained mysteries. It is extremely unlikely that this UFO came from another planet. A planet that would have an advanced civilization with such technology would probably be at least ten thousand light years away. A probe that large could only travel a fraction of the speed of light, say one tenth. That means it would take at least one hundred thousand years to arrive at Earth. It would take another ten thousand years to send signals back to the home planet to report its findings. No civilization would want to wait that long. And besides, who would remember anyway? A wormhole shortcut is very unlikely, but there is another possibility. As I mentioned in my lecture, physicists believe that there is a large amount of dark matter in the universe. Perhaps there are dark planets near us that we are completely unaware of. There is a very small possibility that the probe came from there. Even taking into account these very small probabilities, my conclusion remains that what you saw did not come from an another planet. What can I say? Maybe it was the intensity of the play. Maybe it was the immensity of love."

Chapter 6

Crondike's Interview

A tall, extremely handsome and well-built man in his late twenties walks through the rotating glass doors of a large Manhattan skyscraper. The man has the chiseled features of a Hollywood movie star. In fact, he looks very much like Christopher Reeves in his superman role. Although he has leading-man good looks and is wearing a finely tailored suit with a tasteful silk tie, there is something a little strange about him. He has an impeccably kept ample head of hair but there is no hint of a beard or hair anywhere else. His ears are slightly larger than usual and come to a point at the top and his hands are a little larger than usual. After entering the large granite reception hall, he checks the occupant list on the facing wall. He runs his index finger down the alphabetical list until it reaches Walter Crondike 5252. He steps into the elevator, presses the button for the 52nd floor and seems amused as the elevator quickly rises to his floor. The man gets off and briskly walks down a long door-lined hallway until arriving at office 52.

On the door of the office is printed in gold letters, *Walter Crondike, News Anchor and Investigative Reporter.* Upon entering, he quickly surveys his surroundings. On his right there are three small, glassed walled offices. Each office door says Investigative Reporter and the names Gerald Plesant, Molly Bahl or Crystal Bahl. Each office has a desk piled high with papers behind which there is a diligently working person. Straight ahead is a dark mahogany paneled wall with an impressive mahogany double door sporting shiny gold doorknobs. Next to the door is a light cherrywood desk. The desk is neatly kept and on it there is a phone with an intercom, a typewriter, in and out baskets containing some papers and a brass rectangle that says Dolly Hubbard, Walter Crondike's Receptionist.

Approaching the desk, the man sees a stunning blond woman with a captivating smile. "Are you Miss Hubbard?"

The woman meets his gaze and says, "yes I am. How can I help you?"

"My name is Brian Landy and I have an urgent message for Mr. Crondike."

"Do you have an appointment? I don't see your name in our schedule book."

"I am sorry, but I do not have an appointment. I must assure you, however, that this message is of the utmost importance. Mr. Crondike would be very disappointed if he does not receive it and there may be dire consequences."

Dolly perceives a slight British accent and hesitates for a moment. She finds this young man a little weird but appealing. She lifts her phone and presses a button. "I'm sorry to disturb you, Walter, but there's a gentleman here who would like to see you."

Without looking up from his work, Walter asks, "what's his name? Does he have an appointment?"

"His name is Brian Landy and he doesn't have an appointment. He says he has an urgent message of utmost importance for you."

"Oh well, I have a half-hour until my interview with Ford. Send him in."

"Mr. Crondike will see you now, Mr. Landy."

Dolly ushers Brian into Walter Crondike's large book-lined office. Besides impressive shelves of books, many with leather covers, there are trophies, medals and pictures of famous statesmen and world leaders. On a massive desk is a clutter of papers, books and models of rockets and satellites. Next to the desk is a wooden stand filled with pipes and a canister of tobacco. Walter Crondike is seated behind the desk in a large leather chair. He rises briefly and says, "good morning Mr. Landy, please sit down. Tell me, what is this important message?"

"I am an angel and I have a message from God," Brian says, with his hand outstretch.

Walter is a little stunned but he's been around and seen and heard practically everything. He clears his throat, hesitates and looks Brian over a few times. "Look, Mr. Landy, you may not know this, but I'm a very busy man and I don't have time for this kind of nonsense. I've got to leave in a few minutes to conduct an interview with Vice President Ford."

"First of all, God would like me to convey to you that he has great respect for the press and in particular, great respect for you. He believes that a free press is necessary for the proper functioning of any civilization."

"Mr. Landy, I'm sorry, but I'm going to have to ask you to leave." Completely ignoring Walter's request, Brian continues, "God agrees that the press is the fourth estate and is needed to keep the executive, legislative and judicial branches of government honest. The people have a right to know."

"All right, Mr. Landy, I'll admit that's something I like to hear. I'll tell you what. I'll call your bluff. If you can convince me in five minutes that you're an angel, I won't call security and have you thrown out." He fills a pipe with tobacco, lights up and leans back in his chair engulfed in a plume of smoke.

"I could use my powers of higher dimension space-time to disappear or to levitate in the air, but I was instructed to keep a low profile and not draw attention to myself. However, I will use brain waves or as we call them, thought waves, to read your mind. We can do this in an unobtrusive way and no one else will know about it. I would like to ask you to concentrate and think as far back as you can about your early childhood."

62

"Okay, I'll humor you. Here goes." Walter takes a puff from his pipe, closes his eyes and concentrates for about thirty seconds.

"I think I have enough. You and your parents lived in the small town of Saint Joseph, Missouri, in a white wooden house. Your family had a black cocker spaniel named Bobby. You had a large back yard with lots of big trees, a flower garden and Bobby's dog house. You used to like to climb on top of the dog house and as high as you could up in the trees. One time you were pretending to fly and jumped off the roof of the dog house. You landed on a tree stump which resulted in a nasty cut on your leg. You still have the scar today to prove it. You were a difficult child and got into trouble a lot. You and your friend, Freddie Lincoln, were playing with matches in the back yard and started a fire. The fire began burning the wooden fence in your yard and your parents had to call the fire department. A fireman said they got there in the nick of time before the fire got to the house and burned it down. On another occasion, you were running in your driveway with an ice pick and fell down. The ice pick punctured your neck and you staggered into the house bleeding profusely. Your parents were in a real state of panic and Bobby was barking like mad. They tried to control the bleeding by compressing a towel to your neck and they rushed you to the emergency room of the local hospital. When you got there, the attending nurse held some gauze on your neck and started asking your mother questions."

"How much blood did he lose, Mrs. Crondike?"

"I don't know, a lot. Can't you ask these questions later?"

"A shot glass, a cup, a water glass?"

"A cup, I guess. You're supposed to be helping my son. Let's get on with it!"

"Your grandfather had a junk yard with piles of scrap iron and a warehouse full of magazines and comic books. One of your favorite pastimes was lying on a stack of comic books, looking at the pictures and pretending you were a superhero. You always wanted to be a pilot and fantasized about flying planes and rocket ships. Your parents bought you a tricycle shaped like an airplane with wings and a propeller in front. They even bought you an air suit with leggings, a leather pilots jacket and a leather strap down hat with goggles. You would speed around the neighborhood sidewalk, pedaling like mad and making loud airplane noises.

When it was time to go to kindergarten you were not happy about it. It took you away from your comic books, your airplane and other toys. Besides that, you didn't like to talk to teachers. You found them to be bossy and intimidating. For nap time at kindergarten you and the other children had to lie on cots for a half hour and be completely still and quiet. One time you felt a bowel movement coming on but you were too embarrassed to ask the teacher if you could go to the bathroom. Most of the children were sleeping and the teacher did not want any noise that would disturb them. You held it as long as you could, but you eventually pooped in your pants. You tried to ignore it and hoped that it would just go away. But the smell got pretty bad and you were soon discovered. The teacher didn't know what to do with you so she called your mother to come get you. Your mother rushed you home and was not happy about cleaning you up."

Feeling overwhelmed, Walter snaps, "**stop**, that's enough already. I believe you can read my mind. I don't know how you did it but I believe. You recalled some things that I know are true but even I didn't remember. How did you come up with that kindergarten episode? I haven't told anyone about it. I haven't thought about that for fifty years."

Brian answers quietly, "I found it in the deep recesses of your mind."

"All right, I'm not convinced that you really are an angel but you are an amazing mind reader. In the slight chance that you are an angel, where do we go from here? After all, I am a reporter and if there is a story here, I don't want to miss it."

"God would like to grant you an interview. He has never granted an interview to anyone on Earth before, but he feels that you earthlings have progressed a long way and are mature enough to hear his words. He has made it a point not to intervene in human affairs but he feels that you deserve answers to some of your questions and that this will not upset the balance of nature. He knows that there are many people who do not believe in him. These people will think you're crazy and not believe anything you report. Those who do believe in him may gain inspiration from your story. I know one thing for certain, some of his answers will surprise you. They definitely have surprised me. At the very least you will gain a new perspective on life and the universe."

"I can see I'm taking a chance here, but what do I have to lose? The worst thing that can happen is that they'll kick me off the network and Dan Blather will take over. How are we going to conduct this interview?"

"God realizes that you will need some time to prepare your questions. I will return in 24 hours at which time I will escort you to the Academy, you call it heaven, where you will conduct your interview. God is looking forward to this and I'm sure he will enjoy it as much as you."

"Why can't God come here for the interview? After all, being God, he could just appear here if he wanted to."

"God is incredibly busy, even busier than you. But he can explain this better than I. Even God would take time to materialize here in this office. Also, he cannot directly intervene and his presence cannot be known by anyone but you. Finally, if you barely believe that I'm an angel, you probably wouldn't believe that he is God. What's the point then? If you see God at the Academy, there will be no doubt where you are and with whom you are conversing."

"It's a deal. If this is not legitimate we will never see each other again. If it is, I'll see you at 10:00 tomorrow morning."

Brian gets up from his chair and extends his hand to Walter. They shake hands and Walter feels a steel-like grip. "Before I go I would like to present you with a gift from God."

He reaches into his pocket and pulls out a small glowing silver sphere. Walter takes the sphere, gently places it on his desk and watches Brian close the door behind him. Beneath Walter's desk and covering half of the office floor is a thick plush brown carpet. On the carpet are footprints where Brian stepped. An ordinary man's footprints would be barely perceptible. These are deep footprints that could only be made by someone weighing 700 or 800 pounds. Walter stares at the footprints as the carpet springs back and they slowly disappear. He catches his breath and glances at the sphere on his desk. The sphere glows brighter and fills the room with blinding light. It turns a deep red, then orange, yellow, green, blue and violet. It then rises halfway to the ceiling, it becomes striped with a spectrum of colors, starts spinning more and more rapidly and projects a dizzying rainbow around the room. The colors stop and it projects an image on the ceiling saying compassion. Finally, it vanishes leaving a particle of dust that drifts down to the desk.

Walter stares at the ceiling for a minute, takes a few deep breaths and pounds on an intercom button. "Dolly, cancel my appointment with Ford and clear my calendar. Get Blather to take my anchor broadcast tonight and send Plesant and the Bahl sisters in here immediately!"

With a rush of excitement, Gerald, Molly and Crystal enter Walter's office and nervously seat themselves in three chairs in front of his desk.

Leaning against his desk, Walter begins, "I want the three of you to put aside everything you're doing! We are about to embark on the story of a lifetime and we only have one day to do it! I need your complete attention and concentration and I don't want any back talk!"

"What's going on, Walter?" Gerald asks, "I've got work to do, ya know? What could be that important?"

"Is this about that creepy guy who just left?" Molly interjects.

Crystal nods at Molly in agreement, "yeah, he gives me the shivers. Did you see his ears?"

With a nervous laugh, Molly says, "and he walks like Frankenstein. I think I'm going to puke."

Walter sighs, "that creepy guy is an angel and he wants me to interview God!"

The three reporters look at each other in bewilderment and burst out in boisterous laughter. They laugh for a good three minutes until their eyes fill with tears. Molly jumps up and shakes her long black hair up and down until it practically touches the floor. Crystal gets up and does a provocative hula-hula dance. Gerald falls off his chair, lies face down and pounds his head on the carpet.

"Ya know, Walter," Gerald says lightly with a little wink, "I told you to cut down on the booze."

Molly slaps Gerald and adds, "did you put that Irish whiskey in your coffee again?"

Crystal joins in the teasing, reaching out her hand, "let me see that bottle you keep in your bottom drawer. I'll bet it's empty."

Gerald moves closer to Walter, "let me smell your breath. Yes, ya know, it smells of spirits. Where were his wings? Ya know, why didn't he fly out of here?"

Walter waves his hands, he's not in the mood for the reporters' nonsense. "First, stop with the 'ya knows,' Gerald. It's very irritating. Second, he is an angel. His name is Brian Landy and he's coming back tomorrow to take me to heaven to interview God."

Crystal, not ready to let Walter off the hook, "wait a minute, I get it. You've been smoking pot in that damn pipe. The tobacco really stinks and the pot is even worse. Besides that, your office is always full of smoke and I get the second-hand junk in my office. Let's look into that tobacco can of yours. Aha, just as I suspected, it's full of marijuana. We told you to cut down on the merry-merry."

Walter straightens to his full height, "cut out the crap, you guys," he says with a serious sternness. "I'm convinced that Landy is an angel. He read my mind. He told me things about my childhood that were in my brain but that even I had forgotten. He told me about an incident that I had never mentioned to anyone. He gave me a little sphere that glowed, changed colors, rose into the air and projected the word 'compassion' on the ceiling."

"What incident was that, Walter?" Crystal asked.

"It happened when I was in kindergarten. Oh, never mind. You don't need to know."

"Walter," Molly looks at him with concern, "where's the sphere now?"

"Well, it disappeared. It only lasted for a few minutes."

Gerald, still skeptical, "any magician could do parlor tricks like that. Besides, the government has all kinds of records on you. A lot of people can look at your files and come up with that information. How naive can you get, Walter?"

"Now I finally get it." Crystal declares, "it took me awhile but I see what's happening. That Brian Landy character is an FBI agent! Tricky Dicky sent him to spy on you and catch you in a compromising position. He wants to make it look like you've gone off the deep end. He's trying to get even for your Watergate investigations. Not only is he the worst president we've ever had, he's mean, dishonest, vindictive and underhanded. I wouldn't put this whole thing past that lying son of a bitch asshole."

Walter interupts, "that's enough, you clowns. If you don't get serious, I'm going to fire the lot of you and hire some people who will work with me on this. We've got to come up with some good questions for me to ask God and we don't have much time. First of all, I do not want to make a fool of myself and second, one does not keep God waiting or arrive late for an appointment with him."

But Gerald pushes on, "are you fuckin crazy, Walter? In the unlikely event that this is all true and you do interview God, who will believe it? Any decent publisher will want a verification, corroboration and confirmation of your source and how do you purpose to do that? From that well-known guy, Brian Landy? You'll be the laughing stock of the industry. They'll call you names like Crudy Crondike and Walter Weiner. Don't be stupid, Walter."

"First of all, Gerald, tone down the nasty language. This is a reputable business office. Besides, with all this yelling, Dolly's probably listening on the intercom and she doesn't have to hear all that filth. Second, this is a once in a lifetime opportunity and I'm willing to take my chances. Even if nobody believes it and nobody publishes it, just think of the things I can learn and the insights I can gain. It could be a life changing experience. I could be the only person in the world who has talked to God. Let's do some brainstorming.

Think of some penetrating questions."

Crystal pipes in first, "all right, how about this one? Do angels have sex?"

Gerald laughs, "that's a good one. How about this? If I die for my country, will there really be 42 virgins waiting for me in heaven?"

"Do angels wear underpants?" Molly asks. "For that matter, does God wear underpants?"

With a look of glee, Crystal continues, "do female angels have twelve vaginas?"

"Well, I guess that's enough." Molly sighs, "can we go home now?"

Walter, running out of patience, "damn it, you idiots! You know I can't ask God questions like that. Get serious now or get ready for your pink slips."

Gerald, not reading the anger in Walters voice, continues, "how about this? What do I have to do to go to heaven?"

Crystal joins in this new line of questioning, "I shop lifted a pair of earrings five years ago. Will that keep me from going to heaven."

"Do I have to be a Catholic to go to heaven?"

"Is the greatest president we ever had, Harry Truman, in heaven?"

"What about my deceased cousin, Lucille? Is she in heaven?"

Walter allows, "that's a little better, but it still isn't there. I need some questions that are deeper and more comprehensive. I need questions that God would be pleased to answer."

Eventually, the group settles down and even begins to get enthusiastic about the project. They call out for lunch, work all afternoon, call out for dinner and work late into the night.

Brian Landy walks out of the office building onto the crowded Manhattan sidewalk. He looks into the faces of people with interest. He walks for miles, never stopping to eat or go to the bathroom. He walks through Central Park and studies paintings at the Museum of Modern Art. He walks the length of Manhattan, down to the Battery and Wall Street. He takes the Staten Island Ferry, waits in a long line and goes to the top of the Statue of Liberty. He walks back to the Empire State Building, goes to the observatory on top and stays there for an hour, gazing at the majesty of the city. He gives the impression of seeing the city for the first time. By now, it is dark and the city lights emit a dazzling sparkle. He walks awhile longer until it is about 11:00 p.m. He doesn't seem to tire but he slows his pace as he looks into the window of a dimly lit all-night coffee shop. Besides a waitress, there are only two people sitting at separate tables in the shop.

A few feet past the door to the coffee shop, a beautiful young woman is leaning against the building. She's average height, slim and has long, light brown hair and brown eyes. She's wearing a low-cut blouse and a mini skirt, exposing long slender legs, ending with spiked high healed shoes. She flashes Brian an appealing smile and says, "do you want a little company, sweetie?" Brian replies, "yes, I think I do" and motions her into the coffee shop. The waitress ushers them to a small table in the corner of the room. They sit down and stare at each other for a minute, more out of curiosity than anything else. She speaks first.

"What's your name sweetie?"

"Brian Landy, what's yours?"

"My name is Jeanie Roman."

"I heard a song on the radio called 'Jeanie with the Light Brown Hair.' Is it about you?"

"I don't think so. That song's much older than me."

"I heard another song called 'Brown Eyed Girl,' perhaps that one's about you."

"Definitely not. Let's talk about something else. You're not from New York, are you?"

"No, I'm not. I'm an angel and I'm from the Academy. You call it heaven."

"Wow, that's a lot for me to swallow. I've heard a lot of lines in my day, but this is the first time I've heard that one. It's going to take me awhile to get used to this. Do you really want to keep up with this pretense?"

"This is no pretense. I am really an angel and being one, I do not lie."

"I don't believe you, but let's pretend I do. I'm curious to see where this is going. Why are you here?"

"I'm here to deliver a message from God to Walter Crondike. Actually, I'm supposed to keep a very low profile while I'm here but I don't have to see Mr. Crondike again until tomorrow and I thought this wouldn't do any harm. In fact, I'm very interested in learning about people on Earth."

The waitress brings the couple two cups of black coffee, sugar, cream and a small dish of sweet biscuits.

Jeanie sets the coffee in front of Brian, "have some coffee Brian. Do you want sugar or cream?"

"No thanks, I'll just have it black. I usually don't eat or drink but to be sociable, I will." He sips a small amount of coffee as if never having done it before.

"Are you telling me that you're not originally from Earth?"

"That's true. I'm originally from a distant planet whose name is not important. I died about 5,000 years ago and God summoned me to the Academy. My actual name would sound funny to your ears so I took the name Brian Landy. It's the name of one of your historians whom I've read and admire very much."

"But how do you know so much about us besides reading from this historian? How did you learn to speak our language so well, although I do detect a bit of British?"

"We have observation posts at the Academy where we observe inhabited planets. We have cosmic-ray telescopes and we intercept waves from telephones, radio and television. We can even watch your movies. For more accurate readings, we even send probes to the planets. You're not supposed to see them and they usually only come out at night. They're small silver disks about $3\frac{1}{2}$ feet in diameter. We recently sent one to London."

"I still don't believe you but you are very convincing and you're very nice. How would you like to come to my apartment? It's very plush and has a great view of the city and the Hudson River. We can enjoy the view and make love. I've never made love with an angel."

"I'm sorry but I can't make love with you."

"Why not? I am attractive to you aren't I? You do like me, don't you?"

"Yes, you're very attractive and I like you very much. But I'm sorry, I don't have the male body part for lovemaking."

"I don't believe this. You're freaking me out, Brian. Why not?"

"I didn't think it would be necessary for my visit here. After all, it doesn't have anything to do with my mission which is to convey a message from God to Walter Crondike. Now that I'm here I can't just manufacture one out of thin air. But I'm very interested in hearing about you and would like to just stay here and talk if you don't mind. I'll pay you anything you would like."

"That's a shame. I think you would make a very good lover. All right, we can stay here and talk. What would you like to know about me?"

"Well, how old are you and what's your life like?"

"I'm 21 years old. My life with my drug addict mother and nonexistent father stunk so as soon as I graduated from high school three years ago, I got out of there. For three years now I've been on my own and as you can see, I'm a prostitute. I've got a pretty good life. I've got a swanky apartment and I make good money. It is getting to be a drag though. Some of the Johns are real creeps and I can't do this forever. With my lousy hours and terrible diet, my good looks won't last long and in five or six years I'll have to find something else."

"What would you do?"

"Well, I love animals and I've always wanted to be a veterinarian. I figure I can stand this unsavory profession for five more years, save some money and go to veterinary school. At least that's my dream. I think everyone should have a dream, don't you?"

"Yes I do. I think you're a wonderful person, Jeanie, and I hope your dream comes true."

The couple talk for hours about heaven and earth. They laugh and sometimes gently touch. To an outsider they would appear as young lovers. They continue all night and into the morning. They watch the sun rise above Manhattan skyscrapers. Although they wish these moments would last forever, they know their time together is limited.

"It's 9:00 a.m. and I have to leave soon for my appointment with Walter Crondike. Before I go, I would like to give you something. I shouldn't do this and I might get into trouble, but it's worth it. Let me have your hand."

Brian reaches into his pocket, pulls out a brilliant five carat diamond and places it in Jeanie's open hand. "This diamond is worth over $100,000. It's a perfect diamond and it's not from Earth. It's from my home planet and I've carried it around for 5,000 years. Do not take it to a pawn shop. I would like you to take it to one of those fancy Fifth Avenue jewelers. They will know what it's worth and give you a check. Deposit the check in a bank. I want you to quit this job, leave your apartment and register at a good veterinary school. You might have to get a part-time job but with this money you can do it. You will have a good life and when it's over, you will go to heaven and I will be waiting for you there."

Brian closes Jeanie's hand around the diamond. A tear trickles from one of her eyes down her cheek. Brian touches the tear and whispers, "I love you." She silently mouths, "I love you too." Brian places a crisp $100 bill on the table, they leave through the shop door and walk in opposite directions.

At 10:00 a.m. Brian opens the door to Walter Crondike's outer office with great flourish. Barely noticing the stares of Dolly, Gerald and the Bahl sisters who are standing almost at attention, he walks into Walter's office and closes the door behind him. Walter sits behind his desk, an exhausted expression on his face. "Are you ready, Mr. Crondike?"

Grabbing some papers from his desk, Walter says, "I'm as ready as I'll ever be, Mr. Landy."

"I'm sorry but you can't take papers. They won't make it through the trip. Also, I have to ask you to empty your pockets. Those things won't make it either."

Walter empties his pockets, takes off his watch and stands in front of Brian.

"What do we do now?"

"I'm going to ask you to turn around." Brian who is six feet five inches approaches Walter who is five feet nine inches, from the back and wraps his arms around Walter's chest. Walter feels like he is enclosed in a steel vise and can barely breathe. Brian's body transforms into a spaceship shaped object with a pointed cone top. There is a flash of sparks and they disappear. A few seconds later, four anxious figures burst into the empty room. They see Walter's keys, watch and wallet on his desk. Knowing the door is the only way out, they tussle each other to get to the window. They see what might be a speck in the sky that rapidly vanishes, but it isn't clear.

Gerald calls out, "Holy shit. It's true. Dolly, tell Blather he'll have to take over as anchor for awhile."

And what a ride it is. Walter, who wanted to be an astronaut all his life, has a most amazing journey. He sees flashing lights and psychedelic patterns. He sees fireworks better than any Fourth of July. He sees erupting volcanos and swirling tornados. He sees dodecahedrons, octahedrons, icosahedrons, paraboloids, hyperboloids and four-dimensional cubes. It seems like they have traveled for days, but who knows, maybe it was for hours or seconds.

As Walter sees higher dimensional objects that are impossible to describe, he gets the idea that he is slowing down. Sure enough, he lands lightly alone inside a huge marble temple. He doesn't feel tired. In fact, he feels rested and exhilarated. His body feels light and the pains and itching he had on Earth are gone. There are two white leather chairs in the room. One is empty and the other is occupied by a jovial Santa Clause looking figure in a flowing white robe, who says, "welcome to the Academy Mr. Crondike. I hope you don't mind if I call you Walter. I am God and that is what I would like you to call me. This is not what I really look like. In fact, if you could see the real me, all you would see is a three-dimensional projection consisting of elementary particles and energy. I have chosen this form because I think this is what you expected to see and what would make you feel most comfortable. I promise I won't give you my 'ho ho ho' Santa Clause imitation. Please have a seat so we can begin our interview."

Walter clears his throat and says in a weak voice, "your honor, I mean God, is it all right if I take notes?"

"I'm sorry, but as with your trip here, paper would not survive your trip back to Earth. You're a very intelligent man, I'm sure you will remember all you need to know. As Brian told you, I have a great respect for you and your work. Some people on Earth believe in me and some, that don't, might change their minds after hearing your report. Please begin."

"Tell me about the Academy and how it is organized."

"Unlike Earth and the visible universe which is a $3 + 1$-dimensional space-time manifold with three dimensions of space and one dimension of time, the Academy is a $4 + 2$-dimensional space-time manifold. The Academy is a place of higher learning. We call our members academicians and we form a society of scholars. We study everything that is of interest to a higher intelligence. One of our primary studies is the cosmos itself, which is the grandest experiment of them all. We have millions of apprentices, angels and archangels viewing screens attached to powerful quantum computers with huge memories. These computers monitor the greatest quantum computer of them all which is, again, the cosmos itself. We are investigating the enormous complexity of the cosmos with its various patterns and mysteries. On rare occasions, problems occur which can result in disastrous inconsistencies. On these occasions, a group of archangels and I must work to overcome these problems. Sometimes there is a minor inconsistency on a set of measure zero and we monitor it to make sure it works itself out with no consequences. We conduct many seminars on a plethora of subjects and have many discussions and arguments in both large and small groups. We study all the sciences and mathematics. We study languages, literature, poetry, politics, history, civilizations and all forms of life. One of our favorites is music. We have many choirs, symphonies and, of course, harps. With all this going on, we never get bored and, of course, we have that marvelous balm that keeps everything running smoothly, *humor*."

"Would you give me an example of Academy humor."

"By all means. Many academicians say I am a mathematician. This may not be exactly right, but mathematics is my favorite subject. Mathematics is the one true reality and the power that controls the cosmos. In any case, here is a mathematical joke in the form of a theorem. The steps in the proof are self-evident. The reasoning and logic between the steps are perfectly correct. Yet the statement of the theorem is bewildering.

Theorem. *All cats have nine tails.*

Proof. No cat has eight tails.

A cat has one more tail than no cat.

Therefore, a cat has nine tails.   □

"That's a good one, God. Besides humor, what else do you do for fun at the Academy?"

"For one thing we have lots of parties. I myself give a huge number of parties because I want to eventually include everyone but having too many folks at one party makes it unmanageable. We also have refreshments that make us quite happy. One is called cosmic tea and the other is dark matter chocolate."

"Can you describe the hierarchy of academicians for me?"

"At the first level we have the apprentices. They are newly elevated souls who originate from planets that support intelligent life. They are 4+2-space-time dimensional beings and we have trillions of them. Most of their time is spent learning, observing and experimenting. They can also indulge in our planet replicators, our virtual athletics and our game centers. We have many apprentices who are content where they are. Depending on their progress, others may be promoted to the next level, that of angel, within 100 to 1,000 years. We have billions of angels and they are 4+3-space-time dimensional beings. They can participate in all the activities of the apprentices, but they also attend higher level seminars and conduct research in a variety of fields. On rare occasions, an exceptional angel is promoted to the highest level, archangel. They are 4 + 4-dimensional beings and there are about 100,000 of them. They spend a lot of time in research and monitoring the cosmos. Of course, there's also me. I am a 5 + 5-dimensional creature and I have the power to raise or lower dimension. I have also bestowed this power upon my archangels. We have rotating panels of archangels and angels who consider others for promotions."

"I don't understand this higher dimension business. Can you explain it to me?"

"You are well aware that you exist in a three-dimensional space. You have forward-backward, that's one dimension. You have left-right, that's another dimension. Finally, you have a third dimension, up-down. Even though you can't observe them, you can imagine in your mind, that there could be other dimensions in space. Take your right hand and point your thumb straight up. Now stick your index finger forward and your middle finger to the left perpendicular to your index finger. You now have three perpendicular axes meeting at a point that is a little below and forward from the base of your thumb. These axes form the basis for a 3-dimensional coordinate system. You can use this coordinate system to locate points in three-dimensional space. But what about your other two fingers? They're curled up and don't point anywhere. You might wonder why you have five fingers on your hand. Four or six fingers would serve your purposes just as well. Could it be that your ancient cave-dwelling ancestors needed those extra two fingers to point in two more directions? Could it be that these ancestors lived in a 5-dimensional space that has since shriveled down to three dimensions? Why is your little finger smaller than the rest? Will it get smaller and smaller and after 10,000 years eventually go away. Is it like your appendix that is no longer of any use to you? Will humans eventually have only three fingers? Just as the five fingers on your right hand are primordial reminders of five space dimensions, the five fingers on your left hand are reminders of five time dimensions. If you think about it, this all might make sense."

"Do academicians ever die, do you have bodies?"

"Academicians do not die, they come from a soul that cannot be destroyed. They also do not have bodies in the usual sense and are composed of pure energy. However, they can take any form they want by converting their energy to matter. Many of them are comfortable in assuming a form similar to their appearance when they lived on a planet. If they want, they can converse by talking but this is not necessary because they can communicate faster and easier through thought waves which are a high frequency radiation like x-rays. In many ways, I am exceptional among the academicians. I have existed since the beginning of the cosmos and I did not come from a soul. My power comes from my control of dimension and my vast experience. You see, the Academy is only a few billion years old and I am about 14 billion years old."

"Since academicians don't die, isn't the Academy getting overcrowded?"

"It is very difficult to obtain and sustain conditions that support life on a planet. Besides that, these conditions vary in time and even if there are life forms present, intelligent life is very rare. For example, on your planet, most of the life has been in the form of insects and dinosaurs. In your universe there are only about 10,000 planets that have intelligent life inhabitants. These planets are very widespread and it is highly unlikely that they will communicate. Also, intelligent life civilizations only last for about 50,000 to 60,000 years. After that the beings on a planet either destroy each other or destroy their planets or deplete their resources. So you see the number of worthy souls is limited. In any case, there's plenty of room. A one-dimensional space is like a straight line on a plane which is a two-dimensional space. You can see the amount of extra room on the plane. In fact, you could place an unlimited number of lines on the plane. Now you could place an unlimited number of planes in your three-dimensional space. In the same way, we could place an unlimited number of your three-dimensional earths in our four-dimensional Academy. Moreover, we don't need to worry about resources because we don't eat (we can pretend to eat if we want), don't breathe oxygen and so on. So we have room."

"What's going on with these extra dimensions of time?"

"As I said, an apprentice has two dimensions of time, an angel has three and an archangel has four. These extra degrees of freedom give them more room to manipulate. Your one-dimension of time is linear. That is, if you take two different times A and B, then one of them is earlier and one is later. That is, either $A < B$ or $B < A$ and we say that A and B are comparable. If A and B are two-dimensional, they don't have to be comparable. Think of two points on a plane. One doesn't have to be smaller than the other like two points on a line. For one dimensional time, there's only one way to go from one time to a later time. In two-dimensional time there are many ways to go from one time to another. A two-dimensional time being can do very tricky things in the eyes of a one-dimensional time being. He can disappear and then reappear at a later time. He can appear to go backward in time. You can imagine what a three, four and five dimensional time being can do."

"In the scriptures we read things like, God is one, God is eternal, God is everywhere. Are these true?"

"Yes they are true. A religious person accepts these statements on faith. There are also scientific explanations, but they are rather technical and I cannot go into them now. When you come to the Academy, you can attend my cosmic seminar and hear the complete story."

"Is it hard to get into heaven?"

"If you follow my single commandment, thou shalt have compassion, then you will most likely be elevated to heaven. As usual, there are exceptions and we have rotating panel of angels who decide who is worthy of heaven. If you do not get into heaven, your soul, which cannot be destroyed, is placed in a holding zone where it is periodically reviewed."

"Is there a hell?"

"I should have mentioned that. I suppose I didn't because it's kind of disgusting and we don't usually discuss it. We do have a type of purgatory. It's a $2 + 1$-dimensional space-time manifold. These souls are converted into beings that are completely flat. All they can do is crawl around on a two-dimensional surface. I seldom go there but it's maintained by a couple of angels. We also have a special place that's really grotesque. It's a $1 + 1$-dimensional space-time manifold. These creatures are like worms moving on a line. All they can do is crawl forward or backward and bump into each other. That's where we keep Adolf Hitler and his Nazi hoodlums."

"Do dogs go to heaven?"

"I'm sorry dog lovers, dogs do not get to go to heaven. Dogs are very loving and loyal animals, but they do not have souls. This applies to cats and other animals. Also to trees, flowers, insects and grass. So far only intelligent beings have souls. Chimpanzees are getting close but they're not there yet."

"Do fetuses have souls? When do they get one?"

"Fetuses obtain a soul when their umbilical cord is cut. Before that, the fetus is part of the mother's body. It is not our business what she does with her body as long as she shows compassion."

"Do you hear our prayers? Do you care whether we believe in you?"

"No, I don't hear your prayers. Look at the size and complexity of the cosmos and the Academy. Even I have trouble keeping track of all that. Do you think I have time or the ability to listen to a bunch of prayers? And even if I did, I couldn't do anything about them because I do not intervene in human affairs. I would like people to believe in me because I exist and I think the truth is always best. However, whether you believe in me or not will not change the universe and will not make one bit of difference. Also, it's ridiculous to think that I care what religion you choose. Moreover, I wish folks would stop saying that the scriptures which they quote from constantly, are written by me. I deal in facts and not in nonsense."

"What about homosexual unions?"

"What is more beautiful than two people in love? Marriages are not made in heaven, they are made on your planet and they are about love. Having babies is easy, love and family are what's worthwhile."

"On rare occasions, someone like Albert Einstein, who is head and shoulders above everyone else, appears. It's almost as if they come from another planet with higher intelligence. Does the Academy have something to do with this?"

"Yes, the Academy is involved with such happenings. We have a program whereby an angel or archangel can request a visitation to an inhabited planet. Great care must be taken, however, to avoid any inconsistency and I cannot overstate the disastrous effects an inconsistency can cause. We can't just place someone on Earth. People would ask where did he or she come from? Who are his parents? Where are the records? A bad contradiction could occur. The event must occur along a natural progression of nature. What happens is that an angel implants a soul into an egg of a carefully chosen woman. When the egg is fertilized it becomes a special child who inherits genes from the mother and father and traces of the implanted soul. These traces usually have little effect on the child, but sometimes the child inherits special traits which are unpredictable. There have been a few hundred of these people on Earth. Most of them have not been exceptional. Some that were exceptional are the obvious ones like Moses, Jesus and Mohammad. Others were Archimedes, Leonardo da Vince, Joan of Arc, Isaac Newton, Leonhard Euler, Frederick Gauss, Wolfgang Amadeus Mozart, Ludwig van Beethoven, Albert Einstein, John von Neumann, Mother Teresa and Richard Feynman. We usually watch these special people rather closely. For example John von Neumann was a mathematical genius. These people aren't supposed to remember anything from the Academy, but something went wrong and he did. He was spewing out new mathematics too fast. The world wasn't ready for this. He was beginning to upset the balance of nature. I had to call him back early. He later told me he wasn't ready and I informed him that he should continue his work at the Academy. He is still incredibly productive."

"What's going to happen to our civilization on Earth?"

"Even I cannot tell the future and I do not have the ability to go forward in time. But I do have the experience of observing many civilizations like yours. Some have flourished for hundreds of thousands of years and some have decayed rapidly after about 10,000 years. On average, a civilization has lasted 20,000 to 30,000 years. I am not optimistic about conditions on Earth and I anguish over all the greed and hatred there. Sometimes I think there must be a defect in the human makeup. Other times I think it is due to the tribal history of your ancient ancestors when destroying other tribes was necessary for survival. This might have produced an inborn fear and hatred in your genes. I apologize for this state of affairs. Although I am not directly responsible, I think religious intolerance has something to do with it.

If you do not kill each other off, I think that in about 70 years your civilization will begin a 200 year golden age. I say this for two reasons. The first is that I think you will harness nuclear fusion in about 70 years. Although your scientists understand the theory of nuclear fusion, they cannot contain and control it. The problem is that nuclear fusion produces so much heat that no vessels have been developed to contain it. However, in the next 70 years, your scientists will develop extremely strong magnets that will contain a fusion reaction in a small space. The heat generated can then be used to perform a huge amount of work. The hydrogen fuel for the reaction will come from water. Can you imagine filling your automobile tank with water and driving 100,000 miles without refilling? Once you have harnessed nuclear fusion, you will have an unlimited source of clean, inexpensive energy.

The second reason is the quantum computer. Your computers now do not use quantum mechanics in their hardware or software. They are based on using electric voltage to produce on and off states and magnetism for data storage. Also, the circuit chips in your computers are getting smaller and more compact. This is beginning to produce too much heat. Eventually, in the next 70 years, electronic components will get so small that quantum theory will take effect. This will inevitably result in quantum computers. Quantum computers will not dissipate heat and will operator much faster than conventional computers. But their real power will be in their memories and software. They will be able to store one bit of information per atom in the memory device. Since there are about 10^{23} atoms per cubic centimeter, this gives a lot of memory. Their software will execute exponentially faster than conventional software. This is because they can entangle and form superpositions of states which result in massive parallel computations.

Combining nearly unlimited sources of energy and great computational power, your civilization should begin a 200 year golden age. But then the situation will rapidly deteriorate. Your planet will become overpopulated. Your farmland will diminish further and you will deplete your planet's resources. The irreversible consequences of man made global warming will make the deserts larger and cause almost complete melting of the polar icecaps. The oceans will rise over two feet, causing flooding of all coastal cities. The polar bears, elephants and great cats will vanish except for in zoos. Due to overfishing and pollution, life will disappear from the oceans, except for jellyfish and a few small fish species. The overuse of antibiotics will result in drug resistant diseases, causing widespread epidemics. Of course, pockets of people will survive for thousands of years more, but your civilization will never return to its previous glory. I'm sorry to deliver such a pessimistic message. But this will all happen unless you work hard and begin now to reverse these processes."

"I'd like to ask you a couple of questions about science. Is time travel possible and is traveling faster than the speed of light possible?"

"Time travel into the past is impossible. This is against a fundamental principle of nature called causality, which states that the cause must precede the effect. In other words, the past can influence the future, but the future cannot influence the past. This principle is so self-evident that it's almost unnecessary to state it. What you do today certainly can influence what happens tomorrow, but what you do tomorrow can have no influence on what happens today. If you could build a time machine and step out into the past, even if you don't do anything, your very presence will have an effect. In this way the future would affect the past.

Even worse, if you could overcome the causality principle and travel back in time, it would cause contradictions or inconsistencies that would tear the fabric of the universe.

Suppose you get into your time machine and step out five minutes earlier. You would see a person who looks like you getting ready to step into the time machine. Which person is really you, the one stepping into or out of the time machine? Suppose right after you step out of the time machine five minutes earlier, you take your keys out of your pocket and place them on the table. Five minutes later you will be back to the time when you first stepped into the machine. Your keys will be on the table and at the same time they will be in your pocket. Even stranger, you will now be forced to step back into the time machine because that's what actually happens now. Thus, you and the rest of the universe will be in an infinite repeating loop every five minutes. This clearly cannot happen. Similar, but more subtle inconsistencies would occur if you went back further in time, like a century.

You have heard me speak of inconsistencies before and I cannot over emphasize the importance of the fact that they not occur. If one inconsistency occurs, then, it usually causes another which causes another and so on. This continues quickly, until the whole universe collapses and disappears. Let me give you a simple example that illustrates this point. Suppose we have the inconsistency:

$$1.00000000000000000001 = 1 \tag{6.1}$$

where there are twenty zeros after the decimal point. You may think that this is a very minor inconsistency. No conceivable measuring instrument could distinguish between the two numbers in (6.1) so for all practical purposes it's true. Subtracting one from both sides of (6.1) gives

$$0.00000000000000000001 = 0 \tag{6.2}$$

which is again a minor inconsistency. Now multiply both sides of (6.2) by ten to get

$$0.0000000000000000001 = 0 \tag{6.3}$$

Now there are 19 zeros after the decimal point and we can hardly tell the difference between (6.2) and (6.3). Keep multiplying by ten until we arrive at

$$0.1 = 0 \tag{6.4}$$

which is no longer a minor inconsistency. Multiplying by ten again, (6.4) becomes

$$1 = 0 \tag{6.5}$$

This is really bad because we can multiply both sides of (6.5) by $2, 3, 4, \ldots$ to get

$$2 = 3 = 4 = 5 = \cdots = 0$$

In this way, all of our numbers have collapsed into zero and have disappeared. You might now say, "That's bad, but it's not a catastrophe. It may not be easy, but I could still survive without numbers." My answer is, perhaps, but you would have to give up all your electronic gadgets, your car, machines, house and buildings, because they are constructed using mathematics based on numbers. But could you survive without time? If $1 = 0$, then 1 seconds = 0 seconds. As before, all intervals of time collapse to zero. But without time, you cannot have change and without change you cannot have motion. The blood in your veins stops flowing, the air stops moving into your lungs, the earth stops orbiting the sun, the sun, which is composed of moving hot plasma ceases to exist. The entire universe becomes a gigantic contradiction and disappears.

To complete my answer to your question about time travel, travel into the future is possible. You could almost do it now with today's technology. Build yourself a cylindrical cabinet with a turntable floor. Get in the cabinet and set the motor to spin the floor at thousands of revolutions per second. Keep increasing the number of revolutions until you are moving near the speed of light and then stay in the cabinet for a couple of hours. According to the theory of special relativity, when you get out of the cabinet, days, years or centuries will have passed on Earth, depending on your speed. You have thus traveled forward in time by days, years or centuries. If you don't like spinning that fast, you can accomplish the same thing by climbing into a rocket ship, going out and coming back to Earth at speeds close to that of light.

Finally, you asked whether traveling faster than the speed of light is possible. The answer for human beings is no. This is because faster than light speeds would contradict some of Einstein's special relativity equations. However, members of the Academy and I can and frequently do travel faster than the speed of light. This is possible because we are higher dimensional beings and we are not constrained by the equations that hold in your lower dimensional space-time. These higher dimensions are also related to dark matter and dark energy that your scientists know exists but cannot detect."

"I apologize in advance, God, but there are a few questions that my staff would like me to ask you. It's against my better judgement but here goes anyway. Do angels have sex?"

"Angels don't have bodies or genders so they don't have sex in the usual sense. However, they have something better that we call connecting. Two or more angels get together and connect to form a single unit. They meld to form a fluid cloud of energy and particles. They produce myriads of particle-antiparticle pairs that explode into tiny puffs, resulting in sparkles of energy. They experience tingling sensations and huge orgasms. This can go on for hours or days. It is quite pleasant and I must admit I do it too."

"Please excuse me, God, but I just have to ask you this. Would you show me what you look like under your robe?"

"All right, but you'll probably be disappointed." God stands up and opens his robe. There are the usual head, arms and legs but in between there is nothing but a smooth metal like cylinder.

"As I said, I have taken this form to make you comfortable. I didn't think it was necessary to have a complete body because it would be covered with a robe."

"Getting to a more serious subject, would you tell me something about the cosmos and its origin?"

"Now that's probably the greatest question of them all. It would take until eternity to answer that question completely but for now, I can give you an outline. It goes almost like poetry.

In the beginning there was an empty void.
Then powerful reality began to operate.
This reality generated numbers sequentially.
It began with $1, 2, 3, 4, \ldots$
At each number tick, a vertex is formed.
These vertices produce universes.
Not one universe, but a multitude in parallel.
First there is one universe with a single vertex.
Next there are two universes, each with two vertices.
Next there are five universes each with three vertices.
Then there are 16 universes, each with four vertices.
This process continues sequentially forever.
The vertices are connected in various patterns to form sites.
A universe becomes a path through the sites.
A plethora of paths creates a plethora of universes.
The paths crisscross in complicated ways,
form in a beautiful, elegant framework.
The dynamics of the paths is not deterministic.
It is a probabilistic process,
governed by the laws of quantum mechanics."

"Wow, I can't say I completely understand it, but that was beautiful. Is there anything else you would like to convey to us earthlings?"

"Just one more thing and it is very simple. It is the power of a smile. Your psychologists have concluded that smiling is good for your mind and body. Studies have shown that the average child smiles about 400 times a day while the average adult smiles less than 20 times. Some adults never smile at all. Your children begin life very happy and innocent. As they grow older, they become jaded and less carefree. Learn from your children and be more like them."

"This conversation has been the highlight of my life. I have never felt more secure and relaxed. Can I stay with you here forever?"

"You know that you must return to Earth to report on our interview, Walter. But later, I think we can make some kind of arrangement. Your report will be very important and I hope people will learn from it. So we must say goodbye until we meet again."

Chapter 7

Crisscrossing Universes

Mary Kay Bennett and Charles Randall enter the office of David Fowler in the mathematics department at the University of Massachusetts, Amherst. Fowler is a tall distinguished looking professor in his fifties with graying hair and horn-rimmed glasses. Randall is about the same age but is scruffy, considerably shorter and has hair flying in every direction. Bennett is a single, attractive, newly promoted associate professor in her thirties and was a Ph.D. student of Fowler.

Fowler closes his office door after they enter, "I emailed you guys to come here because I have a very important project for us. Since it's July and you don't have any classes to teach, I want you to devote your entire attention to this."

"Look Dave," Charles interrupts, "I'm really busy with my research right now and don't have time for a new project. I've just discovered an operational manual representation of empirical logic and am anxious to see where it will lead. This may result in our long sought after interpretation of quantum mechanics."

MK agrees, "I'm busy with my research too, Dave. I want to work on a generalization of orthomodular lattices called effect algebras. It gives a noncommutative version of fuzzy logic. I find this to be very exciting and I really don't have time for anything else."

Waving his hands excitedly, Dave says, "forget about that research for now. This is really important and I'm only asking for one month."

"What could be so important? Why can't it wait?", Charlie wonders.

"I'll tell you what would be so important. On August 10 a once in a lifetime event will occur. In fact, this is the only time an event like this will occur in the lifetime of the universe! I'm talking about something of cosmic proportions."

"Give me a break, Dave," MK says impatiently. "The lifetime of the universe? Cosmic proportions? I think you're getting carried away. What is this thing and how do you know about it?"

Dave presses on, "I'll tell you in a minute what it is and how I know, but first, I need to tell you why you both should drop everything and work like mad with me on this. With your help, I am going to make us all millionaires. In fact, we will each get about eight million dollars, tax free. We can each invest our share in tax-free municipal bonds and get something like $400,000 a year. We could quit our jobs teaching these knuckle heads and just do research. You can then devote all the time in the world to your empirical logics and effect algebras."

"Speaking of knuckle heads," Charlie says skeptically, "I'll bet this scheme of yours is a real beaut. I'll give you ten minutes to tell us your hair brained idea, let's hear it."

Ignoring Charlie, Dave continues, "I got the idea from my work on discrete quantum gravity. This is a theory that unifies quantum mechanics and general relativity. According to this theory, every cosmic instant our universe bifurcates into billions of other universes. A cosmic instant is about 10^{-81} of a second. This is $0.000\ldots01$ of a second with 80 zeros."

"Dammit Dave," Charlie says, impatience coloring his tone, "don't treat us like idiots. We know what 10^{-81} is. How does this bifurcation occur?"

"It goes like this." Dave is undeterred, "at each instant our universe is structured with a scaffolding of interconnected points called vertices. The interconnections are formed in various ways to form a causal set that I call a site. The sites are graphs with the additional structure of a partially ordered set. Every cosmic instant, a new vertex is created and there are myriads of ways this vertex can be connected to previous vertices. Each way forms a different site. In this way, a site divides into billions of new sites every cosmic instant. A universe is really a path through these sites. The sites on a path expand by one vertex every cosmic instant. This results in not just one universe, but a plethora of expanding universes. This is called a multi-universe theory and a path is sometimes called a universe history time-line. We happen to belong to one time-line, but there are a huge number of others. The number of these time-lines is increasing exponentially in time, which makes their description almost unmanageable. Luckily, I've developed some theorems that discern certain patterns in their behavior."

Softening, MK says, "okay. We kind of get it. But what is this great occurrence that you were talking about?"

Dave nods to MK and continues, "well, the paths are very complicated and the only theory available to describe them is quantum mechanics. But quantum mechanics only provides us with the probabilities of the paths and various events. The computations of these probabilities are very tedious and I have utilized our university computer to do a huge amount of number crunching because doing these calculations by hand would be virtually impossible. Of course, I am interested in the path of our particular universe and I have obtained some preliminary results. Not surprisingly, our path crisscrosses many other paths all the time. When we cross another path our universe instantaneously coincides with another universe. Using my calculations and some computer simulations, I found that our path crossed another path 35 years ago. Let's call our universe A and the other universe, whose path we crossed 35 years ago, B. So 35 years ago, universe A and B were identical for an instant. That's no big deal, it happens all the time. But now we come to an absolutely phenomenal occurrence. My simulations show that this August 10th universe A

and B will cross again. But this time the paths will remain together for about one second and then divide and never recross. Now a second is incredibly long compared to a cosmic instant and the probability of such an event is astronomically low. It's like flipping a coin a trillion times and having every flip come up heads or getting a trillion reds in a row at a roulette table in Las Vegas."

Charlie, is interested, but still unsure, "so what? I think that's great that you may have found a very unlikely event, but what good could this possibly do for us? How is this going to make us millions of bucks? By the way, I'm not interested in going to prison because of some dumb-shit stunt you've concocted."

Dave's voice is steady, "I'd rather not tell you more now because my calculations are preliminary and need to be checked. I assure you that nobody is going to prison and if I'm right, this plan is foolproof. I'm just asking you to indulge me for a few days and go to a little trouble. If this works, it will be well worth it. Just to wet your appetite, I'll give you a little hint as to what this is all about. It has something to do with diamonds in Boston."

Somewhat reluctantly, MK says, "all right, Dave, I think Charlie will agree with me. We'll both humor you for a little while. I for one am always interested in a new adventure, but this better be good. If it isn't, your name will be mud around here. What do you want us to do?"

Dave sits down, "Charlie, I'd like you to verify my simulations and get more accurate data. As we know, the computer here at Amherst is a piece of shit. It's very slow and doesn't have much memory. With your NSF grant, you have a lot of computer time with the supercomputer at MIT. I'd like you to run up there and verify my work. We especially need to know the amount of time that universes A and B coincide on August 10th and at exactly what time this will happen. MK, I have two jobs for you. I know that you are vice-president of our Eastern American Mathematical Society chapter and they sent you a fancy, official card designating this. I'd like you to flash your card at the convention center office in Boston. Tell them that the AMS is planning their annual meeting for 2020 and Boston is one of the cities in contention. They'll fall all over themselves for you because they're always interested in new conventions. Tell them you'd like a preliminary view of their facilities but you need to make an appointment in two weeks to bring a colleague for a closer look. The other job may sound a little strange. I'd like you to meet a fellow named Richard Greechie. I know him, but not well. I do know he comes from an old Boston family and his father manufactured ice cream cones. After selling cones with his father, for awhile, Richard went to work in my father's jewelry store. Now he's a broker for BGC, the Boston Gem Company. You can tell him you know me and you're interested in purchasing a diamond ring. He's a charming bachelor and I'm sure he will be happy to talk to you. I want you to get to know him. I think you'll like him and he might even ask you out on a date. All right, you have your jobs. Remember, it's hard to make a lot of money doing mathematics, but if we're really clever, we can break the trend. I'd like you to report back to me in a week. In the meantime, I have a lot of planning to do."

A week later, the three colleagues meet again in Dave's office.

"Okay," Dave begins, "we don't have much time guys, how did it go?"

"Your calculations were correct," Charlie says. "I had to do a lot of programming and number crunching and I had to pour over pages of output data, but I've arrived at the following results. Universes A and B will coincide for precisely 0.957 seconds and it will occur at 7:05 a.m., August 10th."

Nodding, MK adds, "everything went well at the convention center. I have an appointment to meet with them and a colleague in two weeks to view their facilities. I talked to Dick Greechie. I think he's great and like him a lot. We went out on a date and got along fabulously. He just got back from New York and told me that he bought a perfect five carat diamond from a young lady for \$150,000. He said he had never seen a diamond like it and that it looked like it came from another planet. He told me that the young lady informed him that she got it from an angel. I think it's more likely she got it from a sugar daddy. Also, Dick loves mathematics and said he always wanted to be a mathematician. Unfortunately, he didn't have enough money to go to graduate school when he was young. Anyway, we talked for hours about orthomodular lattices and effect algebras. He even gave me some ideas for my research. We have a date to go out again."

Dave smiles with satisfaction, "great work guys, that's excellent. It's even better than I expected. Before I tell you the master plan, here's why it's going to work. If you were going to break into a bank vault at night and steal the money, what is the main obstacle you would have to overcome to get away with it and not get arrested?"

Charlie jumps to his feet, "fuck it, Fowler, I'm leaving. I'm not having any part of robbing a bank. I knew this scheme of yours was going to be crazy."

"Calm down, Charlie, you're not going to rob a bank. This is only a hypothetical analogy. Answer my question."

MK, ignoring Charlies outburst, ponders the question, "you'd have to get through the door, get through the bank security, break into the vault and get out without leaving a clue."

"You didn't really answer my question, MK, I asked for the main obstacle, not a bunch of little ones. Actually getting through the door, through the security and into the vault are relatively easy and I've got those covered. The biggest obstacle is not getting caught and arrested after you leave the bank. The bank notes are usually marked or have recorded serial numbers, so how do you convert them to usable cash? Even if you do convert them, how do you spend the money without raising suspicion? There might be witnesses seeing you enter or leave the bank or seeing your car while you're in the bank. Even if you're wearing masks, hats and gloves, you might leave your DNA from a cough or a sneeze. The list goes on and on. Well, guess what? I've got that covered too."

Charlie grumbles, "Dave, will you quit jerking us around and give us the plan? My patience is running thin here."

"Here it is. I don't think I've told you my life story before. My father started working as a golf pro. In fact, when I was a kid, I used to caddy for him. He wasn't satisfied with that work, so he saved some money and used it to open a small jewelry store in downtown

Boston. He worked very hard, was quite successful and bought a larger jewelry store. Thirty-five years ago, I was 21 and just graduated from college. My father asked me to go into business with him. I told him that I had a passion for mathematics and wanted to go to graduate school and get a Ph.D. It was a very difficult decision for me and I could have gone either way. In fact, I would say the probability of my choosing graduate school was 51% versus 49% for the jewelry store. My father understood and gave me his blessing, so off I went to graduate school."

"Dave, that's all very nice but what does it have to do with this great plan of yours?" says MK with exasperation. "Can you please get to the point?"

Dave motions for his colleagues to calm down and listen. "The point is that 35 years ago is precisely when the Universes A and B crossed. From the probabilities I just mentioned and some calculations I made about our universe, I came to the conclusion that in Universe B I made the decision to go into business with my Dad. So here we are in two parallel universes. In our Universe A, I go to graduate school and in the other Universe B, I go into the jewelry business. Let us call me Fowler A and my counterpart in Universe B, Fowler B. About 15 years ago, my father closed his store in Universe B and retired. At that time Fowler B went to BGC to become a diamond broker. I got this information from further computer simulations. At about the same time, my father also closed his store and retired in Universe A. But now Richard Greechie in Universe A was out of a job and he also went to BGC to become a diamond broker. Since Universes A and B are due to cross on August 10th, three weeks from now, our Greechie A has a counterpart Greechie B in Universe B."

"Let me get this straight," Charlie interjects. "In Universe A, we have you, Fowler A and Greechie A, while in the parallel Universe B, we have two diamond brokers Fowler B and Greechie B. At intersection, on August 10th, the two universes will coincide so you and Fowler B will coalesce for one second and also Greechie A and Greechie B will coalesce for one second. But what about all the other people in the universe? What will happen to them?"

Dave nods excitedly, "everyone in our universe will have a counterpart in Universe B and the two will coalesce for one second. In most cases the pairs are almost identical and no one will notice what's going on. I don't have time to calculate what will happen with the others. The computations are very complicated and it was hard enough to work out what will happen with me."

"This seems to be going on forever, Dave. What in the world are you getting at?"

"I'm sorry this is taking so long. Here's the main point. It just so happens that August 9th and 10th are the dates of the International Diamond Festival to be held at the Boston Convention Center. This amazing coincidence is the key to my plan. Diamond dealers from all over the world will be there. They will display a huge number of loose diamonds for retailers and wholesalers to view. I know because I've attended some of these festivals with my father. Typically, there will be slews of black velvet trays each containing fifty or more loose diamonds on display. Most of the diamonds will be three or four carats worth $40,000 or $50,000 apiece, wholesale. According to my plan, I will go to the festival on

August 10th. Of course, I will look just like the diamond broker Fowler B. During the second of intersection, I will steal diamonds from Universe B and take them back to our Universe A. It's the perfect crime. There will be no diamonds gone from Universe A, so in our universe, there will be no investigation. The diamonds will come from Universe B but Fowler B will not have them so he won't be arrested for the crime. Nobody will be harmed because the diamond companies have insurance and besides, they'll get a lot of publicity from the mysterious disappearance. Everything is airtight. It's a work of genius!"

"Work of genius, my ass!" Charlie bellows. "That's the most cockamamie plan I've ever heard. If you're trying to illustrate the fine line between genius and insanity, you're doing a very good job. The only problem is that you're tilted toward the latter. And airtight, my ass, again. This plan is so full of holes, an elephant could crawl through it. Dave, you're not playing with a full deck here. This is like jumping onto a speeding train, staying for one second and jumping off. How are you getting through security into the room where the diamonds are? How are you going to grab millions of dollars worth of diamonds in one second? How will you know that the diamonds you take are from Universe B and not from our universe? How about other people in the room? Are they just going to stand there while this is going on? What about security cameras? All I've got to say, Dave, is that you're really crazy."

"You didn't give me a chance to explain the details. I didn't work them all out completely because I will need more information but for now, here's what I know. Because the two universes will coincide for almost a second, I have calculated they will be in close approximation during a two minute window, one minute before and one minute after intersection. This will give me time to empty about twelve trays of diamonds into a large briefcase. Except for the exact second of intersection, I'll be in Universe A and Universe B will appear slightly blurred during the two minute window. In fact, Universe B will get more and more blurred until it finally disappears. The Universe A trays will appear sharp and the Universe B trays will be a little separated and a little fuzzy. I'll just empty those trays. Does that make things clearer, Charlie?

Now here's what I need you guys to do in the next week. Charlie, I need you to check my calculations and run computer simulations to find out exactly where Fowler B will be at 7:05 a.m., August 10th. MK, I need you to get as much information as you can from Dick Greechie about the festival. Maybe you can start by mentioning it casually to him. Most importantly I've got to know the room where the main diamond display will be and the layout of the room. I hope you both agree that this plan is workable and has a good chance of succeeding. See you in a week."

"I'm going along with you for one reason," Charlie says. "Since you're doing the stealing, it's your ass that's on the line. If somebody asks me, I'll say I don't know you."

One week later, MK and Charlie report back to Dave. Charlie tells Dave that his calculations are correct and that Fowler B will enter the display room at 7:00 A.M on August 10th. MK tells Dave that the Ben Franklin Room is where the diamonds will be displayed and that Greechie plans to arrive there at 8:00 a.m. Greechie told her that there will only be a couple of people in the room at that time and the room will be opened for the public at 9:00 a.m. The displays will be set up the day before, so everything should be ready. A little before 9:00 a.m., security guards will arrive to watch over things.

Dave then instructs them to go to their appointment with the convention people the following week. They should ask the convention people to see the Ben Franklin Room. This will be a week before the festival, so the room will be empty and it shouldn't be a problem. Dave asks them to scout out the room and to especially note the security arrangements.

After their appointment, they again report back to Dave and tell him about the layout of the room. They inform him that there will be no security guard at the door to the room, but that there is a fingerprint pad which must be activated to open the door. There is one security camera in the room and it takes about five minutes for a complete scan. On August 9th, they meet one last time to finalize their plans. At the end of the meeting, Dave concludes, "We're very fortunate, it looks like the timing works just right. Well, I guess we're ready, see you later."

MK hesitates, and then speaks up, "Dave, I have one last question. I know that Fowler B will enter the Ben Franklin Room at 7:00 a.m. in Universe B. Since the universes cross at 7:05 a.m., his counterpart in Universe A, namely you, will have to be there to coincide with him at 7:05 a.m. But what if you didn't have this plan and you weren't there? After all, we do have free will don't we? Your actions are not predetermined. There are a zillion things you could be doing instead of driving up to Boston and performing a bizarre ritual like going to the Ben Franklin Room at 7:05 a.m."

"Yes, there are a zillion other things I could be doing. These things happen on other universes with various probabilities. However, on our universe, I will be in Boston to meet my destiny. Meet me back in my office tomorrow at 11:00 a.m. and you should each bring an empty briefcase."

"Wait a minute. I also have a last question. What will it feel like to people around 7:05 a.m.?" Charlie wonders.

"A lot of people on Earth will be asleep and won't feel a thing. Those who are awake will feel like they're having a spell of vertigo. They will start seeing double and will get dizzy. They will feel slight changes in their surroundings. It will be a little like an earthquake. This will go on for about thirty seconds, stop and go on again for about thirty seconds. The whole thing will be perceptible for only about a minute. I hope there won't be any bad accidents. We could warn people, but that would probably cause more harm than good. You might try taking a video. It would be an interesting sight. See you tomorrow. Wish me luck."

That evening, Dave drives to Boston and checks into a hotel near the convention center. He wakes up early the next morning and arrives at the entrance door to the Ben Franklin Room at 7:00 a.m. with an empty briefcase. He's nervous and his hands are shaking. He can feel some sweat dripping down his forehead. He presses a button on the chronometer of his wristwatch. It is set to beep at 7:04, 7:05 and 7:06. He stares at the fingerprint pad near the door. He knows that Fowler B will press his thumb against the pad at 7:00

and enter the door, but that is in Universe B which is invisible to him. At the 7:04 beep, the pad begins to separate slightly into two pads, one sharp and one fuzzy. He presses his thumb against the fuzzy pad. Since Dave and Fowler B are almost identical, so are their thumb prints. The door opens and Dave enters.

There are only three other people in the room and they are busily arranging a row of black velvet lined trays, each containing about fifty sparkling diamonds. Closest to Dave is a fuzzy Fowler B. At the other end of the room are two brokers, one sharp and one fuzzy. Each tray is really two closely separated trays, one sharp and one fuzzy. Dave quickly empties the first fuzzy tray into his briefcase. He then empties the second fuzzy tray. Although Dave is moving quickly, the rest of the world seems to be going in slow motion.

Fowler B shouts, "what is going on here? Who are you? What are you doing?"

Dave ignores Fowler B and empties the third fuzzy tray.

Fowler B continues, "stop that, I'm calling security."

Dave quickly empties fuzzy trays four and five. The tray pairs are getting closer and closer and get harder to distinguish. Dave feels a tie materialize around his neck and a dark suit jacket appears over his shirt. Dave and Fowler B get closer and begin to coalesce. Dave's watch beeps at 7:05 and he becomes motionless as they become one person. Almost immediately they begin separating. Dave empties tray six. Fowler B grabs Dave's arm and they begin scuffling. Dave pushes the fuzzy Fowler B to the floor and immediately empties six more fuzzy trays into his briefcase. Fowler B brushes himself off and starts getting up. The other broker pair move toward Dave to investigate the commotion. Dave notices his arm getting fuzzier and is aghast to see his body getting fuzzy.

"Oh shit, I'm in the wrong universe!"

Dave realizes the disaster that is about to materialize, thinks quickly and touches the sharper part of the wall. He immediately becomes sharp again. His watch beeps 7:06 and he opens the door and walks out, briefcase in hand.

In Universe A, everything now appears normal. All the diamonds are there and arranged just as before. The other broker is now alone in the room. He shakes his head as if he's recovering from a dizzy spell. He remembers seeing Dave enter, fiddle with some of the trays and leave. He remembers a shadowy figure saying something incomprehensible, falling to the floor, getting up and disappearing. The security camera only shows a portion of this scene and it looks like some static from a computer blip. Since nothing was stolen, there's no reason to report the incident.

In Universe B the situation is chaotic. Fowler B and the other broker look around in bewilderment. Half of the trays are empty and they're alone in the room. Fowler B collapses into a chair behind the counter. He's in a state of complete confusion and panic. He presses a button below the counter to call security. A security guard comes running down the hall to the Ben Franklin Room. He sees a few people in the hall and asks them if they saw anyone leave the room and they say no. He enters the room and asks the two occupants what happened. The two brokers are still in a stunned condition but are able to blurt out their account. They tell the guard that a shadowy figure entered the room, emptied some trays, pushed Fowler B to the ground, emptied more trays and left. Fowler B tried to stop him, but it happened so fast there was little he could do. It was almost as if the diamonds vanished into thin air. The security camera corroborated their story. The headline story in *The Boston Globe* the next day, is:

Mystery of the Disappearing Diamonds

In a sensational robbery, 24 million dollars worth of diamonds went missing yesterday from the Boston Convention Center. No clues to the identity of the robber were found and the two brokers who were present were completely exonerated. The police stated that they would probably never find the perpetrator. The diamond companies involved were insured.

Dave drives from Boston back to Amherst, shaking with excitement. He arrives at Amherst about 10:00 a.m. and stops at a coffee shop to calm down. The coffee shop is practically empty, with only two customers at the counter, a waitress and a cook. Dave sits down in a booth next to the window. The perky, blond, young waitress approaches.

"What would you like, sir?"

"I'll have a cup of coffee and a Danish please."

"You seem a little nervous and your hand is shaking. Are you all right, sir?"

Dave holds his quivering hand with the other hand to steady it and tries to relax his body. "I'm really okay. I haven't had breakfast yet, so I'm a bit hungry. I think I'll feel better after you bring me my order, so could you hurry it up a little?"

"Okay, okay, keep your pants on. You know, that's a funny expression now that I think about it."

"I promise you, I won't take my pants off if you bring my order."

"To tell you the truth, I wouldn't mind if you took your pants off, but it would be better if we were alone someplace. I think I've seen you before in here. You're one of those professors from the University aren't you? I really like professors, they're so fascinating and intelligent. They talk about exciting things and are always enthusiastic. They aren't all as handsome as you are, though. We've been open since 6:30 this morning and you're the only interesting person I've seen, so far. What's your name, dear, mine's Marge."

"Glad to meet you Marge. My name is Dave and I'm a math professor at the University. Tell me, did you notice anything unusual about 7:00 this morning?"

"Now that you mention it, I did. We don't have many earthquakes around here but I felt something like one. I didn't feel the floor shaking and nothing fell off the shelves, but I got a little dizzy for a minute. I was serving a customer some coffee and I thought I briefly saw two cups. The customer said he noticed it too. Our cook was breaking some eggs on the griddle and he told me he was seeing double. Also, I looked out the window and saw a car almost jump over the curb. Luckily, I didn't see any accidents. It all happened very quickly and I almost forgot about it. Do you know anything about what was going on?"

"I just so happen to be one of the few people in the world that knows what occurred. If you will please bring my order, I'll tell you about it."

The waitress leaves and quickly returns with Dave's order.

"Here's your coffee and Danish, Dave. Now please tell me your story. It might cut down on the boredom in this joint."

"Well, it's going to come out anyway so I guess I can tell you what occurred at 7:05 this morning. Our universe crossed another universe and they stayed together for a second. What you saw for about a minute was the blurred image of the other universe. It all happened very fast and now the two universes are separated forever. This is the only time that such an event will occur in the lifetime of the cosmos."

It isn't often that Marge is involved in a high level conversation. She gets very excited and starts breathing heavily. Her breasts seem to get larger and bulge against her tight low-cut blouse. She scoots into the booth so her hand is on Dave's knee. Dave tries to stay calm and act cool as he sips some coffee and bites into his Danish.

"Wait a minute, wait a minute. Are you telling me that there is more than one universe and we just collided with another one. How come there wasn't more damage? This sounds more like science fiction than fact. How did you know about this anyway?"

Marge's hand moves slowly while Dave tries to continue the conversation.

"There is not only more than one universe, there are trillions and trillions of them. They cross all the time, but only for less than a billionth of a second and no one notices it. I know about this because it is predicted by my theory of the cosmos. It's based on quantum mechanics and probability theory."

Hearing all these high powered words nearly drives Marge crazy. She grabs Dave's hand and places it on her thigh.

"When the two universes were together, this morning, was it possible for someone from one of the universes to grab a souvenir from another universe and bring it back to his own?"

Dave finishes his coffee and Danish with his free hand. He watches as Marge closes her eyes and sways back and forth with the motion of his hand. Her mouth opens and her breathing gets very heavy. Her chest heaves and the buttons on her blouse appear about to burst.

"I suppose so. A lot of things are possible. Why do you ask?"

Marge turns toward Dave and moves very close to him. "I don't know. I just have a great power of intuition and I have this feeling about you. My other great talent is my ability to love. You might say, I have a head for people and a body for pleasure. I've got a lot more questions for you. For example, what makes these universes move around the way they do? Is it jet propulsion or something?"

Dave looks at his watch and sees that it's 10:45. He reluctantly pulls his hand away and gently removes her hand. "I'm very sorry but I have an important appointment at 11:00. I'll come back another time and answer all your questions."

"Are you sure you're coming back? I really enjoyed our conversation and being with you."

"You bet I'll be back."

He briefly thinks about giving Marge one of the diamonds sitting in his car, but decides that a $40,000 diamond would create more suspicion and publicity than he wants. He reaches into his wallet, gives her a crisp $20 bill and walks toward the door thinking: "Wow, that was really worth it." As he looks back, he sees Marge waving goodbye with the $20 bill in her hand. With her other hand she undoes buttons on her blouse and flashes her assets. The temptation to go back in is so great that Dave has to summon all his will power to continue on. His colleagues would literally kill him if he didn't show up for his appointment.

Marge turns toward the cook who is busy preparing food behind the counter. "Hey, Alfonso, do you remember this morning when you saw double and had a little dizzy spell?"

"Yeh, I was just thinking about that. I've decided it was caused by the stuff I was smoking last night."

"Well, that wasn't the reason. It happened because our universe collided with another universe and we stayed together for a few minutes."

"Are you crazy, Marge? Where in the world did you get that wild idea?"

"It came from that customer who just left. He's a math professor at the University. He's very smart and knows a lot about the universe and stuff. He said he'll explain more about it to me later. I've got this feeling that he's going to ask me out for a date. You know, I would really like to learn more about math and science. Maybe I'll take some courses at the University. I might even get a degree and make something of myself."

"That sounds like a great idea. Maybe I'll take some courses with you."

Dave leaves the coffee shop and drives to the Mathematics Building at the University of Massachusetts. When he gets to his office he sees MK and Charlie standing in front of his office door talking excitedly. They both start to say something, but he puts a finger in front of his lips to shush them down. They all rush into the office and close the door. Barely able to contain himself, Dave exclaims, "We did it, we did it! I have 24 million dollars worth of diamonds in this briefcase!" The three grab each other in a big bear hug and jump up and down like excited teenagers. They look at each other, burst out in laughter, grab each other and do it again. It takes them a good ten minutes to regain their composure. Dave sweeps the books and papers from his desk and dumps the diamonds into a large pile on his now empty desk. They divide the diamonds as closely as they can into three equal piles, which they then deposit into their three briefcases.

Dave says, with a grin, "I propose that we go over to the Amherst Pub to get drunk and celebrate. The beers are on me!"

Charlie shakes off his colleague and says, "I'm sorry, Dave. I've neglected my research for a month now. I've got to get back to work. I apologize for doubting you and saying all those nasty things. See you later."

"I'm sorry too," MK says, "I've got to drive up to Boston. Dick Greechie and I have a dinner date. He's going to show me some diagrams that can be used to represent orthomodular lattices. I think we'll call them Greechie diagrams."

"Okay guys, I understand. When we get back together in a few days I want to discuss setting up a fund to pay for people's expenses caused by accidents during the incident."

For the first time in a month, Dave sleeps very well that night. He dreams that God gives a seminar presenting his work on the theory of the cosmos. The dream soon fades and he starts thinking about having coffee and Danish the next morning.

Chapter 8

The Cosmic Seminar

About 40 angels assemble in one of the many seminar rooms of the Academy. A Santa Clause like figure stands before them at a white board and begins speaking. "As you know, I am God and this will be the first lecture of the cosmic seminar. In this lecture, I will outline the basic structure of the cosmos. In later lectures I will discuss more details. Before we proceed with this structure, I must describe some of the elements of space-time geometry. Space-time is a world of four dimensions, three dimensions of space and one dimension of time. We first establish an origin $(0,0,0,0)$ which serves as a base point from which other points are measured. An arbitrary space-time point is given by a 4-tuple (x_0, y_0, z_0, t_0) where x_0 is the x-coordinate, y_0 is the y-coordinate, z_0 is the z-coordinate and t_0 is the t-coordinate. We call (x_0, y_0, z_0) the space coordinates and t_0 the time-coordinate.

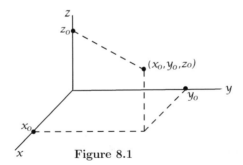

Figure 8.1

The coordinates can be any real numbers representing space and time in convenient units. For example, we could take the origin as a corner of a room at 12:00 noon. If you are sitting in a chair 2.5 feet high, located at an x-coordinate five feet from the corner, y-coordinate seven feet from the corner and the time is 3:00 p.m., then your space-time coordinates are $(5, 7, 2.5, 3)$. We could measure (x_0, y_0, z_0, t_0) in miles and seconds or any units we would like. Figure 8.1 shows a space point (x_0, y_0, z_0) located in terms of an origin $\mathcal{O} = (0, 0, 0)$ and x, y and z-axes.

Some of the numbers x_0, y_0, z_0 can be negative and if $t_0 > 0$ we think of t_0 as being in the future and if $t_0 < 0$ we think of t_0 as being in the past. For example, if you were sitting in the same chair at 11:00 A.M. one hour before we started counting time, your space-time coordinates would be $(5, 7, 2.5, -1)$.

According to Pythagorus' theorem, the distance from the space point (x_0, y_0, z_0) to the origin $\mathcal{O}$ is given by

$$d\left(\mathcal{O}, (x_0, y_0, z_0)\right) = \sqrt{x_0^2 + y_0^2 + z_0^2}$$

This is illustrated in Figure 8.2. More generally, if (x_0, y_0, z_0) and (x_1, y_1, z_1) are two space points, the distance between them is given by:

$$d\left((x_0, y_0, z_0), (x_1, y_1, z_1)\right) = \sqrt{(x_1 - x_0)^2 + (y_1 - y_0)^2 + (z_1 - z_0)^2}$$

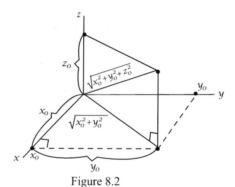

Figure 8.2

One of the basic laws of nature is that the speed of light in a vacuum is a constant c where c is approximately 186,000 mi/sec. That's fast. If an object flew directly over the Earth's equator at the speed of light, it would circle the globe more than seven times in one second. For two space points $p_0 = (x_0, y_0, z_0)$ and $p_1 = (x_1, y_1, z_1)$, let's compute the time t it would take for a light signal to travel from p_0 to p_1. Since speed equals distance divided by time, we have

$$\frac{d(p_0, p_1)}{t} = c$$

so $t = d(p_0, p_1)/c$. Put another way, suppose we have two space-time points (p_0, t_0) and (p_1, t_1) where $t_0 < t_1$. If

$$\frac{d(p_0, p_1)}{t_1 - t_0} = c$$

then a light signal sent from (p_0, t_0) will exactly arrive at (p_1, t_1). If it happens that

$$\frac{d(p_0, p_1)}{t_1 - t_0} > c \qquad (8.1)$$

then either $d(p_0, p_1)$ is too large or $t_1 - t_0$ is too small for a light signal from (p_0, t_0) to reach (p_1, t_1). On the other hand, if

$$\frac{d(p_0, p_1)}{t_1 - t_0} < c \qquad (8.2)$$

then a signal traveling at less than the speed of light can be sent from (p_0, t_0) to (p_1, t_1).

Another basic law of nature states that no physical object can travel faster than c. We conclude that if (8.1) holds then the space-time point (p_0, t_0) cannot signal the space-time point (p_1, t_1). In this case, nothing that happens at (p_0, t_0) can influence anything that happens at (p_1, t_1). On the other hand, if (8.2) holds, then (p_0, t_0) can signal (p_1, t_1). If $t_0 < t_1$ and (8.2) holds, we say that (p_1, t_1) is in the causal future of (p_0, t_0). First $t_0 < t_1$ means that t_1 is later than t_0, so (p_1, t_1) is in the future of (p_0, t_0). Secondly, since (8.2) holds (p_0, t_0) can signal (p_1, t_1) so an event at (p_0, t_0) can cause an effect at (p_1, t_1). If (p_1, t_1) is in the causal future of (p_0, t_0), we write $(p_0, t_0) \prec (p_1, t_1)$.

First notice that $(p_0, t_0) \prec (p_1, t_1)$ does not mean that (p_0, t_0) is less than (p_1, t_1) in the usual sense of numbers. We call $\prec$ an order relation on the set of space-time points of the form (p, t) where $p = (x, y, z)$ is a space point and t is a time. The order relation $\prec$ has two important properties. The first is called irreflexivity and means that $(p, t) \prec (p, t)$ does not hold. The second is called transitivity and means that $(p_1, t_1) \prec (p_2, t_2)$ and $(p_2, t_2) \prec (p_3, t_3)$ imply that $(p_1, t_1) \prec (p_3, t_3)$. It is easy to check that these two properties hold and I will leave it to you to verify these.

In general, if we have any old set of elements $S = \{a, b, c, \ldots\}$ together with a symbol $\prec$ that satisfies:

(1) $a \not\prec a$ for all a in S (irreflexivity)
(2) $a \prec b$ and $b \prec c$ implies that $a \prec c$ (transitivity)

then we call $(S, \prec)$ a *partially ordered set* or *poset*, for short. We use the term partial because it may happen that $a \not\prec b$ and $b \not\prec a$ for two elements of S. If for any two different elements a, b in S we have either $a \prec b$ or $b \prec a$, we call $(S, \prec)$ a *totally ordered set*. The set of space-time points together with the causal order $\prec$ is an example of a partially ordered set that is not totally ordered. To see that it's not totally ordered, suppose $a = (p_0, 0)$ and $b = (p_1, t)$ are two space-time points with $p_0 = (0, 0, 0)$ and $p_1 = (x, 0, 0)$ where $x > 0$, $t > 0$ and $\frac{x}{t} > c$. Since $t > 0$, we have that $b \not\prec a$ and since

$$\frac{d(p_0, p_1)}{t - 0} = \frac{x}{t} > c$$

we have that $a \not\prec b$. This shows that the set of space-time points is not totally ordered.

Besides space-time, there are many examples of posets. For example the set of real numbers $\mathbb{R}$ together with the usual order $<$ is a poset. Clearly, $a \not< a$ for any real number a. Moreover, if a, b, c are in $\mathbb{R}$ and $a < b$, $b < c$ then, of course, $a < c$. Also, if a and b are different real numbers then either $a < b$ of $b < a$, so $(\mathbb{R}, <)$ is a totally ordered set.

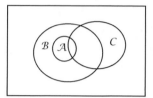

Figure 8.3

For another example, let S be all the subsets of a sheet of paper. Figure 8.3 illustrates three subsets A, B and C. For two sets E and F in S we write $E \subset F$ if E and F are different and every element of E is also an element of F. For example, from Figure 8.3 we see that $A \subset B$ but $A \not\subset C$. Now $(S, \subset)$ is a partially ordered set. It is obvious that $E \not\subset E$ for any E in S and if E, F, G are in S with $E \subset F$, $F \subset G$ then it is clear that $E \subset G$. This transitivity is illustrated in Figure 8.4. From Figure 8.3 we see that $C \not\subset A$ so $(S, \subset)$ is not totally ordered.

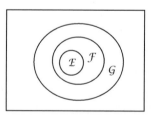

Figure 8.4

There is a handy way of representing a poset $(S, \prec)$ called a Hasse diagram. We represent each element of S by a small circle called a vertex. If $a \prec b$ and there is no c in S with $a \prec c \prec b$, then we call a a *parent* of b and b a *child* of a. If a is a parent of b we draw a rising line from the vertex representing a to the vertex representing b. We call this line an *edge*. The Hasse diagram is the picture of these vertices and edges and it completely describes the poset. Also, a Hasse diagram is an example of a graph as considered in

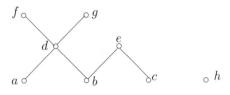

Figure 8.5

Chapter 4. However, a Hasse diagram is more specific than a general graph because it not only has vertices and edges but it also has an ordered structure given by the rising edges.

Figure 8.5 illustrates a Hasse diagram. In Figure 8.5 we see that a is a parent of d and d has two children f and g. Also, e has two parents b and c while h has no children. We can determine the order relation by inspection. For example, we see that $a \prec f$ because a is connected to f by rising edges. Moreover, notice that $b \prec g$. An element a of a poset $(S, \prec)$ is called *maximal* if there is no b in S with $a \prec b$. For example, in Figure 8.5 we see that f, g, e and h are the only maximal elements.

I am now ready to discuss the structure of the cosmos. To begin, I will invoke another law of nature. I call this the law of finiteness. This law states that there are no infinities in the real world. At first you might think that this cannot be true. For example, we frequently talk about the set of natural numbers

$$\mathbb{N} = \{1, 2, 3, \ldots\}$$

and say that the natural numbers are real. However, the set $\mathbb{N}$ is part of the world of intellect: it is only in our minds. We really only need to consider finite subsets of $\mathbb{N}$ and these are what we actually use. The other ingredient that we need is the observational fact that the cosmos is expanding. Astronomers have been observing this phenomenon for a long time. Of course, the cosmos may continue expanding forever or it may stop and then start contracting. We can treat this latter possibility later, but for now we will assume an expanding cosmos.

Taking these two principles, finiteness and expansion into account, we develop a sequential growth model for the cosmos. Now ordinary space time is infinite because there are an infinite number of possible space-time points. Invoking the finiteness principle, we replace space-time with a finite poset $(S, \prec)$. To remind us that we are working with the causal order, we shall call a finite poset a *causet*. The sequential growth model begins with the empty causet $\emptyset$; that is, the causet with no elements. At the beginning, time is set at 0 and then ticks $1, 2, 3, \ldots$, each tick being called a *cosmic instant*. At each cosmic instant a causet grows by adjoining one new maximal vertex and this growth comes from the expansion principle. The vertex is maximal because no other vertex should have a later time and this new vertex should not have a causal effect upon previous vertices. Thus, at cosmic instant one, we have a causet with one vertex. At cosmic instant two, this causet can grow into a causet with two vertices in two different ways. This is illustrated in Figure 8.6.

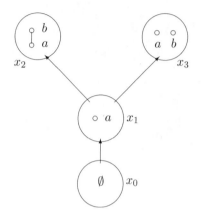

Figure 8.6

In Figure 8.6 we have the causet x_1 with one vertex a. Since there is only one vertex we need not be concerned with the causal order. At cosmic instant two, we have two possible causets x_2 and x_3 because we can add a maximal element b to a in two possible ways. Notice in x_2 we have $a \prec b$ while in x_3, a and b are not causally related. We call x_1 the neutrino and call x_2, x_3 the positron and electron, respectively.

Look at causet x_1. That's me for God's sake! That's me, God! I am unique. I was present at the beginning of the universe, at the big bang. I am the neutrino. To be precise, neutrinos are part of the four-dimensional shadow of my ten-dimensional self. Since neutrinos are everywhere in the cosmos, so am I. Since neutrinos compose most of the matter of the cosmos, so do I. Since trillions of neutrinos pass through the bodies of every human being, so do I. Some of these neutrinos are absorbed into their bodies, so I am there. Neutrinos will exist as long as the cosmos exists, so I am eternal.

At cosmic instant three, both x_2 and x_3 can grow by adjoining a maximal element in three ways. This is shown in Figure 8.7. We call x_4, x_5, x_6, x_7, x_8 quarks. The number 2 on the arrow from x_3 to x_6 is called the *multiplicity* of the transition $x_3 \to x_6$. The multiplicity 2 comes about because x_3 can grow or transition into x_6 in two ways. The best way to see this is to consider labeled causets. Suppose we have a causet $A = \{a_1, a_2, \ldots, a_n\}$ where $a_1, \ldots, a_n$ denote the n vertices of A. A labeling of A is obtained by numbering the vertices with the numbers $1, 2, \ldots, n$ in such a way that if $a_i \prec a_j$, then the number labeling a_i, namely i, is smaller than the number labeling a_j, namely j. Figure 8.8 gives a labeling of x_3 and the two possible resulting labelings of x_6.

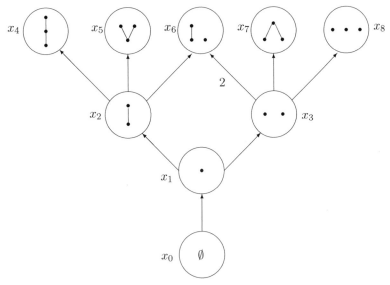

$$\text{Figure 8.7}$$

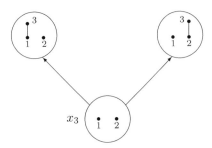

$$\text{Figure 8.8}$$

We conclude that there are six causets with three vertices including multiplicity, so there are six quarks.

If a causet x grows into a causet y by adjoining a maximal element we write $x \to y$ and say that y is an *offspring* of x. Figures 8.9–8.12 illustrate labelings for x_5, x_7 and x_8 of Figure 8.7 together with labelings for some offspring.

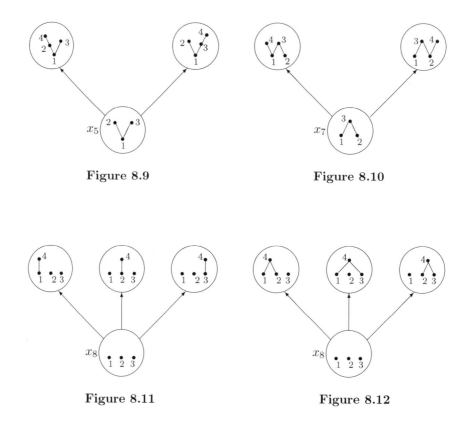

Figure 8.9

Figure 8.10

Figure 8.11

Figure 8.12

Figure 8.13 shows the cosmos at cosmic instant four. Notice there are sixteen new causets produced and twenty-two including multiplicity.

Each causet in Figure 8.13 represents an instantaneous universe. For example, x_5 represents a universe at cosmic instant three while x_{16} is a universe at cosmic instant four. A *path* or *history* is a sequence of causets $y_0, y_1, y_2, \ldots$ where $y_0 \to y_1, y_1 \to y_2, \ldots$. Every path starts at the big bang x_0, so we always have $y_0 = x_0$, $y_1 = x_1$, but after cosmic instant one there are many possible paths. For example $p = x_0 x_1 x_2 x_5 x_{15} \cdots$ and $q = x_0 x_1 x_3 x_6 x_{15} \cdots$ are paths that happen to cross at cosmic instant four. A completed universe or simply a universe, for short, is a path that goes on without end. Thus, a universe is not just an instantaneous universe at a particular cosmic instant, but it includes the entire history and future of a universe. Even if two universes are identical at some cosmic instant, they are different if they have different histories or futures. The universes p and q considered previously cross at cosmic instant four, but they have different histories.

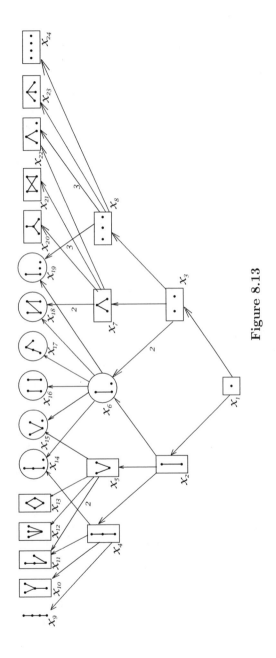

Figure 8.13

101

The causets $x_1, x_2, \ldots x_8$ represent the elementary particles: neutrino, positron, electron and quarks. These were the early constituents for the various possible universes. Of course, there are myriads of possible universes, one for each path. In fact, even at an early time like cosmic instant ten, there are billions of universes with partial histories up to that time. These universes form complicated crisscrossing paths that continue without end. The positron x_2 is an example of an antimatter causet and the electron x_3 is an example of a matter causet. If a causet y is on a path that passes through x_2 but is not on a path that passes through x_3, we call y an *antimatter* causet. If a causet y is on a path that passes through x_3, but is on no path that passes through x_2, then y is a *matter* causet. A causet that is on a path that passes through x_2 and on another path that passes through x_3 is called a *mixed* causet. Every causet except x_0 and x_1 is exactly one of these three types. For example, x_{13} is an antimatter causet, x_{14} is mixed and x_{20} is a matter causet. In Figure 8.13, the causets in the vertical rectangles are antimatter, the causets in the circles are mixed and those in the horizontal rectangles are matter.

I should mention that even though there are many parallel universes, there is only one Academy. We at the Academy have the luxury of being able to observe the entire cosmos, to study its vast complexity and try to solve its deepest mysteries. Intelligent beings inhabit only one universe and even if it crosses another universe, this other universe is almost impossible to detect.

One of the deep mysteries of the cosmos is the matter-antimatter asymmetry problem. This problem considers the question of why there is so little antimatter present in most universes. Put another way, why is it that the amount of matter vastly dominates the amount of antimatter in most universes? A clue is given in Figure 8.13. Notice that this figure is fairly symmetric about a vertical line through its center. Thus, the left antimatter side is quite similar to the right matter side. However, there is an important difference. Most of the multiplicities occur on the right side and this phenomenon becomes more pronounced as we continue vertically in time. A more detailed analysis which we will go into in later seminars shows that this asymmetry of multiplicities results in a preponderance of matter over antimatter. Roughly speaking, the higher the multiplicity of a transition, the more weight that transition has.

Of course, if a path stays on the left side of Figure 8.13, which is the antimatter side, then that universe will have a lot of antimatter. But this only accounts for a relatively small set of universes and the probability of such a set is minimal. In fact, the probability of a single universe is zero and the only way of getting nonzero probabilities is to consider fairly large sets of universes. It turns out that the set of paths that stay in the mixed sector of causets have the predominate probability.

Suppose X is an intelligent being. The main concern of X is: which universe (that is, which path) am I on? Now X can obtain a partial answer to this question by studying the history of his universe. The main tool for such studies is astronomy. Astronomical data can be employed to construct the evolution of X's universe up to the present time. The reason this works is that light travels at a finite speed c so it takes time for light and other electromagnetic radiation from a star to reach X's planet. Since light from a very distant star takes a long time to reach X's planet, X's astronomers are viewing this star as it appeared in early phases of his universe. Thus, his astronomers can view the early history of his universe. From this information, X can then predict his future and thus his complete universe. However, X cannot predict his future exactly. He can only compute probabilities of various possible futures. That is, X can only compute the probabilities of various sets of paths whose initial partial path is the same or similar to his up to the present.

Why can't intelligent beings make exact predictions, but only probabilities? One reason is that there are many paths that their universe can take and it is not clear which path their universe will continue on. The main reason is that the dynamics of the cosmos, that is, the way the cosmos changes, is governed by the laws of quantum mechanics. In fact, what we are discussing here is sometimes called discrete quantum gravity. Quantum mechanics is a purely mathematical theory with a physical interpretation and mathematics is the only true reality. According to the tenets of quantum mechanics, only the probabilities of results can be given. Even I, God, cannot make exact predictions and must use quantum mechanics to obtain the probabilities that events occur.

Quantum probabilities or, as they are sometimes called, quantum propensities are quite different than ordinary probabilities. One reason for this difference is that they are computed using complex numbers instead of real numbers. We will discuss quantum probability in later seminars, but for now I will give you a taste of ordinary probability theory or, as it is also called, classical probability theory.

In classical probability theory, we have an experiment or situation with various possible outcomes and each outcome has a probability of occurring. The probabilities are numbers between zero and one and they describe the chances that the outcomes happen. The probability of a set of outcomes is the sum of the probabilities of the outcomes in that set. Since at least one of the possible outcomes must occur, we specify that the sum of the probabilities of all the outcomes is one.

To make things very simple, let's consider a hypothetical toy cosmos in which we only have five times, instants zero, one, two, three and four. The universes are the various paths $x_0 x_1 y_2 y_3 y_4$ in Figure 8.13. Even in this toy cosmos, we have a huge number of paths. Examples of paths are:

$$p_1 = x_0 x_1 x_2 x_4 x_9$$
$$p_2 = x_0 x_1 x_2 x_4 x_{10}$$
$$p_3 = x_0 x_1 x_2 x_4 x_{11}$$
$$p_4 = x_0 x_1 x_2 x_4 x_{14}$$
$$p_5 = x_0 x_1 x_2 x_5 x_{11}$$

Our main task is to compute the probabilities of the various paths or equivalently the probabilities of the universes. Now, a path $p = x_0 x_1 y_2 y_3 y_4$ consists of the transitions

$x_0 \to x_1$, $x_1 \to y_2$, $y_2 \to y_3$ and $y_3 \to y_4$. Each transition has a transition probability $P(x_0 \to x_1)$, $P(x_1 \to y_2)$, $P(y_2 \to y_3)$, $P(y_3 \to y_4)$ and the probability $P(p)$ of the path p is given by

$$P(p) = P(x_0 \to x_1)P(x_1 \to y_2)P(y_2 \to y_3)P(y_3 \to y_4) \qquad (8.3)$$

Doesn't Equation (8.3) make a lot of sense? This is the standard multiplication law of probability theory. It says that the probability of going from x_0 to y_4 along the path p is the probability of first going from x_0 to x_1 times the probability of next going from x_1 to y_2, times the probability of next going from y_2 to y_3 and finally times the probability of going from y_3 to y_4.

There are two requirements for a transition probability $P(x \to y)$. The first is that $P(x \to y)$ be a number between 0 and 1, inclusively. If the offspring of x are $y_1, y_2, \ldots, y_n$, then x must make a transition to one of its offspring so the sum satisfies

$$P(x \to y_1) + P(x \to y_2) + \cdots + P(x \to y_n) = 1 \qquad (8.4)$$

Notice that starting at x_0 there is only one possible transition $x_0 \to x_1$ so $P(x_0 \to x_1) = 1$. We can therefore replace (8.3) by

$$P(p) = P(x_1 \to y_2)P(x_2 \to y_3)P(y_3 \to y_4) \qquad (8.5)$$

Just for fun, let's put in some concrete numbers. The numbers can be anything we want as long as they satisfy the two rules for transition probabilities. Instead of choosing arbitrary numbers, we shall choose numbers that seem reasonable. By symmetry, we let $P(x_1 \to x_2) = P(x_1 \to x_3) = 1/2$. Notice that these numbers are between 0 and 1 and since x_2, x_3 are the offspring of x_1, the numbers add up to one as required by (8.4). We now let

$$P(x_2 \to x_4) = P(x_2 \to x_5) = P(x_2 \to x_6) = 1/3$$

and again our two requirements hold. Since $x_3 \to x_6$ has multiplicity 2, we give this transition more weight and let $P(x_3 \to x_6) = 1/2$ and

$$P(x_3 \to x_7) = P(x_3 \to x_8) = 1/4$$

Continuing, we let

$$P(x_4 \to x_9) = P(x_4 \to x_{10}) = P(x_4 \to x_{14}) = 1/4$$
$$P(x_5 \to x_{11}) = 2/5$$
$$P(x_5 \to x_{12}) = P(x_5 \to x_{13}) = P(x_5 \to x_{15}) = 1/5$$
$$P(x_6 \to x_{14}) = P(x_6 \to x_{15}) = P(x_6 \to x_{16}) = P(x_6 \to x_{17})$$
$$= P(x_6 \to x_{18}) = P(x_6 \to x_{19}) = 1/6$$
$$P(x_7 \to x_{18}) = 2/5$$
$$P(x_7 \to x_{20}) = P(x_7 \to x_{21}) = P(x_7 \to x_{22}) = 1/5$$
$$P(x_8 \to x_{19}) = P(x_8 \to x_{22}) = 3/8$$
$$P(x_8 \to x_{23}) = P(x_8 \to x_{24}) = 1/8$$

We are now ready to compute probabilities of paths. Since they're simpler, let's first compute the probabilities of paths to time instant three. There are only six of these and we have

$$P(x_0 x_1 x_2 x_4) = P(x_1 \to x_2) P(x_2 \to x_4) = \tfrac{1}{2} \cdot \tfrac{1}{3} = \tfrac{1}{6}$$

In the same way we have

$$P(x_0 x_1 x_2 x_5) = P(x_0 x_1 x_2 x_6) = 1/6$$

Similarly, we obtain

$$P(x_0 x_1 x_3 x_6) = P(x_1 \to x_3) P(x_3 \to x_6) = \tfrac{1}{2} \cdot \tfrac{1}{2} = \tfrac{1}{4}$$

and

$$P(x_0 x_1 x_3 x_7) = P(x_0 x_1 x_3 x_8) = \tfrac{1}{8}$$

We conclude that the mixed path $x_0 x_1 x_3 x_6$ is the most probable. Notice that the sum of the probabilities of these six paths is one, as it should be.

To compute the probabilities of the complete paths in this toy cosmos, we can use what we already did. For the path p_1 considered earlier, we have

$$P(p_1) = P(x_0 x_1 x_2 x_4) P(x_4 \to x_9) = \tfrac{1}{6} \cdot \tfrac{1}{4} = \tfrac{1}{24}$$

In the same way

$$P(p_2) = P(p_3) = P(p_4) = \tfrac{1}{24}$$

and

$$P(p_5) = P(x_0 x_1 x_3 x_5) P(x_5 \to x_{11}) = \tfrac{1}{6} \cdot \tfrac{2}{5} = \tfrac{2}{30} = \tfrac{1}{15}$$

Since this is so much fun,let's compute a few more:

$$P(x_0 x_1 x_2 x_5 x_{12}) = P(x_0 x_1 x_2 x_5) P(x_5 \to x_{12}) = \tfrac{1}{6} \cdot \tfrac{1}{5} = \tfrac{1}{30}$$
$$P(x_0 x_1 x_3 x_7 x_{20}) = P(x_0 x_1 x_3 x_7) P(x_7 \to x_{20}) = \tfrac{1}{8} \cdot \tfrac{1}{5} = \tfrac{1}{40}$$
$$P(x_0 x_1 x_3 x_6 x_{18}) = P(x_0 x_1 x_3 x_6) P(x_6 \to x_{18}) = \tfrac{1}{4} \cdot \tfrac{1}{6} = \tfrac{1}{24}$$
$$P(x_0 x_1 x_3 x_7 x_{18}) = P(x_0 x_1 x_3 x_7) P(x_7 \to x_{18}) = \tfrac{1}{8} \cdot \tfrac{2}{5} = \tfrac{1}{20}$$
$$P(x_0 x_1 x_3 x_8 x_{19}) = P(x_0 x_1 x_3 x_8) P(x_8 \to x_{19}) = \tfrac{1}{8} \cdot \tfrac{3}{8} = \tfrac{3}{64}$$

We conclude that p_5 is the most probable path.

Isn't life wonderful, that we can do all these great calculations? We now conclude with an interesting observation. We call a path that terminates at x_9, x_{10}, x_{11}, x_{12}, or x_{13} an *antimatter path*. If A is the set of antimatter paths, then the probability of A becomes:

$$P(A) = \tfrac{3}{24} + \tfrac{1}{15} + \tfrac{2}{30} = \tfrac{31}{120} \approx 0.26$$

We call a path that terminates at x_{20}, x_{21}, x_{22}, x_{23} or x_{24} a *matter path*. If M is the set of matter paths, then the probability of M becomes:

$$P(M) = \tfrac{3}{40} + \tfrac{3}{64} + \tfrac{2}{64} = \tfrac{49}{320} \approx 0.15$$

We call the other paths mixed paths. If B is the set of mixed paths, since $P(A) + P(B) + P(M) = 1$ we have

$$P(B) = 1 - P(A) - P(M) \approx 0.59$$

We conclude that in this toy cosmos, the universes that are a mixture of matter and antimatter are the most probable.

Computing probabilities for the real cosmos is much more complicated than what we have done in this toy cosmos. This is true for two reasons. First, the real paths go on forever and do not stop at time four. Second, the probabilities are quantum probabilities and not these simple made up classical probabilities that I used for illustrative purposes. This concludes our first cosmic seminar. See you next time."

Chapter 9

God's Party

As God said in his Crondike interview, he gives lots of parties. He does not want the parties to be too large and unwieldy, but he wants to eventually include everyone in the Academy. After everyone is included he begins the party cycle again. With billions of apprentices and angels in the Academy, how does he have time to include them all? The answer is that, unlike on Earth, time in the Academy is at least 2-dimensional. Events that occur at different times in the Academy might appear to be simultaneous on Earth. This gives time for thousands of parties at the Academy in one Earth second. Most parties consist of merriment, conversations, stories, jokes and even some serious puzzle solving. If you've ever wondered what angels and God do for fun, here is your answer. The following is a typical God party.

"Welcome to my party, angels and archangels. As you know, I give lots of parties. That's because there are so many of us and I want to keep these parties down to a manageable size, while eventually including everyone. Before we begin our festivities, I'd like to tell you a little story about a new apprentice, Jonathan.

Jonathan attends his first seminar and sits down next to another apprentice in a large lecture room.

"Hi, how are you? My name's Jonathan."

"Hi, I'm Patrick. I haven't seen you before. Is this your first seminar?"

"Yes, it is, I'm one of the new guys." Jonathan smiles and shakes Patrick's hand. "Wow, there's a lot of apprentices here. It looks like over a hundred."

"Yes, there are about a hundred here. This is one of our most popular seminars. There are others that aren't this well attended. It will be about ten minutes until the lecturer arrives. In the meantime, everyone is just socializing."

After a minute, someone yells out a number, 68, followed by a huge roar of laughter. After another minute, someone else yells out a number, 123, followed by another roar of laughter. This continues two or three more times.

"What's going on here, Patrick? What's with the numbers and all the laughing?"

"Most of us have been together for a long time, some for a couple hundred years. We originally started telling jokes, but we've known each other so long and we know our jokes so well, that we numbered them. To save time we just call out the numbers. Everyone instantly recalls the joke and laughs."

"That sounds like fun. Can I try?"

"Sure, go ahead."

So Jonathan yells out the number 57 and there is complete silence. He tries again with the number 75 and again, complete silence. In desperation he calls out 198 followed by nothing.

"What's happening? What am I doing wrong?"

"There are some that are good at telling jokes and some that aren't."

In a booming voice, God yells, "okay, let the fun begin. I invite you to do some mingling and socializing. Also, you should enjoy some cosmic tea and dark matter chocolate. But don't overdo it. Later we'll have some party puzzles and you'll have to do some thinking to solve them. In a while we'll get back together for some stories and jokes. Have a good time."

What do you think heavenly partygoers talk about? Seated at this table are Jennifer, Rebecca and Dota. Let's listen to what they are saying.

"I've been trying to figure out how I got to heaven." Jennifer says thoughtfully, "In my youth I was really wild. I drank and did drugs. I shop lifted and had lots of affairs. I guess I got here because I later settled down. I got married and was a good mother. I feel guilty because some of my friends aren't here. They were just as good people as I was. Maybe I'll talk to some of the angels on the review committee."

Nodding, Rebecca says, "I know how you feel. I got pregnant out of wedlock and my parents sent me to a home for unwed mothers. Nuns ran the home and they were really mean. I had a very difficult childbirth. The nuns were cruel and wouldn't give me anything to relieve the pain. They said it was punishment for my sins and that I would burn in hell. I don't see any of those nuns here so I guess they were wrong about who's going to hell."

"What about you Dota? How did you get to the Academy?" Jennifer inquires.

Dota was from the planet Ardon and had a different appearance than Earthlings. He was tall and had very long arms and fingers. But what made him completely different was his head. It was completely smooth with no hair, eyes, nose, ears or mouth.

"As you can see, most of the beings at this party are former Earthlings," he says, "but I'm from Ardon. I'm as aware of my surroundings as you are but I rely entirely on mind waves for communication. My planet is much smaller than Earth and we have less than a million Ardonians. Ardon is very hospitable and bountiful. We are peaceful, friendly beings. We would never think of harming anyone. Words for war, hate, jealousy and revenge do not exist. Rare disputes are settled by a rotating committee. We have

108

no diseases and our bodies just shut down after about 100 of your years. Essentially all Ardonians are elevated to the Academy."

Rebecca's face lights up as she listens. "Wow, that's wonderful. I didn't know that such a planet was possible. I have lots of questions about how things work on Ardon but we can talk about that later."

"Do you know who were sitting next to me at the last political science seminar?" Jennifer asks Rebecca.

"I have no idea."

With a confident chuckle, Jennifer reveals, "Thomas Jefferson and Abraham Lincoln. I recognized them immediately and started asking them questions. I asked Jefferson if he really had slaves. He said he did and even admitted that he had a slave mistress. He said those were different times and he feels terrible about what he did. He wishes he could go back to Earth and make it up to the slave descendants. I asked Honest Abe if he ever told a lie. He replied that he told lots of them. When he reviewed the troops he would praise them for their great job, tell them they should keep fighting and he was sure they would win the war. Well, they weren't doing that great of a job and he wasn't sure they would win. In fact, he was scared to death they would lose. After all, the Confederates had better trained soldiers and superior officers. He had to appear to be a strong leader and put up a good front."

Later, an archangel addresses the merry party makers.

"Greetings everyone. You all know me, I'm Norton Kronomer, your master of ceremonies. Before I introduce our first presenter, I'd like to tell you about an episode I observed on Earth.

While I was watching the planet, a colorful hot air balloon caught my eye. The balloon supported a basket containing two men, Ed Tobin and Sam Krupnick and was flying over an isolated mountain forest.

"I told you that we should have landed earlier, Sam," Ed shouted. "Now we're hopelessly lost. How are we going to find our way back?"

Sam shakes his head, "if we had landed earlier, we would have missed this beautiful scenery. I suggest we find someone and ask for directions."

"That's the stupidest, most ridiculous suggestion I've ever heard. First of all, we're 4,000 feet above the ground. Second, we're flying at 30 miles per hour over a dense forest. How the fuck are we going to ask someone for directions?"

"Don't you know anything about ballooning, you idiot. All we have to do is let some air out and the balloon will lose altitude and slow down. Look, we're coming to a clearing in the woods. There's a guy walking in the clearing. Let's go down and ask him."

So Ed and Sam let some air out of their balloon and make their way down until they are hovering a few feet above the lone figure in the clearing. The man is slowly walking in deep thought and is unaware of their presence. It turns out that he's the famous philosopher, Jeffrey Bub, who's thinking about his latest theory of quantum correlations, called banana land.

"Hey, mister," Ed yells, leaning over the edge of the basket, "sorry to disturb you, but can we ask you a question?"

Jeffrey looks up and is startled to see two men in a balloon hanging right above him. "All right, you can ask me a question. What is it?"

Sam yells down, "can you tell us where we are?"

Jeffrey studies the two men for a few minutes. He paces back and forth for a few more minutes. He strokes his chin and thinks for still another few minutes. Finally, he answers, "You're in a basket hanging from a hot air balloon." He wanders off into the woods and the two balloonists blast hot air into their balloon and quickly gain altitude.

"You know Sam, that guy must have been a philosopher."

"We don't even know that guy. Why do you say that?" Sam asks.

"Well, first it took him a very long time to answer our question. Second, his answer was absolutely correct. Third, it didn't do us a damn bit of good."

The crowd laughs and Norton bows his head gratefully.

"Thank you Norton," God takes the stage, "that was great. I would like to interrupt now to present my first party puzzle. Here it is. You and your wife live on Earth and you both arrive at a party at which there are four other married couples. Soon after you arrive, various handshakes take place. No one shakes hands with himself or herself and no one shakes hands with his or her spouse. After the various handshakes take place, you ask everyone else at the party including your wife how many hands he or she shook. To your surprise, everyone gives a different answer. How many hands did your wife shake? I'll give you ten minutes to figure out an answer. Anyone who gets the right answer and can explain it correctly gets a special prize. It's all right to consult with others. Good luck."

Some of the angels and archangels break up into small groups, others at the party remain alone to think about the problem. Some converse noisily, some go into deep thought. A few break out pads of paper from nowhere and others concentrate deeply in their own thoughts.

The time passes quickly and God speaks again, "your ten minutes are now up. From your thought waves, I conclude that twelve of you got the right answer with a correct explanation. After the party is over, the winners will get their special prize which is a glimpse into the fifth space dimension. I'm sure you'll find it fascinating. Now for the answer. At first you probably thought that I didn't give you enough information. That there is no simple answer. Your wife could have shaken any number of hands. But I did give you enough information and there is only one possible answer. Angel Jason, did a very good job of solving the puzzle, so I'll let him explain it."

"I used a graph to solve the problem." Jason responds, "there were a total of ten people at the party and I represented each person by a vertex. If two people shook hands, I drew an

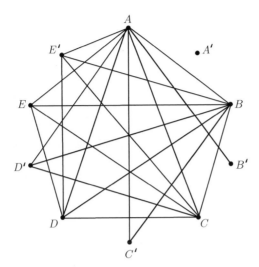

Figure 9.1

edge between their representing vertices. Since no one shook hands with themselves or their spouse, the most number of hands a person could shake was eight and, of course, the least number was zero. Since you asked nine people and they each gave a different answer, you heard the answers $8, 7, 6, 5, 4, 3, 2, 1, 0$. The graph I drew is shown in Figure 9.1. Someone gave the answer 8 and I labeled that vertex A. Now A didn't shake hands with one other person so that person must be A's spouse, who I labeled A'. Since everyone else shook hands with A, A' must be the person with no handshakes. Next, someone gave the answer 7 and I labeled that vertex B. Now B already shook hands with A and couldn't shake hands with A' because A' shook no hands. Also, B didn't shake hands with his or her spouse B'. Hence, B shook hands with everyone else. We conclude that B' has only one edge as in Figure 9.1. Continuing as in Figure 9.1, we see that C shook six hands and C' shook two hands. We then have that D shook five hands and D' shook three hands. Finally, both E and E' shook four hands. Since you heard all different answers you must be either E or E'. So you and your wife both shook four hands and the answer is four."

Norton waits for the crowd to calm and says, "thank you for the great presentation, Jason. Our first story will be presented by Charles Holland."

"I am Charles Holland, president and CEO of Charlie's Chocolate Factory and I am going to tell you about the history of the world.

In the beginning the Earth was void. There was no structure and there was no life.

111

Then along came Charles. On the first day he created the ground on which to build his factory. On the second day he created the great and famous Charlie's Chocolate Factory. On the third day he created light to see his factory. On the fourth day he created air for people to breathe. On the fifth day he created people to work in his factory and on the sixth day he created more people to eat his chocolate. Finally on the seventh day he rested and all was well. Life was good and chocolate was abundant. As your creator, I will now give you some tenets to help you achieve a fruitful and fulfilling lifetime. I call these sacred canons the ten condiments.

(1) I am Charles, President and CEO of Charlie's Chocolate Factory.

(2) Mine is the only worthy factory and thou shalt not partake of chocolate from any other factory.

(3) I have brought thee out of the house of Brussel sprouts and asparagus and have delivered thee to the house of pasta and chocolate.

(4) Thou shalt not take from the chocolate box of thy daughter for that is an abomination.

(5) Thou shalt not take from the chocolate box of thy neighbor's wife for that is a sin.

(6) If thou has a photographic memory, then thou shalt not think of negatives.

(7) If at first thou does not succeed, then thou shalt not skydive.

(8) Thou shalt not leave chocolate out in the sun for it will melt and decay.

(9) Thou shalt not eat chocolate in a tornado or under water.

(10) Thou shalt set aside a day for rest and eating chocolate.

If you follow these condiments, you will lead a long and successful life and you and your seed will multiply. (If you're lucky, they may add, subtract and divide too.) Amen."

The group of party goers burst out in laughter and applause. No one laughs harder and applauses longer than God.

Wiping his eyes, Norton says, "thank you, Charles. Our next story will be presented by Brian Landy."

"Thank you, Norton. It's a pleasure to be here with you, my friends. I would like to tell you a love story. This is an unusual love story because it's not about two people. It's about a diamond and me. I found a five carat diamond on my native planet. It was so flawless and beautiful that I carried it with me all my life. Unlike the raw diamonds that are found on Earth, this one was already cut and polished. It had the brightest sparkle I had ever seen and I could feel it vibrate when I held it. I was so attached to it that after I died, God allowed me to keep it at the Academy. I know that angels do not usually have possessions and in fact we have no need for them. But God agreed that this was an exception and it has been with me for 5,000 years. God told me that diamonds are the most perfect of all the minerals. They are composed of pure carbon and carbon is the main component of life. For this reason, diamonds and life are closely related and diamonds are almost living beings. For obvious reasons, I called my diamond Di and we were in love. Di vibrated at various frequencies and in this way we were able to communicate. I had concluded that Di actually possessed feelings. Although diamonds do not have a gender, I thought of Di as being female because she seemed to be very sensitive.

About fifty years ago, I went to Earth on a special mission for God. I was only there for a day, but during that short time I became enamored with a beautiful Earth-Child named Jeanie Roman. It was a different kind of love than what I have for Di. It was deeper and more emotional. It was sensual and intellectual at the same time. It was amazing. I was so taken by this Earth-Child and her plight that I gave Di to her. In this way I gave up one love for another and I lost them both. But my hope was that this would be temporary. I thought that Jeanie would sell Di for a lot of Earth dollars so she could live the life that she deserved. The plan was that she would go to college and become a veterinarian.

Jeanie followed the plan and sold Di to a jeweler in Boston named Richard Greechie. Richard, in turn, sold Di to a lady friend named Mary Kay Bennett a.k.a. MK. It turns out that MK was a rich mathematics professor at the University of Massachusetts in Amherst, Mass. How she got so rich is a mystery but it happened suddenly and it is believed that it had something to do with two other rich mathematicians in her department. MK had Di mounted in the setting of a ring that she wore for the next 35 years until her death. Di didn't mind being in MK's ring. After all, diamonds love to sparkle and show off.

Richard thought that MK and he would marry and that the ring Di was mounted in would be MK's engagement ring. But life does not always turn out as expected. MK fell in love with a waitress named Marge who was taking an abstract algebra course from her at the university. Marge later got a Ph.D. in mathematics and she and MK moved into a big house in Amherst. They wrote important joint papers on lattice ordered groups and became famous in the mathematical community. They traveled all over the world and mingled with many other famous people. Di could really show off and was greatly admired. She was happy.

The happiness continued for thirty years, but then tragedy struck. MK was on her way to London to receive an award. The airplane she was on exploded, broke into a thousand pieces, fell into the Atlantic Ocean and sank to the bottom. The explosion was so violent that it blew Di out of her mounting. She landed alone at the bottom of the sea. She was completely intact because practically nothing can destroy a diamond. Di thought that no one would ever find her there on the ocean floor under a pile of sand. She became depressed and lonesome.

But then a miracle happened. It may be that diamonds have souls or perhaps she was carried up by the hundreds of sparks and bubbles from the souls of the passengers. It could be that since Di had already been at the Academy for 5,000 years, she was just returning home. Whatever the explanation, and I really don't care, Di ended up here at the Academy with me and we are very happy.

What about my other love, Jeanie? I'm still waiting for her. She didn't become a veterinarian after all. She went to medical school and got a doctorate of physical therapy. She runs a very successful clinic in Portland, Oregon. Is Di jealous that I have another love? No, she isn't. Jealously is not an emotion that diamonds have. How do I know all this, you might ask. I know all this partly from Di herself and the rest I observed through one of our neutrino or cosmic-ray telescopes."

"Thank you, Brian," says Norton, "that was very touching. I'll let the next speaker introduce himself."

"Greetings everyone. I don't know about you, but I think this is one of the best parties I've attended. We're having such a great time. For those of you who don't know me, my name is Job Tobedone. Now you may think this is a strange name, but as I shall explain, it is quite logical. Actually, I didn't get this name until after I grew up on Earth about 3,000 years ago. At that time I was twenty years old. You see, I was a jack-of-all-trades. If there was a **job to be done**, I would do it. Well, that's not exactly true. What I'm referring to are physical jobs. When it comes to mental jobs, that's a different story and it's the story I want to tell you now. This happened a long time ago when I was about fifty and my memory is not very good. Besides that, I've drunk a lot of cosmic tea, but I'll try to be as coherent as possible.

About 3,000 years ago, I was one of the wandering Jews. There were about 200,000 of us wandering around in this awful desert some forty years after we fled from slavery in Egypt. This story concerns a conversation that I overheard between two of my fellow nomads. Moses and Shlomo.

"I'm sick and tired of wandering around in this terrible desert, Moses. It's dry, hot and desolate. We're all thirsty and barely have enough food. All we can see is sand and a few rocks. It's boring. There are no trees, lakes or mountains. You are the worst leader imaginable. You've been leading us around in circles for forty years and I can prove it. See that rock over there? See those two sets of initials in that rock? I carved the first set thirty years ago and I carved the second set ten years ago. Who knows how many other times we've been in this area? I don't think you know what you're doing. I think you're a completely lost screwup. Besides that, what is this promised land crap you keep talking about?

I'll bet there is no promised land. It's a piece of nonsense that fell out of your screwed up brain."

"Calm down, Shlomo," Moses says, "I'm sure we can discuss this in a civil manner. You don't realize what a difficult job I have. This desert has no markers, except for a couple of rocks, to guide us. The promised land is our place of destiny. It is the beautiful land of milk and honey. God told me that he would point the way, but I haven't heard from him for forty years. It doesn't help when I constantly hear bitching and gripping from everyone. I'm 120 years old and I'm getting tired of all this nonsense. If you think you can do a better job, you are welcome to take over. You can be the leader. If that doesn't suit you, at least tell me what to do.'

"Well, its quite simple. All we have to do is walk directly north and we'll be out of the desert in two or three weeks."

"That sounds good. Which way is north?"

"I don't know. I haven't had much education and I'm not very smart. You're the great Egyptian scholar prince. You tell me."

"We could use a compass to tell us which way is north. Do you have a compass handy?"

"Compasses haven't been invented. Any other ideas?"

"I've heard that all we have to do is look at the night sky and find the north star, but damn, all the stars look the same to me. Maybe it's my old eyes."

"That's right, Moses. I've been told that we first find the big dipper, look up from there and that's the north star. But where is the big dipper and which way is up from there? Besides that, stars move around in the sky. How can they tell us which way is north down on earth?"

"There's another way. The sun rises from the east and sets in the west. Since the sun is now setting, this way is west. Now all we do is turn right and we're facing north. Let's go."

"Wait Moses, how far right should we turn? And that's fine for you cause you're right-handed. I'm left-handed. Should I turn left?"

"It doesn't make any difference which handedness you are. All you have to do is turn ninety degrees right."

"But degrees haven't been invented yet. What do we do about that? Besides, what does this have to do with temperature anyway? We all know it's hot here."

"Shlomo, you are very silly. For God's sake, turn right by a right angle."

"I know the Pythagoreans and the Egyptian surveyors talked about right angles, but I really don't know what that means. Does it have anything to do with left angles? Is turning left by a left angle the opposite of turning right by a right angle? Being left-handed, I have a right to know. Or is it a left to know? I'm really confused. What should we do, Moses?"

"Why don't we ask this guy standing next to us? Hey, Job Tobedone, which way should we go?"

"Don't ask me. I'm just listening to your conversations, I'm an innocent bystander."

The crowd murmurs, and Norton steps back on the stage, "thank you, Job. It was great to have some first-hand history. Our next story will be presented by Pamela Milan."

"I would like to relate a story about the famous mathematician, Friedrich Gauss, that took place when he was about eight years old.

The teacher of his second grade class decided to give the students a lengthy task so she could take a break from teaching and have some time for herself. She asked them to add up the first 100 positive integers. Thus, she asked them to find $1 + 2 + \cdots + 100$. She thought this would occupy them for about an hour, so she could get some rest. Well, young Friedrich worked for about two minutes and wrote his answer 5050 on his slate, declaring, "There it lies".

The astonished teacher saw that his answer was correct and after waiting for an hour for the rest of the class to respond, she found that it was the only right answer. How did this young genius do it? He quickly decided that adding $1 + 2 = 3$ and $3 + 3 = 6$ and $6 + 4 = 10$, etc., would take too long and be prone to mistakes. He chose to add in a different way. He chose to add the first to the last, the second to the second to last and so on to get $1 + 100 = 101, 2 + 99 = 101, \cdots, 50 + 51 = 101$. So he got fifty 101's. But $50 \times 101 = 5050$ the answer. Another way of looking at this is

$$
\begin{array}{ccccccccc}
1 & + & 2 & + & 3 & + & \cdots & + & 50 \\
100 & + & 99 & + & 98 & + & \cdots & + & 51 \\
\hline
101 & + & 101 & + & 101 & + & \cdots & + & 101 & = 50(101) = 5050
\end{array}
$$

This story brings up a very interesting question. What is the sum of the first n positive integers? That is, find $1 + 2 + 3 + \cdots + n$. Notice for $n = 2$ we have $1 + 2 = 3$, for $n = 3$ we have $1 + 2 + 3 = 6$ and for $n = 4$ we have $1 + 2 + 3 + 4 = 10$, but this doesn't help very much. We shall proceed using a method similar to the one employed by Gauss. Let $S = 1 + 2 + \cdots + n$ be the sum we are seeking. We then find $2S$ to be

$$
\begin{array}{ccccccccc}
1 & + & 2 & + & 3 & + & \cdots & + & n \\
n & + & (n-1) & + & (n-2) & + & \cdots & + & 1 \\
\hline
(n+1) & + & (n+1) & + & (n+1) & + & \cdots & + & (n+1) & = n(n+1)
\end{array}
$$

Under the addition line the number of $(n+1)$s is n, so we obtain $2S = n(n+1)$ so that

$$S = \frac{n(n+1)}{2}$$

This is an amazing result because it works for any positive integer. If we let $n = 100$, which is the problem that the young Gauss solved, we get

$$S = \frac{100(101)}{2} = 5050$$

But we can let $n = 1234$, for example, to obtain

$$S = \frac{1234(1244)}{2} = (1234)(622) = 773,146$$

This illustrates the great power of mathematics. Rather than performing the tedious sum $1 + 2 + 3 + \cdots + 1234$, one term at a time, which could take weeks, we can quickly calculate the answer $S = (1234)(1244)/2$ in a few seconds."

"That was fascinating, Pamela. Thank you. Our next presenter is Steve Cone."

Steve begins, "for some reason, I enjoy stories about animals. Maybe it's because they are so interesting and funny. My first animal story goes like this.

Scientists at the Scripts Institute in San Diego have studied dolphins for a long time. After years of research they have discovered a special diet that will enable dolphins to live forever. The diet consists of fresh seagulls which have to be gathered daily. One day, two of the scientists went out on the beach, caught some seagulls and placed them in a cage. On the way back to the Institute, they had to negotiate some large boulders on which there were sleeping sea lions. They gingerly crossed over the sea lions and were immediately confronted by a police officer.

"I'm sorry gentlemen, but I'm going to have to arrest you."

"What's the charge, officer?" The scientist asks.

"Crossing sedate lions for immortal porpoises."☺

The crowd responds with some chuckles. Undeterred Steve continues, "here's my second animal story."

A penguin waddles into a bar and says to the bartender, "Got any eggs?"

The bartender says, "I'm very impressed that you can talk, Mr. Penguin. In fact, you're the first talking penguin I have ever met. But I'm sorry, we don't have any eggs. I can offer you beer, wine, whiskey or other alcoholic beverages, but no eggs."

The penguin waddles out, but the next day he returns. "Got any eggs?"

"I told you yesterday, we don't have any eggs. The answer is still the same and we won't have any eggs tomorrow."

The penguin, again, waddles out, but the next day he returns. "Got any eggs?"

Losing his patience, the bartender says, "damn it, my patience has worn out. I'm getting sick and tired of you coming in here and asking for eggs. I get it now, you don't really talk. All you can say is that same thing over and over again. If I see you in here again, I'm going to get out my hammer and nail your fuckin web feet to the floor. Now beat it."

Still again, the penguin waddles out, but the next day he returns. "Got any nails?"

The bartender has had enough and shouts, "Fuck, no." To which the Penguin responds, "got any eggs?"☺

An awkward silence fills the hall. Steve proceeds, "my next story involves my favorite animal, a panda."

A panda walks into a restaurant and orders a hamburger. He eats the hamburger, pulls out a gun, fires two shots into the ceiling and walks out.

A man in the restaurant watches all this in amazement and follows the panda out. The man says to the panda, "what in the world was that all about? What's going on?"

The panda hands the man a book and says, "read this. It explains everything." The panda walks away and the man looks at the book. It's a dictionary and there's a marker in it. The man opens the dictionary to the marked page. It reads, "panda, bear like animal. Habitation, southern China. Eats, shoots and leaves."☺

This story is received with uproarious laughter.

"Here's my last animal story." Steve says, waving for quiet.

A rabbit meets a snake, a turtle and a lizard at a party and they get along famously. It turns out that the snake, turtle and lizard live together and they invite the rabbit to come to their house the next day for a visit. The rabbit shows up at their house the next day and is surprised to see that it is a large mansion surrounded by acres of woods and gardens. The rabbit rings the bell next to a huge hand carved mahogany door. A stuffy formal looking English butler opens the door.

"Good morning, sir. May I help you?"

"The rabbit replies, 'I'm here to see Mr. Snake."

"I'm sorry sir, but Mr. Snake is out by the lake."

"Well, what about Mr. Turtle?"

"He's not available now. Mr. Tur-tel is out by the well."

"Okay then, can I see Mr. Lizard?"

"He's presently predisposed. Mr. Liz-ard is out in the yard."

"Please tell Mr. Snake, Mr. Turtle and Mr. Lizard that Mr. Rab-bit is here with the shit."☺

When the laughter dies down, Norton says, "thank you Steve. Maybe animal stories are so popular here at the Academy because we don't have any real ones. Now God would like to present his second party puzzle."

"As with my first party puzzle, anyone who solves this one will receive the special prize of a glimpse into the fifth space dimension. The puzzle goes like this. Show that, at any party with six participants, there are three mutual acquaintances or three mutual strangers. That is, there are three participants, all of whom know each other or three participants, all of whom do not know each other. Of course, this includes the possibility that there could be both. As before, I'll give you ten minutes. Good luck."

Ten minutes later God returns. "This puzzle was a little harder. Having received your thought waves, I conclude that only four of you got it. Here's the solution. We will again use graphs to solve this problem. Recall that a graph is a collection of vertices and edges. If two vertices are joined with an edge, they are called *adjacent* and otherwise they are called *nonadjacent*. We will represent the six participants by vertices of a graph. If two vertices represent acquainted participants, they are joined with an edge, so they're adjacent. Two nonadjacent vertices represent strangers. Suppose the participants are Alice, Bob, Clara, Dan, Eve and Fred. We'll represent them by vertices A, B, C, D, E and F, respectively. Figure 9.2 is a possible graph G_1 for this party. In this particular party, Alice, Dan and Eve are mutual acquaintances. There are not three mutual strangers.

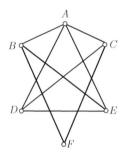
Figure 9.2 (Graph G_1)

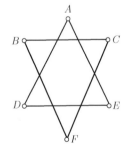
Figure 9.3 (Graph G_2)

Other possible graphs for this party are G_2, G_3, G_4 of Figures 9.3, 9.4, 9.5, respectively. In G_2, A, D, E are mutual acquaintances as are B, C, F. In G_3 there are not three mutual acquaintances, but there are the three mutual strangers A, D, E and B, C, F. In G_4 there are three mutual acquaintances A, D, E and also the three mutual strangers B, C, D and B, C, E. Also in G_4 A, B, F and A, C, F are mutual acquaintances.

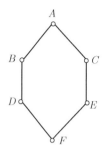
Figure 9.4 (Graph G_3)

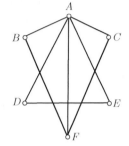
Figure 9.5 (Graph G_4)

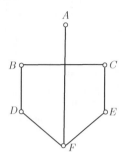
Figure 9.6 (Graph $\overline{G_1}$)

The *complement* $\overline{G}$ of graph G is defined as having the same vertices as G, but vertices in $\overline{G}$ are adjacent if and only if they are nonadjacent in G. For example, the complements of the graphs G_1, G_2, G_3 and G_4 are illustrated in Figures 9.5–9.9.

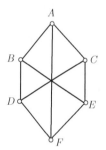
Figure 9.7 (Graph $\overline{G_2}$)

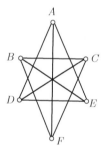
Figure 9.8 (Graph $\overline{G_3}$)

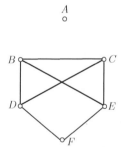
Figure 9.9 (Graph $\overline{G_4}$)

Notice that there are three mutual acquaintances if and only if the corresponding graph has a triangle and there are three mutual strangers if and only if the complement of the corresponding graph has a triangle. For example G_1 and G_2 have triangles while $\overline{G_1}$ and $\overline{G_2}$ do not; G_3 has no triangles; $\overline{G_3}$ does have triangles; and G_4 and $\overline{G_4}$ both have triangles. Thus, the problem is solved by the following theorem.

Theorem. *For any graph G with six vertices, G or $\overline{G}$ contains a triangle.*

Proof. Let v be a vertex of G. Now v is adjacent to three vertices u_1, u_2, u_3 of G or $\overline{G}$. The reason for this is that if v is not adjacent to at least three vertices of G, then v is adjacent to at least three vertices of $\overline{G}$. Suppose u_1, u_2, u_3 are vertices of G (Figure 9.10). If any two of the vertices u_1, u_2, u_3 are adjacent, then they are two vertices of a triangle whose third vertex is v (Figure 9.11). If no two of the vertices u_1, u_2, u_3 are adjacent in G, then they are vertices of a triangle in $\overline{G}$ (Figure 9.12). If u_1, u_2, u_3 are vertices of $\overline{G}$, the proof is similar. □

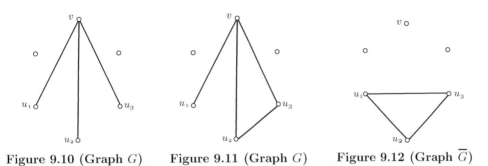

Figure 9.10 (Graph G)   **Figure 9.11 (Graph G)**   **Figure 9.12 (Graph $\overline{G}$)**

"Thank you God. As usual, that was very enlightening. Our next presenter is Alice Tall."

"I would like to tell you two stories about elderly people.

A perky elderly woman skips down the hallway of an assisted living nursing home. Her hair is all fixed up and she's wearing a sleeping gown. She comes across an old man in a wheelchair and flips up the hem of her gown and says, "supersex." The old man stares blankly into space and says nothing. She shrugs her shoulders and continues down the hall until she meets another old man in a wheelchair. She flips up her gown a little higher and says, "supersex." The old man looks at her briefly, his head droops down and he falls asleep. Undaunted, she skips further down the hall until she finds yet another old man in a wheel chair. She flips up her gown still higher and says, "supersex." The old man looks at her for a minute and opens his mouth. A little drool comes out and he says in a very low voice, "I'll take the soup." ☺

"Here goes my second story.

Two elderly women are walking down a garden path of an assisted living nursing home.

The first woman says, "isn't it wonderful, dear, that two old friends like us are able to spend our golden years together like this?"

"Yes, it is wonderful," the second woman responds. "I especially enjoy all of our walks together and all the years we've spent playing bridge with our other friends."

"As I recall we've known each other since kindergarten. Our families lived close to each other and we played together as children. You know my memory is not as good as it used to be and I'm very embarrassed to say that I don't remember your name, my dear. I hope you find it in your heart to forgive me. Please help me and tell me your name."

After thinking for a minute, the second woman replies, "when do you need to know?"☺

"That was great Alice, thank you. I think it is appropriate to have at least one God story so here's my contribution."

Hershel prays to God, "dear God, I know I haven't prayed to you very often and I know I'm not very observant but I hope you can hear me now. I really need some money and I'm asking you to let me win the lottery this week. Thank you for your consideration."

Hershel doesn't win the lottery that week and prays again. "I didn't win the lottery last week and I'm asking you to reconsider. Please, I'm begging you to let me win next week's lottery. If I win, I promise I'll make you proud of me."

Again, Hershel doesn't win the lottery, so he appeals in prayer "dear God, I'm really desperate and about to give up. Please, help me to win next week's lottery. I'll do anything if you grant my request."

Hershel looks out his open window and sees big dark clouds welling up in the sky. Lightening strikes nearby and there is a huge clap of thunder. He then hears a mighty voice come out of the clouds, "give me a break here, at least buy a lottery ticket."☺

"Before I introduce our next presenter, I'd like to tell you a religion joke."

Cannibal Adam is chatting with his friend Ben. "You know, Ben, I've been having indigestion all day."

Cannibal Ben responds, "I'm sorry to hear that, Adam. What did you eat yesterday?"
"As usual, I ate a missionary."
"How did you cook him?"
"Like I always do, I boiled him in a big pot."
"What was he wearing when you captured him?"
"He was wearing a dark brown robe and a brown skull cap."
"Well, that's your problem, you cooked him wrong. He was a friar."'☺

"Our next presenter is Jerry Bamberger."

Thank you, Norton. I would like to tell you about an experience I had when I was sitting at the bar of the Tadich Grill in San Francisco. As you may know, the Tadich Grill is an elegant old restaurant in the heart of the financial district. It is noted for it's seafood. The bar is a huge mahogany structure that occupies one side of the restaurant whose walls are impressive dark paneled wood. The bartender came up to me and I ordered a scotch on the rocks. While waiting for my drink, I looked up at the shelves behind the bar. The shelves contained a large array of liquors of all types, but on the top shelf, I noticed an ornately carved wooden box. When the bartender returned with my drink, I asked him what was in the box. He replied: 'Oh, that, let me show you.' The bartender stepped up on a stood, retrieved the box and set it down before me. He took a silver key from his pocket and placed it in an intricate gold latch on the box. He turned the key and opened the box. To my surprise, he pulled out a beautiful miniature piano that was exact in every way. He pressed down a few of the keys with his finger nail and the sounds were flawlessly in tune. But what really astonished me was that he then reached into the box and gently lifted out a perfect little man. The little man was wearing a tux and I was amazed to see that he was alive! The little man walked around the piano a few times, flexing his very small fingers. In the meantime, the bartender pulled a miniature chair from the box and place it before the piano. The little man sat down and started playing a Bach sonata.

I told the bartender that this was the most incredible thing I'd ever seen and asked him how this all came about. He told me this was the result of a wish he made to a Genie. "A Genie?" I replied, "now you're really pushing it. This whole episode is so impossible, I must be dreaming. If you want me to believe you, you"ll have to show me this Genie." "Sure," said the bartender, "and according to the rules, the Genie will grant you one and only one wish." The bartender took down a metal urn that was also on the top shelf and told me to rub the urn with my sleeve. Nothing could surprise me anymore and sure enough out poured a huge Genie. The Genie said something about being glad to get out of that cramped urn and asked me to make a wish. I told him I'd like a million bucks.

Well, I was wrong. The next thing did surprise me. The whole damn room was filled with ducks. There were ducks quacking on the floor. There were ducks flying around in the air. There were ducks on the tables and ducks on customers' heads. There were waiters and busboys mopping up duck poop everywhere. The din from all the quacking and clucking ducks and cursing from the waiters and busboys was unbearable. I yelled to the bartender above all the noise. "What happened? Doesn't that Genie hear well?" The bartender replied, "well, no, he doesn't. You don't think I asked for a ten inch pianist, do you?"☺

After the laughter subsides, Norton addresses the party goers. "I would like to present our next speaker, a fabulous story teller, Janet Finly."

Many years ago, a native American chief was stricken by a serious illness. The chief summoned his best medicine man, Bluebear to his teepee. Bluebear carefully examined the chief and asked him about his symptoms.

"Oh great medicine man," the chief began, "I feel terrible. I have a bad headache and high fever. Besides that, I have this awful rash. Can you help me?"

Bluebear thought for a few minutes. He looked up at the sky and meditated. He hummed some incantations and asked the gods for consul. He then pulled out a long thin strip of deer hide from his medicine bag. "I think I have a cure, great chief. Take this strip of deer hide. I want you to cut a one inch piece from the strip each day and chew the piece until it is gone. Continue this for one month and then I will return to check your progress. I hope this works for you, oh brave and nobel chief."

The chief duly follows Bluebear's instructions and one month later Bluebear returns to the chief's teepee. "Oh, great chief, how fare thee?"

"Not so good Bluebear. The thong is over, but the malady lingers on." ☺

"That was a good one, Janet." Norton says, giggling to himself. "Our next presenter is Lester Richmond."

I would like to tell you a story about a friend of mine when I lived on Earth. My friend's name is Hymie and his wife is Ethel. who Janet mentioned earlier. One day, Hymie announced to Ethel, "it's Friday and I feel a need to go to synagogue for services this evening."

Ethel replied, "I don't think that's a good idea, Hymie. The last time you went to services, you got into a fight with Stanley Golden and vowed never to go again. I don't remember exactly what happened, but you said something to Golden and he got really mad. You know what a bad temper he has."

"I don't care. If Golden is there I won't say a word to him. I'll just ignore him and sit as far away from him as possible. I can't let that jerk bother me, I'm going."

"Okay, go. I'm playing bridge tonight, so I'm not going with you."

So Hymie goes to synagogue. When he comes home that night, Ethel greets him at the door.

"Why are you covering your eye, Hymie? Let me see."

"Oh, it's nothing."

"Hymie, you've got a black eye. What happened? Did you get into a fight with Golden again?"

"No Ethel, Golden wasn't even there. What happened was this: I was sitting behind the Lowensteins, minding my own business. Unlike some people I know, who are always talking, I was very quiet. When we got up to say a prayer, I noticed that Mrs. Lowenstein's dress was stuck in the crack of her tuchus. Being the gentleman that I am, I pulled it out. Well, she hauled off and punched me in the eye."

"Well, I hope you've learned your lesson, Hymie, you big schmuck. You claim to be a gentleman, but you completely lack social graces. You should know better than pulling on someone's dress like that. It's completely inappropriate."

Things went smoothly for Ethel and Hymie until the next Friday.

"Look Ethel, I'm a Jew and I have a right to go to synagogue and pray if I like. I know, I know. You're going to tell me I'm asking for trouble. Well, I'll tell you two things. First, I've learned my lesson and I won't pull on any dresses. Second, I'll take my good friend Moishe with me. He'll watch over me and protect me. Besides, God will be there and he won't let anything happen to me."

"All right, it's against my better judgement. But I'm telling you, stick close to Moishe and don't do anything obnoxious."

Hymie goes to synagogue and he comes home that night with his other eye all black.

"Good heavens, Hymie. I can't believe this. What happened this time?"

"Well, Moishe and I went to synagogue and we sat behind the Lowensteins. When we stood up to pray, Moishe noticed that Mrs. Lowenstein's dress was stuck in the crack of her tuchus. Being the gentleman that he is, Moishe pulled it out. Now I know how inappropriate that is and how much she hates that so I pushed it back in."☺

Lester continued, "since Jewish stories are so popular here, I'll tell you another one.

It's Germany in 1936 and a train is traveling from Berlin to Frankfort. There are four people sitting in a first class compartment car. On one side is a beautiful young woman and her mother. On the other side facing them are a German officer and a Jew. The atmosphere is very stiff and no one speaks. The officer sits almost at attention, causing the others to sit very straight, too. No one smiles and they all stare directly ahead, avoiding eye contact. Suddenly, the train goes through a long tunnel and it becomes pitch dark in the car. After a few seconds, there is a kissing noise and a loud slap. The train comes out of the tunnel and a large red welt is apparent on the officer's face. Each of the four occupants has a silent thought.

The daughter wonders, "why did that handsome officer kiss my mother and not me?"

Similarly, the mother wonders, "why did my daughter slap that handsome officer when he kissed her?"

While the officer thinks, "it's the Jews who are causing all the trouble in this country. He kissed her and she slapped me."

To himself the Jew says, "it's a good thing I made that kissing noise before I slapped him."☺

Norton, smiling, says, "it's getting late, my friends and the party is almost over. Our last speaker is Chandra Lear."

"I'd like to tell you two absent-minded professor stories. Although it seems unlikely, these stories are supposed to be essentially true. The stories concern two famous mathematicians, David Hilbert and Norbert Wiener. Here's the first story.

> Mrs. Hilbert enters her husband's study, "I'm sorry to disturb you while you're in your study, dear, but I have to remind you that we're going to the opera this evening."
>
> "Oh no, how am I supposed to finish my work on complete inner product vector spaces with all these interruptions," David grumbles. "Besides, you know how I feel about getting all dressed up for these stuffy operas."
>
> "Now dear, you'll have plenty of time for your vector spaces later. I suggest that you shower and start getting ready. We have to leave in two hours."
>
> So David showers and puts on his tux, while Mrs. Hilbert carefully applies her makeup and slips into her formal evening dress. A car and driver are waiting in front of their house to take them to the opera. Mrs. Hilbert gets into the back seat of the car and David dutifully follows. As he gets into the car, Mrs. Hilbert exclaims, "David, look, there's a spot on your shirt! You can't go to the opera like that. You know how important this is to me. Run back in and change shirts. Hurry up or we'll be late, I'll wait for you here."
>
> David goes back into the house. Mrs. Hilbert waits and waits. After about 20 minutes she rushes back into the house and finds David asleep in bed in his pajamas. "David, wake up. What's going on? We're supposed to be going to the opera."
>
> David looks up at her groggily and says, "well, I went into the house. I guess I was thinking about vector spaces. Anyway, I took off my jacket, my tie and my shirt. After that I usually go to bed, so I did." ☺

After the laughter dies down, Chandra continues, "the second story is about Norbert Wiener, Professor of Mathematics at the Massachusetts Institute of Technology (MIT).

> Professor Wiener, his wife and their young daughter live in a house near the MIT campus. They decide to sell their home and move into a nicer house a few blocks away. It's the morning of the day they are to move into their new house and Norbert prepares to leave for work at the Institute.
>
> "Now, Norbert," his wife says, "remember this evening you're supposed to come home to our new house. I'm writing our new address on this piece of paper. Put the paper in your pocket and look at it before you come home to remind yourself to go to the right place."
>
> "Don't treat me like an idiot, dear. I certainly know we're moving to a new house today. But I'll take the paper to humor you. Kisses, bye."

126

He puts the paper in his pocket and off he goes to MIT. His mind is occupied all day with his work on Brownian motion and stochastic processes. He has to make a calculation, so he fumbles in his pocket and pulls out the paper. He scribbles furiously on the paper, looks at his watch and sees that it's 3:05. He realizes that he is supposed to teach his class on functional integrals at 3:00, so he puts the paper on his desk and rushes out of his office. After his class is over, he leaves MIT and starts walking home. Norbert arrives at his old house and remembers that he doesn't live there anymore. He doesn't recall his new address so he reaches into his pocket but the paper isn't there.

He looks around to check his surroundings hoping for some clue that would indicate which direction to walk to get to his new house. Squinting through his thick glasses, Norbert, notices a young girl playing in the front yard. He approaches her and says, "little girl, do you know where the Wiener's new house is?"

"Daddy," the little girl responds indignantly, "it's me. Mommy sent me here to get you and take you home." ☺

The applause is wild and God once again takes the stage. "I hope you had as good a time as I did. The winners can come see me to collect their prizes any time they want. You know where to find me. Everywhere! See you all later."

Chapter 10

Sammy and Poke

When Walter Crondike's report of his interview with God appeared in newspapers around the world, the reception was mixed. Of course, there were the skeptics and the admirers. Some said it was an elaborate hoax and others said it was the story of the century. On average, the reception was polite but not overwhelming. The topic that drew the most attention and outrage was God's remark that dogs and other animals do not go to heaven. This even drew a protest from the National Humane Society, which established a "March of Dogs" campaign to raise money for their cause. One of their slogans was: "I Believe in Dog." Another was: "God Spelled Backwards is Dog." In order to clarify the situation, God asked Sammy Templeton to report on his experiences with animals. Here are the results, with God speaking first.

"I have said that there are no real animals in the Academy. This is mainly because animals do not have souls, so they can not be elevated to a higher level. Since many of our academicians have fond feelings for them, we do have very realistic replicas of animals. They seem real in many ways except they are not derived from preexisting living creatures. Why don't animals have souls? There are many who believe that animals deserve souls more than people. After all, animals only kill for food. Animals do not have the emotion of hate. I wish I could say the same for people. Like the universe, the Academy is evolving and animals may soon develop souls and be admitted to the Academy. This is what the story of Sammy and Poke is about. I'll let Sammy tell you the story in his own words."

My name is Samuel Templeton, but everyone calls me Sammy. I am 24 years old and I live in Oklahoma City. This story begins 18 years ago when I was six. At that time, my father, Jason, mother, Carol and I lived in a plain but nice house in Stillwater, Oklahoma, which is about 70 miles from Oklahoma City. We had a large fenced back yard with lots of trees. There was a small stream about 100 feet behind our back yard that emptied into Boomer Lake which was about a mile away. This lake was in the middle of a large city park called Boomer Park. Besides the lake, Boomer Park contained some dense woods and walking trails. Stillwater was a quiet little town, except it was the home of Oklahoma State

University. This was a medium sized university and many of the towns-people made their living working at the university or at businesses supported by students and staff from the university. In particular, my Dad was the maintenance supervisor for a large engineering building at OSU. Jason and Carol were not well educated people. After they graduated from high school, their parents could not afford to send them to college because it was during the great depression. But they were well-read, worked hard and we were a happy little family.

For my sixth birthday party, my parents invited five children from the neighborhood. After the games, ice cream and cake, I opened presents from the other children. Then my parents gave me a present that would change my life.

"Happy birthday, dear. Your Dad and I thought you might be getting a little lonesome with just the three of us here, so we decided to get you something to keep you company. It might be a little work for you, but we think you're old enough now to handle it."

My Dad added with a grave tone, "even though this is a present, it will require some responsibility. If you want to keep what we are giving you, you will have to take care of it."

I unwrapped a small rectangular shaped glass aquarium. Inside were some green plants, a little water pond and the cutest thing I'd ever seen. It was a small green turtle about one inch wide. Its back was light green with a pattern of dark green stripes and its underside was a dark yellow ribbed shell. I lifted it up very gently because I could feel that its shell was fairly soft. When I placed it on my palm, it immediately stood up with its legs and head out of the shell and began licking my finger. It was an instant bond and for both of us, this was love at first sight. My heart melted and I went into a state of pure joy. This was the best present they could have given me and I will be forever grateful. I asked my Dad whether it was a boy or girl turtle and he said it was hard to tell but he thought it was a boy. I put him back in the aquarium and could see him trying to climb up the side of the glass to get back to me. I asked my Dad to put the aquarium away because I knew the other kids wouldn't be as gentle as I was. My parents also gave me a box of turtle food and I diligently fed him a small amount every morning.

At my request, my Mom and Dad read me some books from the library on the care and upkeep of turtles. I kept the aquarium on a shelf in my room and every day after school, I would rush into my room, close the door and we would play. He would walk around on my palm and lick my fingers. He would crawl up my arms and try to lick my face. Sometimes I placed him on the floor and he would slowly crawl around sniffing and exploring but after a few minutes he would always return to me. When I came into my room, he was excited and overjoyed to see me. We were the best of friends. I talked to him a lot and he seemed to listen. It was almost as if he understood what I was saying. I told him some of my favorite fairy tales that my Mom had read to me. After a while he started moving his lips as if he wanted to talk too. He did not walk very fast and he almost never wanted to run, so I thought I'd call him 'Slow Poke' but I later shortened it to 'Poke.'

A year later, Poke was about three inches wide and his shell was much harder. I

130

supplemented his turtle food with extra vegetables we had in the house like lettuce, spinach, turnips, zucchini, carrots and celery. I cleaned his aquarium once a month and delighted in watching him grow. We still played in my room in the afternoons and weekends. He was more confident now in exploring my room and crawling under the bed. He also liked to sit in my lap and stare up at me. He looked at me admiringly, as if I were the greatest thing in the world. It made me feel big and important. I had these fantasies about being a king while Poke and my toy soldiers were the subjects.

When Poke was two, his shell was a full six inches wide and he grew too large for the aquarium, so we bought him a larger one. By this time, I took him outside in our back yard so he could get more exercise. He loved it out there and would walk around for hours smelling everything he could find. He came to me when I called and he had an almost human presence. When I looked into his eyes, he stared back at me and I could see that there was some kind of intelligence there. It was sort of erie. I had the feeling he was some kind of alien from a distant planet.

I was nine years old and in fourth grade when Poke turned three. His shell was as hard as a rock and was a good nine inches wide. He had a large triangular tail that dragged on the ground when he walked. Poke was now too big for an aquarium so he had the run of my room. He must have weighed over five pounds and was hefty for me to lift. He didn't mind when I picked him up and watched him move his legs back and forth in the air. In fact, I could tell he thought it was great fun. Even my room got too small for him and he was soon walking around the house. But these excursions only lasted a few months.

"This is not working out well, Sammy." My Mom complained, "I can't have a turtle crawling around the house. He's making messes on the floor and carpet and he's getting into food and other stuff. Poke is an outdoor animal now and you'll have to keep him in the back yard."

Of course, my Dad had to put in his two cents as well, "I'm sorry son, but your Mom is right. It's not fair to keep him cooped up in the house all day and you know how much he likes it outside. An adult turtle needs a lot of room to roam around. You can go out and see him whenever you like. I'll build a box with a blanket in it so he can stay warm in the winter. If he doesn't like the box, he can sleep wherever he wants, like under our back porch. To tell you the truth, I didn't expect him to live this long and get so big. I thought pet turtles only lived a year or two. I guess it's because you've taken such good care of him and given him so much attention. Also, I have to admit that Poke is not an ordinary turtle from a pet store. I got him from the biology lab at the University and I didn't think of asking what kind of turtle he was."

What my parents said was true. Poke loved it in the back yard. He loved all the smells. He enjoyed munching on grass, leaves and twigs. I even saw him eating apples that fell from our tree. He liked watching the insects, birds and squirrels. I spent a lot of time out there with him and fed him vegetable snacks. He was getting even bigger. I read in my turtle book that turtles and tortoises can live over a hundred years and they continue to grow most of their lives but at a slower rate, as they get older. In the summer, Mom and

Dad let me set up a pup-tent and sleep in the back yard. Poke would crawl into the tent and sleep next to me. He was a great companion and it was fun having him there.

One night it got a little hot in the tent. There was a nice breeze outside, so I threw my sleeping bag onto the grass and slept on top of it. It was a beautiful night and the sky was filled with stars. The moon was half full, so it wasn't completely dark. As usual, Poke crawled up near my head and went to sleep. A few hours later, a miracle happened. I still can hardly believe it happened, but it did. I heard a small voice, "Sammy, do you see those stars?" I looked around, startled. There was only Poke and I. I got a little scared and thought of running into the house. Then I thought there must be an explanation for this. Maybe it was a ghost or maybe I was hearing things. I could see that Poke was awake and moving his lips but there was no sound coming out. "Who said that?" I exclaimed.

The voice was coming from Poke. "It was me, but you really didn't hear me. You received my brain waves."

"I must be going crazy," I thought, "I'm conversing with a turtle. Poke, what are brain waves and how did I receive them?"

"They're kind of like sound waves but they don't make noise. They're more like light waves or radio waves. They go from one brain to another and we have receivers that accept them. Some living beings use them to communicate. You can converse with me without talking. All you have to do is think what you want to say. I can't actually read your mind. I only receive the signals that you want to send."

"But why haven't you sent me brain waves before?"

"I've tried many times, but this is the first time your brain has been receptive. You are very special because most people never learn to use brain waves. It takes a lot of skill and practice. You will get better as you use it more. It's a great way to communicate. When you get good at it you can converse this way over a long distance, a mile or more."

"This is all really amazing. I can't believe that we're actually kind of talking together, Poke. Do all animals converse with brain waves?"

"I guess people never really developed brain waves because they could talk to each other and it was't necessary. But animals don't have the proper vocal cords for speech, so they've developed an ability to use brain waves to communicate. Of course, this has evolved over long periods of time. Animals of the same species easily converse using brain waves. If they are different species, it's harder. I'm pretty good with squirrels and dogs but birds have a very strong accent and insects are impossible."

"Can I converse with my parents this way?"

"You can try, but it probably won't work. You're the only person I've been able to communicate with. Maybe if you don't learn it as a child you can't learn it. I really don't know. The only things I know is what I've experienced. Now are you ready to answer my question?"

"What question?"

"Do you see those stars?"

"Yes I do. They're really bright tonight and they're beautiful."

"Do you know what they are and how they got there?"

"I really don't know exactly but I think scientists can answer questions like that very accurately. We talked a little about stars in my science class at school. My teacher said that our sun is a star and they're big globs of hot gasses called plasmas. The reason they're so bright is because they're burning very hot due to nuclear fusion reactions. We can't see them during the day because of all the light from the sun. I have no idea how they got there but it has something to do with the big bang."

"Wow, that's amazing. You human beings are really incredible. You can think and reason about abstract things that are completely beyond my capabilities. You can think about beauty, science and stuff like that. I won't even ask about nuclear reactions, plasmas and the big bang. They'd be way over my head. The only things I think about are smelling, eating and getting away from danger. I wish I were more like you. I think you're wonderful. I remember when I was a baby in the palm of your hand. Why is it that you know so much more than I do?"

"Listen Poke. There's a lot of things that people don't know and I also believe there's a higher power than us. You are wonderful in your own way and we all play a part in nature's plan. Tell me, what's it like being a turtle?"

"That's a hard question, Sammy. What would you say if I asked you what it's like being a human? Anyway, hard questions are good and I'll try to answer. For the most part, my life is pretty ordinary. I spend most of my time eating, sleeping and exploring the back yard. I guess I enjoy just being. I like to lay here in the sun and watch the birds and insects. Every once in a while a rabbit comes into the yard. Rabbits get around and they're very interesting. I like it when you spend time with me and feed me snacks. It would be nice if I could visit with some other turtles sometime."

Poke and I talked, I mean communicated, for hours that night. It was the most amazing experience of my short life. I camped out in the back yard a lot that summer and we spent many hours flashing brain waves back and forth. As one might suspect, he was very limited. He could not comprehend things like math, geography and history. He didn't have a very good sense of humor and didn't understand the point of most jokes. But he knew a lot about squirrels, rabbits and the dog next door. He even gave me some gossip about our neighbors that the dog told him. He told me about his urges to get out of the back yard and explore some of the rest of the world.

That fall, I took Poke for walks in the woods behind our house. He was delighted with all the new smells and vistas that opened up to him. When he saw the stream, he was overcome with delight. He jumped right in and swam and paddled with abandon. He bobbed up and down, dove down deep and gobbled water plants. I was amazed by how long he could stay under water. He was in seventh heaven and didn't want to leave. After each of our excursions into the woods he thanked me profusely for bringing him there. I told him that I enjoyed it too and I really did. I thought it was time to tell my parents about having conversations with Poke. They patted me on the head and said it was nice to have fantasies while I was young.

Early the next spring, Poke discovered that he could dig a small hole under the fence and get out. I told Mom and Dad and they said it was all right. After all, it was his choice and if he wanted the freedom he could take it. Besides, the woods and lake were more of his natural habitat than our back yard. Sometimes I would find him in the stream and he followed me home. Other times, I couldn't find him but he came home later for his vegetable snacks in our yard. Later, he started leaving for a week or two at a time and I missed him and our conversations. Then I didn't see him for two months.

That summer I was riding my bike on the trail around Boomer Lake when I saw two large turtles in the water. I stopped to investigate and saw that one of them was Poke.

"Is that really you, Poke?"

"Hi, Sammy. Yes, it's me and this is my mate Margery."

Margery said, "Hi Sammy, I'm glad to meet you. Poke has told me so much about you. He idolizes you and thinks you're the best person in the world. He asked me if I minded whether he comes by to visit you and I said it was all right with me. Do you want to see our babies?"

I couldn't believe my eyes. Swimming behind them were 10 or 12 little baby turtles. They were so cute and they looked just like Poke did four years ago. Margery and Poke were clearly very proud of their babies. I watched as they all proudly swam around in a large circle. I sat down by the side of the lake. Poke and Margery came out and laid down beside me. Some of the babies were very shy but a couple came out of the water and crawled around on my hands and lap. Soon, most of them were there with me. I gently played with the babies for the rest of the afternoon. It gave me a real warm and fuzzy feeling. I wanted to take one of the babies home but I was sure their parents wouldn't have approved.

I didn't see Poke or his family much for the rest of the summer and I was lonesome. Most of the times I rode around Boomer Lake, I couldn't find them. I knew that they had to hide their babies from strangers and predators like hawks and eagles. I also knew that Poke had family responsibilities so he couldn't come by to visit me.

Luckily, I wasn't lonesome very long because of two events. The first was that my Dad answered an ad in the paper and brought home the cutest puppy I ever saw. He was six months old and was a black long haired Dachshund. His favorite sport was playing tag. I would run after him and tag him. He would then run after me and touch my leg with his paw. This would go on for half an hour. When I saw him I would say, "hi, do you want to play tag?" It became clear to me that we should name him Hitag. Of course, Hitag and I were the best of pals and for the most part, he filled the void left by the missing Poke.

The other event happened that September. I was ten years old and in the fifth grade. I walked to school and back every day. It was six blocks away and it took me about ten minutes. I could have ridden my bike but I guess it was so close that it wasn't worth it. Well, walking home one day, I saw this girl who was also walking home from our school. I'd seen her before but I didn't pay much attention. Before then I thought girls were the most useless creatures on Earth. What were they good for? They weren't interested in baseball, toy soldiers, cars and construction equipment like normal people. All they did was whisper, giggle and gossip. They played with dolls, cared about clothes and put on lip stick and disgusting makeup. I didn't want to have anything to do with them.

That all changed when I saw this girl. Her name was Lilly Johnson and she lived about three blocks from me. She was nine and was in fourth grade. She was thin, had blond hair, blue eyes and she was beautiful. I was very shy in those days, but I got up enough courage to say hi. She said hi in reply and told me she noticed me at school before. Lilly said she also saw me walking Hitag and thought he was really cute. She told me she had a year old puppy named Zelda who looked a lot like Hitag. Zelda was a black, long haired Poodle Dachshund mix. She had long droopy ears, big brown eyes and large paws. Lilly said we should get our dogs together sometime so they could play. I said, sure and needless to say, I walked Lilly home. I had never really talked to a girl before and was surprised to learn how easy it was with this one. I was also flattered by the attention she gave me and she seemed to like me.

After that day, I went a block out of my way to meet Lilly and we walked to school and back practically every day. She was a lot of fun to be with and I liked being with her. We soon became very good friends. We would go to each others houses and play in our rooms. Our dogs got along great and we walked them together and watched them frolic in our back yards. The better I knew her, the more I liked her. Even though she looked delicate and fragile, she was strong and tough both physically and mentally. This doesn't mean she was boyish in any way; she was, in fact, quite feminine. She loved to fight and wrestle which her mother said came from her father who was a tall blond handsome man with a playful manner. Lilly's favorite game was to pretend she was a tiger. She would make a fierce roar and scratch and bite hard, but usually without breaking the skin. She would grab my finger and bite it hard until I yelled, "ouch, that really hurts." Although she tried to act ferocious, it was impossible for her to look that way and she was usually just funny.

After I met Lilly, I didn't see Poke for about six months. I didn't miss him very much because I was busy with school and homework. Also, I had devoted parents, Lilly and Hitag to keep life interesting. But then one Saturday, Lilly and I were running around in the woods behind my house with Hitag and Zelda. All of a sudden, something crawled out of the stream. It was Poke! Hitag ran over to investigate and Zelda hung back a little cautious. Poke retreated into his shell and closed up. Hitag sniffed all around the shell and even stuck his nose underneath to get more smells. But then Poke's head and legs popped out and Hitag gave his face a big dog lick. Then Zelda came up and licked Poke's paws and tail.

"Who are these guys, Sammy?" Poke asked, with a bit of a panic in his voice.

"The first one is my dog, Hitag, and the second one is Lilly's dog, Zelda. This is my friend Lilly, by the way."

"I'm glad to meet you, Lilly. You, too, Hitag and Zelda. Any friends of Sammy are friends of mine. I really didn't need a bath though. I get plenty of water from the stream."

"I can't believe this," Lilly said. "That turtle is talking. At least I think he's talking. Come to think of it, he wasn't speaking because I didn't hear a sound. Whew, this is all very confusing. You've got some explaining to do, Sammy. What's going on here?"

"This is really exciting, Lilly. You have the power to communicate with thought waves. Poke is sending you signals from his brain and you're receiving them. If you practice, you'll be able to send thought waves back to him. I've been conversing with Poke this way for years, but you're the only other person I know who can do it. Pretty soon, I bet, you and I can do it too. That way we can converse without making a sound. Isn't that cool?"

Lilly exclaimed, "wow, is that really true? Does that mean we can talk to each other without moving our lips and no one else will know what we're saying?"

"That's right. Animals do it all the time, but most people can't do it. Animals are much better at it than I am because they've been doing it for millions of years. They can communicate for blocks or even miles. I have to be right next to animals to understand them."

"Can dogs use thought waves too? What about Hitag and Zelda?"

Hitag chimed in, "you're darned right we can do it. Zelda and I have been conversing with thought waves for a while now but we didn't know we could do it with you and Sammy. This is great, we can all talk to each other."

"Wow, this opens a whole new world of communication for all five of us. Hey Poke, I haven't seen you for a long time. Why don't you come over more often and we can all hang out together?"

"That would be great, Sammy. I've had family responsibilities until now. But our little turtles are getting big now and they can take care of themselves. I think I can get away more often. You know I have a very good sense of smell? Even better than dogs like Hitag and Zelda. I can smell things miles away and sort out individual odors. I may not have the mental capacity of people, but my sense of smell is far superior. If you put some carrots and zucchini outside your back fence, I'll smell them and come over. I'm getting kind of tired of eating grass and leaves and would certainly enjoy some delicacies."

The next four years were the best of my life and since I'm now 24, that's saying something. On weekends and after school the five of us would frequently hang out together in our back yards or in the woods and we would have the most wonderful adventures you can imagine. Sometimes Lilly and I would talk out loud and other times we would use thought waves. One of our fantasy trips was to pretend we were in a zoo. Lilly, of course, was a tiger, I was the zookeeper, Hitag was a panda, Zelda a zebra and Poke a giant Galapagos tortoise. Lilly and I made make-believe cages out of cardboard boxes and other kids in the neighborhood would come to our zoo to look at the animals. The animals soon tired of being cooped up in boxes, so we progressed to our Africa game. In this case the others were the same animals as before, but I was a hunter. Lilly would attack me and scratch and bite me. We didn't know anything about sex in those days but I enjoyed it when she jumped on me and bounced up and down. She didn't mind if I put my hands on her butt. All we knew was that it felt real good. The animals would also jump on me and lick my hands and face.

"Now that we have this great gang, we should have a name. We have a turtle and I like doves so why don't we call ourselves the Turtle Doves?" Lilly smiled to herself.

I answered, "that's a good start, but I think it would be more descriptive to call ourselves the Turtle Dogs."

Zelda's scratchy voice joined in, "Turtle Dogs, I like it. It's kind of catchy."

So Turtle Dogs we were. We must have looked like a motley crew. Two kids, two dogs and a turtle marching through the woods looking for adventure. After a while our fantasies got more sophisticated than zoos and African safaris. We pretended to be superheros out to save the world. We actually did find a few injured birds and squirrels that we nursed back to health. We rescued a mouse being attacked by a cat. Another time we found Mrs. Clark's dog tangled tightly around a tree. Mrs. Clark kept him in her front yard with a rope attached to his collar and the other end tied to a stake. He got loose and ran into the woods with the rope dangling behind. He must have been stuck there for hours because he was weak and whimpering. We untangled him and took him back to Mrs. Clark. She was very grateful and gave us some milk and cookies.

There was one time when Hitag and Poke helped me do something really important. At 2:00 a.m. Hitag jumped on my bed while I was sleeping and licked my face. I woke up with a start and said: "Hitag, what's going on? Don't you know it's the middle of the night?"

"I'm sorry, Sammy," Hitag said, "but Poke's in the back yard and he's sending some strong thought waves. I can't tell what it's about but he's very agitated. He doesn't act that way very often so we should find out what's happening."

"All right, Hitag, I'll put on some clothes and shoes and we'll go out there to see what the problem is. With all this trouble I'm going through, this better be good."

When we reached the back yard, Poke was pacing back and forth and he was clearly quite upset. "Something really bad is happening. I smell an awful oder and I don't like it."

"Where is this smell, Poke?"

"Over there. Follow me."

This was one of the few times I'd seen Poke run. Usually when we're walking or running through the woods, Poke would straggle behind and catch up when we slowed down or stopped. We never worried about him finding us because of his great sense of smell. But this was different. Hitag and I had to run to keep up with him. We made our way through about 600 yards of woods and came to a street. About a block away we saw black smoke rising into the sky. As we got close, I saw that it was coming from the back of Lilly's house! I rang the bell and knocked on the door as hard as I could. Mr. Johnson opened the door and said, "Sammy, what's wrong. Don't you realize it's two in the morning."

"Mr. Johnson, your house is on fire! You all have to get out now!"

"Oh my God, I do smell smoke. I'll go get Mrs. Johnson; you run upstairs and get Lilly."

When I got to Lilly's room I saw Zelda jump up from her sleep at the foot of Lilly's bed. She started barking excitedly. As I shook Lilly I could see smoke and flames coming up the back wall of her room. Lilly was in such a deep sleep, I had to pull her up by her arms to get her to wake up. She was wearing a thin night gown and I could see for the first time that she was developing breasts. There wasn't time to get aroused about that now as I grabbed her hand and led her down to the front door and then outside. Mrs. and Mr. Johnson, Hitag, Zelda and Poke were there waiting for us.

Mr. Johnson moved to greet Sammy, "Sammy, how did you know about the fire? You're a big hero, you saved our lives."

"It wasn't me, Mr. Johnson. Poke smelled the smoke and he and Hitag led me here. They're the real heroes."

The Johnson's gave me a big hug and Lilly kissed me on the lips. I wanted to hold her real tight and kiss her back but I thought I'd better not.

"Thank Hitag and Poke for us, won't you, Sammy," Mrs. Johnson said gratefully. "When we get the house back together we'll have you all over and give them some big treats."

A few minutes later the fire department came and put out the fire. It took about five months to rebuild the house. Most of this time, the Johnson's stayed at Lilly's grandparents' house. When Lilly complained it was too crowded there, she got to stay with us for a month in our guest bedroom. We would sneak into each others bedrooms at night. We didn't have real sex but we did a lot of snuggling, hugging, kissing and petting. It was really nice.

After the fire, the Turtle Dogs were even closer than before. We were famous superheros as we strutted around patrolling the woods and streets of our neighborhood. But about six months later disaster struck. I hadn't seen Poke for a month and all of a sudden I saw him in the corner of our back yard. He was all closed up in his shell and he laid there motionless for hours. Finally I got some vegetables and placed them next to him, but he still wouldn't come out. I left him alone that night. The next day was Saturday and I didn't have school. I went out that morning to check on him. He was still there and the food was untouched. Hitag licked his shell and I sent him some strong thought waves.

I called out, "what's wrong Poke? Please come out so we can talk to you."

"Okay, I'll come out, but I won't be very good company."

"What happened Poke? Why are you so sad?"

"I think Margery's dead. I haven't seen her for two weeks."

A tear formed in one of Poke's eyes and dripped down his face. He lowered his head to the ground and sobbed.

"How do you know Margery died? What's going on, Poke?"

"We were happily swimming in Boomer Lake. Margery and I were having a great time. We dove down to the bottom, nuzzled together and came back up. Then along came this big, mean, ugly man in a boat. He had a net and he used it to trap Margery. He put her in a metal box in his boat. He tried to get me but I dove down and hid in some reeds. I could see his awful face peering into the water, looking for me. Even when I was underwater, I could smell him. He reeked of sweat, blood and excretion. Luckily, our offspring are older now and they were able to swim away and hide too. I'd seen this man before but I don't know his name. I heard him mumble something about making turtle soup. Isn't that terrible? I could sense his hate, scorn and cruelty. I didn't know such things existed. What recourse do I have? I looked all over for her and I don't know what to do."

"I'm so sorry Poke. I know how awful you must feel. Even though turtles don't like to hug I'm sending you a mental hug and hope that helps. We'll get the Turtle Dogs together and look for Margery."

We looked for Margery that afternoon and all day Sunday but couldn't find her. We even waded into Lake Boomer and checked through the reeds to no avail. We also looked for the mean man but we didn't know who he was and we couldn't find him either. I was surprised that Poke couldn't smell him anywhere but it might have been that Poke had some kind of emotional block. Since Margery never did show up, we were sure that he killed her. Now that Poke didn't have Margery and his kids were grown up, we were his main family and he spent a lot of time in our back yard. Of course, he still went under the fence to the stream and Boomer Lake when he felt like it. When we were alone or with Hitag, he and I had some pretty deep conversations.

"Sammy, do you think Lilly and you will get married and move away?"

"That's a pretty hard question, Poke. Lilly and I have a really good time together and we like each other a lot. But getting married? That's a different story. I honestly don't know. We're still kids and haven't thought about it. Even if we got married, we couldn't move away from our families and friends like you. I'm afraid you're stuck with us for a long time."

"I've tried to communicate with your parents but I can't seem to get through. Maybe there's a blockage or something. Hitag told me he also tried but he couldn't get anywhere. The only thing they ever respond to is a bark and they don't understand that either. Hitag said he thought he briefly got a message across to your Mom but her face turned red and she walked away. How come it's so easy to converse with you and Lilly but not with your parents?"

"I think when people get older, they get very serious and lose their ability to imagine and play. They don't think it's possible to talk to animals, so that area in their brain shuts down. It's too bad because they lose a whole world of knowledge and adventure. The animals lose a lot too."

"Have you talked to other animals besides Hitag, Zelda and me?"

"Yes, I've talked to some other dogs but it's been very superficial. Let's face it, a lot of them aren't very smart. All they want to talk about is bones, dog food and getting petted and scratched behind their ears. I've talked to a couple of squirrels and rabbits but they're very wary of people and don't want to get too close. I've tried to talk to a couple of cats but they're very snobbish and not very friendly. My best communication has been with animals in the zoo. They've had a lot of experience and know about exotic places. Some of them don't like being stuck in cages and yearn to be free. Some complain they don't like the food and their handlers aren't very nice."

"I know what you mean about cats. I don't like them at all. The only thing they're good for is chasing. Just like you, I think our zoo is nice. I hear that the Oklahoma City zoo is very impressive but our little Stillwater zoo is all we have. I've snuck in there five or six times. The monkeys are fun to watch but they're too busy swinging, running and jumping around to talk. The tiger is too mean and ferocious for my taste. The red panda spends most of his time lolling around in the branches of a tree. He looks more like a giant red squirrel than a bear and he isn't interested in conversing. My favorite used to be an Oklahoma sage grouse. I said, 'used to be,' because he isn't there any more and the reason why is quite a story.

The first time I snuck into the zoo was after closing so there were no people around. Because it was in the summer it was still pretty light outside. After wandering around for awhile, I happened upon the sage grouse cage. It was just a plot of ground enclosed by a wire fence like humans have for their back yards. It also had a wire top so the grouse couldn't fly out. There were three grouse in the cage, two males and a female. I could tell because the males were large and had very colorful plumage, while the female was smaller with simple brown and white coloring. Two of the grouse were at the back nuzzling each other and the other male was in front looking out of the wires of the cage. I crawled up to the cage and said, 'hi, I'm Poke. What's your name?'"

"No one ever gave me a name. They just call me Sage. Those two back there are Roland and Rita. You'd better be careful. Only zoo animals are allowed in here. One time I saw the zookeeper, Zook, catch a raccoon who came in looking for food. Zook split him open with an ax and threw him in the trash to die. He was whimpering in there for a whole day."

"Thanks for the advice. I don't see anyone around now so it's safe. Besides, if someone comes along I can run and jump into that creek over there. How is life treating you here in the zoo?"

"Fair, I guess. Zook isn't very friendly. He just feeds us, does repairs and keeps things clean. We have to look good for the paying customers, he says. The hard, dirty work, like scooping up poop is done by the assistant zookeeper. Zook calls him Assistant. We call him Assie."

"What about Roland and Rita. What are they like?"

"Well, I'm the only one with any brains around here. They're about as dumb as they come. Roland is a little more colorful than me. He struts and prances around like he's really hot stuff. Rita is very impressed and she doesn't pay any attention to me. They do a lot of mating and I'm left to myself. Rita lays an egg everyday or two and sits on them like she knows what she's doing. Zook collects the eggs and I think he cooks and eats them. Roland and Rita don't notice the eggs are gone and wouldn't care if they did notice. I don't think Zook wants any more grouse. It would cost him more to feed us. Not that the food is that good here. All we get is some dried millet and some seeds and insects we find in the grass. All in all, my life stinks and I would like to get out of here."

"Would Roland and Rita like to get out too?"

"They're not smart enough to think about it. They like being taken care of and fed by someone. There are no predators here so they will probably live longer than out in the wild. Life is easy for them here. I would like to fly and be free in the wild. I'd take my chances out there. I want to live the life I was created for."

"We heard someone coming so I had to get out fast. A few days later, I went to visit my new friend. He was standing there where I left him. I asked him how things were going."

He replied, "about the same. I'm glad you came back. I like talking to you. Things are so boring here."

"I'm sorry, pal. Is there anything I can do?"

"Well, now that you mention it, there is. You can help me get out of here. I can't do much scratching with my little feet but you've got big sharp claws. You could dig a hole under this stupid makeshift fence."

So I started digging a hole. I got pretty far, but then we saw Assie coming along with his bucket and scoop. We quickly covered the hole with leaves and I scampered away. I went back two more times to continue my work. While I was digging, Sage and I had long conversations. I told him about Margery and my little turtle family. I told him about the adventures of the Turtle Dogs. He told me stories he heard from the eagle in the cage next door. The eagle had a long adventurous life until a hunter shot off part of his beak. He was rescued by the Humane Society and they gave him to the zoo. Some veterinarians from the University constructed a plastic beak to fit over his stub. The beak works pretty well, but not good enough for him to live in the wild. He told me that he is indebted to the vets for giving him a new life. This is not the best life be could imagine, but it's better than none at all. Sage also told me about his dreams of someday having his own family. By now the hole was almost large enough for Sage to get through.

But then disaster struck. We saw Zook at the other end of the cage. He had an ax in one hand and was testing and shaking the fence with the other hand. He was coming toward us. I had to think fast. There was no time to cover the hole with leaves. I did the only thing I could. My shell was the same color and texture as the ground. I jumped into the hole and I fit perfectly. Sage moved to the back of the cage. He pranced around and made honking bird noises to distract Zook. Miraculously, the camouflage stunt worked and Zook didn't notice anything unusual. After Zook left, we again covered the hole with leaves because we were afraid he would return.

I went back the next morning before the zoo opened. I squeezed through the hole and went into the cage. When Sage saw me, he jumped on top of my shell and flapped his wings wildly. I ran around the cage as fast as I could with Sage on my back. Then we chased each other for a few minutes while Rita and Roland watched with dumbfounded expressions. We both decided that we'd better stop because we were making a lot of noise and it could get dangerous. Sage told me that this was the best time he'd ever had. I finished digging the hole so Sage could squeeze through. After he was out he turned and looked at me with a sad but excited expression. He gave me a peck on my shell and said he would remember me forever. He flew into the air, circled me once and dove down to look me in the eyes a last time. Then he was off in the sky to meet his destiny. I never saw him again and never went back to the zoo."

I told Poke that was a wonderful story and it made me cry.

He then said, "Sammy, have you ever told your parents that you've communicated with Hitag, Zelda and me?"

"I tried to, several times, but it's very discouraging. I told my Mom a long time ago and she started crying. My Dad told me not to talk to her about it because it upset her. He said that people who say they talk to animals are considered to be crazy. He mentioned a big word like schizophrenia or something. Dad said he might have to take me to a psychologist if I kept this up. He said it's great to live in a make-believe world when I'm young, but at some point I had to learn to distinguish between fantasy and reality. I didn't mention it to him again."

"I hope when you get older you won't stop talking to me. I don't want to ever lose you."

"I won't be like other adults because I know how to use thought waves and I always will. I'll do everything in my power to make sure we'll be friends forever."

"I love you, Sammy. Is it all right for animals to say that?"

"It's perfectly okay, Poke. I love you too."

I gave Poke a little scratch behind the ear. He never admitted it before but I could tell he liked it. Everything went smoothly with my little gang and me for another year. I was then fifteen and a high school sophomore. Lilly and I were very close. We were excited about entering adulthood and learning about each other and our bodies. We undressed each other and played around. We did everything short of intercourse. Neither of us was ready for that yet. It was even more intense because we could communicate without speaking and we knew that in this sense we were unique. We both felt wonderfully light hearted. Like we were in heaven, flying.

But soon, everything changed. One evening after dinner, I heard Hitag barking frantically in the back yard. I went out to investigate and found him jumping up and down against the fence.

"I got some waves from Poke and he's in very bad trouble. He really needs our help. Poke's pretty far away so you better get your bike."

I hopped on my bike and followed Hitag as he ran down the street. Hitag and I rushed like mad for about a mile until we came to a small park. The stream from Boomer Lake ran through the park and we followed it for about a block. Hitag stopped at the back yard of a shabby little house. In the yard we saw something that made our jaws drop. There was this big, mean, yellow and brown cat named Scab that I'd seen before. About two years ago, we found Scab toying with a little mouse. Scab would pounce on the mouse, then let the mouse run away a few feet and pounce on him again. We chased Scab away and were sure the mouse escaped before continuing our patrol of the woods. Scab belonged to a grouchy man named Mr. Crabtree, who nobody in town liked. I'm sure the feeling was mutual because Mr. Crabtree hated everyone in town except possibly Scab and himself. What we were aghast to see was that Poke was lying upside down on his back with his head and feet flailing in the air. Scab was hissing, growling and snapping at him and Poke retreated into his shell. But as soon as Poke came out and started rocking to right himself, Scab would bite at him. Hitag growled, barked and chased Scab away while I gently picked Poke up, turned him over and placed him on the ground.

"Ugh," Poke grumbled, "that awful cat jumped on me and flipped me over. When I was younger, I could quickly right myself but it keeps getting harder as I get older and heavier. Thank you guys for saving my life. I'm sure that cat was going to eat me."

But then things got worse. Mr. Crabtree heard us and came running over from his house. Poke started to run but Mr. Crabtree grabbed him and held him high in the air. Crabtree was the ugliest man I'd ever seen. He was tall and fat and his face was covered with an unshaven stubbly beard. He was wearing dirty, old overalls and a tattered red and white flannel shirt.

Crabtree gave Poke an evil smile and said, "this is a nice big turtle. He'll make a delicious soup, even better than the turtle I caught in Boomer Lake last year."

Hitag growled and grasped his jaw around Crabtree's leg. Crabtree kicked Hitag hard with his other foot and knocked him off. Hitag laid on the ground whimpering in pain. Crabtree was much more agile and athletic than he looked. He held Poke high with one hand, put his other fist in the air and gave a triumphant laugh. I grabbed him around the waist and tried to wrestle Poke out of his hand but he was much bigger and stronger than I was and he threw me to the ground.

"You should know better than to mess around with me, kid," Crabtree growled. "If I find you in my yard again, I'll get out my shotgun and fill your stupid little ass with lead."

Crabtree left in a huff holding Poke tightly in his large grubby hands. By now it was dark and I watched as Crabtree took Poke into his garage. I saw a light go on in the garage for a minute and then it went out.

I turned away and asked Hitag, "are you all right? That was a very brave thing you did."

"I'm okay, Sammy," Hitag answered, licking his paw, "it's just a bruised rib. I wasn't that brave, it was mainly instinct. I didn't think about it and did what I had to do. What's our next move?"

"Let's wait a few minutes until we're sure he's in his house. Then we'll go check out the garage."

After a few minutes, we quietly snuck up to the garage. There was a full moon and I could see into a small window in the garage. I brushed aside a bunch of ivy covering the window and I saw a large metal box on a wooden work bench. I knew that Poke was inside the box. I was terrified to see a long row of turtle shells hanging on the wall behind the bench. I saw that the window was unlatched and tried to lift it but it was stuck with years of old paint. I got out my pocket knife and scrapped off as much paint as I could. With a lot of effort, I was able to raise the window. I climbed through, got Poke out of the box and climbed out holding Poke in my hands.

Poke slowly pushed his head out of his shell, "thank you for saving my life again, Sammy. I don't think I can ever repay you. We've got to get out of here fast. Put me down and I'll run over to the stream. I'll swim under water and he'll never find me."

I did what Poke asked and hopped onto my bike. I looked back and saw the light go on in the kitchen with Crabtree looking out the back window. Hitag and I got out of there fast. When I got home I told Mom and Dad about that terrible Mr. Crabtree and asked them what we could do.

"That Crabtree character is well-known as the meanest guy in town," Dad explained, "but there's nothing we can do about him unless he does something illegal. I want you and Hitag to stay away from him. Anyway, I just told your Mom something that might solve your problem with that jerk. I just got an offer to head the maintenance team for a large office building in downtown Oklahoma City. It will mean a lot more money and Mom and I decided I should take the job. We'll have to move there in one month."

"But Dad, we can't move to Oklahoma City. We have a lot of friends here. What about Lilly? She's my best friend and I can't leave her."

"Look, Sammy," Mom said reassuringly, "it's only 70 miles away and we can come back often for visits. Of course, we'll take Hitag with us so you'll have him and you can make new friends. This is a great opportunity for your father and we can't ask him to give it up. These kinds of chances don't come up often and he may never get another one. Besides, we can now move out of this little town and go to an exciting big city."

"Can we take Poke too?"

Dad looked at me impatiently, "I've told you before, Sammy, that Poke is a wild animal. He's not domesticated like a dog. He can't live in a big city. He needs a habitat of woods and lakes that's more suitable for him. There's a lot of traffic and crowds in Oklahoma City and it would be too dangerous."

I had a nagging feeling that there were some things that my parents weren't telling me. There was more to this move than met the eye. Did they think that Lilly and I were getting too intimate? Did they believe that my relationship with Poke was unnatural? Did they think that this Turtle Dogs gang was getting out of hand? Maybe we were recruiting other kids and dogs and were forming a large unruly gang. I never did find out whether there was this motivation for the move or whether it was just my wild imagination. If I asked my parents now, they would probably say they don't remember.

The next afternoon, I found Poke in our back yard.

"At least I now know what happened to Margery. I hope he didn't make her suffer much. How do people like Crabtree get so cruel?" Poke already looked so sad, I didn't know how I'd break my news to him.

"I can't explain it, Poke. I do know that he's not the worst. I've read that a few hundred years ago, people would sail from Europe down to Africa and South America and trap thousands of giant tortoises. They would put the tortoises on their backs in the holds of ships without light, food or water. The tortoises would be like that for weeks or months until they got to Europe and were slaughtered. Today there are very few giant tortoises left. A hundred years ago there were millions of carrier pigeons and bison in America. People used to shoot them for fun. I saw pictures of people riding trains through the west, shooting bison for sport out of open cars and windows. Due to this senseless slaughter and loss of habitat, carrier pigeons are extinct today and there are very few bison left. I won't even go into the clubbing of baby seals and the inhuman slaughtering of cattle."

"That's really terrible. I'm glad I don't read books and learn about that awful stuff."

"I've got some bad news to tell you, Poke."

"Oh great, thanks for cheering me up, Sammy."

"My parents and I are moving to Oklahoma City."

"You'll take me with you, won't you?"

"I'm sorry, Poke. I begged them to let me take you, but they said you can't go. They told me it's too dangerous for you there."

"But I'll miss you terribly and I don't feel safe here anymore. This is not a good place for me with that mean cat and awful Mr. Crabtree."

"You're a very smart turtle, Poke. You can stay under water in the stream and hide in the reeds at Boomer lake. Cats hate water and Mr. Crabtree is too dumb to find you. You'll be happy here. You might even find another mate and have more babies. Besides, I'll come back a lot and visit you. It's not very far by car."

"Goodbye, Sammy. Don't forget me, please."

The next few weeks were busy with moving plans. We had to pack things up and make arrangements with movers. My parents went to Oklahoma City a couple times to look at houses and we put our house up for sale. Toward the end of the month, they bought a nice house on the outskirts of the city. It had a large fenced back yard with lots of room for Hitag to run around. It was a few blocks from a quiet cemetery and was away from the noise of the city. I told Mom and Dad that this would be a nice place for Poke to live but they wouldn't listen. The day before we left, I said goodbye to Lilly. It wasn't easy. She cried and I didn't want her to see it, but I cried too. We held each other real tight for a long time. I couldn't find Poke and hoped he was all right. I didn't think I'd ever see him again.

Hitag was a great dog but he had one major problem. Unlike most dogs, he was afraid to ride in cars. Every time he rode in a car he would get very carsick. Because of this, we never took him for a ride, except when we had to take him to the vet. The hour and a half trip to Oklahoma City was no different. He kept his head out the window and threw up a few times. We stopped a couple of times so he could poop on the grass by the side of the road.

We all liked our new house. Hitag was especially pleased with the large back yard.

It had lots of trees and a great variety of new smells. One reason for this was that the previous owner had three dogs. I took Hitag on many walks so he could investigate the neighborhood. My high school was fine and I made some new friends. I soon became very busy with school work and activities. At the back of our house was a large sunroom with big windows on three sides. I liked sitting there doing my homework and looking out at our back yard. About a month after our move, I was staring out the window and I saw Hitag running around the yard excitedly. He was pawing at the ground and his nose was bobbing up and down near a circular object. The circular object was Poke! I grabbed some carrots and ran out to him.

"Hey Poke, I'm really glad to see you. How did you find us?"

Poke shook his head and smiled, "it was a long way and it took me a long time but I just followed Hitag's smelly trail. The hardest part was crossing some roads and dodging a few cars. You didn't think you'd get rid of me that easily, did you? I'll have some of those carrots now."

When I told my parents about Poke they said they couldn't fight the inevitable and he could stay in our back yard as long as he wanted. We went back to Stillwater for visits every couple of months and I spent as much time as I could with Lilly. We also exchanged letters and built up sizable phone bills. The old Turtle Dogs gang had broken up and our interests were different now, anyway. We both dated other people but our hearts always belonged to each other. Lilly was beautiful and in high school a lot of good looking guys were interested in her. When I say guys I don't mean twerps her age, but high school seniors and college guys from Oklahoma State. She had her choice of any of them but deep down she chose me, even though I couldn't compare to those guys in looks. For me she was always the only one. When it was time to go to college, I went to Oklahoma State and so did Lilly. We were a couple for four wonderful years. In those days, unmarried couples didn't live together, so we stayed in University dormitories. She majored in sociology and I majored in business. It was a good thing we didn't have any classes together, because we could easily have cheated on exams by exchanging answers using thought waves.

After we graduated from OSU, Lilly and I got married. We bought a condo in downtown Oklahoma City and we both work in nearby office buildings. Well, my dear friends, you are now up to date. I am 24 and Lilly is 23. Right now we're visiting my parents. We're all sitting in the sun room, talking and looking out the window at the backyard. It's a beautiful fall day and the leaves on the trees are brilliant red, orange and purple. We see Hitag sleeping in his favorite spot under a tree at the corner of the yard, with Poke right next to him. Hitag is 15 years old, which is quite elderly for a dog. In the last few months, his arthritis has gotten much worse and he can barely walk. Most of the time he spends sleeping right where he is now. My parents tell us that they'll take him to the vet tomorrow if he doesn't get up.

"How are you doing, old pal?" Poke said to Hitag.

"Not so good, Poke. I'm in bad pain. All my functions are shutting down and I'm dying. I can feel the earth calling my body to return. After I die, what will happen to me,

Poke?"

"That's a hard question my dear friend. I don't think even Sammy knows the answer to that and he knows practically everything. It's all part of nature's way. All your pain will disappear and you will become one with the earth. The grass above you will be greener and the nearby flowers will grow brighter. You'll be completely at peace."

"I love where I am now. I don't want to go to the vet. Can I stay here?"

"I'll ask Sammy to bury you right here. When the grass gets real green, I'll eat some of it and you'll be part of me. We'll be together forever."

"That makes me feel good. I'll miss you, Sammy and Lilly but I feel content. I don't have the pain any more and I'm getting drowsy. Will you stay with me here for awhile, so we can talk some more?"

"As long as you want, my friend. As long as you want."

Hitag dies peacefully that night and as Poke relays his request, Sammy buries him in his favorite spot under the tree. The next spring the grass is extra green there and according to Poke it's delicious.

A few years later, Lilly and Sammy have a baby boy whom they name Jaxon and two years after that they have a daughter named Erin. This family is loo large for the condo so Sammy and his parents do the logical thing. They switch mortages and the family takes the house and Sammy's parents move into the condo. Unlike when Lilly and Sammy grew up, this family leads a normal existence. There are no Turtle Dogs and no extraordinary adventures. Even though Sammy and Poke try to teach them, Jaxon and Erin never master the art of thought waves. According to Poke, the children are too busy running around and playing to take the time to stop and talk to a pokey old turtle. Besides, they have each other and their friends to talk to and it takes some concentration to communicate in other ways.

Thirty five years later at the age of 65, Sammy dies in his sleep from a sudden and unexpected heart attack. He's buried in the cemetery a few blocks from their house. A month after he's buried, Lilly visits his gravesite. She's not completely surprised when she sees Poke sleeping on the grave, right below the tombstone.

"We lost him, Poke and I miss him terribly. I always thought we'd retire and grow old together. We had plans to travel and spend time with our grandchildren."

A tear swells up in Poke's eye and Lilly begins to cry too. She places Poke on her lap and gently strokes his head.

"I miss him too, Lilly. There never will be anyone else like him. I do get comfort lying here where I can smell his essence. The smells bring back memories of when we were together. When I close my eyes I can visualize all the great times we had."

"I envy you Poke. I wish I could smell him too. I want him to hold me and love me again, but I guess that will never be. I miss his kiss and his touch. This happened way too soon."

"I want him to talk to me again and scratch me behind the ear. Can I ever see him again? I think that there must be more than living a short time and dying. As great as you humans are, I have this feeling that there is a still higher power. Is that possible?"

"I believe that there is a God who lives in heaven. I believe that the souls of good people go there when they die. If anyone has a soul, then you do Poke. Even if you don't have a soul, I believe that there is an angel in heaven named Samuel who can come to Earth and instill you with one. When you die, your soul will go to heaven so you and Samuel will be together again."

"Thank you Lilly, I like that. What you said gives me great comfort. I may only be a turtle but sometimes I'm capable of deep thoughts. Will you be in heaven too, Lilly?"

"Yes, I think I will, Poke."

"Is there such a thing as turtle angels in heaven?"

"You're getting way beyond my capacity to answer, Poke. Let's make that one of our deep thoughts."

Lilly visits Sammy's grave every month and Poke is almost always there. For many years they talk and reminisce about their times with Sammy. During that time Poke gets this strange feeling that he has acquired a soul but he is never sure. Lilly lives for 30 more years and Poke lives 40 more years, until he is 100.

If you visit Oklahoma City today, you will find a magnificent metropolis. Two places that you must visit there are the Cowboy and Western Culture Museum and the Botanical Gardens. The gardens are administered by the Oklahoma City Botanical Garden Society. The president of this Society is a striking, elegant, gray-haired lady named Lilly Johnson Templeton. The Gardens are in the center of the city and contain a complex system of waterways. The waterways empty into a river with a parallel river walk surrounded by shops, restaurants and theaters. You will see lots of ducks paddling in the waterways and below the surface you will see fish and turtles. If you look closely into the central pond, you will see a massive turtle, two feet wide, crawling along the bottom. This turtle is the granddaddy of them all and his name is Poke. At the edge of the pond is a brass placket on which is inscribed:

"Profound wisdom comes from the humblest creatures."

Chapter 11

An Angel on Earth

The angel, Solomon, stands alone before a tall bench-like desk, behind which are seated three stern white robed figures. In front of each figure is a small wooden placard with the names Peter, Paul and Mary neatly inscribed. It is not often that an angel feels nervous, but Solomon senses a shiver of anxiety as he surveys this august assembly.

Peter speaks first, "Angel Solomon, you have come before this committee of archangels to request instatement as a human on Earth. As you know this is very unusual and we take this quite seriously. This action could have consequences, both for yourself as well as the people on Earth. Tell us why you think we should honor such an extraordinary request."

"I have been a member of this Academy for 2,000 years and have been an angel for over 1,000 years. I believe I have been a model angel and have done everything expected and requested of me. I have served on committees, have attended seminars, have taught classes and have made many accurate measurements of the cosmos. But I'm beginning to burn out. I feel restless and I need stimulation and revitalization. I feel like I lack a creative spark and have not been able to perform original research. This is probably the reason that I have not been promoted to archangel. I have observed and studied the people on earth for a long time. I identify with them and would like to join them for one of their lifetimes. I believe that my soul contains an attribute of goodness and that I could make things a little better on Earth without upsetting the balance of nature. If you give me this sabbatical and allow this request, I think that I will come back refreshed and be a better contributing academician."

"You, of course, realized that life on Earth is not perfect," Paul intones. "Quite the contrary, life is very messy there. You could suffer from one or more of the four p's: pain, poverty, pestilence or puberty. You would have to endure rejection, sickness and itching. You might also experience hunger, depression and loneliness."

Mary adds, "you would have to contend with people around you smoking, getting drunk, getting drugged, cussing, coughing, sneezing, burping and farting. There will be pests like mosquitos, flies, ticks, chiggers, flees and lice. There will be constant noise, honking cars, loud music, barking dogs and scratching cats. You would have to put up with bodily functions like urinating, defecating, vomiting, puss, pimples and nose bleeds."

"Let's not forget dandruff, boogers, earwax, halitosis and diarrhea," Peter says. "Also, there's a lot of greed, hate and jealousy there. They have criminals, dictators and psychopaths. Besides all that, you will have to die, which may not be very pleasant. In short, it could be disgusting and awful. Why you want to do this is beyond me."

"To be fair, there are some beautiful things on Earth," Paul observes, "like mountains, lakes, flowers, birds and butterflies. Also, they have the best pasta in the universe and the chocolate isn't bad either. Besides that, I hear that the sex is really good."

Watching Solomon intently, Mary says, "you also have to realize that if we implant your soul into a human egg, you will lose essentially all your memory of the Academy. All that you have learned and experienced here for 2,000 years will be lost. Depending on your conduct on Earth, you may not be allowed to return to the Academy. If you do return, you will have to start from scratch as an apprentice. Also in the unlikely event that something goes wrong, your stay on Earth will be aborted. Do you agree to all these terms?"

Solomon nods his head, "I gladly agree and I relish the prospect of such a grand adventure. I want to experience the ups and downs of mortal life. I understand that the Academy is a wonderful place and we can reproduce qualities of life on Earth, but there is still something missing. I am ready to go."

"Are you sure you have thought this over carefully?" asks Peter.

"I am certain and I have most carefully considered all the consequences."

"Then," Paul says, hammering his gavel, "the three of us consent and grant your request."

And so it came to pass, Solomon the angel disappeared and was reduced to a tiny spark that contained his soul. The angel, Michael took possession of the spark and delivered it to the egg of a recipient on Earth.

A short time later, God happens on Mary taking a walk. "Hail Mary, how goes it with our friend Solomon on Earth?"

"Dear God, after much searching, Peter, Paul and I found a suitable recipient on the planet Earth. Her name is Sara Freeman and her husband is Mendel. They have been married for two years and they want to have a child. Michael implanted Solomon's soul into her egg that was ready to be fertilized. Last night Sarah and Mendel performed a mating ritual and we got a hit! They should have a child in nine months."

"Congratulations, Mary, we're going to have a baby! There will be an angel on Earth."

Nine months later in 1934, Sarah gives birth to a beautiful baby boy. He looks like a little cherub and they name him Robert. Robert is the joy of their lives. He is quite precocious from the very beginning. He starts walking at one year and talking at two. He talks in long sentences at three and is reading entire books at four. He has brown eyes and long curly blond hair. He looks like a perfect angel. He has an incredible sense of humor and is telling jokes at five. But Robert's greatest talent is in mathematics and figuring out how things work. He is constantly asking questions, many of which stump his parents.

When this happens, he goes to their encyclopedia set to find the answer. By the time he is six, he can add, subtract, multiply and divide and when he is seven he is doing algebra problems. Robert's blond hair turns brown and it soon becomes evident that he isn't a perfect angel after all. He has a mischievous streak, craves attention and loves practical jokes. On the other hand, he is affectionate and only plays practical jokes on people he likes or loves. If someone pulls a joke on him, he laughs as loud as everyone else.

When Robert is three, his parents mysteriously go to the hospital and bring home a tiny baby girl. They name her Francine but she is soon called Fran. After she grows old enough to understand such things, Fran has to endure a myriad of Robert's practical jokes. There are plastic spiders on her pillow and plastic lizards and snakes in her clothes drawers. The toilet paper in their shared bathroom goes suddenly missing or even worse it becomes glued together. Still worse, she might find glue in her panties. Then there is the whoopie cushion that he places under her desk chair pillow, which makes farting noise when she sits down. We won't even discuss what happens when she starts wearing a bra.

Beginning at about seven, Robert can not resist his burning desire to understand how things work. His first experiment is the family toaster. He takes it apart, examines everything in it and then tries to put it back together. Everything goes back except for one little piece, but the toaster never works well again. This goes on with other appliances until Sarah puts her foot down and tells Robert to keep his hands off her electric appliances, including the vacuum cleaner and washing machine. It helps a little when his parents and grandparents buy Robert an erector set, a chemistry set and an electric train for various birthdays and occasions.

Robert is always the smartest person in his school, including his teachers. In fact, his teachers have a devil of a time keeping his active mind challenged. His great genius really comes to the fore when he is twelve. He never has to do homework (boring, boring), so he has plenty of time to help out at his father's furniture store after school. Freeman's Fine Furniture is in Queens, New York. The family lives a few miles away. The store is not a big success, but it provides the family with a middle class standard of living. However, things change when Robert comes up with his idea.

"Dad, these wooden bed frames that we use really stink."

"What's the problem, Robert? Nobody's complained about our bed frames and it's what all the other furniture stores sell. People have been using these frames for a hundred years."

"That's the problem, Dad. This isn't a hundred years ago, this is 1946. We're in the modern age now. We should be using metal frames and not just any metal, we should be using light metal alloys."

"You're driving me crazy with your newfangled ideas. There is no material better than good old-fashioned wood. What in the world is light metal alloys?"

"Never mind that now, I'll explain it to you later. Anyway, look at the design I've drawn on this graph paper. Not only are these metal frames lighter and stronger than the old wooden frames, they're adjustable. See these bolts here? We can unscrew these bolts, adjust the width and length of the frames according to these spaced holes and then screw them back. Remember the problems we've had with nonstandard box spring and mattress sizes? Well, this solves that problem. Best of all, the cost of the metal and its fabrication are cheaper than for wood. Look at my figures. We could patent this and make them ourselves."

Mendel examines Robert's design plan and studies his math computations. He sits down slowly in one of his large armchairs and stares up at the ceiling. He shakes his head and mutters to himself, "what planet did this boy of mine come from?" The Freeman Bed Frame, as it is now called, is a huge success and sells all over the world.

In high school, Robert excels in math and science without working very hard. He does get an occasional B in English, History and Social Studies, because he does not consider them worth bothering with. In his spare time he has a small business fixing radio and television sets. He converts his family's basement into an electronics shop complete with tools, supplies, voltmeters and oscilloscopes. When a friend asks him how he can fix broken radios and TVs, without electronics training, he answers, "most of the time it's a burned out vacuum tube or wire that I can see just by looking. It's easy to replace the tube or solder in a new wire. Sometimes it's more challenging and that's when I really have fun. When this happens, I just pretend I'm an electron going through the various resistors, capacitors, inductors and cathode ray tubes. I then use my voltmeter or oscilloscope to test the circuits. Then I ask myself, what's stopping me from completing my circuit and reaching my destination? When I answer this question I can fix it."

When he is a junior in high school, Robert finds an old guitar in the upstairs attic. He tunes it and starts strumming and singing along. He teaches himself to play, begins to write songs and compose music. His favorites are bluegrass and folk music. Classical music doesn't seem to interest him. What really interests him are girls, but we'll wait until he goes to college to tell about that.

The logical university for Robert to attend is Cornell, because his friends are going there. It is in upstate New York, less than 200 miles from home, yet far enough away for him to feel independent. He double majors in math and physics and lives in the men's dormitory, Raleston Hall. He can think very fast and wherever he goes he is the smartest person in the room. He is tall, handsome and popular. He comes across as a brash, wise guy, and jokester. But beneath the brash veneer, he is a math and physics genius. During his junior and senior years at Cornell, he takes part in the Putnam Competition. This is a mathematics exam, taken by a few thousand of the best mathematics students in North America. The exam is a grueling two-day test of math skills. Students are given six hours on each of two days to solve twelve difficult, original problems. Most students solve only one or two of the problems and no one had ever attained a perfect score. In his junior year, Robert comes in second in the nation. In his senior year he takes first place with a perfect score.

But it isn't his genius at math and physics that makes Robert famous at Cornell. It is an incident that occurs during his sophomore year. Robert is taking a course in hydrodynamics, the study of the flow and forces of water. The course gives him the idea of studying the flow of water into and out of Raleston Hall. He first makes careful measurements of the size of the pipes in the building and their water pressure. He then designs diagrams of the water system and performs some complicated computations. Using this information, he comes to a remarkable conclusion. Raleston is three stories high. On each floor there are dorm rooms and a large central lavatory. Each lavatory has four showers, five toilets, five urinals and eight sinks. If all the showers, toilets, urinals and sinks in one of the lavatories were turned on full force at the same time, the water pressure would be so high that the main water pipe under the lawn in front of Raleston Hall would blow!

Robert takes his newly gained information to the Dean of the College of Sciences. He shows the dean his diagrams and computations. The Dean, who is a former chemistry professor understands what he is seeing. He thanks Robert for his diligent work and takes his papers. He assures Robert that he will consult with the University engineer and get back to him with their findings. A month later, the Dean summons Robert to his large book-lined paneled office.

"Mr. Freeman, I consulted with the University engineer. He studied your papers and told me to tell you that there is no problem. First, your calculations apply to only one lavatory in Raleston Hall and that dorm has three lavatories. Second, there is no way that every fixture in one of the lavatories would be running full force at the same time. Third, even if they were, the pipes are designed to withstand twice that water pressure."

"That may be true of brand new pipes, but these pipes are over 50 years old. In that amount of time, they have probably weakened considerably. Also, there are a lot of large trees in the vicinity and tree roots are known to compromise the integrity of water pipes. I think you should ask the engineer to investigate this situation personally. He should inspect the pipes at Raleston Hall and make sure they are up to code. For that matter, he should inspect the other dorms as well."

"Mr. Freeman, do you realize what the expense of digging up ground and cutting into walls to examine pipes would be? It would create a huge mess and cost thousands of dollars. We are on a very tight budget and there are better ways to spend our money. For example, I'm a strong advocate of scholarships for disadvantaged applicants. I have known our engineer for a long time and I trust his judgment. He's had years of experience in these kind of matters and he knows what he's talking about. I'm sorry, but I have to agree with him."

"Well, at least you should warn people about the possible danger of a water pipe break. Besides water damage, someone could be badly injured."

"I don't think that's necessary. My decision stands. Good day, Mr. Freeman."

The next day, Robert places a sign on the lawn in front of Raleston Hall that says "STAND CLEAR." Then he and nine of his buddies congregate at the second floor lavatory. They turn on all the showers and sinks at full blast. At Robert's signal, they flush the five toilets and five urinals simultaneously. Immediately, there is a loud explosion and water shoots out of the ground in front of the building in a gusher reminiscent of Old Faithful. The water main is turned off, the dorm is evacuated and it takes the engineer and his crew a week to clean up the mess. A red-faced Dean never takes any disciplinary action.

Meanwhile in Heaven, God calls Peter in for a meeting, "have you been keeping track of Freeman (a.k.a. Solomon)? I'm a little worried about him. He's not acting human. In fact, he's acting superhuman. I'm afraid something went wrong and he's retrieving knowledge from the Academy. Is it possible that his soul retained more memory than we expected it to?"

"I've been watching him closely, God," Peter responds. "He does have some special talents and he stands out but not in a spectacular way. I'm not overly concerned yet and I've taken his actions as youthful exuberance. I'm hoping he'll settle down to normality as he ages."

"I hope so. I don't want him to push too fast and upset our delicate balance. As you know, I'm always concerned about consistency. If it gets much worse, I may have to recall him."

And sure enough, almost as if he heard, Robert does settle down and he becomes more human. It all begins at a fraternity party soon after the Old Faithful incident. Robert arrives at the party with one of his buddies, Jon Hirsch. The party is loud and boisterous. There is a lot of animated conversation and many attractive coeds. People are singing fraternity songs around the piano and guzzling a strong vodka punch from a huge punch bowl. And then Robert sees her. She is seated on a couch, slim, blue-eyed and has long, curly, dark blond hair that falls in ringlets about her shoulders. Her perfect complexion is light, like a Dresden doll. Robert's eyes widen and his mouth falls open. His throat goes dry and for once in his life, he's speechless. After staring for a minute, he's barely able to blurt out to Jon, "Who is she? Do you know her?"

"Yes, I know her, she's in my English Literature class. Her name is Elaine."

"Jon, can you introduce me to her?"

Robert's knees go weak as they walk over to the young ladies seated on the couch. Jon breaks the ice by mentioning something about the English Lit class. He then introduces Robert to Elaine. She recognizes Robert from the famous Old Faithful incident when his picture was plastered over the front page of the school newspaper. He's tall, dashingly handsome and a local hero. He's also brilliant. They both fall in love immediately. The rest of the evening they only have eyes for each other. They talk, they sing songs and they dance. First a fast jitterbug and then a slow close-in dance. It feels so natural to be in each others' arms, they could have danced all night.

Up until then, Robert had been quite a ladies man and dated a lot of girls. After he meets Elaine, he knows that this is it. They take long walks together, they go to movies, they eat out at restaurants. Elaine opens a whole new world for Robert. She is also brilliant, but in different ways. She is an English major and knows a lot about literature. She is well-versed in history, social science and politics. Subjects that Robert couldn't be bothered with before. They discuss these subjects and talk about philosophy and astronomy. They go to plays, political rallies and concerts. She opens the world of classical music and he becomes enthralled with opera. He becomes softer, more reflective and quieter. He adores her. When she talks, he listens. She begins to call him Robbie. To everyone else, he's Robert, but to her he's Robbie.

Elaine and Robert are a couple for two and a half years and the night after they both graduate from Cornell he asks her to dinner at their favorite small French café. Robert prearranges for the waiter to bring out his guitar after dinner. Robert gazes into Elaine's eyes, strums his guitar and begins singing a song. The song consists of three stanzas:

You are the Earth beneath my feet,
You are my dark blue sky,
You are the air that I breathe,
You are the one who makes me fly,
You give me love, you give me pain,
You are Elaine, you are Elaine.

You are the gift that always gives,
You cause the smile that's on my face,
You are the flowers that I smell,
You are the thoughts that I chase,
You make the sun, you make the rain,
You are Elaine, you are Elaine.

You are the one who receives my songs,
You are the one who makes my heart sing,
You are the one who gives me the words,
You are the one who makes the bells ring,
You are melody, you are refrain,
You are Elaine, you are Elaine.

"That was beautiful, Robbie," Elaine croons. "How long did it take you to write it?"

"I've been thinking about you for a long time, but it only took me about twenty minutes to write it."

"I don't care, Robbie. It took my breath away and made my heart stop. I love it and I love you."

After leaving the café, they go back to Elaine's apartment, where her roommate is conveniently gone for the night. Robert asks her to marry him. She says yes and they share a long kiss. He turns her around and gently caresses her. He kisses her on the back of her neck and starts to slowly lift her thin silky dress.

"Robbie, we shouldn't be doing this until after we're married."

"I don't think a little practice will do any harm. Anyway, I'd like us to get married right away."

155

How can she resist? She gives in and completely relaxes. Then they make love. An image of white marble temples flashes through Robbie's mind but soon passes. They both think, "Is this what heaven is like?"

"Do you want to try it from the other side?" Robert asks shyly.

"Oh Robbie, why not."

"Do you want to have a baby with me?"

"If he looks like you, yes. Oh my God, what if she's a girl?"

"If she looks like you, yes."

Elaine turns around and they do it again. It's more delicious than the first time. They laugh, moan and groan with abandon. This time takes longer and they finally collapse in utter ecstasy, satisfied and exhausted. They fall asleep in each others arms for the rest of the night.

Elaine and Robert get married in July and take a two week honeymoon in New Orleans. This is made possible by Mendel's success in selling bed frames. In August they move into the graduate student housing complex at Princeton University. Robert, being the genius that he is, has to go to graduate school at one of the top universities in the world. Elaine gets a job teaching English at the local high school and Robert is awarded a graduate research assistantship in the physics department at Princeton. Although Robert thoroughly enjoys mathematics, his passion for understanding how things work convinces him to study physics. Besides, theoretical physics is practically all mathematics anyway. It's just mathematics slanted toward applications in the real world. Robert soon meets the famous physicist, Archibald Wheeler, at the Institute for Advanced Study. They both have similar original and off–mainstream minds that complement each other beautifully. They spend hours together in deep discussions and arguments. The research pours out spontaneously and naturally.

Elaine and Robert share four idyllic years at Princeton, learning, experiencing and growing together. Robert conducts research under Wheeler and is awarded a Ph.D. in physics at the end of their fourth year. His work is later recognized internationally and is known as the Freeman Fusion Field Theory.

Next stop is the California Institute of Technology where Robert gets a position as assistant professor in the physics department. Elaine still teaches English, but she yearns to have a family and settle down as a full time mom. Robert likes the idea of being a father as well. He has mixed ratings as a teacher at Caltech. On the one hand, he is a stimulating lecturer. He draws the students into his lectures and keeps their attention. He is very popular with good students. On the other hand, he does not have patience for average or mediocre students. He hates giving exams and hates, even more, grading homework and exams. He even goes to the extreme one semester of not giving any exams and awarding an A to every student in his class. He has a great dislike for administration and committee work. He hates the endless department and division meetings and frequently skips them. In short, he abhors pomp and circumstance and just wants to do physics.

Promotion and tenure at Caltech are based on three elements: research, teaching and administration/committee work. Luckily, Robert's research is going well, he's publishing lots of papers, he's invited to speak at many conferences and his international reputation is growing. After three years, his teaching and administration problems are overlooked. He is awarded tenure and promoted to associate professor. This is vary fast for Caltech but there were rumors that another university was interested in hiring him and Caltech does not want to lose such a valuable member. In fact, a similar situation occurs three years later when he is offered a position at another prestigious university. Caltech immediately promotes him to full professor.

Although life at home is happy, Elaine and Robert are disappointed that they cannot conceive a child. After a few years of trying they start reading books and taking classes on techniques of fertilization. It just makes love making seem stiff and controlled. Instead of a joy it makes sex seem like work. In desperation, Elaine sees a gynecologist and gets a prescription for fertility pills but that doesn't help either. They begin talking about adoption, but neither of them is ready for that.

About three years into his Caltech career, Robert's research hits a big breakthrough. Based on his thesis work, he derives an important equation called the fusion flow formula or F^3. This formula has the potential for developing a method to contain a nuclear fusion process. The great unsolved problem of nuclear fusion is the containment problem. A controlled nuclear fusion process can only be contained for a few thousandths of a second and if the process is to generate usable power, much longer times are necessary. The difficulty is that the materials become so hot that no known vessel can contain them. The F^3 formula describes magnetic fields with quantum fluctuations that can contain these materials for a long time period. This is the reason for the formula's enormous potential.

The mathematical physicist, Jean-Paul Marchand, occupies the Caltech office next to Robert's. Jean-Paul is a handsome, debonair Swiss physicist who got his Ph.D. from the University of Geneva under the direction of the great Swiss physicist, Josef Jauch. Jean-Paul is a few years older than Robert and was hired at Caltech a few years earlier. Soon after they meet, the two physicists become good friends.

"That F^3 you derived is incredible, Robert," Jean-Paul exclaims. "In order to get F^3, you had to think and visualize in four dimensions. How in the world did you do that?"

"To tell you the truth, Jean-Paul, I really don't know. It seems to already be in my mind. Every once in a while I get these four dimensional images in my head. I try to keep them there because they're so structured and beautiful, but they soon disappear. If I concentrate very hard, I can sometimes bring the images back. One time I was doing this and F^3 just popped into my head. It's as if I have some kind of memory of a previous life, but usually I can't access it. If I could, I have the feeling that I might discover even greater things."

Although Jean-Paul is a very good physicist, he is a little quirky and absent-minded. For one thing, he has a problem with keys. Every few days he forgets to bring the key to his office and he has to borrow the secretary's key to let himself in. After a while the secretary would accompany him to his office, because he usually forgets to give her back the master key. Then there's the time he leaves his car key in his locked car with the motor running. He rushes into Robert's office in a panic and asks him what to do. Robert calmly grabs a hanger from the hook on his door and goes back with Jean-Paul to his running parked car. After a considerable amount of juggling with the pulled apart hanger in the closed front car window, they are able to open the door. They turn off the motor and retrieve the key, averting the disaster of a burned out motor.

A few months later, another amusing incident occurs. Robert is sitting at his desk in deep concentration, probably thinking about four-dimensional space-time manifolds and path integrals. He is startled to hear a big commotion in Jean-Paul's office. He hears drawers opened and banged shut, books falling from shelves and long bouts of cursing. Robert rushes next door.

"What in the world is going on, Jean-Paul? What's the commotion all about?"

"I can't find my car keys and I've got to drive to an important appointment in an hour."

"Calm down, Jean-Paul, if worse comes to worse, I can drive you to your appointment. In the meantime, we can look for your keys."

They both search Jean-Paul's office. They find some things that Jean-Paul lost earlier, but not car keys.

"Remember the time you left your keys in your car? Why don't we go out to your car and check?"

Just in case, Robert grabs his trusty hanger and they go to Jean-Paul's locked car. They peer through the front window and there is no key in the ignition.

Jean-Paul looks around quizzically, "even if you drive me to my appointment, I still need my car keys. What do I do about that?" He pats his pockets to check again for his keys.

"Well, we could call the Ford dealer. They probably have your car record on file and they can bring you another key."

"That would take too long. I've got a better idea. I can call my neighbor. He's got a key to my apartment and I can tell him where I keep my spare car key. I'll just ask him to bring it here."

So the two start back to their offices with Robert in the lead. Jean-Paul hangs back, he is still peering into the car window. He strokes his chin in puzzlement thinking that perhaps he left the key on one of the car seats. Robert looks back to see if Jean-Paul is following him. He glances at the trunk of the car. There, plain as day, sticking out of the trunk lock are Jean-Paul's keys.

"Jean-Paul, look at your trunk!"

Jean-Paul's face turns red, he grabs his keys, jumps into his car and with barely a goodbye, drives off. He even makes it to his appointment and Robert can have the rest of the day in peace and quiet.

Six years into Robert's Caltech career, he and Elaine are still not able to conceive. They begin talking about adoption. They find that there is a considerable amount of red tape involved and the process could take six months to a year. Still, they start filling out papers. In the midst of this, Elaine complains to Robert about severe abdominal pains. On Robert's insistence she goes to her gynecologist, who examines her and takes blood and x-rays. A few days later the doctor calls and says that he would like to see them both as soon as possible. When they ask him for more details, he tells them that he would rather talk to them in person. For the first time in his life, Robert is frightened. Not frightened like a child who thinks she sees a monster in her closet, but frightened to his very core. If something happens to Elaine, he doesn't think he could handle it. Elaine is also frightened. Life until now has been so beautiful, she doesn't want it to ever end.

The wait in the gynecologist's reception room that afternoon seems to last for hours. They hold each other's hands very tight and reassure each other. "It's probably nothing" they both keep saying. The doctor ushers them into his office and asks them to be seated. Wild thoughts rush through Robert's mind. He thinks about an electron. According to quantum theory, before a position measurement is performed an electron is free to have any position it wants. After the measurement, the electron's position is determined within a specific range. Before the doctor speaks, everything is as wonderful as it has been. After he speaks, their lives might be abruptly changed with no return. Maybe he shouldn't let the doctor speak. But that wouldn't do any good.

As they would prefer, the gynecologist does not mince words. He tells them that he is very sorry, but it appears that Elaine has ovarian cancer. He says they should not be overly concerned at this point. The diagnosis is preliminary and his test may have given a false positive. He advises them to go to an oncologist for further tests. After further consultation, the oncologist confirms that Elaine has a fast growing strain of ovarian cancer and without treatments she has about six months to live. With radiation and some experimental drug therapy, this might be stretched to a year, if she is lucky.

The ride home is very quiet with each in their own thoughts. They go into their modest home near the Caltech campus, fall into each other's arms and cry. They kiss, embrace for a long time and cry again.

"You've got important work to do Robbie," Elaine says with her calm steady voice. "You can make a difference in the world. I don't want you to be burdened with a dying wife."

"You'll never be a burden to me, my darling. You're the love of my life. You *are* my life. I want to take care of you. I *will* take care of you. We'll get through this thing together. We're a team. This is going to be the best damn year of our lives."

And it is. Elaine quits her teaching job. Despite the pain killing drugs, she is active and strong for a few months. Robert comes home from work early every day. If he isn't teaching that day, he doesn't go to work at all. He barbecues and they laugh, tell jokes, horse around and wrestle. They giggle, embrace and make love.

Even as she becomes weaker from the radiation, drugs and disease, they don't care. They make love anyway. Robert neglects his research and his teaching suffers. The faculty and staff at Caltech are incredibly supportive. When Robert has to take Elaine to a radiation or therapy session, Jean-Paul or another faculty member teaches his class. They even make up his tests and proctor them. Above all, they grade exams and homework and decide the grades. The next semester, Robert is given a sabbatical with full pay so he can stay home to care for Elaine. After about eleven months, Elaine becomes very weak. She can barely lift her head and is bedridden. The doctors put her on a heavy dose of morphine and tell Robert that the end is near.

A few nights later, Elaine becomes delirious and Robert tells her he has to take her to the hospital. Until that moment, Robert felt he could do anything, but now he feels helpless. This is the most important person in his life and there's nothing he can do. As they slowly pack up a few things, she glances around their bedroom. This is the place that they spent many joyous hours together and she knows she will probably never see it again. Then a thought crosses her mind. Could this have been a gift from God? Could I have been married to an angel? But before she can say anything to Robert, the thought quickly vanishes.

After a few days in the hospital, her condition worsens. The morphine cuts the pain but she can only speak in a whisper.

"Robbie, this place is awful. The lights are always on. There's constant noise at the nurse's station. They keep disturbing me with shots and pills and taking my temperature and blood pressure. I can't stand all these monitors, wires and tubes in me. I don't want to die here."

"You're right, Elaine. I'm taking you home."

Robert insists that she be released. After much arguing and discussion, they take out the tubes and check her out. Robert drives her home, carries her to their bedroom and gently tucks her into bed. She is very frail and thin and she lost her hair from the treatments, but she is still beautiful.

"Robbie, I'm not ready for this."

"I'm not ready either, darling. Maybe you'll be a little better tomorrow."

"I don't think so. I can barely breath and I feel myself going. Will we ever be together again, Robbie?"

"I don't know where they're coming from but I have these visions of us together. We're wearing white robes. So I'm sure we will be together again, darling. I'm sure we will."

"Robbie, would you sing that song that you wrote for me again?"

Robert goes to the closet, pulls out his guitar and sits on the bed very close to Elaine. He strums a few notes and begins to sing:

"You are the Earth beneath my feet,

$$\vdots$$

Halfway through the song, he hears Elaine gasping for breath. He sets down his guitar and holds her tight. Elaine takes one last breath, closes her eyes and dies in Robert's arms. Robert cries uncontrollably and doesn't notice the little spark rising through the ceiling and into the night sky. He cries for what seems like hours. He pulls himself together for a while, kisses her lifeless lips and cries again. He wants to die too. Somehow, he feels that if he does, he will be with her sooner. There's a bottle of morphine pills in the medicine cabinet. He can swallow them all and put an end to it right now. But then he thinks, the adventure is not over. He can carry on for her. He has things to do. He can actually help people. He can help the world. That's the way she would have wanted it. He holds her tight and finally falls asleep for the rest of the night in her arms. Even though she is gone, her body seems to stay warm and he feels a little bit of contentment.

And help the world he does. After a few months of grieving and despair and after a few more months of feeling sorry for himself, Robert starts doing research again. This is largely made possible by the generosity and patience of his colleagues who realize his great potential. Beginning with his F^3 work, Robert is able to devise some experiments to achieve containment. Of course, this is only a paper and is far from being actually realized. Robert begins consulting with some Caltech experimental physicists and they are enthusiastic about setting up the experiments in their laboratory. Word gets out that Robert's research is taking off and he gets grants from the National Science Foundation and the Naval Research Institute. He even gets some grants from private and municipal power companies. Robert gets enough grants to release him from teaching responsibilities and hire assistants to help with his work. His experimentalist colleagues get tens of millions of dollars in grants to build their experiments. He's on top of the world again.

But there's a big catch. Robert despises security regulations. His work involves nuclear fusion for peace time power but nuclear fusion can also be used for bombs. So now his research is classified! He keeps saying, "I'm not interested in nuclear bombs. I'm just interested in basic research and how the nucleus works. I'm interested in harnessing nuclear power for peaceful use." Robert hates the word bombs. He hates killing and he hates war. But whatever he says doesn't help.

Robert is aghast when the Caltech security department tells him that his latest paper can't be published because it's classified. He believes in the free distribution of knowledge. He believes that security classifications stifle the distribution of knowledge and inhibits worldwide collaborations necessary to advance science and physics, in particular. After his second paper is classified "top secret" he exclaims, "what do those idiots in security know about which papers should be classified and which should not? Just because they've taken freshman physics, they think they know everything. I had one of those guys in a physics class and he was an ignoramus." To make things worse, the granting agencies start classifying his work. He retaliates by turning down grants, much to the chagrin of money conscious department chairpersons and deans who rely on the grants overhead to cushion their budgets. He also amuses himself by putting obscure scientific titles on his papers like "Covariant functional integrals of anhomomorphic spacetime trajectories." to throw security officials off. He is able to get a couple of papers past them this way.

To top things off, Robert starts noticing security officers patrolling the hallways outside his office. This is when his practical joke personality resurfaces. One of his favorites is to put on a large black hat that covers most of his face. When he sees a security officer approaching, he runs down the hall the other way and quickly turns a corner. He peers back around the corner and when the officer sees him he suddenly pulls back. Of course, the officer rushes to the corner but by then Freeman is around the next corner. This continues until Robert gets bored. Another time when Robert sees an officer approaching from a distance he quickly goes into a broom closet. When the security guy opens the door to investigate, Freeman jumps out from behind the brooms and yells, "Boo." Recognizing him as the famous Professor Freeman, the officer has no choice but to walk away. Then there's the time that Robert places a suspicious looking box in the hall outside his door. When a security officer deftly opens the lid, a coiled-spring clown jumps out practically to the ceiling. A day after this incident the department chairman, Bill Darn comes to Robert's office.

"Robert, you've got to stop messing around with the security officers. Especially that last one with the box. They almost brought out the bomb squad. These guys are deadly serious and they carry guns."

"I'm serious when I say that guns should not be allowed in this building. If you want to see me around here any longer, you will get these guys off my back and out of my sight."

"I sympathize with you, Robert, but I don't know if I can do anything about it. Anyway, I'll do my best."

After that there are fewer security officers in the building and, except for emergencies, none in the sight of Professor Robert Freeman. But this is all minor compared to what happens next. Robert is instructed to keep his office door locked when he isn't there and worst of all, he is issued a safe with a thumb print pad. The safe is bolted to the floor and he is told to keep his research papers locked in there when he isn't present. That is the last straw! Robert is in the habit of keeping research papers and notes piled high on his desk, in his book shelves and even on the floor. At times, when his fan is on, there are papers flying in the air and people have difficulty navigating the cluttered floor. He is not about to change now and he doesn't. In fact, the safe door is always open and he finds the safe to be a handy place to stack even more papers.

There are a few physics faculty members whom Robert does not like. This is mainly because they are stiff, inflexible and pompous. The physics professor he dislikes the most is Calvin Wilson. Wilson thinks he is the most important person in the world. He does good research, is a dedicated teacher and serves on many committees, some of which he chairs. He has been chairman of the tenure and promotions committee as long as anyone can remember. He spoke against Robert when he was up for tenure and promotion to associate professor because of Robert's teaching and administration record. It is rumored that he cast the only dissenting vote at the department meeting. Robert tells the story of when Elaine and he went to a party at Wilson's house. The party was given by Mrs. Wilson to celebrate Calvin's birthday. Well, Calvin never showed up. He was too busy working at his Caltech office on a very important paper that had an impending deadline. Everyone could see the embarrassment and disappointment in Mrs. Wilson's eyes.

Calvin Wilson also does classified research, but he is very meticulous. At the end of the day his door is locked, his desk is cleared and all his research papers are locked in his safe. By this time, some of Robert's brashness returns and his practical joke streak really fires up. He goes to Calvin's office and engages him in some small talk. This even leads to a discussion about physics. While they are talking, Robert leans against the back of the door and unlocks it. Later in the day, Robert goes to the faculty lounge where Calvin and others are drinking coffee. After Calvin leaves, he discretely purloins his coffee cup and deftly places it in his briefcase. Returning to his office, Robert takes out the cup and examines it carefully under a bright light. Sure enough, he finds a perfect thumb print. Robert dusts some fine graphite onto the print and lifts it off with a wide piece of transparent tape. He then transfers the print onto the thumb of a latex glove. That evening after Calvin leaves his office, Robert tries the door. It's still unlocked. Robert enters, closes the door and places his gloved thumb on the safe's pad. It opens. Robert places a piece of paper on top of the other papers in the safe. On his paper is written in large printed letters: R. F. WAS HERE. He locks the safe, turns the latch on the door to lock it and leaves.

Calvin's office is on the floor above Robert's. As Robert suspected, the next day there is a lot of clamor and commotion on that floor. There are security officers and campus police up and down the halls, talking to each other and into walkie-talkies. Calvin Wilson is shouting that he can't understand how this happened. He's saying that he's taken every precaution and there's no way such a thing could occur.

When Bill Darn sees Robert watching this spectacle in amusement, he winks and says with a smile, "do you know anything about a note saying R. F. was here?"

Robert replies, "beats me, it must be a different R. F. It could be Richard Feynman, he's known to do things like that." Security decides, since nothing is missing, they'll drop the whole thing. The situation gets more serious when other notes start popping up around the department, but that's another story.

A few years after Elaine's death, Robert begins enjoying the social scene. He becomes quite a ladies man. He goes to parties and bars and picks up women. He takes them home for one-night stands. It's as though he's looking for something that he never finds. After a few years, he tires of this kind of life and decides to settle down. He remarries a nice woman named Arlene Popper and their marriage is good but it's not quite the same. She is not Elaine and he misses Elaine terribly. Even with this sadness and his problems with security, his research in fusion physics continues unabated.

One afternoon, Robert receives a phone call in his office, "we did it, we achieved containment! Come to the lounge to celebrate."

When he arrives at the lounge there are a bunch of physicists jumping up and down like children. They are popping Champaign bottles and glasses of Champaign are being passed around. One of the experimentalists that Robert is consulting with raises his glass and toasts, "This morning, we maintained a nuclear fusion containment for two seconds! This is a monumental breakthrough. With more work, we are confident that we will achieve containment for much longer periods of time. This is the beginning of a new era. We are at the threshold of attaining a cheap, reliable, clean, safe and almost unlimited source of energy. This will free mankind from its dependence on fossil fuels and give us the ability to generate enough power for all our needs. None of this would be possible without the pioneering theoretical work of Robert Freeman. Professor Freeman, I toast you."

Robert and a small group of his experimentalist colleagues soon become famous. Laboratories all over the world reproduce their experiments and carry them further. But there are serious engineering obstacles blocking the path toward an economical and practical method for generating nuclear fusion power. At this time the methods are just too expensive. Nevertheless, progress is being made and the time will come.

Robert continues his research on nuclear fusion but he is slowing down a bit. Also, his interests are expanding. He is doing work on the physics of liquid helium and quantum computation. Besides that, he is devoting more time to teaching and lecturing. Caltech asks him to design and teach a new quantum mechanics course and he accepts enthusiastically. He always thought that there was a better way to teach quantum mechanics and he wants to do it right. The course is a little difficult, but is a big success and results in Robert publishing a three volume series of quantum mechanics texts. These books are well received throughout the world and are still being used for quantum mechanics instruction.

Ten years after the containment breakthrough, Robert receives a long distance call in the early morning. He always likes to stay up late and sleep late, so he's not happy with this early call.

"Yes, what is it?"

"Is this Professor Robert Freeman?"

"Yes, it is. What are you calling about?"

"This is Professor Sven Erickson from the Nobel Prize Committee in Stockholm, Sweden."

"Oh yes, Professor Erickson. I recently read your paper on the canonical commutation relations. It was very interesting. Do you want to talk about it?"

"I'm sorry but this is not a good time for that, we can talk about it later. I'm actually calling to inform you that you and two of your colleagues are to be awarded the Nobel Prize in physics this year. The award will not be officially announced until tomorrow, but I'm calling you early so you can be prepared for all the notoriety. The prize is $1.2 million, so each of you will have a $400,000 share. We have sent some acceptance papers by diplomatic courier for you to complete. They should also arrive tomorrow."

"This comes as a complete surprise to me. I didn't even know I was nominated. Thank you very much for the honor."

"We try to keep these things a secret until they're announced. Congratulations, Professor Freeman. Goodbye."

In one way Robert is excited and honored by this announcement. In another way, he doesn't relish all the attention and notoriety. He would have to talk to reporters and explain his research to laypeople. He would have to patiently receive endless congratulations and handshakes. He would have to attend boring ceremonies. It is going to be such a bother. His research and teaching would be interrupted for, who knows how long. He decides to talk to his friend Jean-Paul whom he trusts and respects.

"Jean-Paul, I have something important to discuss with you."

"Is it about another of your incredible ideas? Have you discovered another formula?"

"No, it's not about that. I've just been informed that I'm going to be awarded the Physics Nobel Prize."

"Wow, that's fantastic. That's the most wonderful thing that's ever happened. I'm proud of you, you certainly deserve it. Congratulations, let me shake your hand. I want to give you a big hug."

"Thank you, Jean-Paul. But I have a problem. You know how I hate pomp and circumstance. I'm going to have to endure months of publicity. I'm going to have to talk to reporters and go through interviews. I'm going to have to explain to a bunch of idiots what I'm doing and what my work is all about. I have my teaching and research to worry about. I don't have time for all this. Besides, I don't like prizes and I find this one to be political and arbitrary. There are a lot of deserving people who haven't gotten it and some jerks who have."

"Listen to me Robert. This is a prestigious and well-deserved honor. You've gotten prizes, awards and honors before. You know what to do. Just go through the motions and humor them. It will all be over before you realize it. Then you can go back to work and enjoy the past glory."

"There's a little technicality, I won't get the prize unless I sign the acceptance papers. This is my chance to protest all this nonsense. I'm not going to sign them."

"Robert, are you crazy? Oh, I know, this is one of your ridiculous jokes. You're pulling my leg aren't you?"

"It's no joke. I'm serious."

"Look, Robert, don't act like you're insane. Consider this carefully. If you think you'll get a lot of publicity from getting the Nobel Prize, just imagine what would happen if you don't accept it. That's never happened. You'll go down in history for being the only person who has not accepted the Nobel Prize. People will never forget it. Just think of the questions you'll have to answer. You'll be hounded the rest of your life. Accept the prize now and it will all be forgotten in a year. Most people don't remember old Nobel Prize winners. After all, there are hundreds of them."

Robert finds this argument convincing and he accepts the Nobel Prize. It isn't so bad and he enjoys talking to the king of Sweden who is very knowledgable about physics. He later says that the only thing good about getting the Nobel Prize was that it enables him to buy the ocean cottage that he always wanted. He is disappointed that Elaine isn't there to enjoy it with him. She would have been very pleased and very proud.

Chapter 12

Nuclear Disaster

After being awarded the Physics Nobel Prize, Robert Freeman continues with a long and distinguished career at Caltech. He and his wife, Arlene, never have children but they are cherished companions who travel together to meetings and conferences. They also enjoy sabbaticals in various foreign countries and frequent getaways to their ocean cottage. Robert retires from Caltech at age 76 and even though he no longer is active in research, he keeps up with the physics literature and gives lectures on popular science. He and Arlene welcome the serenity of their golden years. But six years into retirement, all hell breaks loose.

DENVER POST   **May 12, 2017**
NUCLEAR DISASTER OCCURS

Yesterday morning at 10:30 a.m., May 11, 2017, a strong tornado made a direct strike on the nuclear power plant in southeast Missouri. The tornado hit the plant with sustained winds of over 160 miles per hour. The roof of the plant collapsed and cracked the casement of the main nuclear containment vessel. Dangerous radiation was released into the atmosphere and the surrounding soil. Three workers at the plant were killed. The power plant has been shut down and nuclear engineers in protective suits are now investigating the damage. Executives from the Southeast Missouri Power Company, that runs the plant, assures us that everything is under control and the plant can be repaired. They state they are doing everything possible to ensure that the plant will safely return to operation. However, as a precaution, the area is sealed off and residents of nearby communities have been asked to evacuate. The President is appointing a Senate Committee to investigate the disaster. Their objective will be to determine why it happened and how to prevent such accidents from occurring in the future.

"I'm not only concerned about the radiation in the atmosphere that may spread to surrounding communities, but also the radiation that might contaminate the water. After all, the plant is only 60 miles from the Mississippi river, which is the main waterway

167

of the country. Contamination into nearby streams could reach the river and become a problem as far away as New Orleans. I hope they are taking water samples now, so they can control the situation at an early stage," said Gary Hartman of the prestigious firm Hartman Environmental, Denver, Colorado.

A week later, Robert receives a call at his ocean cottage.

"Hello, this is Robert Freeman."

"Hello Professor Freeman, this is John Watson of the United States Senate. You're a hard person to get hold of."

"Well, yes. My cell phone is turned off and I like to spend time at my cottage to get away for some peace and quiet."

"I'm sorry to bother you, Professor Freeman. Under ordinary circumstances, I wouldn't be breaking into your peace and quiet. But I'm calling about a matter of national emergency. I'm a member of a Senate Committee appointed by the President to investigate the Southeast Missouri Nuclear Power Plant accident. We are in the process of forming a panel of ten distinguished nuclear experts and environmental engineers to help with our investigations and report directly back to us. Many sources have recommended you for this panel. Would you be interested?"

"I've read about the accident and I'm very concerned. However, I've got to tell you that I am now retired and I'm getting along in age. Besides, my field is nuclear fusion and not nuclear fission. There's a big difference and this is a nuclear fission plant. I think you have the wrong man."

"We think you are the right man. Your experience and wisdom will more than compensate for any lack of youthful energy, so age is not a concern of ours. What is important to us, is that you are one of the world's experts in nuclear power. You are a Nobel laureate and your word would carry a lot of weight. Your presence would provide prestige to the panel and our committee. Being retired, you will have the time and freedom to devote to this national emergency. There is a sense of urgency here, and we need a complete, careful and thorough report from the panel. We would like to wrap this investigation up in about six months and then you'll be finished except for maybe a small amount of consulting if later questions come up. We will cover all of your travel and expenses, plus a generous consulting fee. Also, we will pay expenses for your wife to accompany you if you wish. I can't overemphasize the importance of this project. I have heard that you have a great desire to help the world and I know that you have participated in many worthy causes. Your country needs you and I appeal to your patriotic duty to come to our aid. The entire Senate committee and the President would be most grateful if you would accept this important challenge."

"You've made a very good case that I can't refuse. All right, count me in. But if I'm going to do this, I will need some things from you and I need them fast. I would like you to email me all the available information you have on the accident. I want the plans and blueprints of the plant. I want specifications and aerial photos of the site, both before and after the accident. I want the name of the company that built the plant. I want the names and phone numbers of the company's officers and also, of workers who were involved in the plant's construction. One thing you will have to know about me is that if I do something, I do it right."

"Thank you for agreeing to participate, Professor Freeman. Your country owes you a great debt of gratitude. Unfortunately, I'm not sure I can get you all the information you are requesting. Some of it is classified."

"Don't give me that classified shit. If you can't get me all I need, you can count me out. I'll send you my secure email address. I assume the United States Senate has secure lines. I'll expect to hear from you within the next two days. By the way, when it's completed, I would like a list of the other panel members, together with their credentials and phone numbers. Let me leave you with a friendly warning, Senator Watson. I do not like to be messed with and I do not like red tape!"

"I'll do my best, sir. My staff will get to your requests immediately. Goodbye, Professor Freeman."

Robert hangs up and thinks to himself, "maybe I was a little too strong with a U.S. Senator. Well, he probably expects that kind of behavior from a world renowned Nobel Prize winner." He then rushes into the kitchen where Arlene is preparing lunch. He's more excited than he's been for years. He gives her a big kiss and exclaims, "all hands on deck, Matie. We've got a mission to accomplish."

"Aye, aye, captain and what is this important mission?"

"We're going to investigate the Southeast Missouri Nuclear Power Plant disaster."

"I've been reading about that. It's been in the newspapers and on television news every day. Evidently the radiation is spreading and they're having a hard time containing it. What can I do to help?"

"Right now I need you to sit tight while I plan a strategy. In a week or so we might have to travel, so be ready."

Two days later, Robert receives a long email from Senator Watson containing blueprints and specifications. A day after that he receives a large packet from a special delivery courier. The packet is well-sealed and labeled confidential, top secret. It contains a huge amount of information, including names, addresses, phone numbers and aerial photos. There's even a dramatic photo of the plant during the tornado. He pores over the information for a week. He studies the photos with a magnifying glass and makes frequent calculations on his laptop computer. At the end of the week he gets another email containing a detailed list of the ten panel participants. Upon examining the list he notes that four of the panelists are diplomats who are political appointees and he mumbles, "what a bunch of bullshit."

One of the panelists is another physicist whom he knows but doesn't respect very much. Another panelist is a nuclear power plant manger whom he suspects might be biased. Two other panel members are a meteorologist and an environmental biologist who might be important later, but would probably not be useful for him now. Then his eyes fix on a name: Gary Hartman, Ph.D., environmental engineer, Hartman Environmental,

Denver Colorado. Hartman's credentials are very impressive and he's involved with many environmental causes, including global warming. Robert calls Dr. Hartman and makes an appointment to meet with him in four days at his Denver office.

Robert takes off his shoes and runs down to the beach to where Arlene is seated in a lounge chair by the ocean, reading a book.

"How would you like to go to Denver?" I've got business there during the week, but we can take the weekend off and go to the mountains. The Aspen Institute of Physics is there and Aspen has great hiking and restaurants. You might remember we were there 20 years ago for a conference. I'll fill you in on the business later."

"I remember, I love that place. They also have summer concerts. Let's go."

Arlene and Robert check into the Brown Palace Hotel in downtown Denver. The next morning, Robert leaves Arlene to shop and sightsee. He walks a few blocks to Hartman's office in a high-rise building. Robert and Hartman greet each other and quickly decide to dispense with the formalities and continue on a first name basis. There is almost instant chemistry between the two men.

"I was founder and president of this firm for a long time," Gary explains, "but now I'm retired and just do consulting and special projects. That's why I have this little office. It's cozy and it's all I need. I was originally a lawyer, but I had saved up some money and after my wife passed away, I went to the University of Colorado and got my Ph.D. in environmental engineering."

"How old was your wife when she died?"

"She was only 35. She died in the Big Thompson flood. You might have read about it a long time ago. More than 140 people drowned in that flood. Two of my children, Diane and Jimmy, also died. I guess I never really got over it. I'm still very sad when I think about it. I love mother nature, but she took most of my family away. Maybe it's that dichotomy that got me interested in learning more about our environment. I never remarried, but my daughter Emma and her husband Connor and I are very close. They have two children, Jeff and Madison, who are the joy of my life. They call me Papa and we spend a lot of time together."

"That's terrible about your wife and two children. I'm very sorry and I know how it feels. My wife, Elaine, died of cancer, when she was 33. She died in my arms and I still feel her presence. We had some wonderful years together and my heart still aches for her. I remarried a wonderful woman, Arlene, a few years after Elaine's death. I want you to meet her. She's here in Denver with me. I think she'll be a big help with our investigations. I love Arlene and we have a great time together, but it isn't quite the same as my relationship with Elaine was."

"Of course, I know you're a famous physicist and that you've won the Nobel Prize. I read a lot about you in the newspapers when that happened. I'm not as famous as you are, but we do have a lot in common besides the tragedies of our wives passing. We're both 82, we're both retired and we're both members of this investigative panel."

"Yes we are and that's why I'm here. I'm not that pleased about some of the other members of the panel. Four of them are political appointees and I know the other physicist, Norman Blackborn. Blackborn is known for being more interested in getting funding and grants, than doing real physics. This is an important job and I think the two of us can work together on this. I get the feeling that we can be good friends and trust each other."

"I have the same feeling. Getting to the job at hand, I've read in the latest reports that the situation is much worse than first described. The radiation has spread to surrounding towns. Cape Girardeau is threatened and might be evacuated. There are radiation readings in Carbondale and even as far away as St. Louis. Higher levels of radiation than usual have been reported in the Mississippi River. What is your take on the situation?"

"I'm worried about the radioactive contamination but I'm also concerned about some discrepancies I've found with the plant construction. I've studied the plant blueprints and aerial photos and something just doesn't add up. I think we need to go to Missouri to find out for ourselves. I also don't think we should wait to see what the panel decides to do. There's a lot of bureaucracy and inertia there and we can't afford to waste time."

"I agree and I would like to take the nuclear expert from our firm, Walter Dowd along to take some readings. He's a good man and I have confidence in him. My field is chemical and biological pollution and I'm not an expert in this nuclear stuff. I hate to bother you with this but could you briefly explain the difference between nuclear fission and nuclear fusion?"

"Well, all of our present nuclear power plants, and there are hundreds of them throughout the world, are based on nuclear fission. This is a very dirty process that involves knocking enriched heavy uranium atoms together. When this happens, the uranium atoms break up and this is called fission. When they break up, lead, a lighter form of uranium and a lot of radiation and heat are produced. The radiation, of course, is dangerous but the heat can be used to produce steam, which runs gas turbines that generate power. If the fission is done quickly, you have a bomb. But if it is done slowly, using control rods immersed in water, you have a power plant. If everything goes smoothly, the radiation dissipates into the water, which can be disposed of fairly safely. A problem is that the spent uranium is still radioactive and lasts for a thousand years, so it needs to be safely stored some place. Nuclear fusion is much cleaner and is not quite ready for commercial use, although fusion power plants are in the design stage. In nuclear fusion, light atoms like hydrogen are fused together. In this process, very little radiation is produced but a huge amount of heat is generated. If this is done in something like a tank of water, there would be so much heat that the water would boil off immediately. Thus, methods have to be devised to contain all that heat. This is what we're working on now. I hope that helps your understanding."

"That helps a lot. Let's get ready for our expedition to Missouri."

Gary and Robert meet every day for the rest of the week, plotting their Missouri strategy. Arlene, who is anxious to help, is asked to set up a meeting in St. Louis with the president of the Southeast Missouri Power Company and the CEO of the Continental Construction Company that built the nuclear power plant. In the evenings, Arlene, Gary,

Robert, Emma, and Connor spend time together visiting and eating. Some of their discussions get quite deep. They get along famously. On Friday evening they all go out to a restaurant for dinner and take a long walk along the mall in downtown Denver. Emma and Robert find themselves walking together.

"My Dad told me that you were with your wife when she died." Emma offers.

"That's right, she was very ill with ovarian cancer and we knew she didn't have long to live. I was singing a song that I had written for her and she died in my arms."

"Did you see anything when she died?"

"My eyes were too full of tears to see anything. Why do you ask?"

"When most of my family drowned in the river, I saw three sparks come out of the water. They circled around for a while and then flew up into the sky. Could they have anything to do with God or with heaven?"

"You're getting way out of my realm, Emma. I'm a physicist and I deal with the real and rational. These spiritual things are quite above me. I have given it a little thought though. It's not clear to me how I know this but I know that if there is a God, then he has something to do with neutrinos."

"I don't understand, Robert. What are neutrinos?"

"They are tiny particles that are everywhere. They're in you, they're in me, they're in otherwise empty outer space. They fly around at close to the speed of light and nothing can stop them. They contain most of the known mass of the universe. I also have some ideas about extra dimensions but it's a little complicated. We can talk about it when your Dad, Walter and I get back from St. Louis."

"I'd like that Robert, thanks. As you can tell I'm searching for answers and they're very hard to find."

"I know how it is. I've been searching for answers for almost 80 years now. Every once in a while, I get a flash of insight but not very often. I think it's easier to find answers in the physical world than in the spiritual one."

"Robert how did you get so smart? How did you accomplish all those incredible things?"

"I don't think it was all me. I think I had some kind of track to a higher plane. I also think that everyone has the ability to reach a higher level. There is more to a person than their body, mind and spirit. This is a case of a whole being more than the sum of its parts. To reach this higher level requires work, dedication and concentration. I think future generations will get better at it than mine has been. Perhaps your generation or your children's generation will reach higher in large numbers. We spoke earlier of God. Perhaps God is our ability to make our lives move to a higher place. Some people call this higher plane, salvation."

"Robert, you are a very wise man. I could talk to you forever."

"Emma, even though I have not known you long, I can tell you are destined for greatness. I know this because you have the guts to ask questions, really hard questions. Sometimes the questions themselves are more important than the answers. In any case, the road to knowledge begins with the right questions. I hope we'll be together again real soon."

Saturday and Sunday Arlene and Robert spend a glorious weekend in Aspen. The weather is beautiful and the mountain hiking is spectacular. After returning from a hike late Saturday afternoon, Robert announces, "dress up dear, I'm taking you for dinner, my treat. Besides, I've got something serious to discuss with you."

"Your treat? Does that mean this is a date? Something serious, that's a switch. Now you've really got my curiosity aroused. Give me an hour, I've got to take a shower first."

Robert takes Arlene to a charming little French restaurant that he noticed earlier, when they were walking around town. They are seated in a secluded corner where they can talk in private. The maître d' gives them a menu that they study for a few minutes.

A tall thin waiter with slicked down black hair and a thin, broad mustache approaches their table. "Welcome to La Petite Gourmet. May I have your order?"

Arlene asks Robert to order first. Robert is on a low cholesterol diet and tries to avoid red meats. He orders the cheapest selection on the menu.

"I'd like the grilled eggplant with mixed vegetables." Robert says.

"No, no, no. That's the worst dish on our menu," the waiter scolds. "I assure you, you won't like it. It's terrible. If I serve you that, I'll never forgive myself. We only have that for people who want to spend their money on wine. Please, Monsieur, order something else."

"Okay, Okay, I'll take the red snapper."

"Don't do it. That's the second worst dish on our menu. I tried it yesterday and it was awful. This isn't red snapper season and that fish has been sitting around in our frozen food locker for weeks. Besides that, the sauce is thick and spicy to disguise the fish smell. I beg you to order something else. But not the chicken, it's dry and chewy."

"Look here my good man, if these things are so bad, they shouldn't be on the menu. I give up. I'm afraid if I try to order something else, it will be the third worst dish on the menu. Just bring me whatever you recommend, but please no red meat. My wife is going to order next. I'm warning you, whatever she wants she gets, I don't argue with her and I don't expect you to. What she orders, you bring."

The waiter takes the rest of their order in silence and leaves in a huff.

"I'm glad that's over," Arlene sighs. "You really handled it well, dear. Now what is this serious business about?"

"As you know, our next stop is St. Louis," Robert explains. "Gary, Walter and I are going and I'd like you to stay in Denver. Emma and Connor told me that they would love for you to stay with them and I think that would be best. Their kids are off at college so they have plenty of room."

"But I want to be with you, Robert. I thought we were a team. We're the crew of a ship, remember? We work together. Besides, I think I'll be a lot of help."

"This trip is going to be strictly business. We're going to be working day and night on this project and there won't be any time for a vacation. But more important, we don't know these St. Louis guys and we don't know if they can be trusted. I have some suspicions about the plant construction and there might be trouble. For all we know, we might be dealing with the St. Louis Mafia here. I'm not saying there will be danger but I need to know that you're safe. If something happened to you, I wouldn't be able to stand it. Besides, you'll be a big help if you set up a headquarters at Emma and Connor's house. You have your laptop and I'll be sending you notes and files for backup from my laptop. We'll need you to make a lot of calls and your cell phone will be more secure than mine in St. Louis. We also need you to be in a safe place to do research for us on your computer."

"When you put it that way, what can I say. I'll miss you, darling. Call me every day, okay?"

The waiter brings their meal and it is quite good. After dinner and wine, Robert informs the waiter that they are in a bit of a hurry and asks for the check.

"I hope you enjoyed your dinner. May I ask where you are going next."

Robert is hesitant to answer because he's afraid that the waiter won't approve. He holds his breath and replies, "we are going to a concert in the Festival tent. They're playing Schubert."

"Excellent choice, enjoy the rest of your evening."

They heave a sigh of relief and leave. Sunday is another glorious day in Aspen. They drive back to Denver Monday morning. Monday afternoon, Gary, Robert and Walter fly to St. Louis and check into the Park Plaza Hotel.

Tuesday morning they take a cab to the downtown office of the president of the Southeast Missouri Power Company. The office is on the top floor of a 40-story skyscraper. Instead of solid walls, there are huge floor to ceiling glass windows with breathtaking views of the St. Louis Arch and the Mississippi River. One can see ornate bridges crossing the river and barges and cargo ships moving up and down the waterway. There is ample room in the office for Gary, Robert and Walter to sit in large comfortable black leather chairs facing a shining mahogany desk.

Behind the desk sits president Blanford Jennings. Jennings is a chipper, slightly overweight gentleman in his mid fifties. He's wearing a black pinstriped suit with a crisp white shirt and colorful silk tie. Seated next to him is the CEO of the Continental Construction Company, Allen Ramsky. Ramsky, about 65, is wearing a rather bland sports jacket with no tie. Standing behind them are two rugged looking individuals with strong builds who appear to be former construction workers. Jennings, with a large smile on his face, cheerfully introduces himself and Ramsky. They shake hands with Gary, Robert and Walter. Jennings, then introduces the men behind him as Clay Jackson and Bill Glickerson, who don't shake hands, but remain stoically at the back of the room. Jackson has a large bald head with a black eye patch over his left eye. He's wearing a heavy gray turtleneck shirt. Glickerson, who has a large scar on his neck, is wearing a plaid shirt and a tweedy brown sports jacket.

"Welcome to St. Louis gentlemen," Jennings says kindly, "I hope you have a pleasant stay here. We at Southeast Missouri Power apologize for this tragic accident. Although it was an act of nature that could not have been prevented, we want to make sure that nothing like this ever happens again. We want to find the underlying causes of this disaster as much as you do. We will cooperate with your investigation to the fullest extent possible. All of our resources are at your disposal and if there is anything that I or my company can do to help you, please let me know."

Ramsky nods his head in agreement. "I agree that we have to get to the truth of this matter and I echo Blanford's statement. We at Continental Construction will cooperate as much as we can. Continental Construction is an old St. Louis company, founded over 100 years ago by my grandfather, later run by my father and now here I am. We are proud of our past reputation and want to continue it into the future. We have constructed many buildings and monuments in St. Louis. In fact, if you drive through Forest Park, you will see some of our greatest works. We have a history of building power plants both nuclear and fossil fuel. We built the Southeast Missouri Nuclear Plant 45 years ago. I am now free to tell you that we have a bid submitted for construction of a four billion dollar nuclear fusion plant near the Missouri-Kansas border. That's nuclear *fusion*. You know what that means Professor Freeman. That plant could supply the power for half of Missouri **and** Kansas. Four billion dollars is a lot of money, so you can see why our reputation is important."

"I'm glad that you gentleman are being so cooperative," Gary says. "We will stay out of your way as much as possible so you can proceed with your cleanup work. My colleague, Walter Dowd and I would like to go down to the site to take some readings. Can that be arranged?"

Feeling relaxed, Jennings says, "no problem. Just tell me when you want to go and one of my company vans will pick you up at the Park Plaza and take you there. It's about a two-hour drive to the site. You can take unlimited readings for over a mile from the plant. From between 100 yards and a mile you are limited to one hour because of the radiation danger. Closer than 100 yards will require special permission and protective suits, together with a 30 minute limit. We have a camp set up there with trailers, where our technicians can suit up and take radiation-eliminating showers. If you and Dr. Dowd need anything else, just let me know, Dr. Hartman. By the way, our firm has a glass enclosed air-conditioned suite at the top of Busch Stadium. The next three nights, the St. Louis Cardinals will be playing home games there. We also serve the best meals in town at the suite. If you would like to go, just let me know and I'll send a car to pick you up."

"Thanks anyway, but we'll be too busy to go to baseball games," Robert says. "Now I'd like to tell you what I need. I would like to go into the building and inspect the reactor core."

Jennings voice takes on a more serious tone, "I'm sorry, but I'm afraid that's impossible Professor Freeman. Only experienced nuclear technicians wearing bulky highly protective suits are allowed in there and only for less than five minutes. What you are talking about is very dangerous. There's not much you can see in a couple of minutes and I can't accept the responsibility."

Undeterred, Robert says, "I think I could be called an experienced nuclear technician and I'll bet they have a suit that will fit me. Also, I absolve you of any responsibility, Mr. Jennings. What I would like from you, Mr. Ramsky are the following: the type of cement used in the nuclear core and in the ceiling, the specifications and type of steel used in the reinforcement rods, the grade of uranium used in the fuel rods and their carbon-steel ratio."

"I'm sorry Professor Freeman, but some of that information is classified," Ramsky explains. "I also resent the fact that you seem to be insinuating that we constructed the plant with inferior materials. I'll have you know that upon completion, this plant was inspected by members of the Atomic Energy Commission and it has been inspected every year since then. This plant was designed to withstand tornado winds of 200 miles per hour and why 160 miles per hour winds caused so much damage is beyond me. My opinion is that the plant has been totaled and will never be used again. The radiation danger is so bad that it should be sealed in concrete with it's grounds closed forever."

Now Robert is becoming impatient, "I've heard that classified crap before and I don't want to hear it again. If you don't cooperate fully, you'll have the U.S. Senate and the President of the United States breathing down your neck. If I don't have this information available when I return tomorrow morning, you'll receive a subpoena personally from a U.S. Marshall. And by the way, some news reporters have been talking to us. I don't know how they knew we were here, but they did. You wouldn't want us to say something that would give you bad publicity, would you? Good morning, gentlemen."

As the three get up to leave the room, the other four look at each other in stunned silence. After the door closes, there are two simultaneous conversations.

Ramsky leans into Jennings and whispers, "I don't like those guys and I don't like what they're doing. Blanford, you've got to think of something fast. Jackson and Glickerson, I want you to watch them. Watch them very closely."

Jennings eyes narrow, "perhaps some perks or cash would interest them. Everyone has their price."

"I don't think that would work," Ramsky says, with panic in his voice. "They don't seem to be that type."

The other conversation is with the team who has just departed the room:

Gary laughs quietly, "that was a great little story about the reporters. How did you think of that, Robert?"

"I don't know, it just came to me. I don't like to lie but it wasn't any worse than the bullshit they were feeding us."

Walter looks over his shoulder, "it was a nice touch and it got their attention. Anyway, I saw a guy in our hotel lobby who could have been a reporter."

Robert's thoughts were still on the conversation, "did you hear what Ramsky said about sealing the whole thing in concrete? Can you imagine how much concrete that would take and that asshole is in the concrete business! Who do you think Jennings would request for the job, for God's sake? To top things off, it would seal in the evidence forever. The U.S.

176

government would pay Ramsky to destroy evidence against him. It would be just perfect."

Their suite at the Park Plaza has a large living room that Robert calls the war room. They clear the desk and table to set out their papers and plans. Robert calls Arlene, who is eager to help. He tells her he is emailing her his notes and impressions of the meeting for backup. He also tells her that he is emailing her a list of names and phone numbers of past employees of Continental Construction. He is especially interested in people who worked there 45 years ago. He asks her to call as many on the list as she can and if she can find anyone in the St. Louis area, try to set up an appointment for Robert to meet with that individual on Wednesday, the next day. Arlene calls back that afternoon to tell Robert that she could only find one person who is still alive and lives in the area. His name is Richard Senture and he lives in East St. Louis, Illinois which is right across the Mississippi. The appointment is at 11:00 a.m., Wednesday morning.

Robert arrives at Richard's house by cab at the appointed time. The house is a small wooden shack in an old rundown neighborhood. Richard opens the door. He's a thin, but wide-framed, gray-haired man of about 75, who is hunched and appears frail.

"Good morning, Mr. Senture, thank you for meeting with me on such short notice. As my wife said on the phone, my name is Robert Freeman and I'm investigating the Southeast Missouri Power Plant accident."

"Yes, I've read about the accident. It's very tragic. We get some tornados around here, but that one was especially bad. It did a huge amount of damage. I've heard of you, haven't you won a prize or something? I'm not a well-educated man, but I read a lot. I like to keep up with what's going on. Anyway, I'll do anything I can to help you."

"You're right, I did win a prize. It was the Nobel Prize, but that happened a long time ago and most people have forgotten about it. I appreciate your willingness to help with my investigation. I have some questions to ask you and I need you to answer with complete honesty. I'm representing the U.S. Senate and any untruthfulness could result in a serious perjury charge that could lead to a long prison term."

"I'm a God fearing man, Professor Freeman and I believe in complete honesty. I go to church, I read the Bible and I know the ten commandments by heart. I follow God's teachings to the best of my ability."

"That's what I like to hear. Were you a worker for Continental Construction 46 years ago, when they built the Southeast Missouri Nuclear Power Plant?"

"Yes, I began working for them 48 years ago. I worked for the firm for 40 years and retired about eight years ago. When I first started Allen Ramsky's father, Saul, was CEO. Then I worked under Allen for a number of years. My wife died a few years ago and our only child lives in Oregon, so I'm kind of lonely now. As you can see from my house, I'm having a hard time making ends meet. All I get is $15,000 a year from Social Security and a measly $20,000 a year retirement from Continental Construction. Do you know what it's like to live on $35,000 a year? I spent 40 hard and loyal years with that company and this is what I'm left with. Every once in awhile, I see one of those fat cat executives in his big mansion, corporate jet and fancy car and I really get ticked."

"During the construction of the plant in question, did you notice any discrepancies or inconsistencies?"

"I don't have any hard evidence and can only tell you what I recall from a long time ago. I remember we were always under tight deadlines. If we didn't meet the deadlines, the company would lose certain bonuses. Of course, we workers never saw any bonuses, so I can't tell you for sure. I remember one time we didn't have enough cement but we had a lot of extra sand. It would have taken weeks to bring in the needed cement, so the project manager decided to substitute sand for cement. Another time, we didn't have the right size bolts. It would have taken months to fabricate larger and stronger bolts, so we used the ones we had. I remember the foreman bragging that the company saved $10,000 on that deal. In those days, $10,000 was a lot of money, it's like $100,000 now. Another time, I remember the foreman and project manager arguing about the thickness of some cement walls. They had to bring in old man Ramsky to settle that one. I never did find out what they decided. In general, they placed great emphasis on how the structure looked from the outside. The inside wasn't so important."

"Do you know of anything underhanded going on in the company during the time you worked there?"

"Again, I have nothing solid or any hard evidence, but I can tell you some things I heard from a secretary and you know secretaries have their thumbs on everything. On several occasions, she told me that the firm had given bribes to obtain contracts. The firm has made large political contributions and there are rumors that Ramsky has some government officials in his back pocket. The company has done a lot of work for Southeast Power and he and Jennings are real cozy."

"I have one last question, Mr. Senture. Do you know anyone else who I might contact who would have more information for me?"

"All my construction coworkers from that time have passed away. As I said, secretaries know everything, but most of them were older and they're probably dead by now, too. A couple were younger, but I heard that one died in a fire and another died of cancer. Something about asbestos in the building. Sorry I can't help you more."

"Thank you very much, Mr. Senture. You have been very helpful. You may get a call from the U.S. Senate to be a special witness. Of course, you would be compensated for any travel expenses. I assure you, that our conversation will be completely confidential except for my conveying your information to other investigators whom I trust completely."

"I don't know much about science, Professor Freeman, but I have read some books and know you are famous. It has been an honor to meet you."

"I know you didn't have to answer these questions, Mr. Senture and you gave me honest and direct answers. This was very brave and I respect that. During our brief meeting, I've come to like you and would like to express my thanks. I don't want to insult you by offering you money, but I'd like to give you this presidential medal that the U.S. Senate sent me for being on this panel."

"Thank you, Professor Freeman, I'll cherish it forever and I'll never forget you. God bless you, sir."

Looking down on the scene, God thinks to himself, "I like it when people do my work for me. See you next chapter, dear reader."

That evening Robert, Gary and Walter meet in their war room to discuss plans for the next day.

"Jennings is sending a van to pick us up early tomorrow morning for a trip to the site," Gary tells Robert. "He insists that Ramsky's security guys, Jackson and Glickerson, go along for our safety. I guess we can live with that as long as they don't get in our way."

"Okay," Robert answers. "I met with a former employee this morning and he confirmed all my misgivings. I believe they used inferior materials for the construction of that plant. Not only that, but I have made some careful measurements of aerial photos taken after the accident. According to the blueprint specifications, the main walls and ceiling of that plant should be constructed from steel reinforced concrete four feet thick. My measurements indicate that they are about three feet thick. These two facts alone could easily account for the disaster. I've got to go down into the core of that plant to make our case."

"You're scaring Gary and me, Robert," Walter says anxiously. "We're worried about you going down there. We don't think you should do it. Why can't we send a technician?"

"First of all," Robert says calmly, "I don't know who we can trust around here. Most of the technicians are employed by Southeast Missouri Power. Second, I'm the only one who knows what to look for. Five minutes is not much time and I know exactly what to do. Third, I haven't told anyone about this, not even Arlene, but I've been diagnosed with prostate cancer. The doctors tell me it's a slow growing strain and I've got about four years to live, maybe five with radiation and chemo. I told them I'd rather have quality than quantity of life, so I'll take the four. Anyway, what could happen? I might get a huge dose of radiation (not in the right place, I might add) and die from leukemia in four or five years. What difference would it make? Oh yes, I'm telling Arlene when we get back."

Gary rolls his eyes, "with logic like that, who can argue?"

Robert continues, "this is really big and complicated. I don't think we can handle all of it ourselves. We'll need some help, but we've got to keep this secret. I don't trust Ramsky and Jennings and don't want to put anyone else in danger. I can't call on any of my colleagues at Caltech because they have a direct link to me. However, I know some very competent people in the east who might be willing to help. I've met them at conferences but we've never written any joint papers. They are not in my research field, so no one knows we have a connection. One is Itamar Pitowsky at Princeton and two others are David Fowler and Charles Randall at the University of Massachusetts. Pitowski is an expert on nuclear fission and nuclear power. I can send him the information that I possess. He also has security clearance and access to government records. I can ask him to look more closely into the power plant situation. Fowler and Randall are mathematicians who are computer experts. They are now retired and very successful businessmen who know a lot about finance. I can ask them to hack into Ramsky's financial files. I know these guys are looking for new challenges and this might be right up their alley. We not only have to keep this discrete, but it's got to be legal. With our Senate connections, I'm sure we can clear this with Homeland Security."

"I have a friend who is a U.S. circuit judge," Gary states. "I can ask him for a court approved injunction to open files."

Robert's face lights up with hope, "that sounds good. Let's do it!"

They arrive at the site at 10:30 a.m. Thursday morning. The drab gray sky is made even darker by heavy black clouds that seem to just hang over the disaster site. The view looks like a picture from a war zone. A massive monolith of a building dominates the frame. Its monstrous proportions are lopsided because of a roof that's caved in on one side. There is practically no sound in the surrealistic gloom and doom atmosphere. No birds or insects are visible and one gets the feeling that if you look at the ground you couldn't even see an ant. The building has concrete parking lots on three sides and is entirely fenced in with an eight-foot high chain-link fence topped off with a foot of barbed wire. A perimeter of about 100 yards from this first fence is contained within a more temporary second bamboo fence. Three fire trucks can be seen moving in and out of the parking lot in one-hour shifts. The trucks are spewing large amounts of water from hoses into a huge hole on the top of the building. The water is being used to cool the fuel rods because the original water can be seen leaking out of cracks in the side of the building. Outside of the bamboo fence, tents are set up, together with about a dozen trailers. Some of the trailers are clearly used for bathrooms and sleeping and eating quarters. Three of the trailers are more official looking with Southeast Missouri Power Company logos on their sides, one trailer says Homeland Security and another says Atomic Energy Commission.

The van driver is instructed to go directly to the Atomic Energy Commission trailer. Robert, Gary and Walter present the credentials they received from the Senate Committee and are told they will have total support of the staff. Gary and Walter immediately begin taking readings using instruments they brought from Denver. They later don protective suits and take readings within a hundred yards of the desolate, brooding building. Steam rises from the building and surrounding area due to the evaporating hot water, giving it an eerie glow. In the meantime, Robert gets fitted into a huge lead-lined suit similar to what bomb squad officers use. This takes almost an hour even with the help of three men. He also gets equipped with a powerful flashlight and an encased radioactive protected camera with a strong flash.

Robert has to stand while he is driven in the high-cabbed van to the building. He is escorted to a heavy lead door and is told that all the electricity is off in the building. Close to the door, he will find a one-person construction elevator powered by a battery generator. He is again warned that he can stay for at most five minutes. It's dark, cold and misty inside the massive building. Robert quickly takes flash pictures of the gruesomely distorted ceiling with the large irregular hole. He enters the cage of the elevator, presses a button and is down to the lower floor in about ten seconds. The eerie light from the hole in the ceiling is no longer visible at this lower level and it is almost pitch dark. He turns on his flashlight and starts walking along a narrow corridor between the steel core of the reactor and the reinforced concrete casement surrounding it. He takes pictures of cracks in the core and casement. He can see water dripping and there is about two inches of water on the concrete floor. He suddenly slips and falls down. The suit is so bulky that it is very difficult to get up. For a second, Robert has visions of being stuck there for an hour before rescue workers can get to him and dying of radiation poisoning. But with a great effort he gets up and shines his flashlight down to see why he fell. He sees a shiny metal object on the floor below the water. It's a bolt about a foot long. He picks up the bolt and holds it with his thick lead-lined gloves. Robert looks at the timer on his wrist and notes that he's been there for five minutes. He takes one last picture and moves quickly to the elevator. He presses the button but the elevator doesn't move. He presses the button ten more times. The elevator is stuck! He gets out of the cage and frantically swings his flashlight around the walls. "There must be another way to get out of here," he thinks. He sees a sign on the wall with an arrow that says emergency stairs. He swings open a heavy lead door and climbs the stairs as fast as he can. He reaches the top and is out of the building after a total of nine minutes.

Atomic Energy Commission agents rush him back to their trailer. Robert immediately places the bolt on a steel table, takes off his helmet and asks them to decontaminate the bolt as much as possible. The agents take the bolt, strip Robert of his protective suit and place him in a decontamination shower. He showers for a good 40 minutes and then waits for Gary and Walter to return. During this time he talks to the agents to get their assessment of the situation. The ride back to St. Louis is fairly quiet with a small amount of idle conversation. That evening there are again two simultaneous meetings. The first meeting is in Blanford Jenning's office.

"What were those guys up to yesterday?" Ramsky asks Jackson and Glickerson, who had been keeping an eye on the visitors.

Jackson looks at his notes, "Hartman and Dowd went to the library and looked at old newspaper files and a bunch of maps. Then they went to their hotel room and didn't come out the rest of the day."

"After Freeman came here to get the information he wanted from you, he hopped into a cab and went someplace," Glickerson added. "I couldn't get to my car in time to follow him, so I don't know where he went."

Ramsky is impatient and anxious, "did you get the name of the cab or the license plate number so we can trace it?"

"No sir," Glickerson admits, "I didn't. They were too far away."

"Well, that takes the cake," Ramsky slams his hand down on the desk. "If you clowns don't do a better job than this, you're out on your asses. What about today, what did they do at the site?"

Jackson looks at his boss defensively. "The guards wouldn't let us closer than the bamboo fence, but we watched them with binoculars through slats in the fence. Hartman and Dowd were looking at instruments with lots of dials and buttons. They got real close to the building and did a lot of writing in notebooks. They acted very excited. Then they

181

went behind the building to that stream where the waste pipes empty. They were really excited there too."

"I watched Freeman go in and out of the plant," Glickerson offered. "He had a camera and when he came out he was carrying something. It looked like it might have been a bolt of some kind."

Ramsky shakes his head, "I don't like this at all. It doesn't sound good. Did they say anything on the ride back?"

"I asked them how everything went," Glickerson added. "They said they couldn't talk about it. They asked us how we liked working for the firm. We told them it was great, the firm has a good reputation, that everything is done professionally and honestly. All the employees are happy, the benefits are good and there's never a sign of any impropriety."

At this point Jennings jumps in trying to calm the situation. "I wouldn't worry about anything, Allen. We've got two guys on the panel who look out for our interests. We've got one of those diplomats and that physicist guy, Blackborn in our back pocket. They'll counteract anything Hartman and Freeman do. Besides, that panel will be tied up arguing and discussing for months. We'll have plenty of time to react if we have to."

"Just in case," Ramsky says, "I'd like you to talk to them again, Blanford. Maybe you can bring them around."

The other meeting is at the Park Plaza Hotel "war" room.

Robert takes out a small but heavy, lead-lined-steel case with an aluminum handle. "I want you two to see what's inside this case. You can look at it for 30 seconds, but you can't touch it because it's still a little radioactive."

"It looks like a large steel bolt," Walter says after peering into the case.

"It may look large," Robert replies, closing the case, "but the blueprint specifications call for a bolt twice as long and twice the diameter. There are no specs for a bolt this size. We've got enough to nail these guys! How did the readings go?"

Gary nods, "the readings are off the scales. They're much higher than previously reported. We've got a major national catastrophe here. We think the best thing to do is seal the whole plant off forever."

"That clinches it!" Robert exclaims. "We've got to move decisively and we've got to move fast. We can't wait for that cumbersome ten-person panel to get its act together. I hear they want to meet in ten days to start discussing the matter. I think Gary and I should fly to Washington immediately and make our case before the Senate Committee."

The next morning, the three colleagues meet with Jennings alone in his office because he insists on seeing them one last time.

Jennings leans casually on his desk. "I would like to congratulate you gentlemen for your great work. I hear that you have been working day and night and that you came up with some important findings yesterday. I will not ask you what you found because that would not be proper. However, I know you must be exhausted after that pace. I would like to offer you a little getaway at our company's expense. Our company jet is at your disposal. We could fly you to Denver to pick up your families and then we can fly you all to our Villa in Florida where you can enjoy some rest and relaxation by the ocean. You can stay as long as you like. How does that sound?"

"We can't accept a gift like that," Gary says, anger seeping into his voice. "We have to remain completely impartial during our investigation."

"I can certainly understand that," Jennings says with a tense smile, "but how about this? In six months, after the investigation is over, we would like the three of you to join our company as part-time consultants. Our consultant fees are very generous and you don't even have to be here, you can work from home. With all your expertise, we feel that you would be very valuable additions to our firm. Since this will happen after the end of your investigation, it won't interfere with your impartiality. We can work up contracts now if you would like."

Robert rises to leave, "I'm sorry," he says, "but we are very busy and have other consulting jobs to do. Thank you for meeting with us, Mr. Jennings, but we have more work before us. Good morning."

That afternoon Gary and Robert are off to Washington. A closed hearing before the Senate Committee is scheduled for five days later. They wanted to make it earlier but getting all the senators together is not an easy task. Gary and Robert check into the Washington Hilton. That evening, Jackson and Glickerson meet in Ramsky's office.

Ramsky looks more edgy than usual. He says, "my sources tell me that Hartman and Freeman are in Washington, D.C."

"We knew they checked out of the Park Plaza and took a cab to the airport, but we couldn't find out where they were going," Glickerson says apologetically. "What are they doing in Washington, anyway?"

Ramsky slams his fist against his desk. "You idiots. All you had to do was follow them and watch what plane they got on."

"But how would we get through airport security?" Jackson said defensively.

"I can't believe this," says Ramsky turning his back to them. "You guys are ignoramuses. Do I have to spell out everything? You could have bribed the ticket agent to find out where they went. Or one of you could buy a cheap ticket and go right through security. Anyway, this is really bad. My sources tell me they've scheduled a Senate committee hearing in five days. You two have got to go to Washington right now and stop them. The future of the company and, in particular, your futures depend on it. You've got to take care of this and you've got to do it right. Do you hear me? Take care of it!"

The next day, Jackson and Glickerson check into a small dingy hotel in D.C. They enter their room and stare at each other.

"Okay," Jackson says, dropping his overnight bag, "we have four days to stop them. What did Ramsky mean by 'Take care of it?'"

Glickerson sits on the edge of the bed, "we've worked for Ramsky for twenty years, you know what he means when he says 'Take care of it.' We've got to kill them."

"Kill them! Are you insane? You want to kill a Nobel Prize winner? They'll have the U.S. Marshals, the Secret Service, the FBI and the CIA after us. This is international stuff, they might even sic Interpol and the Swedish Guard on us."

"It's the Swiss Guard, you idiot. Anyway, they'll never figure out who did it. During the two hours you were staring out the airplane window, I've been working on a foolproof plan."

"Since when are you such a genius that you can be working on a foolproof plan? Look, I've beat up some people in my day, but I've never killed anyone. I'm not cut out for this. I can't do it."

"Since I've started working for Ramsky, I've been involved in three killings. It's hard at first but it's easy once you get used to it. Just think of it this way. Everyone has to die sometime. You're merely delivering them to heaven a little earlier."

"But I want to go to heaven and if I kill someone, I'll go to hell which is really a bad place."

"You won't necessarily go to hell you can be forgiven. After I kill someone, I confess my sin to my priest and he forgives me. I trust my priest and know he won't tell anyone. He's taken a solemn oath of silence."

"That makes me feel a little better. What killings were you involved in?"

"Before I started working with you, about ten years ago, I worked with Tom Mooney. If you think I'm mean, you should have seen Tom Mooney. He was the meanest person I'd ever met. He was the meanest man in town. About fifteen years ago, Ramsky got word from his mole in the Internal Revenue Service that one of his secretaries was squealing on him. A secretary, Evelyn Floret, accused his accountant of cooking the books and the firm of not paying enough income tax. She also had evidence of bribery to obtain contracts. She was going to present all this evidence the next day, and Ramsky told Mooney and me to stop her and that's exactly what we did. I remembered Evelyn from the office. She had a pretty face and said 'hi' to me when she saw me. I wasn't enthusiastic about following Ramsky's orders."

"How did you stop her? Did you kill her?"

"That night we went to her place. She lived alone in this little house with one of those kerosene heaters. We grabbed her and dragged her down to the basement. She screamed, kicked and cried. We violated her and abused her. First, I raped her. Mooney said it was his turn. He was really rough with her. She lost consciousness. I told Mooney I felt real bad. He told me to shake it off, that it would be easier next time. A tear dripped down my cheek, but I didn't let Mooney see it. We went upstairs, spread some kerosene around and torched the place. As we drove away, I could see the house going up in flames. All the cops found was a few chard bones and they declared it an accidental fire. Ramsky told us that he liked our work, we had done a great job. He gave us a good raise and a huge bonus."

"Except for the huge bonus, that didn't sound so good. When did it get easier?"

"About ten years ago, this weasel, Walley Jones, who had worked for Ramsky, turned state's witness and was going to testify before a grand jury. The grand jury was investigating corporate corruption. Ramsky told Mooney and me to take care of him. The problem was that there was a cop stationed at Walley's house guarding him 24 hours a day. One night, Mooney and I broke into the back door as quietly as we could while Walley and the cop were in the living room playing cards. The cop heard us and caught us in the kitchen. He shot Mooney and I shot him. Walley was crying and screaming and I pointed my gun at him and told him to shut up. I checked Mooney and the cop and they were both dead. This wasn't according to our original plan and I had to figure how to get away with this. Then it occurred to me, I'd pin the whole thing on Mooney. I put a bullet in Walley's head. As I told you, it had gotten easy. Then I wiped my prints off my gun, put it in Mooney's hand and took his gun. I wiped my prints off of everything I had touched and left.

It worked! The DA concluded that Mooney broke into the kitchen and shot Walley. The cop came in from the living room and he and Mooney shot each other. They also questioned Ramsky but he convinced them that Mooney had acted alone. It didn't hurt that Ramsky was slipping cash under the table to the DA. Ramsky was very proud of me. He gave me another raise and a big bonus. I figure that after I get a bonus from this job, I'll have enough to retire. Then I can spend more time with my wife and kid. I'm a real family man you know."

Jackson sighs, "all right, maybe I can do it. What's this great plan of yours?"

Glickerson's nervous energy fills the room, "Ramsky told us they're staying in a twentieth floor room at the Hilton. They're not going out and are calling room service for meals. All he knows is that they're doing a lot of planning and a lot of talking to their families in Denver. There are two FBI agents stationed outside their door at all times and there are hotel security guards prowling up and down the halls. We can't get them while they're in the hotel."

"So how are we going to get them, genius?"

"We'll get them on their way to the hearing. I have to admit this isn't really my plan, it's Ramsky's. But I worked out the details. Ramsky's source informed him that an FBI limo will pick them up at 9:00 a.m. to take them to the Capitol building. This source lives in Washington and knows the layout of the whole town. He says the only good way to go to the Capitol is down Pennsylvania Avenue, make a left on Madison and then continue to the Capitol. Well, there just happens to be a manhole cover in the middle of Madison. The night before, we'll grab a street maintenance truck, dress up like city employees and plant a bomb under the cover. The next morning, I'll station myself across the street with a remote control device. When the limo goes over the cover, I'll detonate the bomb and slowly walk away. It's foolproof."

"Bomb! Are you crazy? Do you know how to build a bomb? And now you want to kill FBI agents. They'll really hound us down for that. We're way over our heads here."

"No, I don't know how to make a bomb, but Ramsky knows a guy who does. If you think the FBI will hound you down, try to get out of this now and see what Ramsky does to you. He knows where to find you and I happen to know he'll cut off your cock and balls and watch you bleed out."

"Okay, okay, I get the idea. But when this is over, I want out."

At 9:00 a.m. on the appointed morning, Gary and Robert get into the back seat of a long black limo. They both carry briefcases full of papers and Robert clutches his heavy metal carrier case. On the lid of the case is a metal plate on which is engraved Professor Robert Freeman, Radioactive, DO NOT OPEN. An FBI agent is driving and another agent sits shotgun. As planned, Glickerson is stationed behind a tree across the street from a manhole cover on Madison Avenue. He doesn't notice a security camera on the bank building next door that is slowly panning the area. When the limo crosses over the cover, Glickerson presses a button on his remote. There is a loud explosion and the limo flies ten feet into the air and lands on the pavement engulfed in flames. Gary and Robert, in a state of shock, look through the smoke and flames and see the unconscious agents slumped over in the front seat.

Gary yells over the roaring fire, "the doors are stuck, I can't get them open."

"It's hopeless," Robert cries, "I figure the flames will hit the gas tank in ten seconds. Well, Gary, my dear friend, it's been a great run hasn't it?"

"It sure has, Robert. I love you."

The men hug for about five seconds. They hold each other very tight. Somehow it's easier if they die together. There is a deafening blast and they are together as one as their bodies are blown to smithereens. Debris flies in all directions. Only smoke, flames and rubble remain on the pavement, except, six feet away an intact heavily protected metal case lies calmly on the street. It has a few scratches on its sides, but on it's front there is a deep curved scratch that looks amazingly like a smile.

Luckily, no one else in the area is injured and in the ensuing chaos, no one notices the two tiny sparks rising into the smoke filled air. The sparks land in front of a serene marble temple and transform into white robed figures that look a lot like Gary and Robert when they were younger.

Waiting for them are four white robed apprentices named Ellen, Diane, Jimmy, and Elaine. They call out, "Gary," "Daddy," "Robbie." They rush to each other and embrace for a full earth day.

Chapter 13

God's Puzzle

The next morning, Jennings and Ramsky together with a muscular man with shiny black hair and a dark complexion meet at a secluded bench in Forest Park.

"Blanford," Ramsky says glancing around furtively, "I want you to meet my colleague Orviento Shantez from Mexico City. You can speak freely in front of him because I trust him explicitly. I've had many dealings in Mexico and Orviento has been my main contact there for over 20 years. I've brought him here to replace Jackson and Glickerson. He's smarter than both of those clowns combined and I know he'll do a good job for us. Although he's well known in Mexico City, nobody knows him in the states and that's a bonus. He's also a very skilled hit man. I've seen him take out a guy a mile away with a high-powered rifle and long-ranged scope. You should see what he does with an assault rifle and high-capacity magazine. He could probably whack twenty people in less than a minute. I've asked you to meet me out here in the park because this is a sensitive period and you can't tell who might be listening. For all I know, our offices are bugged."

Jennings clears his throat, "speaking of Jackson and Glickerson, where are they? Are you going to dispose of them?"

"I don't kill people unless it's absolutely necessary. They're on a plane to Paris as we speak. I thought it would be good for them to leave the country until things cool off."

"Paris is not exactly an obscure place for them to hide out. I can just see those assholes traipsing around Paris. They stick out like two sore thumbs. Everyone in France will know they're there. Couldn't you think of someplace more out of the way?"

"If you'll shut up and let me finish speaking, I'll get to that. After they arrive in Paris, they'll hop on a plane to Corsica. Corsica is a sparsely populated island in the Mediterranean Sea. Most people have only heard of it because Napoleon was born there. Anyway, I own a modest villa in a rugged mountainous region of Northern Corsica. The villa is very isolated except for a small village called Sisco about a mile away. It's so hidden that even most people from the village don't know it's there. The villa is listed under an assumed name and it cannot be traced to me. I paid those guys $200,000 each and told them to lay low for at least six months, maybe more. I stressed the importance of not calling any attention to themselves and they understand the seriousness of the situation. If they don't act right and get into any trouble, we'll have to get rid of them. Orviento here is the perfect man to do it. Besides, I wouldn't mind getting some of my dough back."

Orviento's eyes gleam with anticipation, "I'm all packed and ready for anything, Allen. Just give me the word and I'll take care of it."

"Wasn't that bombing a bit extreme?" Jennings asks. "Now the heat will really be on. The authorities won't rest until they find out who is responsible. I heard that half the D.C. police force and a lot of the FBI are assigned to this case. I have a bad feeling about this situation. I'm getting very nervous and I don't like it. Have you heard anything?"

Ramsky waves off his concern. "When the stakes are high, extreme methods are called for and the stakes are really high. I've got everything under control and there is no need to be nervous. Besides, I've got nothing but good news to report. My source high up in the FBI told me they have no leads for the bombing. They've combed the area and all they have is a blown up car and some body parts. Their only evidence is a silly bolt in a metal box and a few bomb fragments. They don't know what the bolt is good for. The fragments are so burned up that there are no discernible fingerprints. They're so desperate that they're looking at the surrounding buildings. They're even appealing to the public for leads. Of course, we've got to be very careful and vigilant in case something turns up. I think that's unlikely and we're in good shape. We can stay one step ahead of those idiots. I've done it all my life. Now here's the second piece of good news. The power plant has been declared a total loss and is shut down. It's off limits to everyone, so nobody can get in there to collect evidence. The government intends to encase the whole mess in cement. This is a really big project worth about two billion bucks. They are opening up a bidding to large construction firms. Since your firm owns the plant, Blanford, you will probably have some influence over who wins the bid. Needless to say, if Continental Construction wins, you will get your usual 10% of the profit making your share about fifty million. That's a lot of money. You see what I mean when I say the stakes are high?"

"I feel a lot better now, Allen. But what about the evidence that Freeman and Hartman were going to present to the Senate committee?"

"Their laptops, papers and files were completely destroyed in the explosion. I don't think we need to worry about that Senate committee. My people on the committee are going to bog them down in petty squabbling until the whole affair just fades away. Well, that's all we need to discuss for now. Let's walk over to the Chase Hotel and celebrate with some scotch. It's only two blocks away."

Orviento stands up tall and says, "let me tell you Allen and Blanford what a pleasure it is to work with gentlemen of your intelligence and caliber."

At about the same time that this meeting was taking place, another conversation relevant to our story is occurring between two people. It takes place in a spacious loft of a refurbished warehouse in the Bronx, New York. Irene Bender is a petite young woman in her late twenties. She's wearing tight jeans and a well-fitted white cotton halter-top.

Gilbert Hughes is middle aged with closely cropped, slightly graying hair. He's wearing black slacks and a red plaid shirt.

"Would you like an omelet this morning Gill? I'm making one for myself and you know they're my specialty."

Gilbert starts walking toward the counter where Irene is preparing breakfast and trips over his untied shoe laces. He catches himself on the counter before he hits the floor, "sure, that will be fine. Let me help you."

Irene breaks eggs into a bowl, "why do you have that large bandage on your thumb, Gill?"

"Oh, I cut myself yesterday evening when I was cutting carrots for dinner. Don't you remember?"

"Oh yes, I remember now. For someone as meticulous as you are, you really are clumsy. You're either tripping over your shoe laces, cutting yourself shaving, choking on your food or something else. And besides that you're continuously farting. We have to keep the overhead fan going or the window open to get rid of the stink. Also, you never remember what I tell you and you always get the wrong things on our grocery list. You're supposed to be this high powered electrochemical engineer and when you're around me you act like a klutz. I notice when you're working in your fancy laboratory downstairs, you wear a white uniform and all your expensive equipment is neatly arranged. The lab is spotless and you mix chemicals and solder wires with great precision. When you're here in the kitchen, you fart and can't hold a knife without cutting yourself. Can you explain this to me?"

Gilbert puts his arm around Irene's waist and says, "I guess I can explain it like this, sweetie. When I'm with you, I can relax and be completely at ease. I can feel your warmth and love. This is where I want to be. When I'm in the lab, I have to be very careful and precise. It's a dangerous place. I'm dealing with chemicals that could explode and I'm working with high voltages. It's stressful and I don't particularly enjoy it, but it's a living and it makes damn good money. My last project took about a week and it brought in $200,000. You must admit, that's not bad."

"It does bring in good money, but how do you live with yourself, my dear? You make bombs that kill people. Come to think of it, how do I live with myself? I guess I'm as guilty as you are. You talk about love and in your lab you make hate."

"I've never killed anyone. All I do is mix some chemicals and attach wires to electronics. After I make a device, I put it in a box and hand it to someone else. I don't know what they do with it and it's not my concern. My only concern is to make lots of money so we can live in style. You don't seem to complain when you buy your designer jeans, expensive watches, fancy jewelry and gourmet meals at high-end restaurants."

"I don't care that much if one of your devices kills a mobster, but what if a little kid is around? What do you say about that?"

"A lot more innocent people are killed by cars than by bombs. Do you blame the automakers for that? What about gun manufacturers? Do you blame them? A huge number of innocent people are killed by guns."

"Have you ever thought of doing something else? Making bombs is such a ridiculous profession."

"I'm good at this work and it's easy for me. I keep up with the latest technology and it's challenging. I'm one of the best at what I do."

"But what if we get caught? We could spend the rest of our lives in prison. You're supposed to protect me. What would you do if the cops or someone wanting revenge knocked on the door right now?"

"I've thought about that. First, it's unlikely. The nice thing about bombs is that they get blown to bits and don't leave any evidence. Second, we have an escape route. The front door is the only visible entrance to our loft. But as you know, we have a secret back door that leads downstairs to a tunnel to the warehouse next door. Third, in case of a real emergency, I have just installed a hinged latch right here below the counter. Lift the latch and you will see a red button. If you press this button, there will be a 30 second delay for us to get out our secret door. After 30 seconds, there will be a huge explosion and this whole place will be gone without a trace. Anyway, you think too much. Lighten up and get over here."

"I read in the paper this morning that a bomb went off in D.C. yesterday, killing four people including a Nobel prize winner. Could that be your work? Oooh, don't stop."

"Shut up, let me concentrate on what I'm doing here."

Time at the Academy is different from time on Earth. Time on Earth is linear. That is, it acts like points on a straight line. For any two different times a and b, one is always before the other; either $a < b$ or $b < a$. In this way, time proceeds in an orderly linear fashion. On the other hand, time at the academy is not one-dimensional, so it is not linear. For example, if you have two points a and b on a plane, there is no meaning for $a < b$, so time can act in strange ways. What seems like a day on Earth could seem like much longer in the Academy and vice versa.

Robert is quite busy in his new surroundings at the Academy. He has orientation and apprentice classes. Elaine and he talk, connect and reminisce. Robert spends a lot of time at an observation building watching what's happening on Earth. Of course, his main interest there centers around what is going on in specific locations in Denver, St. Louis and Washington D.C. In the observation building, there are banks of powerful supercomputers. These are quantum computers that are exponentially faster than computers on Earth. Also, since quantum bits are stored on individual atoms, their memory storage is trillions of times that of Earth computers. By entering the proper commands, one can observe any place in the cosmos. The reception is not always perfect, but by using neutrino beams, one can see through walls and hear with great precision. While Robert is intently watching a computer screen he is notified, via brain waves, that he has an entrance appointment with none other than God. An appointment like this is something one cannot break.

As Robert walks toward God's great hall, everything begins to look vaguely familiar. It's as if he'd been there before. But how could that be? Also, he starts to recall memories of experiences at the Academy but they are very incoherent and fuzzy. As he enters the hall, he sees two comfortable white leather chairs. Seated in one is a now familiar (to us at least) Santa Claus-like figure who beckons Robert to sit in the other chair.

"Welcome to the Academy, Robert. I know that everything is a little strange right now and that you will require some time to become oriented. But let me assure you that you will find the Academy a very stimulating place that will challenge your inquisitive mind. You will also find that you, or at least your soul, have been here before as an angel named Solomon. However, most of your memories of that period have been lost and cannot be retrieved. You are a lot different than Solomon but that's not important now. What is important is that you will have to start from scratch as a new apprentice so you can learn the ways of the Academy and its higher dimensions. We will have ample opportunities to discuss these subjects at later meetings. For now I would like to hear your thoughts and initial impressions. Even though I'm God, I cannot completely read your mind unless you share it with me."

"I am very glad to meet you, God. I must admit that I wasn't sure you existed but now there is no doubt. Although this all could be an illusion, it's too real for that. I also didn't realize that the Academy existed. It is clear to me that this is a much better place than Earth and this is where I belong. I have to apologize because I've been very preoccupied with observing events on Earth. I haven't yet participated in any of the fascinating seminars that are going on, but I hope to get to them soon. I also look forward to meeting some like-minded apprentices and angels so we can interact in stimulating discussions. Also there's my parents and my sister. I have so much to do."

"There is no need to apologize, Robert. You will have plenty of time to do whatever you want here. An eternity, in fact. You will find that except for rare circumstances, there is no sense of urgency here. But tell me what it is on Earth that you find so engrossing?"

"I really don't have to tell you because you're God and you know everything. But I guess it would do me a lot of good if I could get some things off my chest. When I ascended from Earth, I left some unfinished business. There are some very evil people in the world and they need to be brought to justice. These people are literally getting away with murder. Not only that, they're profiting enormously from their evil deeds. I'm not sure that the people of Earth will find out who they are. I don't know that they'll be properly punished. Can I briefly return to Earth to help straighten things out? As you know, I'm very good at fixing things. Or at least, can I send a message to advise them what to do?"

"Going back to Earth, even briefly, is impossible and sending a message is not a good idea. In your apprentice lessons and in seminars you will hear a lot about consistency. I'll just say a few words about it now. As a scientist, I'm sure you realize the importance of consistency. The laws of nature must be reliable, they must not contain contradictions. This is the underlying basis of the scientific method. Within certain parameter limits and boundary conditions, natural laws hold without exception. If you perform an experiment and the result does not comply with a natural law, then something must be wrong. Either the experiment was performed incorrectly or the natural law must be revised. Consistency must be maintained or everything will collapse. It is the foundation on which the universe is constructed. If you were to return to Earth, it would likely result in a contradiction. You are certainly aware that even the slightest cause will result in an effect. Would you like to be responsible for the destruction of the universe? I am the caretaker of the cosmos and I cannot allow that to happen. As far as justice is concerned, you are new here and your views of justice will undoubtedly change. You are used to thinking about justice relative to a few years, here at the Academy, we measure justice relative to eternity. I think you underestimate the forces of good on Earth. Besides, if these people do not meet justice on Earth, they will certainly meet it here. In the end, everything will even out. You also mentioned profit, but wealth is also only measured in a few years compared to eternity. At the Academy we have no use for material possessions so wealth is irrelevant."

"I understand what you are saying about consistency and justice, but I feel so helpless. If these evil mobsters are allowed to go free they will harm a lot more innocent people. We should be able to do something to protect those folks. Isn't there anything I can do?"

"I also feel the pain that you are experiencing. You have great compassion for what's happening on Earth and that is a very good quality. Consistency and compassion are what makes a universe possible. I don't always do this, but I'm willing to strike a compromise. I will give you a puzzle. If and when you solve the puzzle, you will be allowed to send a subtle message to Earth. The message must be short and not give any direct information. It must be in the form of a code that appears in someone's dream. People have strange dreams all the time and it shouldn't result in an inconsistency. I know because I've done this before."

"Thank you, God, I accept the challenge. What is the puzzle?"

"First the ground rules. You must not use a computer and you can only use your mind and senses. You will not be able to solve this puzzle immediately, but you can take it with you to solve at your leisure. Being God, I will know when you have solved the puzzle and you will immediately have the ability to transmit your message. Do you have any questions?"

"Can I work on the puzzle with my friend Gary? I usually work better if I can discuss things with someone else."

"That is permissible, but no one else. I certainly don't want you to line up a thousand angels and have them work on the puzzle simultaneously. This puzzle is known on Earth as 'Instant Insanity,' but most people have never seen it before. It goes like this. Here are four cubes. Each of the six faces of a cube is colored red, blue, white or green. The object is to make a straight stack of the four cubes one on top of the other, so that each of the four colors appears exactly once on each side of the stack."

"Okay, God, let me try it once in case I have any questions. I've stacked the four cubes. On this vertical side I have two whites, a red and a blue. I'll move one of the whites around until I get a green. Now I have green, white, red and blue on this side, so this side is great. But on this other side, I have red, white, blue, red, so I have to get rid of one of the reds to get a green without messing up the first side. I cannot only turn a cube around but I can turn it over on one of its six faces. Wow, this looks hard to solve using trial and error."

"There is little likelihood of solving this puzzle purely by chance because there are 41,472 possible combinations of the four cubes. Why? You can put the bottom cube down in many different ways, but by symmetry, only three of them are essentially different because there are three pairs of faces that are covered (one on the bottom, one on the top) leaving the other four faces exposed. Now that we've taken care of symmetry, the second cube may be put on top of Cube 1 on any of it's six faces and then Cube 2 may be rotated in four possible ways, giving $6 \times 4 = 24$ possibilities. The third and fourth cubes also have 24 possibilities, so there are $3 \times 24^3 = 41,472$ different combinations. Unless you are incredibly lucky, you need a system and that is the challenge of the puzzle. You have to find a system."

"Thank you, God. I'm anxious to find Gary so we can get to work. See you later, goodbye."

Robert finds Gary at the observation building, deeply engrossed at a computer screen.

"Hi Gary, I thought I'd find you here. What are you watching?"

"Hey Robert. I'm watching some heavenly pornography. You know I'm kidding, don't you? Pornography doesn't work here. Actually, I'm tuned in at the FBI office in D.C. They've got their two best agents, John Horton Conway and Ronald Graham, working on the case. Those guys are the two greatest problem solvers in the bureau. Listen to what they're saying."

Gary sits down next to his friend and watches the conversation unfolding there.

Conway is speaking, "the only definite piece of evidence we have is this metal box containing a radioactive bolt. According to the label, it belonged to Robert Freeman, but we don't know its significance."

"We need to find out why Freeman and Hartman were here in D.C.," Graham says, "and why someone wanted to kill them. I don't believe this was just some random bombing."

"Evidently, the bomb was placed under a manhole cover and remotely detonated. The lab is now trying to piece together the bomb fragments, but they're not making much progress. We need to carefully examine the area under the cover. Also, we've got to check to see if there are any witnesses or surveillance cameras in the surrounding vicinity."

"I'll round up some forensic experts to comb the area and get back with you this afternoon. In the meantime, you need to find out about Freeman, Hartman and that bolt."

"We've got the whole street blocked off. The traffic is a mess and the highway department is after us to reopen. This is a high profile case with the Nobel prize winner and all that. The press is hounding us for developments. Even the president is pushing us for action. We've got to come up with something fast."

Gary turns away from the computer screen and faces Robert. "It doesn't look like they have much yet. I wish there was something we could do."

"They should know why we were in D.C.," Robert says indignantly, "we were riding in an FBI limo for Pete's sake."

"Be patient, give them time. You know they've just started. So what have you been doing lately, Robert?"

"I had a very interesting conversation with none other than God, himself. I told him how frustrated I am with the developments on Earth. He told me that if I solve a puzzle, I can send a short coded message to Earth in the form of a dream. He said you could help me with the puzzle but no one else."

"If you could send a message, that might help break the case. I'm willing to give it a try. Tell me about the puzzle."

"God gave me these four colored cubes. The object is to stack the cubes so that each vertical side shows all four colors. Trial and error doesn't seem to work. We need a system. It will probably have to be a pretty clever system because, after all, this is God's puzzle."

"These are really beautiful cubes. They're made out of some kind of solid precious stones."

"Come on, Gary, I don't think that's relevant. We need to solve the puzzle now. We can admire the stones later. Wait a minute, I have an idea. Moving the cubes themselves around is very inefficient and takes a long time. I think we need to represent the 'unfolded' cubes on a piece of paper so we can see all the colors at once."

"That's a good idea, but how do we unfold a cube? I wouldn't want to break these beautiful cubes open. Besides, we'd have to put them back together later to see if we've solved the puzzle."

"Concentrate here, Gary. We kind of flatten the cube so we see all six faces. If we numbered the cubes 1,2,3,4 and use R,W,G,B to represent the four colors we get something like this (Figure 13.1)."

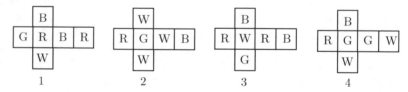

Figure 13.1

"That's great. I see from your diagram (Figure 13.1) that if I cut out one of the crosses and fold along the lines, I get a cube with the faces colored just like the real one. Hey, now I've got an idea! I remember in college I took a course called operations research. This course showed us how to use mathematics to solve real life problems. One of the things the course taught me is how to use multigraphs, which are like graphs, except they can have multiple edges and loops, to organize and manipulate data."

"That all sounds well and good. But how do we use a multigraph to describe the colors of our four cubes?"

"We could use vertices to represent the colors and join two vertices with an edge if they are on the opposite side of the cube. I'll draw it in Figure 13.2 (by the way, what does 13.2 mean?). We'll label an edge by the number of the cube it describes. For example, in Cube 1, green is on the left, red is in front, blue is right, red is back, blue on top and white on the bottom, say. It doesn't really matter where the colors are located, what's important is which color is opposite which. So for Cube 1 we have G opposite B, R opposite R and B opposite W. This gives us Figure 13.2(a). Notice that we have a loop from R to R. If we continue with the other cubes, we get Figure 13.2(b). Notice that we have multiple edges between G and B and between B and W."

"Hmm," Robert says thoughtfully, "I'm beginning to see what's going on here. Figure 13.2(b) tells us all the information about the colors on the cubes. What we have to do is extract information from Figure 13.2(b) about what colors to place on the left-right and front-back of each cube. If this works correctly, it will solve the puzzle."

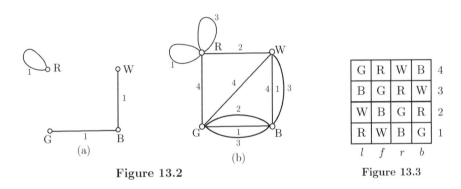

Figure 13.2   Figure 13.3

"It's still unclear how we proceed to extract this information," Gary scratches his chin. "I think we should look at some already solved puzzles that probably have nothing to do with our original puzzle to see what solutions look like. They're easy to make up. I'll draw an unfolded stack corresponding to a solved puzzle with the colors, cube numbers and left-right and front- back labeled as in Figure 13.3. In Figure 3.3, l, f, r, b stand for left, front, right and back, respectively."

Notice that this is some solved puzzle (not our own) because all four colors appear on each vertical column. That is, the colors in the l column are all different and the same is true for the f, r and b columns. Let's see what the opposites are on left-right and front-back. This is done in Figure 13.4."

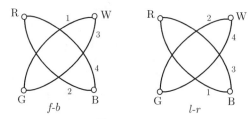

Figure 13.4

"Oh, okay," Robert says, "I think that helps. Let me make up another solved puzzle in Figure 13.5 and see what we get."

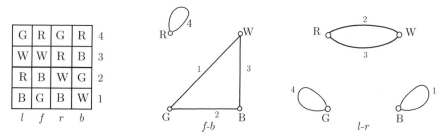

G	R	G	R	4
W	W	R	B	3
R	B	W	G	2
B	G	B	W	1
l	*f*	*r*	*b*	

Figure 13.5

Nodding excitedly, Gary continues, "in Figures 13.4 and 13.5, we see various kinds of *f-b* and *l-r* multigraphs that give solutions to these puzzles. Are other kinds of *f-b* and *l-r* multigraphs possible? Let's see. Since each color appears exactly once on the front, say, and exactly once on the back, they are precisely multigraphs with four vertices, all of whose vertices have degree 2. By degree 2 we mean that a vertex has two edges going to it, where a loop is considered to have two edges."

"We can probably draw all such multigraphs." Robert ponders, "we could have four loops (Figure 13.6(a)) or two loops (Figure 13.6(b)) or one loop (Figure 13.6(c)). That's all the ones with loops. There are only two other possibilities. Two double edges (Figure 13.6(d)) and a square (Figure 13.6(e)). These five multigraphs are the only possibilities. Any other such multigraph can be made into one of these by rearranging the vertices. For example, the multigraphs in Figure 13.4 can be made into the one in Figure 13.6(d) by interchanging G and R."

196

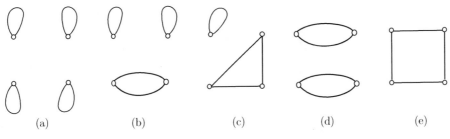

(a) (b) (c) (d) (e)

Figure 13.6

"Let's go back to our original multigraph in Figure 13.2(b)," Gary says. "In order to find a solution,we need to find two submultigraphs with no edges in common, of the type in Figure 13.6 (with each edge labeled differently) to serve as f-b and l-r multigraphs."

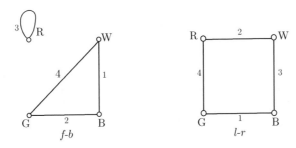

Figure 13.7

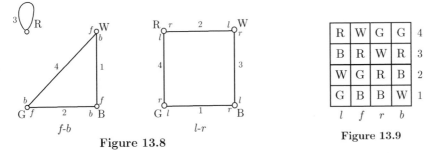

Figure 13.8

Figure 13.9

After a bit of thinking and a few tries, Robert and Gary come up with Figure 13.7.

197

"Yes, yes," Robert jumps in, "now we've got to designate which colors are front, back, left and right on each cube. They have to alternate because one can't have a color appearing twice in the front, say. One way of doing this is shown in Figure 13.8."

Gary slaps his friend affectionately, "we can now read off the solution from Figure 13.8. It's shown in Figure 13.9. Wow, we did it! Even God will be impressed at how quickly we accomplished this task."

Robert laughs, "Arlene is going to have a wild dream tonight. I'll need a couple of hours to figure out a coded message to her."

It's been three days since the bombing incident and Emma, Arlene and Conner are still in a state of shock, bewilderment and grief. Arlene is in no mood to go back to California and her Denver hosts graciously tell her that she can stay with them as long as she wishes. They have a short memorial service for their two loved ones but it is not very satisfying and there is no real closure. That night, after hours of fitful tossing and turning, Arlene finally falls asleep. In her dreams, she begins to feel a presence. The presence becomes more and more realistic. Soon it's quite vivid and it's Robert. He holds her tightly and it feels like he's really there. He tells her that he loves and misses her. It's so real that she even smells his characteristic essence. She feels his encompassing embrace and is overcome with ecstasy and pleasure. He tells her to listen carefully because he has an important message. After she wakes up she should look at his last email correspondence to her. She is to take the last seven words omit the e's, add i and form an anagram. He then asks her to repeat what he just said to make sure she understands. They then make love and it's wonderful. The last thing he says is that they will meet again very soon and be together forever. She has an overwhelming feeling of contentment and falls into a deep restful sleep. Arlene has never had a dream like that before.

The next morning, Arlene wakes up refreshed. After being miserable for the last four days she feels a lot better. At breakfast she tells Emma and Conner about the message part of her unusual dream.

"It's really a long shot," Emma says, "but I think we should try to crack this secret message. It won't do any harm to find out if there is anything to this. Who knows, this might be your subconscious speaking, Arlene. You might have come up with something important without realizing it. I've heard that a person's subconscious brain does a lot of thinking while they're asleep."

Nodding Arlene agrees, "all right, let's do it. I'm sorry to be so stupid, but what is an anagram anyway?"

"An anagram is a transposition of the letters in a phrase to form a different phrase." Conner goes to work, "for example, an anagram for SHE ATE A RUG is HEAR US GATE. They don't make much sense, but they're real sentences. For another example, a famous American author is STAN GUDDER. An anagram is an ancient English king EDGAR DUNST."

Feeling good to have a task, Arlene stands up, "let's clear this table and get to work. I'll retrieve Robert's last email to me."

198

Emma moves closer, "can you believe it. We're going to try to decipher a message from heaven."

"Okay," Arlene says, "the last sentence in the email reads, 'Remember darling, my greatest treasures in order of importance are: I love Arlene, a sky, ice creams.' When I read it four days ago, I thought it was touching, but rather strange. It didn't sound like Robert. But now we know there might have been a reason for it."

"Wait a minute," Emma blurts out, "if there was a reason for it, then why didn't he just come out and say it when he wrote it?"

Ignoring Emma, Conner continues working on the cipher, "the last seven words are: I love Arlene, a sky, ice creams. If we omit the e's and add an i we get the letters in alphabetical order:

A, A, A, C, C, I, I, I, K, L, L, M, N, O, R, R, S, S, V, Y"

"Yes, I see," Arlene says, "now we have to arrange these letters to get something sensible. I have no idea what to do. Should we give up?"

Conner shakes his head vigorously, "let's keep trying. We could see what words we can come up with from these letters. It's a lot like Scrabble. I see a lot of words. For a first pass, I find:

CRYSTAL, CYANOSIS, CYNIC, CYNICAL, CRISIS, SKI, LARVA, VISTA, SOCIAL,SOCIALLY, LIVRY, LILAC, YAM, MANY, MAN, MANLY, ISN'T, CRY, AVARY, IN, MALL, IS"

Emma catches their enthusiasm and moves in closer. "I can see some more:

LARSON, LASS, LASO, SON, YAM, LASSO, MILK, COMA, CAM, CALL, SOLAR, SILLY, SAIL, LARK, SMALL, MILL, MASS, ILL, LOAN, ROAM, SILICON, SILL"

A little dejectedly, Arlene continues, "this goes on and on. I can see:

SACK, KRILL, CRACK, VAIL, MAIL, SIN, KIN, ASS, MAY, KILL, SILK, CAN NILL, NACK, NICK, KNOLL, NAIL, RAIL, RAIN, COCK, ROCK, ILK, SILICA

Can we place any of these words together to get something that makes sense? Of course, we can't put some of the words together because we can only use each letter in our list once. For example, we can't use 'CRISIS IS' because we only have two S's. I don't see anything reasonable. This doesn't seem to be working. Is there a better approach?"

Thoughtfully, Emma suggests, "we could first try to figure out what kind of message Robert would send. It must be very urgent. I'll bet it has something to do with his murder. It might be some kind of clue. Let's play detective."

"If it has something to do with his murder," Conner speculates, "it might contain the name Ramsky. I'm sure that evil man is somehow responsible."

Arlene looks closer, "it does contain the name Ramsky. If we take Ramsky out we're left with the letters:

A, A, C, C, I, I, I, L, L, N, O, R, S, V"

"Okay," Conner continues, "the key now might be the letter V. That letter is a little uncommon. Also, we have two L's and two L's frequently go together. Does that help?"

"How about VILLA?" Emma says, "that works nicely. Let's see, the letters we have left are:

A,C, C, I, I, N, O, R, S"

Arlene nods in agreement to Emma's suggestion. "We have the word 'IN' to get RAMSKY VILLA IN and the letters we have left are:

A,C, C, I, O, R, S

These last letters must give a country or city. Who's good at geography?"

"I am," Conner admits, "and I've got it. It's Corsica! The message is:

RAMSKY VILLA IN CORSICA"

"That's it," Emma says excitedly, "Ramsky might be hiding something or someone in a villa in Corsica. This might be an important clue in the case. We've got to call the FBI and tell them."

"What will we say," Conner wonders, "when they ask us where we got the clue? The whole thing is so far fetched."

"You know how they tell you to inform them of even the smallest details." Arlene recalls, "even if they seem strange or insignificant. We've got to do it. Besides, I've got to get Robert's notes and files from the last month together and put them on a flash drive for the FBI. I'm sure they'll be important for the case and also for the Senate investigation. Emma, will you call the Denver Bureau of the FBI? I don't feel very good right now. In fact I've felt quit weak these last few days. It's probably all the stress and tension we've been through."

Emma gazes at Arlene with sympathy and concern. "I'll do it, Arlene. But after that, I think we should get you to a doctor."

"My first priority is to get the flash drive together." Arlene begins moving on to the next task. "That will take at least a day. Then we can talk about a doctor."

Emma immediately picks up the phone and calls the local office of the FBI.

"Hello, this is special agent Bill Dawn, FBI Denver Office. How can I be of assistance?"

"Hello Agent Dawn, this is Dr. Gary Hartman's daughter, Emma. Are you familiar with this case?"

"Yes, I am Ma'am. The entire national bureau has been alerted and briefed to the case. Since Dr. Hartman was from Denver, we are actively investigating the situation here. In fact, I'm glad you called because we were going to contact you very soon. Do you have any information that might be of use to us?"

"I have two things to tell you that might help your investigation. I probably shouldn't be discussing this over the phone, but I think it is very urgent. You need to act upon this information immediately. My husband, Conner, Arlene Freeman and I have discovered what might be a clue to the case. It's too complicated to tell you, how we made this discovery, but we can discuss this in person later."

"What is this urgent clue, Ma'am?"

"Are you familiar with the name Allen Ramsky, the CEO of Continental Construction Company?"

"Yes Ma'am, he's a person of interest in this investigation."

"We believe that Ramsky is hiding something or someone in a villa in Corsica. We think that whatever it is, it has a direct bearing to this case."

"Do you know who owns this villa or its specific location in Corsica. Corsica is a fairly large island with high rugged mountains. It wouldn't be easy to pinpoint an isolated villa there."

"I'm sorry, I've told you everything I know about this situation."

"Thank you, Ma'am. We'll look into your information immediately. What is the other thing you wanted to tell me, Ma'am?" Agent Dawn asks.

"Arlene Freeman is collecting all the notes and files that she has received from Professor Freeman during this past month. She will download them on a flash drive for you. They will be ready for the Bureau tomorrow afternoon."

"That will be fine, Ma'am. In the meantime, I'm sending an agent to your house, immediately. This is for your protection and safety, so please do not be alarmed. Your house will be under 24 hour surveillance. The agent will be stationed outside, so there should be no intrusion. Thank you for your assistance, Ma'am. We'll be in touch, goodbye."

A few hours later, Ramsky and Shantez meet at the parking lot of Continental Construction.

"I've got you scheduled on the next flight to Denver, Orviento. There are some new developments. I got word from my source in the FBI, that Hartman's daughter, Emma, has Freeman's computer files and she's going to turn them over to the Bureau tomorrow. There'll be a rental car ready for you at the Denver airport and here's Emma's address. Watch out because they have an agent stationed outside the house. Besides the agent she should be alone in their house with her husband, Conner. I want you to get all the copies of the files and I don't want you to leave any witnesses. Is everything clear?"

"Yes sir, I'll take care of everything. What about Freeman's wife, Arlene?"

"I haven't heard anything about her for a week. I think she went back to California to make funeral arrangements. I can't emphasize how important this is. Our future well-being depends on your getting those files. Remember, there'll be a big bonus waiting for you when you return. Good luck."

Late that night, Shantez parks his car a few blocks from the designated address. He carefully checks his gun and attaches a silencer. He slowly approaches the house and examines the surrounding area. He sees a black unmarked car in front. There is a man in a dark suit in the driver's seat. Holding his gun behind him in his right hand, Shantez taps the driver's window with his left hand. The man, holding a gun in his lap rolls down the window and Shantez fires a bullet into his head. He adjusts the body so it is seated upright and rolls the window back up. Shantez then quickly walks up to the front door of the house. He takes a small kit containing some pointed tools from his pocket and picks the lock. Shantez quietly opens the door and walks in. Gun in hand, he approaches Emma and Conner working intently on a laptop on the dining room table.

Conner looks up startled by the intruder. "Hey, who are you? Are you an FBI agent? How did you get in here?"

"I am not an FBI agent," Shantez says with an evil grin. "In fact, the FBI agent is presently indisposed. It doesn't matter who I am or how I got in. The important thing is what I want. I'm going to ask you some questions. I'll know if you are lying and if you are, your wife is dead. Do you understand?"

"I understand. I'll do whatever you want if you don't harm my wife. What are the questions?"

"Are all of Freeman's files on this computer?"

"Yes, they are."

"Are there other files somewhere else?"

"No, we're working now to back them up on a flash drive, but we haven't done that yet."

"Is there anyone else in this house?"

"No, we're all alone."

"Good, now listen carefully. Close up the laptop. I'm taking it with me."

"You're not going to kill us are you?" Emma says anxiously.

Shantez points the gun at Conner's head and says, "I'm sorry it's not personal. I'm very good at what I do and this is just business. I get paid very well by my employer and he told me not to leave any witnesses."

To Shantez's back is the door to the kitchen where Arlene is preparing coffee. Even with the door almost closed, she can hear the entire conversation. She grabs a large kitchen knife. Her hand is shaking so badly she has to bring her other hand over to steady it. As Arlene slowly opens the door, she feels dizzy and her vision blurs. With the knife in both hands above her head, she quietly approaches Shantez from behind. Emma and Conner see her but have enough presence not to react. Arlene feels a wave of nausea and a sharp pain in her chest. Suddenly she makes a quiet gasp and can't breathe. Arlene faints and falls forward onto a startled Shantez who is about to pull the trigger. The knife lodges a few inches into the middle of his back. He drops his gun and screams out in pain. He reaches back with both hands and tries to pull the knife out. Blood spurts all over the hardwood floor. Shantez slips on the blood and falls to the floor on his back. The knife penetrates all the way and he lies motionless as Conner picks up the gun. Emma rushes to Arlene who is turning pale and grasping her chest.

Two days later, there is a lot of activity at the FBI office in D.C.

Agent Graham leans on Conway's desk. "Well John, things are really progressing in our case. Let's review what's happening."

"It turns out that the guys who planted the manhole bomb were pretty clumsy," Conway says, looking up from the file he's studying. "It was a plastic explosive bomb and it appears that one of them sneezed and knocked off a small piece of plastic that we found on the ground in the manhole. We got a fingerprint off the plastic fragment as well as DNA from the gooey sneeze contents. The DNA belongs to a small-time hoodlum with a record named Clay Jackson. The fingerprint belongs to an engineer named Gilbert Hughes. He used to be an army demolitions expert and he probably built the bomb. He's in New York and they're due to arrest him right about now. We sent in a SWAT team and they're alert to the fact that the place might be booby-trapped. We haven't found Jackson yet but there's a warrant out for his apprehension."

Glancing down at the file, Graham adds, "the computer record from the bank surveillance camera across the street shows the image of a man holding an electronic detonator. We have now identified him as another mobster with a record named Bill Glickerson. There's also a warrant out for his arrest."

"Now let's talk about the big shot," Conway says, flipping through the file, "the mastermind behind all of this. What a coincidence that Jackson and Glickerson are both employees of Allen Ramsky. And now we find that our dead assassin Orviento Shantez is also on Ramsky's payroll. We pursued that old saying 'follow the money' and discovered that Ramsky has a huge money laundering account with the Liberty Bank in Costa Rica. We subpoenaed the records and found that hundreds of thousands of dollars from that account recently fell into the hands of Jackson, Glickerson and, you guessed it, Gilbert Hughes. We also found that money is going to members of a Senate Committee, various politicians, judges, district attorneys, police officers and even FBI agents. Besides that, following a mysterious tip, we traced funds being funneled to a source in Corsica. We never would have found this without the tip, but through a labyrinth of contorted routes, these funds terminated in an isolated villa where we believe Jackson and Glickerson are hiding. Would you believe that a large amount of American dollars have turned up in the hands of a prostitute in Sisco, Corsica? We're now working on their arrest and extradition."

"There's on thing that puzzles me, John. How was the Bureau able to act so quickly and sort through Ramsky's money laundered account?"

"I didn't know about this but there were people in our agency who have been working on this case for a couple of weeks. Robert Freeman got two professors at the University of Massachusetts to hack into Ramsky's accounts. How this was done legally, I'm not completely sure. But it worked. Even though some of his assets and transactions were hidden, Ramsky needed an overall view of what was going on and this showed up in one of his accounts. Freeman also got a professor at Princeton to scientifically analyze the structural problems at the doomed power plant. That will be very useful for the Senate investigation."

"That does it. I think we have excellent cases against Ramsky for murder, bribery, perjury, fraud and government extortion. We also have evidence against his associate Blanford Jennings. I'm issuing warrants for their arrest. The Bureau did a good job on this, John."

"There's a lot of evil in the world, Ron."

"Yes there is, John. But some would say that in this world or in the next, there is justice."

Soon after Arlene arrives at the Academy she is met by Robert dressed, of course, in a white robe. She is as beautiful as ever and they embrace for a very long time.

"What happened to you at the end, my darling?"

"I guess I died of a heart attack. I had never pointed a knife at someone like that and I was a nervous wreck. I never killed anyone before, but I think he deserved it. My mind and body couldn't take the strain but it went fast and easy."

"Well, it's over now, my love. We did it, we beat the bad guys! Congratulations, you did a great job deciphering my message."

"I couldn't have done it without Emma and Conner's help. I must admit, your coded message was ingenious. But I have a question for you."

"Anything you ask dear, I will answer."

"You wrote that email to me before you died, of course. That email arrived way before you could have known about the villa in Corsica. How did you know about the future, when you were in the past? Or, put another way, is it possible that the email was sent from the future into the past?"

"Now those are good questions and I have two answers. The first is the standard, logical answer they will give on Earth. The whole thing is just a coincidence. It was an accident that the right letters came up in my email that I needed for my code. The second and correct answer concerns the structure of the cosmos. You may not completely understand this right now, but you will learn in the Academy that time is not linear. Because of that it is not clear what comes before and what comes after. Does that make sense?"

"No, but maybe it will later. I don't know if I ever will be able to understand such things. For now I have a more important question. I know that Elaine was your first love and some say the first is the best. Do you have room in your heart for me?"

"I have a world of room in my heart for both of you, my darling. But let me tell you a secret. There is a special place there for you and heaven is where you are. Come, let us explore heaven together." Hand in hand, they stroll into an enchanted clearing surrounded by dense woods on three sides. A small creek gurgles before them and multicolored butterflies twitter above a grove of wildflowers. They are amused to see a black, long haired Dachshund sitting near the stream next to a large turtle. The two animals appear to be conversing. Knowing that such a circumstance is impossible even in heaven, they share a long kiss and move on.

They feel free and young again. They even start skipping like two carefree teenagers. Robert in particular, forgets that he was once a famous physicist and all that deep physics stuff leaves his mind (or should we say memory bank). Then in the distance, at a far horizon, they see a small object. It attracts their attention and they watch it intently The object gets closer and begins to look like a plastic beach ball rolling along a path toward them. As the ball comes closer, they see that it is almost transparent and has a creamy white, translucent color. It's about a hundred feet away now and it's huge, maybe thirty feet in diameter. It gets closer and closer. They try to avoid it and run in the opposite direction. But it moves faster than they can run and starts bouncing up and down. The ball overtakes them and bounces right on top of them.

The next thing they know they are trapped inside. Our hapless and helpless couple is completely bewildered. The ball starts spinning and bouncing. The two trapped occupants are thrown into the air and find themselves bouncing off the interior walls and each other. They try to cling together but they get knocked apart when they hit a wall. This goes on for at least ten minutes. Loud music starts blaring and they tumble around for another ten minutes.

Arlene shouts, "this would be fun if I knew we could get out of here."

"Wee, what a wild ride," Robert squeals, "this is better than an amusement park. People pay a lot of money for a time like this."

The bouncing and music stop. They hear a voice coming from somewhere inside the ball. The voice has a deep male sound but with a playful tone. "Hello there people, my name is Localized Energy Sphere but you can call me Les. What's yours?"

Trying to catch his strength back from all the tumult, Robert replies: "She's Arlene and I'm Robert."

"What planet are you from?" Les asks.

Arlene giggles, still excited by the ride, "we're from planet Earth."

"That's a nice planet," Les remarks. "Now that I know, I can talk to you in Earthling terms. It feels good to have people inside of me. It's kind of sexy. Don't worry, I won't start digesting you yet."

"I think you're being very rude, Les," Arlene scolds. "You could have asked us if we wanted to join you like this."

Robert whispers to Arlene, "Let's break our way out."

They scratch, punch, push and pull at the ball's walls. They kick with their feet and butt with their heads to no avail. They transform themselves into pure energy and try to squeeze through the pores of the plastic-like, confining material but that doesn't work. Try as they may, nothing breaks their imprisonment.

"There's no use trying," Les snickers, "you can't get out unless I allow it. The harder you push or pull, the greater the resistance. It's like a spring. I have an impenetrable force field. It's called the strong nuclear force. If you want to keep attempting to escape, it's all right with me. I think it feels good."

Arlene sighs, "is there anything we can do to get you to release us?"

"That's a good question and I'll answer it. Yes, there is something you can do. You will remain imprisoned here for 1,000 years unless you solve three simple puzzles. But be careful, if you give me a wrong answer, you will have to wait a hundred years before you get a second try. If you don't get it on the second try, I grow spikes that can tear you to pieces."

Robert groans, "I can't believe this. Gary and I already solved God's puzzle. Arlene and her friends solved that crazy anagram. I know heaven is supposed to be a paradise. But now it has turned into a puzzle paradise."

"In a way, it is. There are thousands of spheres like me and each of us has our own personality. We also have our own sets of puzzles but there are always three. At any given time, you have a chance of one in 44,000 of encountering one of us. The only way to avoid us is to fly away at the speed of light. Unfortunately, you haven't learned how to do that yet. Of course, all three of my puzzles involve spheres. Are you ready for the first one?"

"Oh, all right. Shoot." Arlene says, taking Roberts hand.

"The planet Earth is an almost perfect sphere and its equator is a great circle on that sphere. Suppose we erect poles one foot high along the equator and pull a rope tight along the top of the poles. Exactly how much longer is the rope than the equator? Isn't that a great puzzle?"

"Can we ask for clarification of a puzzle?" Arlene wonders. "Can we ask you to repeat a puzzle? What about hints?"

"No clarifications, repeats, or hints; what do you think this is, a game show? I could repeat it in a hundred years if you would like. Now get to work."

Robert speaks to Arlene, "we've got to be careful and not give a wrong answer. As much as I love you, I don't think it would be very pleasant to spend 1,000 years together in these close quarters. In this carefree teenage mode we've taken, I've forgotten a lot of physics stuff and I don't remember the exact circumference of the equator. In fact, I don't think I ever knew it. I think it's about 25,000 miles but that's not exact. If we have a rope one foot above the equator for the long distance of 25,000 miles, I would guess that the rope is much longer. I wonder if we can use a computer."

"I wouldn't trust our luck asking that. Besides we don't seem to have a computer handy. I'm hoping that we don't need the exact circumference of the equator to solve this puzzle. Let's see. I recall from high school math that the circumference of a circle with radius R is $2\pi R$."

"You're brilliant, Arlene. That's the key. If R is the radius of the Earth in feet, then the circumference of the equator is $2\pi R$. The length of the rope in feet is the circumference of a circle with radius $R + 1$ which gives $2\pi(R + 1)$."

"Let me finish this. Even with my limited high school math, I think I can do it. The difference between the two circumferences is

$$2\pi(R + 1) - 2\pi R = 2\pi R + 2\pi - 2\pi R = 2\pi$$

That's the answer! It's amazing. The solution does not depend on the radius of the Earth R. It's also surprising that it is only 2π which is about 6.3 feet."

Les spins and bounces with glee. "Yeah! Yeah! You did it, you did it! Congratulations, you solved Puzzle 1 and in record time, I might add. This is so exciting. We're having such a good time. Here's Puzzle 2. A farmer on Earth grows spherically shaped watermelons. The watermelons are 99% water. The farmer ships one ton of watermelons to the market. Due to evaporation, when the melons arrive at the market, they are 98% water. What is the market weight of the watermelons? You must admit, this is another cool puzzle."

Robert smiles, "the melons were originally 99% water and they only lost one percent of their water when they arrived at the market so my first guess is that their market weight is little less than a ton. Could the answer be 0.99 tons? We've got to be careful, this might be a trick question. Do you have any ideas, dear?"

"We might not be able to work this out in our heads. I think we might need to make some computations using algebra. Let's take one watermelon whose original weight is W_1. We can write

$$W_1 = 0.99W_1 + 0.01W_1$$

where $0.99W_1$ is the weight of the water and $0.01W_1$ is the weight of the non-water part of the melon."

"You've done it again! You're a genius, my darling. If W_2 is the market weight of the same melon, then

$$W_2 = 0.98W_2 + 0.02W_2$$

where again $0.98W_2$ is the weight of the water and $0.02W_2$ is the weight of the non-water part. Now the important observation is that although the water evaporates, the non-water part stays the same. Hence, $0.01W_1 = 0.02W_2$. We then obtain

$$W_2 = \frac{0.01}{0.02}W_1 = \frac{1}{2}W_1$$

We conclude that the market weight is only one-half of the original weight. Therefore, the market weight of the original one ton of watermelons is one-half a ton. The poor farmer lost half the weight of his melons."

"Magnificent!" Les cheers, "you guys are great. You've solved Puzzle 2. Let's celebrate!"

Les bounces up very high and twirls around. The passengers tumble about, congratulating each other with laughter and fanfare.

"We have arrived at Puzzle 3. As you can see, I have placed five small dots at random on my spherical surface. Prove that you can draw a closed hemisphere on my surface that contains at least four of the dots."

"I have no feeling at all for this puzzle, Robert," Arlene says doubtfully. "I don't even know what a closed hemisphere is. I'm afraid you'll have to solve this one yourself. I'm confident you can do it. If not, we'll have a hundred years to think about it."

"Luckily, I still remember some spherical geometry and I used to be very good at it. First of all, a closed hemisphere is half a sphere that includes its boundary circle. Now, two different points on a sphere have a unique great circle going through them. It's analogous to two points on a plane determining a unique straight line. A great circle is a circle on the sphere with maximal circumference. For example, the equator on Earth is a great circle. Also, a longitudinal line that goes through the north and south poles is a great circle."

Arlene jumps up and down like she's on a trampoline, "I think I'm beginning to get it. Take two of Les' dots and draw a great circle through them. Now there are three dots left. Either all three are on one side of the great circle or two are on one side and one is on the other side. (Some of the dots can be on the great circle but that's all right.) The great circle divides the sphere in half so it is the boundary of two closed hemispheres. One of these hemispheres contains at least four of the dots."

"That's it," Les applauds, "you did it, but I have to tell you that Albert Einstein did it faster. You're out of here."

Les springs up, leaving the couple standing outside with surprised expressions on their faces. Les skips down the lane with a happy-go-lucky gate as he says, "good-bye. I'll miss you. I love you guys."

As he bounces away, they hear him singing in a loud voice:

"There's nothing as perfect as a sphere.

There's nothing as beautiful as a sphere.

There's nothing as symmetric as a sphere.

The planets are shaped like a sphere.

The stars are shaped like a sphere.

The universe is shaped like a sphere.

Rotate a point and you get a circle.

Rotate a circle and you get a sphere.

Rotate a sphere and you get, you guessed it, a sphere.

Do it again and you get, you guessed it again, a sphere.

Nothing is as magnificent as a sphere.

$$\vdots$$

"

Arlene and Robert look at each other and shake their heads. As they continue on their way, Arlene says, "I guess life in heaven and on Earth is one puzzle after another."

Robert replies, "you said it, baby, and I agree." □

Printed in the United States
By Bookmasters